MYSTERY
DRAKE

EGYPT

Also by Nick Drake

Tutankhamun: The Book of Shadows
Nefertiti: The Book of the Dead

EGYPT

The Book of Chaos

Nick Drake

HARPER

An Imprint of HarperCollins*Publishers*
www.harpercollins.com

HarperCollins books may be purchased for educational, business, or sales promotional use. For information, please write: Special Markets Department, HarperCollins Publishers, 10 East 53rd Street, New York, NY 10022.

Maps © Neil Gower

First published in Great Britain in 2011 by Bantam Press, an imprint of Transworld Publishers.

FIRST U.S. EDITION

Library of Congress Cataloging-in-Publication Data has been applied for.

ISBN: 978-0-06-076594-1

11 12 13 14 15   OFF/RRD   10 9 8 7 6 5 4 3 2 1

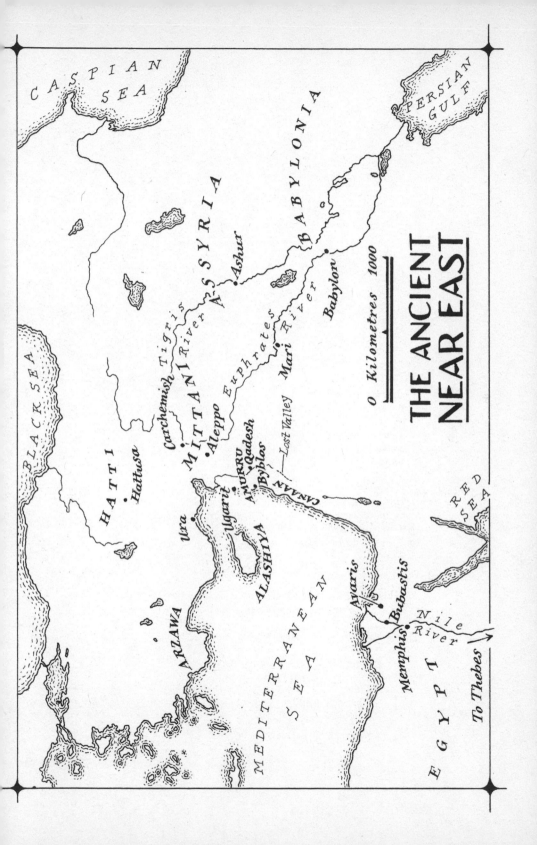

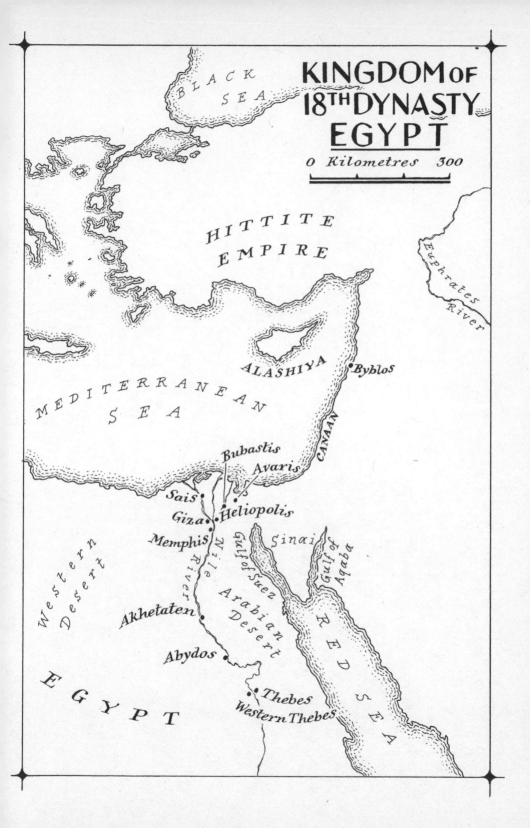

KINGDOM OF 18TH DYNASTY EGYPT

0 Kilometres 300

BLACK SEA

HITTITE EMPIRE

Euphrates River

ALASHIYA

Byblos

MEDITERRANEAN SEA

CANAAN

Bubastis

Avaris

Sais

Heliopolis

Giza

Memphis

Nile River

Gulf of Suez

Sinai

Gulf of Aqaba

Western Desert

Arabian Desert

RED SEA

Akhetaten

Abydos

EGYPT

Thebes

Western Thebes

Cast List

Rahotep – Seeker of Mysteries, detective in the Thebes Medjay (police force)

His family and friends
Tanefert – his wife
Sekhmet, Thuyu, Nedjmet – his daughters
Amenmose – his young son
Thoth – his baboon
Khety – Medjay associate
Nakht – noble, Royal Envoy to All Foreign Lands
Minmose – Nakht's manservant

The royal family
Ankhesenamun – Queen, mid-twenties, daughter of Nefertiti
Ay – King

The palace and other officials
Simut – Commander of the Palace Guard
Nebamun – Chief of the Thebes Medjay

Panehesy – Sergeant in the Thebes Medjay
Khay – Chief Scribe

The Hittites
Hattusa – Ambassador
Suppiluliuma I – King
Crown Prince Arnuwanda – his eldest son
Prince Zannanza – his fourth son
Queen Tawananna

Save me from that God who steals souls. Who laps up corruption. Who lives on what is putrid. Who is in charge of darkness. Who is immersed in gloom. Of whom those who are among the dead are afraid.

Who is he?

He is Seth.

The Book of the Dead
Spell 17

EGYPT

PART ONE

You shall be decapitated with a knife, your face shall be cut away all round. Your head shall be removed by him who is in his land. Your bones shall be broken. Your limbs shall be cut off.

The Book of the Dead
Spell 39

1

Year 4 of the Reign of King Ay, God's Father, Doer of Right

Thebes, Egypt

I stared down at five severed heads that lay in the dust, at the god-forsaken crossroads, in the small dark hour before dawn.

It was cold, and I drew my old Syrian woollen cloak closer around me. The night sky was moonless. The city was all shadows. Doors and windows were shut. No early workers, up before dawn on their way to another long day's labour, paused to observe the spectacle. No one would dare to approach a scene like this. Not in these dark times. The old phrase came to me unbidden: 'The earth is in darkness as if in death . . .' Only the stray dogs of Thebes howled to each other across the districts of the city, from the poor slums to the rich suburbs, as if giving voice to the *ka* spirits of these murdered Nubian boys, hungry for sustenance as they flew between this world and the next.

Under the setting stars shimmering in the ocean of the heavens, a few officers of the city Medjay moved about in the flickering light of their torches, chatting nonchalantly, their shadows wavering on the mud-brick walls of the nearby dwellings. A few nodded at me; others didn't. They had already carelessly trampled their sandals all over the crime scene, destroying any evidence that might have remained. Not that it would matter, for the investigation would be cursory at best. Massacres like this had become commonplace, and the gangs who committed them with impunity seemed to have taken control of the poor districts. They trafficked in opium, gold and human beings, trapping and selling young girls and boys into dead-end prostitution. Their victims even included Medjay officers, fantastically tortured, then decapitated and dismembered for refusing to take the golden opportunity of corruption. Rival gangs slaughtered each other in score-settling bloodbaths along with their screaming girlfriends; the teenage sons and daughters of high-ranking bureaucrats were kidnapped and brutally murdered *after* the ransoms had been paid; and so, despite all the security and high walls gold could buy, no one in Thebes felt safe.

But these decapitated victims were just street kids – Nubian boys, with tattoos and braided hair, and little arrow amulets on leather necklaces to mark their gang membership. They would have run the low-level opium sales for their bigger brothers. They were from the poorest, most dismal of the slums; uneducated, without employment or prospects, vulnerable to the stupid outlaw mystique of the gangs. All bore the wounds of previous street battles: knife-scars on their cheeks, blotted and sunken eyes, blunted, misshapen noses, and ears deformed by beatings. None were older than sixteen – most were younger. Their childish faces now wore the empty look of disappointment common to the newly dead.

The boys' heads were set in a neat row at the feet of their corpses, which had been laid side by side, so that they looked like innocent friends dreaming together. Their dusty hands and feet had been roughly, tightly bound with cheap cord – but when I examined them I was puzzled, for the knots were unusually expert. Also, when a man is beheaded, his blood pumps in arcs from the neck wound; but judging from the absence of any other bloodstains in the street dust, these boys must have been executed somewhere else, and then dumped here as a warning, probably from one gang to another.

I bent down to examine the wounds in better detail: the neck muscles and the spine of each boy had been severed by a single, powerful stroke, which suggested a practised, indeed an exemplary, skill. And the killer must have used a high-quality blade; perhaps a ceremonial *khopesh* scimitar, or a butcher's long yellow flint blade, razor-sharp for eviscerating cattle. Knives have powers of protection and of retribution. The Guardians of the Otherworld carry knives, and so do the minor Gods of that dismal place, with their fearsome faces and their heads turned backwards; and so, clearly, did this killer. I could picture his excellent technique, and his unusual pride in his skill. This did not seem like the work of the usual brutal gang executioners.

In my years on the Thebes force, I had seen every kind of meaningless brutality enacted on the human body. Cruelty, rage, grief – and something others carelessly name evil – can reduce the strange collation of profanity and beauty which makes up each of us to an inanimate lump of decaying meat. I had stood in grim backrooms, and stooped over the twisted bodies of children battered to death. I had considered the ruined remains of young women face down in the still-warm shadows of their own blood. I had seen the matter of the brain – that peculiar ivory jelly, which some say is the repository of our thoughts and memories – dashed across mud-brick walls. I had seen the raw meat of our physical beings exposed as in a butcher's shop; I knew how quickly youth and beauty bloat and stink, when the *ka* and *ba* spirits have departed.

I had seen much worse things than the sight of these five Nubian boys' expertly decapitated heads. And yet it angered me deeply. Perhaps it was our apparent powerlessness to stop this tide of violence. Perhaps it was the Medjay's obvious lack of interest in protecting the poor. Or perhaps I was simply growing old. The hair on my head was grey now, the glossy black of my youth a distant memory; my belly was still trim, but some dawns I felt my bones creaking, and the weight of the skin on my face, and a strange slowness in my blood when I rose to confront the new day.

I shook my head to dispel such pointless thoughts. And then I noticed something, just visible between the pale lips of one of the Nubian boys' heads. I inserted my finger between his white teeth, and retrieved a folded slip of papyrus. It was sticky with blood and saliva. I carefully peeled it open. Neatly drawn in black ink was a strange sign: *a black star with eight radial arrowheads*. Gangs often left scrawled, barely literate messages with their victims' body parts – all part of the grim ritual, the blood-soaked display of power. But usually the messages were banal: *Learn Respect*; *Keep Silent*; *Be Afraid*. This was different. It was not, for one thing, an Egyptian hieroglyph, for our stars have five points, and look nothing like what was before me.

Suddenly, a chariot, drawn by two tired little horses and accompanied by a running guard, clattered up the street, and Nebamun, Chief of the Thebes Medjay, descended. The officers, who until this moment had been sharing their usual diseased banter, straightened up in silence. Nebamun glanced over in my direction. I knew he would want this scene cleared up and the bodies disposed of before dawn broke, and the city awoke. There would, of course, be no proper investigation. Instead, a few likely culprits would be dragged off the streets of the slums, and tortured to confess, and then swiftly executed, as a sign to the world at large that the city Medjay could still do its job. Whatever their petty misdemeanours, these dead boys were still murder victims, and they deserved justice. But because they were poor Nubians they wouldn't get it; Nebamun – 'a man of this world', as he repeatedly claimed, justifying his shortcuts to justice, his casual corruption, and his remorselessly practical violence – would see to that. To talk of justice was to be out of date, old-fashioned and laughable. He was coming towards me. Against the rules, and with a corresponding touch of pleasure, I quickly hid the papyrus in my leather satchel, for further contemplation.

'Shit always travels downhill, eh, Rahotep?' Nebamun said, nodding at the dead boys, and coughing grimly at his tired, old joke. He wrapped his long, finely pleated linen gown tighter around his stately form. He was wearing his gold *shebyu* collar of honour as always, just to remind us of his worldly success. Once impressively muscular, his stocky physique had collapsed into the soft middle age of a man who had succeeded in his profession. His features were blunt, and his hands were not as steady as they had once been, but his eyes still glittered with the pleasure of power. I caught a waft of the sweet smell of beer on his breath. He had never developed a taste for decent wine. I instinctively took a step back from him. He grinned, revealing his poor teeth, and then spat a fat gob of phlegm into the dust a bit too near my sandals. My baboon, Thoth, growled quietly at him.

'Five more dead Nubian street kids. Who cares?' he said, prodding their bodies with his sandals.

I knew better than to respond.

'Let's get this cleared up. No point in distressing the decent hard-working citizens of Thebes with a nasty sight like this, eh?' he said, and he made a sign to the officers to get to work. Then he turned back to me, as if something had just occurred to him.

'What are you doing here, Rahotep?' he said.

'I couldn't sleep.'

Which was true.

Nebamun and I had never seen eye to eye. He had beaten me to the office of Chief of the Thebes Medjay, and immediately proved his innate stupidity by becoming a petty tyrant, intimidating his best men rather than freeing them to do their jobs. In particular he had used his power to sideline me to the point where I was no longer ordered to the scenes of murders, but put to work on petty cases which should have been given to junior officers. And in doing so, he had taken from me the thing I valued above almost everything: my work as a Seeker of Mysteries. Twice before, I had been called upon, over his head and beyond his authority, to solve mysteries by the highest in the land – first by Nefertiti, and then later by her daughter, Ankhesenamun, and her husband, King Tutankhamun. Twice I had been summoned and set to work, independent of his authority. And twice, he would insist, gleefully, whenever he had the chance, I had failed. For Nefertiti had vanished, and Tutankhamun had died. And yet I could never tell him the true story behind these events, to justify myself, for I had promised my silence on those matters.

Suddenly, a Nubian woman ran into the street. She was breathless and desperate. The officers moved to stop her, but Nebamun shook his head, casually giving permission for her to approach her dead child. She fell to her knees before one of the heads and began to keen a high, desperate howl of inconsolable misery.

'I'm sorry for the death of your son,' I said quietly.

She gazed up at me, her face shattered.

'What was his name?' I asked as gently as I could, but Nebamun interrupted me.

'You don't belong here, Rahotep. This isn't your case.'

'It won't be anyone's case,' I said, before I could stop myself.

'Like you said, five more dead Nubian boys? Who cares? End of story.'

'Exactly so. So why don't you fuck off home, before I kick you all the way to the end of the street,' he snapped back, delighted to have antagonized me.

He nodded to his men. They grasped the grieving mother under the arms, and dragged her away, her howls echoing through the dark and silent streets.

Once, I would have owned this scene. Once I was known as the best Seeker of Mysteries in the city. This would have been my case, and perhaps I might have been able to give that mother something, in the end, that looked like justice. I might have discovered why the knots on the ropes were expert, and found the killer who was so strangely skilled at beheading teenage Nubian boys.

I looked around one final time, shading my eyes against the dawn light. Soon the day's heat would take control of the city. Thebes would shimmer and bake under the furious eye of Ra. It would be another day ruled by this world's new gods: gold and power.

I took Thoth by the leash, and we walked slowly away into the last of the shadows.

2

The noble Nakht, tall, slim and elegant, was standing at the top of the entrance stairs of his grand city house, greeting his rich and elite friends as they arrived and passed through into the grand reception hall. He was wearing his finest pleated linens and a magnificent *shebyu* collar – two strands of solid gold rings. Such collars were royal gifts, signs of high favour and office, strikingly beautiful, and very heavy. Such ostentation was a recent development in his personal appearance, which had always been austere; but his rise to even greater eminence, as royal envoy, seemed to have encouraged him to a more open display of personal opulence, about which – as he made very clear – he was not to be teased. Nakht was now one of the most powerful men in the land: the chief official who oversaw the relations between the judiciary, the priesthood, the government and the palace, and who, as royal envoy, represented Egypt abroad. In short, he was the keystone of power. And yet I could never quite square that with the man I knew, who was more interested in studying the mysteries of the stars, and the obscure puzzles of ancient texts, than in the crude, day-to-day business of power and politics. I observed him in action from my bodyguard's vantage, just to his side. His finely drawn face, with its delicate features, moved through exactly the right range of expressions as he greeted each dignitary according to his stature, and by name (for his memory was famously prodigious): the nobles and priests with poised grace, the overseers with a sly, collaboratively subversive wink, the new magnates with respect. And yet, his topaz eyes, alive with intelligence, seemed to observe the pageant of all this, and indeed of all human life, as a slightly remote spectacle. He had the concentrated hunting eyes of a hawk in the smooth face of a gentleman.

Our friendship was unlikely. We had met when we were younger, at a grand reception in Akhetaten, the new temple city built by Akhenaten and Nefertiti midway between Thebes and Memphis. Nakht had been born into a world of gold and privilege, but despite the differences in our origins we had taken to each other immediately.

And now, all these years later, and despite his eminence in high politics and intellectual life, he still seemed to find something amusing and interesting in me. I, for my part, remained intrigued by his life of the mind, his bladed intelligence, and above all by his warm love for my children. Perhaps he borrowed from me the one thing he lacked in his life – a family. And I was glad to share them with him.

Once upon a time, I had been an invited guest at Nakht's famous social functions. Tonight I was here because I was working. Nakht had started to employ me occasionally as his personal bodyguard, saying he could trust my discretion in a way he could trust no one else. With his customary tact, he had made it seem as if it was I who was doing him the favour. And given the unreliable and ever-diminishing payments from my Medjay

11

work, and the spiralling costs of even the most basic of foods, I was absolutely desperate for any means to provide for my family. Many of my fellow Medjay officers, alarmed by the increasing murder rate among our own kind, and the worsening violence in the city, had been drawn into private security work: either at rich men's houses, or rich families' tombs, loaded with treasures and gold – which were always threatened with violent robbery. Some made money on both sides, by collaborating with gangs of tomb-robbers. Others had also been drawn by need or weakness into blackmail, protectionism and extortion. Many times I regretted refusing the Queen's offer to become her private guard, which she had made five years before; but the palace was never my world – I was a Seeker of Mysteries, and no matter what the cost, and no matter how absurd it might seem, I had no choice but to remain true to myself.

Up on the roof, the large terrace was set out with many trays on stands, piled high with the finest of foods in ostentatious quantities: whole ducks in thick glazes; big roasted haunches of gazelle, sliced finely to reveal the pink meat; roasted gourds and shallots; bread rolls; honeycombs; olives glistening in oil on decorated platters; lustrous bunches of shining grapes that caught the evening sunlight; and mountains of figs and dates. Servants dispensed fine wine from the Dakhla oasis. I would dearly have loved a goblet of decent wine, as I could no longer indulge such luxuries at home. My mouth watered; I stopped myself from smuggling a handful of almonds from a dish. After the last guests had departed, Nakht would insist that I take as many of the leftovers as I wished home for the children. 'Otherwise it will just be thrown away,' he would say, trying to find a way to make his charity acceptable, while pressing a small cask of excellent wine upon me. We would eat like kings for the next few days; and for a little while we would not have to suffer the same old onions, garlic, bony fish and gritty bread that had become our staple diet.

As Nakht made elegantly witty conversation with a rich couple, while they fawned over and flattered each other, I gazed out over the city in the glorious evening light. The grey, red and yellow flat rooftops of Thebes, crowded with drying vegetables and broken bits and pieces of household furniture, spread away in every direction. The Avenue of Sphinxes, the vast, straight, paved processional, ran to the north, joining the Temple of Karnak and the Southern Temple, whose towering, painted mud-brick walls reared up near by. I watched as a temple army phalanx laboriously conducted the handover to the night guards in the open ground before the vast pylon. To the west ran the Great River, the source of all life, like a brown and green serpent, glittering silver now as the sunset flowed on its ever-changing surfaces. Further, beyond the cultivation on the west bank, and the stark borderline where the Black Land of the cultivation and the Red Lands of the desert divided, lay the long stone mortuary temples; and beyond them the hills and valleys, now painted in the blacks, yellows and reds of sunset, where the royal tombs preserved the great kings in their stone sarcophagi and gold coffins, timeless and secret. To the south, also on the west bank, I could just make out the squat shapes of the Malkata Palace, home of the royal family, hidden at the heart of the extensive labyrinth of overseers', administrators' and officials' accommodation. And beyond the city's boundaries, beyond the green and black fields, beyond all the monuments and statues made by men upon the face of the earth, lay the great unknown of the Red Lands, that other world of dust and sandstorms and dangerous spirits and death, which had always held such power for me.

The evening sun had dropped low now, and the sky was turquoise, indigo, crimson and gold; the sweet northern breeze of the evening hour had begun to cool the air. At a discreet nod from Nakht, the servants took down the exquisitely embroidered awnings, and lit many little oil lamps. The guests settled on chairs – with low chaises for the women – set out for comfort. I looked at their affluent faces and opulent outfits, gilded by the last of the evening light. They lived in a different world from those in the streets all around them.

I shadowed Nakht as he moved over to a small coterie of close friends who frequented his mansion. Hor the poet was talking, as usual; wittily and bitchily entertaining his friends with scurrilous accounts of high-level indiscretions and scandals, usually of a sexual nature. I used to think poets were dreamers of truth and beauty, with their heads in the Otherworld. But Hor was chubby and self-satisfied, worldly and successful. His little fingers were heavy with valuable gold rings. He was famous for a series of verses, circulated anonymously some years ago, which daringly satirized Ay, once vizier, now King. Today such things would earn him summary execution.

'Friends, I have written a new poem,' he announced ostentatiously. 'It is a trifle, but perhaps I may impose it upon you . . .'

A polite murmur of encouragement followed.

'I hope it is a cheerful one,' said someone.

'There is no such thing as a cheerful poem,' he replied. 'Happiness writes in water, not ink.'

Everyone nodded as if this was a very wise thing to say. He assumed his posture of poetic delivery, head tilted, fingers of the right hand raised, and when he had satisfied himself that he had everyone's attentive silence, he intoned:

> *Who can I trust today?*
> *Brothers are evil, and friends have no compassion.*
> *Hearts are greedy*
> *And each man steals*
> *His neighbour's worldly goods.*
> *Compassion has perished,*
> *Violence walks the ways,*

Evil runs rampant
Throughout the land –
Evil, endless evil . . .

And so it went on. When it was over, his cheerless dirge – which I thought truthful, but repetitive and not particularly original – was met with a worried silence, before the audience applauded hastily. Nakht sensed the mood of the evening was threatening to turn the wrong way.

'Remarkable poem. Concise, memorable and honest,' he said.

'I see I have shocked you all a little. But to be a poet is to accept the responsibility of speaking the truth! No matter what the cost to my personal safety,' said Hor, taking a deep, sustaining gulp from his cup of wine.

'Your relationship with the truth has always been a very flexible and accommodating one,' said Nebi, a well-known architect, dressed in an expensive embroidered tunic.

'Of course it has, in matters of men and this world. I'm a poet, not a complete fool . . .' Hor replied.

'But the truth itself is so complicated these days,' said another.

'The truth is always the truth,' said Nakht, smiling at his own triteness.

Hor waved him away. 'I can't bear platitudes. They actually hurt my feelings,' he said.

All this talk of truth was making me want to go and do something useful.

'However, I have heard some interesting news, friends,' continued Hor, smiling his evil little grin. The others huddled a little closer, checking over their shoulders to make sure no one else was listening. And then, after a carefully timed pause, the poet leaned forward, as if among conspirators, and in a theatrical whisper said: '*He* will soon be with the Gods.'

Everyone understood what he meant but could not say. Ay, the

15

hated tyrant who ruled over the Two Lands, had long outlived the expectation of his natural life.

'But this is hardly *new* news. And even if he were to pass on, how would anyone really know? He's looked dead for years . . .' joked Nebi's wife, to a little round of laughter.

'Mark my words. I have it on authority: it may be only weeks. And none of us will be laughing then.'

The guests glanced at each other and shivered, as if the balmy evening air was suddenly running with strange, cold currents.

'So the moment we have all feared for so very long is about to arrive! The end of this great dynasty – and the end of the age of peace and prosperity!' cried another, mournfully.

'And so at last comes General Horemheb's chance,' said Nebi. 'And with it perhaps the end of the world as we have known it.'

'The general will claim more than the crowns. He will claim everything. And then he will do what he likes with us . . .' said an older man, with his elegantly beautiful young wife sitting subserviently behind him.

'I heard he has a secret papyrus on which he has recorded a list of the names of all his enemies, and all those who have opposed him, or failed to support him, over the years,' whispered Nebi.

'How many of us will be on that list!' replied the older man, looking around at the company.

'It is a dismal prospect,' agreed Hor. Lifting his stubby hand to the west, like a tragic actor, he intoned: 'Like an army of shadows, his numberless soldiers in their divisions will return from their long campaigns against our arch-enemies, the Hittites, and turn their forces instead upon our own great people, to conquer and dominate and suppress our liberty. I see his ships, under blood-red sails, appearing out of the dark night. I see his troops occupying the streets of our city. I see the best men led forth to execution.

I see calamity. I see blood running in the streets. I see the world turned upside down.'

The audience seemed spellbound by his prophecy. I glanced at Nakht, who was observing the poet. We exchanged a slight rise of the eyebrows at the oracular melodrama of the performance. But Hor was serious.

'I have you all amazed. But Horemheb is famous for his cruelties and his passion for revenge. I heard a story, from the mouth of one who was there, that, once, the general ordered a captive Hittite commander to be boiled alive before him, for his entertainment . . . *while he ate his dinner.*'

There were cries of revulsion among the group. More guests had gathered to listen, with their goblets and trays. But at this point, Nakht intervened.

'Come now, friend. Your poetic imagination is a great gift, but as a prophet perhaps you relish your visions of doom too greatly. The future is not so sure. Nor is it necessarily so bleak. No oracle can decide for certain what will happen. Indeed, we have reasons for imagining a different future altogether.'

'Such as? The ascension of Horemheb bringing "order" and "a return to the old values" and so on . . . ?' said Hor, sarcastically.

'His ascension would, in any case, be entirely illegitimate: he has not one drop of royal blood in him. Even Ay himself could claim a bloodline association with the royal family, however debatable. But Horemheb has simply married his way into the family, driven his poor first wife madly to her death, and then made the Queen, last of the true dynasty, into his sworn enemy,' said Nakht.

He rose, and walked among the little gathering. 'Life, prosperity, health to the Queen,' he intoned loyally, to appreciative murmurs from most of those present. And then he continued. 'Friends, is Horemheb truly so powerful? Has he no opposition? Yes, he is General of the army of the Two Lands of Egypt; but do we, the leading men of Thebes, have no faith in our own power and authority? Do intellect and morality count for nothing in the way the future unfolds? Does Amun, the God of our great city, and of the royal family itself, have no power to save us? Can we not save ourselves?'

There was a murmur of support for Nakht's speech from the guests. But only Hor spoke what was on everyone's mind.

'We would not be in this position at all if King Tutankhamun had not died in such tragic circumstances. He would have ruled, perhaps gloriously. There would have been heirs. The empire might have been great again. A new king, son of kings, could have emerged, heralding a bright future. Instead of which . . .'

He held up his squat hands, with their many gold rings, and shrugged helplessly.

'The King's death was an accident. No one could have foreseen it, or prevented it,' replied Nakht, in a manner that warned everyone from contradicting him, or from saying anything further.

Only one person spoke up: 'It is true, there is a crisis in this land. Outside this bubble of affluence and illusion there is desperation. Poverty, cruelty and injustice have done their work on the people; corruption has replaced justice for the poor, and contempt has replaced respect for dignity, labour and integrity. Greed is our king, and corruption is his servant.'

Everyone turned in astonishment to stare at me, because the angry, bitter voice was mine. Nakht stared at me with a remarkably unfriendly detachment. Everyone else clearly thought I was mad and would be instantly dismissed; a servant dares to speak! But someone was slowly clapping. It was Hor.

'I remember you, sir; you are that Medjay Seeker of Mysteries who used to write poetry in his innocent youth.'

'I am Rahotep,' I replied.

'There is truth in what you say. Truth is a dangerous muse. One dies for the truth.'

18

He plucked a silver goblet of wine from a tray, and thrust it into my hand.

'To the truth! And much good it may do us,' he cried sarcastically, and drank the toast. Then he nodded at me, and walked away, quickly followed by the other guests.

'To the truth,' I muttered, and drank from the goblet. I was in for another shock. The wine was superbly rich, with a dark, melancholy beauty. Such were the pleasures of wealth.

When I looked up I saw Nakht was staring oddly at me, but then he turned his back and began to talk to another guest.

3

I should have hurried home through the dark streets, with the bag of leftovers for the family. At the end of the night, Nakht had pointedly said nothing about my outburst. As he handed me my small payment of gold, and the parcel of food and wine, he simply ordered me to accompany him to an important meeting, tomorrow, at noon, in a tone that would brook no discussion. I was about to try to apologize, in my clumsy fashion, but he bade me a brief goodnight, and swiftly shut the door.

The evening had left me in a foul temper. The last thing I needed was to vent my anger on my wife and children. So, taking Thoth by the leash, I headed to a backstreet tavern, an old haunt where I went when I wanted to think, undisturbed. I ordered a small jug of wine, and chose a rickety stool in the corner, where the shadows could keep me company, and no one would approach me. Thoth settled down by my feet. In any case, by this late hour the place was emptying out; the only other drinkers were workmen and labourers. Their exhausted faces looked drawn in the guttering light from the oil lamps; they gripped their drinking bowls with work-damaged hands twisted like claws to the habits of their labours. When the wine arrived in its jug, it tasted exactly how I felt: cheap, crude and bitter.

I took the papyrus out, unfolded it, and pondered the black star. All gangs have their own signs and symbols. They define their identity, and differentiate themselves from their rivals, by gestures, articles of clothing, and codes of language and behaviour – nicknames, complicated handshakes, 'knock three times' types of things. One gang identified themselves by leaving a crisscross slashed across the faces of their victims. Probably this black star was just another such sign, made up for effect. But as I sat there in the shadows with my cheap wine, I couldn't help feeling it suggested something darker and stranger. I told myself to get a grip. I was giving it too much credence; this was almost certainly nothing more than the work of a lunatic with a taste for fancy symbolism.

Suddenly I realized someone was watching me.

'What have you got there?'

It was my old associate, Khety. We had worked together for years, he as my assistant, until promotion had offered him other avenues of advancement, and my unofficial demotion made it necessary for him to move on without me. I'd watched him rise rapidly through the ranks. A strange, slightly uncomfortable distance had grown up between us that neither had attempted to cross for some time. And yet now, suddenly, here he was. He still looked strikingly young – his hair still black, his open face lively, and from the look of him he was still as fit and lithe as a hunting dog.

'Just looking at you makes me feel old.'

He grinned.

'Cheerful as ever,' he replied.

'What are you doing here?' I said.

'I was just passing,' he said.

'A likely story . . .'

He let Thoth sniff his hand, and then stroked his head.

I pushed a stool at him, and poured him some wine. He drank, grimaced, but said nothing, just gazed into the bitter wine, as if it told him everything he needed to know.

'If I'd known you were coming, I'd have ordered something classier,' I said.

He gazed at me. 'It's a disgrace.'

'I know . . .' I nodded in agreement, and refilled my bowl with more bad wine.

'I mean you – you look as miserable as a mule.'

'You're in a good mood, obviously.'

He nodded, and nonchalantly walked over to the landlord. He returned with another jug of wine, and poured us fresh bowls. It was the best the place could offer.

'You haven't turned up here just to flatter me in my self-pity,' I said.

He leaned closer, and raised his bowl. His eyes were alive with delight.

'We're having another child.'

I felt my face light up with a slow, genuine smile. 'You have my congratulations, and my best wishes for the child.' I raised my bowl to him.

'I knew you'd be pleased. It's taken a long time. I'd begun to believe it would never happen again. But the Gods have been kind . . .'

I said nothing, for I dislike talk of the Gods, who taunt us with their promises, and whose disappointments we must always accept.

'Don't look too excited, eh?' he said.

'Sorry. It's been a strange night. Truly, it's a bad world to bring a child into, but I'll do my best not to pass on my customary gloom.'

And we toasted the unborn child with our superior wine.

'What were you looking at when I came in?' he asked casually.

'Nothing.'

'Right.'

He knew how to add the perfect touch of sarcasm to his tone. I showed him the papyrus. He didn't seem at all surprised by it.

'Where did you find this?'

'In the mouth of a beheaded Nubian kid, early this morning,' I said.

He nodded.

'These beheadings are turning into an epidemic,' he said.

'And they're getting better at it. And now they're leaving strange signs . . .' I added.

He leaned forward, and returned the papyrus to me. And then, thoughtfully, he added: 'Do you really think this is just the work of one of the gangs in the city?'

'Probably,' I replied, carefully.

He glanced at me.

'I can't see it.'

'Why not?' I said.

He settled his arms on his knees.

'The Theban gangs are all families. They behave like families: they love each other, they hate each other; they want what the others have got; they kill each other; they make up, they pretend to love each other again; they think they're kings, building empires and dynasties, so they marry their sons to their rivals' daughters; and so on and so on. But the truth is, they're always in cut-throat competition with each other for the same things: manpower, resources, trade routes, political influence, protection, the opium supply. Sometimes the friction becomes too much, so they snap, and there's some predictably messy bloodshed, and then mourning and grieving and furious cursing and threats of revenge; and then

23

they all try to make up, because in the end none of them have the power to dominate the others,' he said.

'So what? Smuggling and trafficking are as old as time. It's no mystery why they're flourishing now, that's just what happens when the legitimate government is as flawed and weak as ours. And, frankly, the powers that be are just letting them get on with it . . . We're living in a failed land, and they're the proof of it,' I replied.

'Sure, everyone's corrupt. Everyone's afraid of the gangs. But something's changed. We're not looking at the usual small-scale stuff. We're looking at something that's evolved suddenly onto another level altogether.' He paused and looked at me meaningfully. 'A mysterious new gang's recently started dominating and destroying the competition . . .'

Khety had always burned more brightly than me in his fascination with conspiracies and secrets, whereas I, the dogged detective, could only look at what was there before me and make my deductions accordingly. But the hairs on the back of my neck were prickling.

'Is this another of your extended conspiracy theories?' I said.

He looked around, and edged closer.

'It's not a theory. I've been investigating this, and I've discovered a few things. No one knows anything about the gang behind these killings. The other gangs – they're like cats fighting in a box because they have no idea who is doing this to them. At first they assumed it was the others, and so there were the usual tit-for-tat exterminations. But they've realized everyone's getting hit. Bit by bit, their organizations are being literally sliced away. It's some other gang altogether. And that really scares them. Whoever these newcomers are, they appear to be attempting to take over the entire opium trade in Thebes.'

'What's your evidence?' I said cautiously.

'The price of opium on the street has gone way, way down;

and yet the quality is better than ever – everyone's going crazy for the stuff. And crucially, for the first time ever, there's as much available as anyone wants to buy. Which means this new gang has accessed a fresh supply route, which could only be the river—' he replied.

'And therefore they're using the ports—'

'Bubastis, perhaps, near the north-east border. And the shipments must come through Thebes. Not Memphis; it's too dangerous, with the army all over the place. And so they must be paying people off, and not just border guards, import officials, local police and low-level people. *The only way this could work is if they have influence at the highest levels.*'

'This is just supposition,' I said, deliberately pushing him. 'Everyone knows the corruption stretches from the gangs to the nobles. They're both getting rich, while everyone else gets poorer. What's new about that? There was even a rumour, years ago, that Horemheb's army was somehow involved in such a secret trade, but there was never any proof. In any case, there's not a thing any of us – certainly not you or I – can do about it.'

He stared at me, shocked.

'This could be the biggest case we've ever worked on. It could make our careers. It could put you back on top. If we figure this out, if we can connect the gangs to the nobles via a new cartel trading in opium, smuggling it without permissions, then Nebamun will have to go on his knees and beg you to go back to work. You could make a real difference. A real change to what's happening. To what's going so badly wrong in this city . . .'

I felt the old, familiar surge of excitement rising within me. A new case. A new mystery to solve. But I squashed it down.

'Listen carefully, Khety. Here's my advice, for what it's worth. Forget the new opium gang. Forget it all. Go home. Work on something else, where you're less likely to get your head chopped off. There's nothing you or I can do that will make any difference to this. It's all been agreed at levels of power you and I will never reach. Anyway, don't people still murder each other in this city in the old-fashioned ways?' I said.

His face was dark with disappointment.

'I'm not walking away from this . . .' he muttered.

I raised my hand.

'Do you really think we could handle it on our own? We wouldn't stand a chance. We can't trust anyone. The city's corrupt, the Medjay's corrupt – look at Nebamun, rolling in gold, he's no fool – no doubt he's taking big fat bribes wherever he can, as well. Don't risk your life for something you can't change.'

He was angry now.

'What's happened to you? I mean, once upon a time you would have jumped at a case like this. It would have *excited* you,' he said.

'Maybe I've finally learned the bitter truth that I can't beat them, even if I'll never join them. But I'm not going to lose the one thing I can still call my own: my life. And you should wise up and do the same, especially with a new child on the way . . .' I replied.

I threw the dregs of my wine on to the dirt floor and, taking Thoth by his leash, walked to the door. Khety followed me out into the dark alleyway.

'I'm going to do this, because I have to,' he said, simply. 'And I want to do it with you. It'll be like the old days. You and me, working on a case that matters. I know you've missed it. You're a great Seeker of Mysteries. The best.'

My heart was a knot of pride and doubt. Somehow his kindness wounded me more than all the insults of Nebamun. I could deal with those; they were just life.

'Go home. Embrace your wife. Think about the new child. Forget all this. Tell yourself it was all just a bad dream,' I said.

He shook his head.

'What sort of man would I be if I just rolled over now? What sort of a father would I be to my kids? I owe it to them. I don't want them growing up in a world where teenagers are kidnapped off the streets or slaughtered every night. And I don't believe for a moment that you do, either. I know you still care. I can see it.'

He knew he'd get me with that.

'Good night, Khety. My congratulations to you and your wife. Thanks for the wine . . .'

I turned away quickly, and kept walking, knowing he was watching me go.

4

I slept badly. Perhaps it was the rotten wine. Perhaps it was the look on Khety's face as I left him in that dark backstreet. It haunted me. But I had other, more pressing concerns. Usually I was the first to awaken in the household, but the light and the noises from the street beyond the walls told me I was late. The space next to me was empty but still warm. I laid my hand briefly on it, wishing Tanefert was still lying there. Some days it seemed we hardly saw each other. Suddenly I felt a deep sadness well up inside me from nowhere. I threw myself out of bed quickly to evade it. I rubbed my face with my hands, to persuade it back into life, and prepared myself to confront another day.

My three daughters – Sekhmet, Thuyu and Nedjmet – glanced at each other quickly, knowingly, as I entered the room.

'Good morning, Father!' they called out, obviously amused by my lateness. I swung my son, Amenmose, five years old, up on to my lap, where he sat, happy in the crook of my arm. The girls were enjoying the luxuries from Nakht's food parcel.

'Good morning, fair ladies.'

They giggled at my clumsy paternal attempt at breakfast banter. Tanefert kissed me lightly on the forehead. Her black hair, threaded with silver, was tied back, and as always she was cheerful; but I could see the weariness and worry in her face.

'Be gentle with your father, girls.' She placed a bowl of milk down beside me. I offered some to Amenmose, who shook his head, so I drank it myself.

The girls gazed at me as they ate their breakfast sweet rolls.

'You look like Thoth in a bad temper,' Thuyu laughed suddenly, unable to bear the silence any longer.

'And do you know what baboons do when they're in a bad mood?' I asked.

'They sulk,' said Nedjmet, the youngest, and herself once prone to such moods.

'They fight. It's vicious,' offered Sekhmet, at twenty-one, the oldest, and by general agreement wisest.

I shook my head.

'They cry,' I replied.

The girls looked surprised by this.

'What's the matter? Haven't you ever seen a baboon cry?' I asked.

'No, show us,' challenged Thuyu.

I pulled my face down in as pronounced a parody as I could accomplish of a depressed baboon.

'There's no difference. You always look like that,' said Nedjmet.

'It'll stay like that if you're not careful,' warned Sekhmet.

'It's true, it doesn't look all that different,' added Tanefert, as she passed by. 'Now leave your father in peace, and get on.'

The girls noisily kissed me farewell, and left to go about their day, while Amenmose and I remained sitting together contentedly in the quietness that had descended on the house.

29

'Father,' he said, seriously.

'Yes,' I answered, wondering what profound discussion of mortality or life was about to begin.

'You know Grandfather's dead?'

My father had died almost a year ago, peacefully, at home. It was what we call a good death. The children had become obsessed with his passing to the Otherworld, and the events that followed, worrying about his resurrection in the afterlife, observing all the rites with exact custom, learning about his *ka*, *ba* and *akh* spirits, and drawing the hieroglyphics for each of them: the two up-stretched human arms for the *ka*, the life force; the human-headed bird of the *ba*, that part of us which is individual to ourselves, which could take any form it desired, and travel between the worlds of the living and the dead; and the ibis of the *akh*, the immortal part of us which returns to the stars after we die. I had of course not told them that the embalmer's high charges, together with those of the priests, who would conduct regular rites, and the burial itself, had taken up all our meagre savings, and that we had had to borrow at an alarming rate of interest to complete and furnish the frankly very ordinary tomb in which my father's body now lay, next to my mother's, as he had wished. If my career had not lapsed into the doldrums, we could have afforded a far finer tomb for him, and I wished it could have been so.

'So what is he doing now?'

'Well, he's finishing his breakfast, and thinking about what to do with the day. He'll probably go fishing. There's plenty of time to fish in the afterlife . . .'

My father had taken me fishing on his reed boat all through my youth, and had delighted in doing the same with my son; they would both sit for hours in a pleasure of patience. Patience was not one of my son's virtues, but he had never been happier, it seemed, than when he was in a boat with his grandfather. Together, they would watch the busy life of the river, with its population of boats

30

and fishermen, lines of poor women in bright robes washing clothes by the shore, animals grazing and lowering their heads to drink, and great flocks of birds flying overhead to their retreats in the reed marshes, diving down to catch fish. He missed the trips, and he missed my father.

'Can *we* go fishing?'

His face was earnest and hopeful.

'Not today. Soon.'

He wrestled himself out of my lap.

'Why not?' he demanded, his little fists and face suddenly clenched with anger.

'Because I have to work today. We'll go soon, I promise,' I said.

'You always say that, and we never do go!' he shouted.

And then he ran out into the yard.

I rubbed my face. Tanefert just shook her head.

'Go and tell him you'll take him later.'

'I can't. I promised Nakht I would help him with something.'

She gazed at me.

'He needs you . . .'

'I know. And we need the payments I earn from Nakht. How else will we eat? What do you want me to do?'

We stared at each other for a tense moment.

'You and that baboon deserve each other. You're both turning into angry old men,' she said, and disappeared with the basket of clean clothes she had been folding.

I made my presence known at Medjay headquarters, as I made sure I did every day. Accompanied by Thoth, I strode under the carved stone image of the Wolf, Opener of the Ways, our standard. The inner courtyard was quiet; just a few people – representatives and petitioners, and women waiting with food for their imprisoned sons or husbands, or bribes for the guards –

31

stood or squatted in the shrinking shadows of the morning. The heat was already scorching. Nebamun's office door was shut. A few Medjay colleagues nodded at me in passing, and Panehesy, the Nubian sergeant, raised his hand to invite me to join him in the morning conference of other officers. I respected Panehesy for his ability to protect his officers from the worst of the politics of the bureaucracy above us all, but these days he had to adhere strictly to the protocols, the deference and the grim compromises required in dealing with Nebamun.

'Another day of fun and games,' he said blithely, as he passed out the day's duties. He handed me down what he could: usually street patrols. Today was the same. It was a long time since I had been given a good, solid murder to get my teeth into. I knew it wasn't Panehesy's fault. But I felt like a stranger to myself.

'What about last night?' I asked.

'Five down, fifty-five thousand to go,' joked a young officer, earning a brief laugh from the others. 'No disrespect intended,' he added, nodding at Panehesy.

'I should hope not,' he replied coolly.

'Let the gangs kill each other off, it saves us the trouble of dealing with them,' said another. The men nodded in agreement.

'Do you have other ideas about last night?' Panehesy asked me. The others waited for my reply.

'No,' I replied. 'Except that one day the gangs are going to be running this city, if we keep ignoring what's happening out there.'

'And just what do you think we can do about that?' asked the first officer.

I shrugged.

'Our job?' I said.

The other men looked annoyed by that.

'Our job is to keep order on the streets of the city. Not to intervene in gang wars we can't win,' said Panehesy quickly. 'And anyway, the culprits have been arrested. They confessed this morning.'

'I bet they did,' I said. 'And presumably they've been executed, too?'

I gazed at Panehesy, and he had the decency to look away first.

5

As I sat waiting for Nakht in the cool courtyard of his city house, I turned the papyrus with the black star over in my hands. I love evidence, above all things. It is the first of the sacred trinity that presides over the success of any investigation – the others being the witnesses, and, finally, the confessors. But I place less value on the second, and almost none on the last. Not for me the grim drama of the interrogation. For me, the crime scene *is* the truth. So my habit is to read each one obsessively for what is there, for what seems to be there, and most importantly for what should be there but is missing. Most are not so mysterious. But a very few have a special atmosphere, a peculiar feeling of meaningful mystery, which I can only call *elusive*. These, I love.

The scene of the decapitated boys was one of those. Death exacted by decapitation. Time of death: the small hours of the night. Killed elsewhere. Witnesses: none. But step beyond that, and all was mystery. Why were these little Nubian street dealers killed in this supremely efficient, audacious and expert way? Why were they left in a place where they would quickly be found? Why had the street been so carefully swept of sandal prints, wheel tracks, and all signs of struggle? That did not speak of the gangs in the city, whose violence was notoriously incompetent, as casually full of error and emotion as the actions of angry children. But if not them, then who? And why, above all, the mysterious sign of the black star? Why had it been left in the mouth of the boy? Who was supposed to find it? Other gangs? The Medjay? Me? I tried to imagine the scene; I tried to see the men who enacted these murders. They didn't seem like gang men, but they remained shadows.

Nakht suddenly appeared on the mud-brick stairs. How long had he been watching me?

'What were you thinking about?' he asked.

'Only about how your house always feels like another world; so close to the chaos of the city just beyond these high walls, and yet so entirely apart,' I replied. 'Two different worlds . . . as different as light and dark . . . order and chaos . . .'

And it was true. Here was order and tranquillity: birds in their cages sang with pleasure; the plants in their clay pots and shallow pools thrived. Servants went about their tasks in a deferential silence, each obviously knowing and respecting his or her place in the great orderly scheme of Nakht's life. Today I noticed he had taken considerable trouble with his appearance. He was dressed in a superb pleated white gown, and the gold *shebyu* collar he had worn at the party. He cast a cool eye over me, taking in my shabby, dusty, street-worn state.

'Order and chaos? Well, you're looking rather chaotic yourself,' he observed, with a brief smile.

'All part of the service, sir,' I replied, realizing my linen tunic was looking the worse for wear.

'Not where we're going,' he responded.

He took me upstairs, and watched as I washed myself from a

basin of cool water, then insisted I borrow a fresh and very fine-pleated, gossamer-thin long white linen tunic, with short sleeves and pleated ends, a fringed kilt, and a standard broad collar – all from his extensive wardrobe. I felt like a stranger to myself in such fine, indeed noble, clothing. It only just fitted, for Nakht is tall and slim as a papyrus reed, and I am thicker-set.

'How do I look?' I asked.

'Better,' he said, satisfied, as he looked me over, making minute adjustments.

'So where are we going?' I asked. 'Why do I have to dress up?'

'Wait and see,' he replied. Then he picked up the standard of his rank – a long ostrich feather, curved at the top, on a beautifully painted pole – and set it against his shoulder. As we left the refuge of the house, his security guards swiftly ordered the crowds back and created a cordon between the street doors and his beautiful, lightweight, gold-gilded, extremely expensive chariot, which was drawn by two elegant black horses. We took our places, standing side by side on the leather mesh floor. The guards fell efficiently into place, running before and behind us, and shouting peremptory commands to anyone who dared to get in our way; and we moved off into the noise of the city.

The ways were crowded with pack mules carrying mud-bricks or vegetables, and serving girls going about their domestic errands, and street children begging. Minmose, Nakht's manservant, held on to the back of the chariot, struggling to protect us from the blaze of midday with a sunshade. People stopped and stared at the sight of the great and noble Nakht, with his standard of office, going about his important business, moving through the sea of humanity like a perfect god in his white pleated robes.

Nakht still had not told me where we were going, but as soon as we approached the docks my suspicions were roused. And when we stepped on to a royal palace official boat, they were

36

confirmed. Nakht took his place in the main cabin, out of sight; and once I had satisfied myself about the security of the vessel and its crew of palace shipmen, I stood guard at the entrance to the cabin. The helmsman at his double steering oars cried out his command, the rowers began their labour, and we slipped past the wharves crowded with larger vessels and barges, and out of the great harbour.

As we steered into the main current of the Great River, I felt the air lift and freshen. I raised my face, relishing the vivid river scents, and from further away to the west, beyond the great stone temples and necropolises, the pure simplicity of the desert air. I knew we were heading towards the vast complex of the royal palace of Malkata. I thought back to the last time I had made this same journey. I had not been wearing a borrowed tunic, nor had I been the employee of another man. I had been Rahotep, Seeker of Mysteries, summoned to the funeral of Tutankhamun by a living god, the Queen of Egypt herself. And now I was going back.

Inside the cabin, Nakht was scrutinizing a set of official papyri; but when he saw me looking in, he invited me to enter the shade, and I sat next to him on the handsome bench.

'You hardly need me as a security guard to take you to the Malkata Palace,' I observed.

'Nevertheless,' he said meaninglessly, as if otherwise pre-occupied.

'It occurs to me I should apologize for my outburst at your party,' I offered, reluctantly.

'You spoke out of turn, if not out of character,' he observed, while continuing to run swiftly through the cursive script on his papyrus. 'You seemed furious about something which is, after all, common knowledge. It was quite inappropriate.'

I shrugged, suddenly feeling like a moody schoolboy before the cool power of a teacher.

'My tolerance for the easy talk of the elite has all but vanished,' I replied.

'So now in your wise middle age you think of yourself as the magnificent, embittered sage of truth.' He looked up, scanning my face.

'Believe me, I see myself very differently,' I replied, perhaps a little stiffly.

He almost smiled.

'My old friend. I know you see the reality of the streets, and the miseries of the people, and that is a valuable perspective. But remember the world of the wealthy, the priests and the nobles also suffers from dangerous tribulations. The two are not mutually exclusive. Much is at stake for everyone these days. We are all bewildered and tormented by the question of the succession. The future seems very uncertain, and that in itself creates conditions of dangerous unrest.'

'But while everyone's talking and moaning, the world we thought we knew and believed in is being destroyed all around us,' I said.

Nakht glanced at me somewhat impatiently, and then wrote rapidly with his reed pen, the cursive characters forming fluently in black ink. I envied him his great skill in writing. My own has never been better than clumsy and awkward.

'And you think you are the only person to notice this, I suppose? And I suppose you also have a proposal to save us all from the abyss of disaster which you foresee? I suppose you know how to solve the problem of the succession? I suppose you know how to balance the vital authority of the royal family against the landed interests and powers of the priesthood and the nobility, and how to protect both against the vaulting ambitions of the army under General Horemheb? Or would you prefer just to stand and watch everything fall apart, and then say, "See? What did I tell you?"'

He could be so frustrating at times, because his rhetoric could quickly trap me into absurdity. And also because he was often right. But I wasn't ready to let this go just yet.

'You're right, of course. But you and your noble friends all sit in your lovely villas, in your clean, fancy clothes, in your fine jewellery, writing your poems and going about your love affairs, and playing your games of politics. You have no idea of what's going on out there, just the wrong side of your villa walls. The rule of law is toothless, it's powerless. The day before yesterday I saw five young Nubian street kids, just low-level opium dealers . . .' I said.

'And?'

'And someone had very efficiently and mercilessly cut off their young, foolish heads.'

He looked up at me with his topaz eyes.

'What would you have me say?'

'Do you remember my old assistant, Khety?' I asked.

He nodded.

'Of course.'

'He came to see me. We talked. At first I thought it was just the usual gang warfare. But he's been investigating. And he's discovered a few things that worry me,' I said.

'Such as?'

Nakht put down his reed pen. I thought I noticed a glint of interest in his eyes now.

'Such as there's a new supply of opium. Suddenly it's widely available. It's high quality. The price is undercutting the usual gang families, who are being wiped out.'

'And is that such a bad thing? Those gang families are extremely destabilizing for the city . . .' he said.

'That's what everyone's saying. But I want to know: who are these new gangsters who kill with impunity and skill? How much power do they desire? Are they the new lawmen of this city?'

'How would I know?' he answered.

His airiness suddenly annoyed me. We had known each other a long time. He could at least relax a little with me, of all people.

'You're the royal envoy. You're at the heart of power. You know everything.'

He observed me with his strange, dispassionate eyes. I could never tell what he was really thinking.

'I have not seen that expression on your face for a long time,' he said, almost amused.

'What expression?'

'The one where you look like a cat watching a bird. Fascinated. Compelled, despite yourself.'

'Well, it matters . . .' I replied.

'Indeed. So what do you propose?' he asked.

'Khety asked me to join him in a new investigation. Find out who this new gang are.'

'And what did you say?'

'I said I would think about it,' I said.

He thought for a moment.

'You should be careful. It sounds extremely dangerous,' he replied.

And he seemed about to say more, but we were interrupted by a call from the captain. We were now crossing the slightly stagnant, unnaturally silent waters of the Birket Habu, the vast artificial lake in front of the Malkata Palace complex, and approaching the long stone quay where those on government or diplomatic business alighted. Beyond lay the royal quarters with their pools and pleasure lake, the vast labyrinth of government offices, and the huge underworld of kitchens, bakeries, granaries, storehouses and stables that served this city within a city.

Nakht rolled up his official documents, straightened his linens, hoisted his standard, and prepared to disembark.

'Whatever happens now, please trust me,' he said unexpectedly. 'And no more careless talk. At the party it was relatively harmless. Here it would be insubordination.'

And then he stepped lightly from the boat on to the stones of the palace quay.

6

I waited outside the Audience Hall, in a long corridor where officers, administrators and priests in their white linen robes came and went, self-important and whispering in the awful hush that seemed to hold the whole labyrinth of the palace in its thrall. In order to reach this hallowed place, we had been ushered through chamber after chamber, stateroom after stateroom, each one ever-more glorious, ornately decorated and filled with ever-more important dignitaries, Priests and Officers, who had bowed and watched us like jackals as we continued on our progress to the heart of the Palace. The sense of gloom was unrelieved by the glorious paintings covering the floor, the walls, and even the ceiling. Elegant fish swam beneath my feet. Wild ducks rose up from the papyrus reed beds of the Great River. The painted water was clean and the painted flowers were perfect. It all seemed like wishful thinking.

With nothing to do but wait, I drifted back to a reverie of one of the last times I had entered this palace. I had returned from the royal hunt with the corpse of Tutankhamun, who had been killed in a hunting accident. For this, I had incurred Ay's wrath, and his unending enmity. And Ankhesenamun, the King's young wife, the daughter of Nefertiti, had known at once that her own destiny was changed for ever. Instead of the new enlightenment which she and Tutankhamun had intended to bring to the empire, she had been forced to marry the vicious old Vizier, Ay. She had had to acquiesce to his ascension to absolute power in order to prevent an even worse outcome: a military coup by General Horemheb. And now, with Ay's impending death, it seemed that that great disaster had only been postponed, and would soon be upon us.

As I was pondering these matters, footsteps approached. I looked up to see a friendly face. It was Simut, Commander of the Palace Guard. A Nubian, he was statuesque and broad-shouldered, and possessed a face of burnished integrity. We had been together with King Tutankhamun when he had died.

'Have you put on weight?' he asked, assessing me.

'Probably,' I said. 'I wish I could say the same of you. You always look so absurdly fit and healthy.'

He laughed quietly and invited me to sit on one of the gilded benches near by.

'What brings you back to the palace after all this time?' he asked.

'I'm accompanying the royal envoy, Nakht. But in a private capacity, as it were. I'm really only here for show . . .'

'Ah,' he said, delicately grasping my meaning. 'Well, it's good to see you. How long has it been?'

'A while,' I replied, carefully.

'Best not to dwell too much in the past,' he offered. 'Although the present isn't promising, either. And as for the future . . .'

He shrugged his big shoulders. And then he added quietly: 'She still asks after you, from time to time, you know.'

I felt ridiculously gratified to hear the Queen still remembered me.

'I hope all goes well with her,' I said.

He glanced up and down the corridor to check we were alone.

'The Queen's position is delicate. She is greatly admired, and many still love her with the old devotion. But when Ay dies she will be extremely vulnerable. People in power are weighing up their alternatives. Without Ay she will not be able to control the army – indeed, no one could. Horemheb is on the warpath all right . . .'

'I thought he was far away, in the northern lands, fighting the Hittite wars?' I asked.

'Indeed, he is supposed to be. But . . .' he leaned in closer, and lowered his voice to a whisper, '. . . no one knows *exactly* where he is. He might be in Memphis, or he might be with his battalions. Things have changed, you know, especially the business of war. He's taken it all into his own hands, built a new network of garrisons, changed the whole management of the conflict. The grand old days of heroic and mighty armies clashing on the field of battle in blood and bravery are a thing of the past. Now there's a new strategy – low-key occupation of cities and towns. The garrisons control the ways and the trade routes. And . . .' he lowered his voice even further, '. . . he's set up a very efficient new system of army messengers. Basically, he's created his own intelligence network, independent of the palace—'

I was about to ask Simut more about this when the huge, gilded ceremonial doors before me suddenly opened. We both leapt to attention. Nakht appeared, but instead of departing, as I had expected, he absorbed the little scene of my dialogue with Simut; and then, to my astonishment, he invited me into the great Audience Hall.

'Life, prosperity, health.'

I offered the royal greeting, on my knees, my head bowed.

My words echoed quietly among the columns of the great, hushed hall.

'Stand up, Rahotep.'

There was a warm pleasure in the voice of Ankhesenamun, She Who Lives through Amun, the Queen of Egypt, as she spoke my name.

I looked up. She sat on a gilded throne set on a dais at the end of the hall. Her face had changed. The soft, delicate, slightly unfocused youthful features I remembered had acquired great beauty and angularity, and more authority, without losing the charismatic glow that became her so well. There was a new depth of understanding in her eyes. She wore a highly fashionable black wig, perfectly curled, cut precise and short under the back of her head, that framed her face perfectly. It enhanced her beauty and added a powerful, stylish severity. Her diaphanous pleated gown was elegant and elaborate, with a knot under her left breast, leaving one shoulder bare. She wore a magnificent, inlaid gold vulture collar and the rearing gold cobra of the uraeus on her brow, to express her royal authority. On her wrist she wore a gold bracelet inset with a large lapis lazuli scarab. She was composed and regal. She had grown into herself. She had become Queen. I felt unexpectedly moved, as if she were a youngster I had once admired, and now met again as a famous and accomplished adult. But as I looked into her eyes, I realized she was also extremely tense, coiled with an anxiety she struggled to disguise.

And we were not alone. On the other gilded throne set upon the dais, I saw a strange bundle of linens. And then I realized the bundle was alive. It was Ay, Doer of Right, King of Egypt. The last time I had seen him he had been suffering from the misery of toothache, sucking on a lozenge. Now, in his shroud of white linen, and with an exquisite gold ankh amulet hanging around his scrawny neck, he looked like something that should have crossed the border between the living and the dead long ago. I observed the blunt facts of his bony skull, his jutting, quivering jaw, and his crippled fingers. He seemed as shrunken and fragile

45

as a wingless, featherless bird. His skin was thin and dry, stretched between bone and bone, blotched and stained purple and brown by time. But there was also a grim tension, a determined force that still held him together, and I realized that that tension was acute physical agony. For the left side of his face was completely disfigured by a vile canker. It seemed to be eating him alive. It was pink, red and black, and in places beaded with blood. It gave off a scent that was not of rotting flesh, but something more acrid and revolting and animal; I knew it would haunt me for the rest of the day. He panted lightly, struggling for each breath. And he could not speak. Only his right eye still seemed alive; and it gleamed with all the hatred of the pain destroying his body. Once, this diminished monster had held all earthly power in his hands; he had controlled kings, he had destroyed great enemies, he had waged war on other empires, and he had aspired to the status and power of a god on earth. And now he was nothing but skin and bone, and the grim black blossom of the canker that would soon destroy him.

In truth, the revenge of time on this tyrant seemed like earthly justice. But even I was shocked when I noticed the open canker's wounds were dotted with tiny white eggs – and that, despite the attentions of the Bearer of the Fan who stood impassively behind the throne, waving the ornate ostrich-feathered royal fan, minute black flies whirred incessantly around Ay's head in a quiet cloud. He gestured for me to approach, as if he wanted to communicate with me. He struggled to speak, but only weak grunts issued from his constricted throat. In a fit of impotent fury, he gradually raised his arm and pointed a quivering, gnarled finger at me, as if concentrating all power and meaning into the gesture. Then his eyes swivelled towards Nakht as if to say something; but suddenly he fell back, powerless, flopping weakly on to the arms of his gilded throne.

With surprising compassion, Ankhesenamun laid her warm,

beautiful hand on his vile claw. This simple gesture seemed to draw him back to consciousness, and he revived slightly. There was a touch of froth on his desiccated lips. He gasped lightly for air like a suffocating fish. He had so desired immortal life on this earth, and now he was brought down to the simplest of truths: he would die, and very soon. The water clock of his life was nearly dry; the last drops were falling, slowly, slowly. He would soon lie in his magnificent tomb, encased in the gold and stone nest of his sarcophagus and coffins, waiting for the life after life. No doubt it was already well prepared.

Ankhesenamun nodded; four servants picked up the throne with little effort, and carried him away, out of the Hall, and into the private apartments beyond. I knew I would never see him again. And I could not help thinking the world would be better off without him, no matter what came next.

I wondered why I had been invited to witness this grotesque spectacle. I glanced at Nakht, who seemed to be unaffected by what had passed, and merely waited for the doors to close behind Ay. Then he bowed his head to the Queen, and waited. She seemed to have something she wished to say to me. She began to pace the great Audience Hall, moving through the elegant pillars, keeping away from the strong light from the clerestory windows, and within the deep shadows that lay across the beautiful painted floor. She gazed at the walls inlaid with coloured tiles depicting the victories of Egypt over her captive enemies – rows of Syrians with their arms behind their backs, Libyans kneeling, and curly-haired Nubians prostrating themselves.

'Do you remember, Rahotep; we sat together, some years ago, out in that courtyard, and I confided in you what my mother once told me?'

Her voice was quiet in the great space of the hall.

'She said if you were ever in any real danger, you should call for me. And you did,' I answered.

She came closer to me. I saw fear in her eyes.

'I was right to do so. I trusted you. My mother trusted you.'

I was suddenly unnerved. I had no idea where this was leading.

'It was an honour to serve you,' I said.

She considered me, then turned and sat on her gilded throne and once more assumed the posture of Queen. The brief intimacy of her manner was gone. This was business.

'What I am about to tell you is absolutely secret. It must remain so, on pain of death. If you fail my trust, I cannot and will not spare you. Is that clear?'

My doubts must have showed on my face, for she glanced at Nakht, who took up the thread.

'The Queen is calling on your duty. This is not a question of volition. Attend the Queen more closely,' he ordered, and we both approached her. I bowed my head. Even if there were spies listening through secret apertures in the walls, they could not hear us now.

'Rahotep, I have asked the noble Nakht to bring you here because I need you once more. I would not have done so unless it was absolutely necessary. I have not asked you here for myself. It is as Queen of Egypt I must once more command your loyalty,' she said, quietly, confidentially.

I nodded as loyally as I could.

'Since Ay and I have ruled the empire together, I have learned a great deal about power, and what men will do to possess it. Of course, he will not live long now. For the sake of the empire, and for the continuation of the civilized values I hold dear, and for the continuation of my dynasty, I will rule alone as Queen after his death. The noble Nakht and I have laid plans for a stable succession. I am a woman, but I have supporters. Many high-ranking men – and women – have made their loyalty known to me. But I must also recognize the honest advice others have given me: there are those whose political and financial interests would be better served by the ascension of another ruler. I am sure you know of whom I speak. General Horemheb has made his ambitions very clear for a long time. I know there are many in the ministries, and in the priesthood, who will go to his side, if they believe he can offer them, and the Two Lands, something better than I can – or more likely if they feel sufficiently afraid. I must recognize the truth of the situation. The nobles and priests wish to protect their powers and possessions. Horemheb has the army under his command, and it is a great force. Without the support of the great battalions of the Egyptian army, it will be simply impossible for me to rule Egypt.'

She paused to look at me.

'I know perfectly well the great flaw in my situation. I am a woman without heirs. There must be a succession. I must produce heirs. I must continue my family line. I must continue my dynasty. But I will choose the father of my child. Of course, with Ay there was never any possibility of that. The general might consider the political advantages of offering me the solution of marriage. But I will never accept him as a husband. I know his merciless ambition and heartless cruelty too well. I remember his treatment of my aunt after he married her. Even if I could find it in myself to have him join me on the throne, I know I would not live long . . . some accident, or a clever, invisible poison, would surely kill me . . .'

She shivered at the thought.

'Were I a king, I would simply take a noble wife. But I am a woman, and I am alone. I have already lost one husband, and suffered another old enough to be my own grandfather. And who is left for me to marry? How can I save my great dynasty? I think, and think, and all I hear are the voices of my parents, and my grandfather, telling me "You are the last, you must save our dynasty from oblivion", for Horemheb would surely annihilate all signs of our rule. Our royal names would be hacked from the stones, and the great monuments of our reigns would be obliterated. Our glories would be annihilated, and our royal names would never be spoken again. The Gods would not know us. It would be as if we had never even existed. But – I must think not only of my family, but also of what we represent: *we are Egypt*. We have created its greatness. We have brought pride, stability, affluence and peace to this empire. And what will Horemheb do with this inheritance, with this legacy of glory? We all know he will dash it to the ground, for the sake of his own glory. His rule would be cruel and tyrannical . . .'

She stopped speaking, and stood up from the throne, as if overwhelmed by the vision of such a catastrophe. She began once more to pace the great shadows of the Audience Hall, and Nakht and I followed her respectfully. Nakht took up the story.

'But there is great opposition to Horemheb. He has no royal blood. The Gods have not yet chosen him. The oracles have not yet spoken in his favour. Many in the priesthood would never willingly accept him as King. Many are loyal,' he added. He bowed his head, I thought rather ostentatiously.

She turned quickly, speaking urgently again.

'Why do you flatter me with gentle words, noble Nakht? You know, as well as I do, that his power is great, and if he decides to enter Thebes to conquer it and take power from me, many will simply acclaim it as the will of the Gods,' she replied. 'Some oracle or other will be deemed to have foretold his rule and given it divine sanction. I mean no sacrilege when I say oracles are easily bought . . .'

There was no answer to this self-evident truth. And there seemed nowhere else to go in this strange conversation. But then she turned to me again. This living god, the Queen of Egypt, was so close I could smell the delicate scented oil she wore on her gleaming shoulders, and on her elegant throat. And with the old spirit in her voice, she suddenly brightened, and whispered into my ear: 'But I have a plan. I have ordered Nakht to explain every-thing to you, and to outline the duties I require of you. I trust him absolutely, and his word carries my authority.'

Nakht knelt, and I followed suit.

'I need you once more, Rahotep. I know you will not fail me,' she said.

Our audience seemed over, but she stayed where she was, hesitating.

'It was good to see you again. Nakht could have communicated my orders to you, but I confess I wanted to see you in person. I have missed you.'

'And I you, Your Majesty,' I replied.

She smiled, for the first time.

'How is your family? Your three girls? They must be beautiful young women now. And your baby son? I suppose he is no longer a baby.'

'They are all well, thanks be to the Gods,' I replied. 'My oldest is studying medicine. She dreams of becoming a doctor.'

'Oh, that is marvellous! Egypt has been dominated by men for too long. I of all people should know this. Women have been underestimated. We need strong, educated women to help us build a better world. If all goes well with us, she will have a bright future under my reign. I will see to it personally.'

'May it be so,' I said quietly.

'I hope to witness her success. Tell her she can count on my personal support.'

'I will,' I replied.

She gazed at me. Such small talk seemed to give her an intense pleasure, as if for once she could share in the things of ordinary life.

'Be kind to yourself, Rahotep,' she said, and then, to my surprise, she pressed a small bag of gold into my palm, and quickly turned away before I could stammer out my thanks.

51

7

As Nakht and I sailed back from the palace to the Thebes docks, the afternoon light had changed; the sun was setting behind us, to the west, beyond the stony hills, in a panorama of gold and red and blue. We sat in the cabin, alone. I felt like a dog waiting on its master to be fed; I watched him finish with his documents, perfect the way his linen gown sat upon him, and take a refreshing sip of his drink. Finally, he was ready to speak, and by this time I was almost ready to strangle him, I was so tense with anticipation.

'Before I begin, I must ask you to keep silent until I have finished. We are old friends. But, believe me, I will not allow friendship to come between us in regard to what I am about to tell you. This is very serious. It is a matter of high state. Is that understood?'

'Of course it is,' I said.

He waited, then finally whispered: 'The Queen has written and sent a formal, secret letter to the King of the Hittites. In this letter, she has requested him to send her one of his sons, to be her husband, and to rule on the throne of Egypt beside her.'

I thought he was joking.

'You're not serious.'

'I am not inclined to make jokes about the fate of the Two Lands,' he replied.

I stood up, deeply shocked, trying to absorb the ramifications of this revelation.

'But that is impossible. No one in Egypt will accept a foreigner of any kind on the throne of the Two Lands – least of all a son of our arch-enemy . . .'

'Keep quiet. And sit down!' he hissed. He was furious with me now. He stood right in front of me, whispering urgently.

'I asked you to listen to me without comment. The proposal is radical, but it has many advantages.'

'Such as?' I demanded.

He was no longer comfortable in the little cabin, unable to be sure we were not overheard. And so we paced along the deck, in the evening light, arguing.

'Firstly, it'll completely wrong-foot Horemheb. He could never anticipate this move. Next, it will solve the vexed question of the succession. There is quite simply no one else in the kingdom for the Queen to marry. This way she will have a husband we can control, and she will beget sons,' he insisted.

'But they will be the half-sons of our *enemies*!' I said.

'And *that* is the stroke of genius! With this marriage, the war between Egypt and the Hittites will be brought to a spectacular end, in a peace that is entirely to our advantage. It has gone on far too long. It is pointless, unnecessary and extremely expensive. It is domestically unpopular, and it no longer brings us any appreciable international gains. In short, we are wasting time and resources on an outdated conflict that should now swiftly be brought to a conclusion. A negotiated settlement is in both sides' interest.

Indeed, the war is only benefiting the enemies of international stability—' he argued, his eyes bright with determination, his finger raised in affirmation.

'Such as who?' I interrupted.

He shook his head, apparently frustrated at my stupidity.

'I don't have time to explain all this to you, you just have to do as you are commanded,' he said.

'If you are commanding me to be part of something, you owe it to me to explain the full reasons for risking my life.'

He stared at me.

'Very well. But *listen*, and *think*. The kingdoms and the city-states of the Levant, with their warlords, their petty tyrants and their disastrous polities, are a cause of great international instability. This, as the pre-eminent empire of the world, we cannot and will not tolerate. Peaceful relations with the Hittites are not only economically advantageous to both sides, but also – and this is the consequence I trust you will particularly appreciate – *will mean the army no longer has a defined enemy.*'

I gazed back at him.

'So you think Horemheb could not continue to claim the army's vast powers and financial necessities if there was no conflict to justify them?' I said.

'Yes! At last you begin to understand. It will remove his main purpose, and therefore deeply undermine his personal power and authority. Conflict defines nations. Enemies justify armies. Wars glorify generals. Without his great enemy to give him purpose and meaning, he will be significantly diminished. He will have to come to terms with us. He will not be able to oppose the Queen.'

Nakht stood there, in the late sunlight, his face like a clever schoolboy's, his smooth features a picture of delight at the audacity of the plan. I had to admit, it was extraordinary. It also seemed to me incredibly risky. But somehow Nakht had taken an idea that sounded preposterous, and turned it into what looked like brilliant politics. He gazed at me expectantly.

'If this was a round of *senet*, I'd say you were going to get knocked off the board very soon, and into the jaws of a crocodile,' I said quietly.

He scowled, irritated and disappointed.

'Your gaming metaphor is crude. But if you insist on using it, yes, we are gambling everything on a last throw of the sticks. And to be frank: what other option do we have?'

'You could fight an open battle for the succession against Horemheb here, in Egypt. In Thebes,' I suggested.

'It will not work. Horemheb commands the two corps of Upper and Lower Egypt: that is, the Ta, Ra, Seth and Amun divisions, each of five thousand troops. The division leaders of the first three are loyal to him. Let's speculate: Horemheb is from the delta, the Seth division are from his home, owe him the most loyalty, and would have the most to gain from supporting him. Say he ordered them back from the war in the north. One division alone would probably be sufficient to take control of Thebes. Memphis he already controls. And if he were able to command one or two divisions more to attack Thebes, what would become of us all?'

I shook my head, and walked away, up towards the prow of the boat, trying to absorb what I was hearing. I saw we were close to the city.

'If you think things are bad now, under Horemheb's rule there would be summary executions, curfews and the wholesale massacre of the palace hierarchy and the priesthood! The Queen and her supporters would be executed. He would simply commandeer everyone's riches for himself, and if the priesthood opposed him they would be decimated. Blood would run in the gutters. It would be the end of everything,' he said, as if to persuade me further.

'Now you sound like Hor,' I said.

'*Hor was right.*'

We confronted each other in silence. We were both angry and alarmed.

'Even if your plan works, even if the Hittite King agrees to this proposal, and to a peace plan, and even if Horemheb does not launch a coup, I still have a question – why are you telling me all of this? Why am I being invited into the great secret?' I said.

Nakht looked quickly around, to confirm no one could hear us, took me by the arm, and spoke into my ear.

'I have been honoured with the supreme responsibility of leading the diplomatic mission to the Hittite capital to negotiate the marriage agreement. It will be a secret mission. We will travel incognito. It is essential Horemheb has no intelligence about us, or our whereabouts. We will travel as merchants on the Way of Horus, as quickly as possible. We will charter a commercial ship from Ugarit to the southern coast of the Hittite lands. Once we arrive in the Hittite capital of Hattusa, I will negotiate the terms of the peace treaty, and of the marriage. If we are successful, we will then bear the responsibility of bringing the Hittite Prince safely back to Egypt. We will be accompanied by Simut, and a retinue of elite palace guards, who have all been carefully vetted for loyalty.'

'And still I do not know what this has to do with me,' I said.

'The Queen orders you to join this mission as my personal bodyguard. Simut and his guards will ensure the safety of the royal letters and the gifts of gold we will carry to the Hittite King, and they will manage the security of the mission in general. But you will be responsible for my personal safety. Let's be clear: if necessary you will be required to give your life for mine. I should add this is not my idea. The Queen insists. And perhaps she is right, for only I can undertake the negotiations. In addition, however, the personal safety of the Hittite Prince will also be your responsibility on the return journey.'

My heart pounded. I couldn't think how to respond.

'You have put me in a position where I cannot say no,' I said.

Nakht's face hardened.

'Not I, but the Queen. But I know you very well, my friend. I can see in your eyes that you are excited. I see something of the sparkle, the gleam of adventure, which has been missing for too long. Do not deny it. You relish excitement. You need mystery. You thrive on it. It is your meat and drink. And if I may be so personal,' he paused, 'you might also value the very substantial reward that will be yours, in addition to the gold she has already given you, if we are successful.'

I gazed out at the Great River's panorama without seeing anything. He was right. I was excited. After these years of frustration and humiliation, and of domestic tedium, the prospect of such a journey, of such high responsibility, and of adventure in other lands, was like cool, clear water to a man lost in the desert.

'I cannot simply leave my family. You *know* that. What would happen to them if . . . ?' I said.

'If we do not return? I have considered that. If we succeed, I have been authorized to offer you the role of Chief of the Thebes Medjay.'

I felt my heart skip a beat.

'Nebamun is Chief of the Thebes Medjay,' I replied, as coolly as I could manage.

'The Queen agrees it is time this city had a police chief whose dignity and worth reflected the power of his high position; someone who was capable of building the force into an organization better suited to its true purpose, which is to uphold the law of the land. Nebamun will accept his retirement with the grace that comes from receiving a large settlement of gold and a royal declaration of official thanks and respect,' he said, in his most persuasive voice.

Nothing in this world would give me more satisfaction than to reclaim my rightful position in the Medjay, and to see my rival, in all his arrogance and vanity, displaced.

'You tempt me with the prize I desire above all others. But you know I promised my wife I would not leave the family again,' I said. Nakht inclined his head.

'Listen to me. If I were to die tomorrow, I would have no family of my own to perform the rites for me. My tomb would not be visited by my descendants, for I do not have any. But I flatter myself that your own family might miss me. Believe me, I love them as my own. I take their well-being into deep consideration. I am aware of the grave perils of the journey ahead of us. The stakes are high, the way is full of dangers. We are going to the heartland of our enemies. We must cross through unknown and highly unstable territories notorious for the worst kind of barbarity. It's possible we will not return.'

He paused for a moment, and looked away at the docks that were approaching now. His eyes assessed everything, as if making an inventory of every ship, every cargo, entering the city. I suddenly saw his memory as a great, hushed scriptorium, its shelves stacked with thoughts and memories, all rolled and docketed like papyrus manuscripts.

'So I propose the following,' he continued. 'Your family shall lodge in my city house during the period of our journey. While they are there, they will want for nothing, and they will be safe and secure.'

'But if I do not return, who is going to look after them? How will they eat? What will become of them?' I asked.

He turned to me, his face gravely sincere.

'In the event of your death, my friend, I will provide for them like a father. I will be generous. You have my word. And if I should die too, then they would inherit my entire estate. They would never want for anything again. In any case, I drew up the relevant documents years ago. The Queen is not the only person in Egypt who has to consider her succession.'

I was so surprised by this that I barely registered the thud as the boat touched the quay.

'There you have it,' he said. 'But remember; everything is at stake. The world we know is hanging in the balance. It is no exaggeration to say the future of Egypt depends upon the success of our mission. We must do all in our power to ensure the right outcome. So, join me not only because the Queen commands you; do it so that your children can grow up in a decent world.'

And he stepped quickly up from the boat, and into his waiting chariot.

'Can I give you a lift?' he enquired, solicitously.

I shook my head. I needed to walk.

8

That evening, I said nothing to Tanefert about my audience with the Queen. Nor did I give her the little bag of gold. All night, as I lay on the couch, my mind toiled like a scarab beetle trying to push its ball of dung into the light, going over and over the conversation with Nakht. And when dawn glimmered on the floor of our bedchamber, I felt as if I had been fighting with myself for hours. Sometimes I have woken from a night's sleep with the solution to a long-puzzled, intransigent mystery simply waiting for me. But that morning, my thoughts were still a jumble of shards.

Tanefert glanced at me as she rose from her couch, and pinned her long black and silver hair around her head.

'You were restless.'

'Did I disturb you?' I asked.

After all the years of marriage, of raising children, of surviving the volatility of my working life, I was still in love with my wife. But recently I had realized that she needed more from me than I had been able to give her. A little distance had opened between us, almost unnoticed, rarely acknowledged. We made love infrequently. The couch was for sleep at the end of exhausting days. I confided in her less often. Perhaps that is the fate of all marriages.

'You can tell me anything,' she said quietly. 'I hope you know that.'

I tucked a stray wisp of glossy hair behind her delicate ear. Outside, the girls were preparing their breakfasts, and taking charge of their baby brother. I could hear their amiable chatter, the banging of the dishes, and my son's early morning protestations. I reached out quickly and embraced my wife, kissing her and drawing her back down to the couch with an open need that surprised her.

'I miss you,' she said suddenly, putting her hand against my chest, near my heart. Her eyes were shining.

'I miss you, too,' I said, and kissed her again.

By the time we appeared in the kitchen, Tanefert winding her hair about her head once more, me rubbing my face as if to pretend I had just woken, the girls were ready to leave for their lessons, and I was late. They allowed themselves a giggle at my expense – for the older two girls were no longer innocents. I washed my face in the yard basin, and then, having taken Thoth from his place and attached his collar and lead, the girls and I walked together down the lane in the shade, and along the Alley of Fruit, where the market was already lively with sellers hawking bright fruit and vegetables.

At the crossroads, I kissed the girls, and watched as they cheerfully made their way off along the street, talking and laughing and arguing, until they merged into the crowds. I stood for a moment, enjoying the warm light of a new day. I had made this family, I loved my wife, and now, thanks to Nakht, I could finally see a way forward for all of us. I felt the stirring of an unfamiliar sensation: I felt alive and confident. I shook my head cheerfully at my own foolishness, and set off with Thoth at my side, moving nimbly and excitedly down a different street, into a fresh day.

But as soon as I entered the Medjay headquarters, I knew something was wrong: several of the men glanced at me, and glanced quickly away. I hurried over to Panehesy.

'What's happened?'

The pity in his face told me the worst.

The body had been dumped in a foul side street of the slums, where locals tipped their stinking rubbish. It was a dismal place to deposit a man's mortal remains, an offence to the spirits of the dead. A couple of younger Medjay officers were peering down the alley in awe. When they saw me, they tried to dissuade me from going any further. But I shoved them away. I had to see.

Khety's head had been severed. It sat calmly in a small puddle of congealed black blood. With the cold habit of a lifetime, I noted the details: the sticky crimson prints of dogs and cats in the street dirt all around him. He must have been killed in the small hours of the night. His lips were blue, his skin inert, and his dead eyes half-open. When I examine a murder victim, I think about the kind of knife that might have made the wounds, but not about the suffering those wounds caused. This is because I owe it to the victim to work efficiently; I am not there for the benefit of my own feelings. I am there only to bear witness, as best I can, to the final truth of their death.

So I crushed the futile tears starting to my eyes, and the cries that stuck in my throat. Some force deep inside me was shaking me hard, but I steeled myself to do the necessary work; I focused, for Khety's sake, for his honour, giving him

62

my final respects. I saw how the blades that accomplished the beheading had been extremely sharp; the cuts in his flesh were precise and knowledgeable. There was no hesitation, no prevarication, no uncertainty. Khety's head had been severed expertly, just like the Nubian boys'. And the killer had had a respect, amounting to an obsession, with neatness of composition: behind the head were the other parts of my friend's corpse, butchered like an animal carcass. His arms and legs were stacked against his trunk, like logs of flesh and bone. His hands and feet had been cut off, too; his fingers, snipped off, were laid on top like a dreadful decoration. And on them, disgustingly, the shrivelled remains of his penis had been placed. The killer had started with his extremities. I realized he would probably have been alive throughout much of the butchery. The world around me was spinning. I turned away and hurried, crouching, into the further shadows of the alley, where I vomited on the filthy ground, bucking like an animal.

A crowd of fascinated little street children had gathered to watch me. I grabbed a handful of stones and gravel, and hurled it at them as if they were dogs. They scattered, shouting and laughing.

I returned to the mutilated remains of my friend. Khety's dead eyes registered nothing. I reached out and took his head between my hands, as carefully as I could. A dead head is heavy. I felt a ridiculous urge to ask him questions, to interrogate him, even to slap his stupid face until his eyes flickered open, his jaw stirred into creaky motion, and he spoke again, if only to curse me for waking him from the dead. Like a madman, I kissed his cold brow, whispering my useless, propitiatory apologies. Two nights ago, my friend had asked for my help. And I had abandoned him. Now he was cruelly slaughtered. Perhaps I could have stopped him behaving recklessly. I could have saved him. Guilt hunched on my back like a vicious monkey, digging its sharp claws into me, and began to whisper its hot accusations into my ears.

And then, even in the midst of my new agony, a thought crossed my mind; although the jawbone was already stiff, I prised open my friend's teeth as carefully as I could, and reached inside his dead mouth. And there it was: another fold of papyrus. I tenderly replaced my friend's head on the ground. I was shivering now, although not with cold, and I forced my hands to do my bidding, to open up the delicate papyrus. Inside was the black star, with its evil arrows pointing in every direction.

I heard footsteps. Nebamun was walking towards me. I hid the papyrus in my satchel. He glanced at Khety's remains and shook his head with no more respect or feeling than if he were looking at a dead dog. Then he took a deep, dramatic breath, as if he had something momentous to convey.

'What a world,' he managed.

His trite little clichés had always incensed me.

'He was a good officer. I know he was your friend. But I can't have you running around the city like a madman trying to track down his killer. I'm instructing you to remain at home, and I'm assigning someone else to this case . . .'

I turned to him.

'He was my partner. He's *mine*. This is *my* investigation. You can assign your arse,' I said.

Nebamun squinted, and spat.

'I've tried to be sweet and compassionate, in your hour of need, and all that . . . and you've thrown it right back in my face. So listen to me carefully, Rahotep. If I hear you're meddling in this, I'll have you arrested and thrown into the darkest cell I can find, and I'll seal you in there for ever, and let some of the more enthusiastic and less fastidious members of the Medjay have a go at you. Understand?'

The blood burned in my hands.

'You have no intention of investigating this, any more than you've "investigated" any of the other murders,' I said. 'What's that about?'

I noticed the twitching of the thin blue veins in the wrinkled skin around his beady eyes.

'That kind of talk will cost you more than you know,' he said, staring coldly at me.

'I've nothing left to lose,' I added. 'What is it about me that alarms you so badly that you've spent the last years stripping me of everything that's rightfully mine?'

'It's because you think you're so fucking special, Rahotep. You seem to think you operate by some code of honour that exalts you far above the rest of us. But you know something? You're not special. Your honour's a sham. You're a failure. I didn't have to do anything. I just had to watch you turn your own career into a joke. I've enjoyed the spectacle. But now I'm bored with you; and when you start making accusations against me, then that's the day you've gone too far,' Nebamun snarled.

'Just try me,' I said deliberately.

He raised his stubby finger at me.

'You think you've still got it, don't you? The truth is, no one cares. You're on your own. Some partner you must have been; you've been doing nothing, and yet here he was doing the real work, and he ends up like this?' And he jerked his head back at Khety's remains.

I only realized what I'd done when he staggered backwards, dabbing at the blood on his lip. The other officers trotted over, stupid as goats, exclaiming at my crazy action. Nebamun waved them away, but I saw to my intense satisfaction he was furious.

'Hitting a superior officer is grounds for immediate dismissal.

So don't bother coming back to headquarters now, or ever. Just *fuck off!*'

He turned away, and then, as an afterthought, called back.

'Oh, I forgot. There is one last thing you can do. *Tell Khety's wife.*' And he laughed.

9

When Kiya saw me standing there, her smile instantly died. She half-closed the door, murmuring, 'No no no no no,' over and over. When she stopped, I stood listening to the terrible silence on the other side of the door. I called her name quietly.

'I can't let you in. If I let you in, it'll be true,' she said, eventually. 'Please go away.'

'I can't. I'll wait here until you're ready,' I replied, through the door.

As I stood there, waiting quietly, the people going about their daily business in the street seemed small and irrelevant. How little they knew, I thought, of the darkness of death behind and beneath and inside everything in their lives. How little they understood their own mortality, as they went unknowingly through each day in the enchantment of new clothes, and appetites fulfilled, and amusing love affairs. They had forgotten that at any moment all we hold dear, all we take for granted, all we cherish and prize, can be torn away from us.

Eventually, the door opened silently. I sat with Kiya in the small room at the front of the house. Khety and I had rarely socialized together; and although I knew where he lived, I had never visited him at home. Now I saw this other side of his life: the ornaments and trinkets, the little divine statuettes, the average-quality furniture, the efforts to make the place look better than it was. A pair of his house sandals waited by the door for his return.

I told Kiya the simple facts. I heard myself swearing and promising I would track down Khety's killer, and bring him to justice. But the words were meaningless to her. She just stared right through me. Nothing I could do would redeem what had been lost, for ever.

Suddenly her focus seemed to swim up from the black depths of despair.

'You were his best friend. He was never as happy as when he was working with you.'

I had to turn my face away. Outside, the noises of the street continued. Somewhere a girl was singing lightly, casually, a phrase of a love song.

'I have to ask you something: did he tell you where he was going last night?' I said, despising myself.

She shook her head.

'He never told me anything,' she replied. 'He thought it was better that way. It wasn't. Not for me, anyway.'

We sat in silence for a moment.

'This new child will never know his father,' she said, as she looked down at her belly.

'I will care for it as if it were my own,' I said.

Kiya was rocking back and forth, as if trying to console the unborn child in her belly for the loss of its father. Then she suddenly looked up.

'You argued with each other that night, didn't you?' There was still nothing accusing in her voice. Only sorrow.

I nodded, relieved to confess it. She looked at me with the strangest expression, a mixture of pity and disappointment; but before I could say more, suddenly the door opened, and their daughter appeared. Her cheerful, delicate face was quickly wide-eyed as she absorbed the strange atmosphere in the room. The sight of the child instantly released Kiya's tears. She threw her arms open, and the child ran into them in confusion and distress, while her mother sobbed, grasping the little girl as tightly as she could.

I stood outside in the futile sunlight, feeling as empty as a clay vessel. I began walking without direction. Every street vendor's cry and call of laughter, every snatch of birdsong, every friendly shout from neighbour to neighbour, reminded me I no longer belonged to the land of the living, but had become a shadow. I found myself eventually facing the glittering imperturbability of the Great River. I sat down and stared at its perpetual waters, green and brown. I gazed at the sun, shining as if nothing had happened. I thought of the God of the Nile, in his cavern, pouring out the waters of the Great River from his jugs. I thought of the long futility of the impossible days ahead. And I felt a new coldness take possession of me: a single-minded impulse, a purity of intention, like a blade of hatred. I would find Khety's killer. And then I would kill him.

10

The stench from the garbage and mess in the street alone could have killed a mule. In the sowing season of *peret* the heat can be sweltering, and in the overcrowded slum on the wrong side of the city, far from the river and its graceful breezes, nothing stirred. All the passageways seemed to lead back into each other, going nowhere. I stood in the shadows on the street corner, and watched. It was late morning; people evaded the heat of the sun as if it were deadly. Old men and women dozed and muttered in grim, dark doorways. Street dogs lay on their sides in the dust, panting. Emaciated, filthy cats stretched out in whatever shadow they could find. Young mothers lazily fanned themselves, while their kids played in the rubbish and dirt that had piled up everywhere, and in the squalid streams that meandered thickly down the alleys. And occasionally young Nubian men – most no more than kids, but already tall and striking in their looks – sauntered past, roving the shadows, watching everything, guarding their territory.

This was one of the slums' streets notorious for the opium trade, where the low-level gang boys would sell to the more desperate addicts – those who dared to come here, despite the dangers, driven beyond fear by obsession. The slums were populated by immigrants from Punt and Nubia, originally drawn to Thebes by the lucrative southern trade routes that brought gold and copper, ebony, ivory, incense, slaves and rare animals – leopards, giraffes, panthers, little brown monkeys, ostriches – from beyond those lands. Others were drawn by the dream of a better life; the lucky ones ended up labouring on big construction projects, or being employed for their prized skills in metalwork. But in these years, the last royal constructions had been completed – such as the Great Colonnade Hall, inaugurated under Tutankhamun – or abandoned under Ay's austerity. It was taken as a sign of the dynasty's weakness that no new monuments or temples had been commissioned – for such triumphs in stone were symbols of power and honour. And so the children of those immigrants, with no prospect of work, and with a keen sense of their alienation from the wealth of the city, turned to the only other option available to them: crime. Not for them the business of tomb robbery, which required surveillance, organization, and effort, and which was in any case the preserve of the older thieving families. These teenagers were messengers, couriers and occasional killers for the opium gangs.

As I watched and waited, Khety's dead face kept flashing through my mind. I remembered Kiya holding on to her daughter for dear life. And I recalled Tanefert's desperate face as she had struggled to console me when I had finally found the courage to walk into my own yard, and sink to my knees before her. My heart was like broken glass in my chest. Would it be like this for ever? I struggled to keep my focus on the spectacle before me: the haggard shadows, the arrogant youths, and the yellow-toothed, ragged addicts, with their dulled eyes. One, obviously a rich boy, shambled along the street, his arrogance undermined by his fear and need. He had the signs of withdrawal: his legs shook with wild energy, and he was scratching at his arms, drawing blood. He wore good clothes, and gold rings on his fingers, and his hair was neatly cut. It was like watching an antelope being stalked by lions: the Nubian boys quickly closed in, tracking him along the street, and whistling to each other. One of them jauntily approached the rich boy. He was maybe fourteen or fifteen years old, already tall but still with a child's bony thinness and awkwardness, wearing a short white kilt, leather tassels, gold earrings, and with his hair immaculately plaited. He was full of bravado. Keeping always to the shade, he nodded, and beckoned the rich boy to follow him up a side alley. The rich boy nodded back. The Nubian boys sniggered, and made their way around the back. Those rings would soon be off the rich boy's hands, most likely with his fingers still wearing them.

I slipped up the alleyway. They were standing close together, but the Nubian boy had his dagger out, threatening the rich boy. I grabbed him from behind. His weapon clattered to the ground. He writhed in my grip like a feral cat.

'Get out of here now,' I hissed at the rich boy.

He was trembling, but not with fear.

'No – I need it, I have to have it . . .'

To my amazement, he actually picked up the dagger and wavered it uncertainly at me. The Nubian kid laughed at both of us with open contempt.

'You stupid idiot. Give it to me!' I shouted.

I looked up the alley. The Nubian boys were gathering. The kid in my grip bit me hard. I whacked him on the side of the head.

'I'm Medjay, and if you don't give me that blade and run, you'll be in prison,' I said to the rich boy. He glanced at me pathetically, gave the dagger to me, and just stood there hopelessly.

'Go!' I yelled. He finally scarpered. I pressed the blade against

72

the Nubian boy's neck vein, which pulsed delicately. He was wearing a carved amulet, bearing the sign of an arrow, his symbol of belonging, and of protection. The same one the dead boys had worn.

'What is it you want, Medjay man?' he demanded.

'I want you to take me to your boss,' I replied.

He laughed in my face, a practised snarl of contempt, smirking and scoffing.

'Who do you think you are?' he said.

I slapped him hard across the face a few times.

'Think you're a soldier, a big man, a brave?' I said, jabbing the blade harder against his skin. He stared at me incredulously, licking the blood from his lips. Now I saw a glint of fear in his eyes.

'I'll kill you for this disrespect,' he said, glancing at his approaching colleagues. I shoved him around, and shouted at them all.

'I'm a man with questions, and I want some answers. And believe me, I'll cut out his eyes before he can blink if you come any closer.' And I raised the dagger to show I was serious.

The boy clicked his tongue. His eyes moved from side to side as he tried to work out what to do next.

'You'll never walk away from this place. The shadows will kill you. You will be cut up into little pieces!' he offered, brazening out the situation.

I punched him hard in the kidneys. He buckled up, and his colleagues drew back a little, spitting, calling oaths and shaking their heads.

'Here's the deal. Either I arrest you for possession of opium, which means you'll end up in prison and I'll personally make sure you never see daylight again, or else you take me to whoever it is runs your gang.'

The boy just laughed with contempt.

'You're a madman. You think you can just go on in and talk to the boss? You? You'd be dead meat before you made it through the door.'

'That's my problem. Show me the door. Or I'll cut out your eye . . .' I said.

And I pressed the point of the blade home right next to his eye, producing a dot of blood, to show him I was serious. Suddenly his bravado vanished, and he started to whisper, 'Don't don't don't . . .'

My hand was shaking, we both realized.

'Now tell your little friends to fuck off, unless you want to let them see you piss yourself,' I said quietly.

He motioned to the other boys to back off. They drifted away into the shadowy passages.

The crude wooden door he took me to gave away nothing of the business inside. The sign of the arrow was drawn on it, big and crude. Someone had added a pair of gigantic balls to the symbol. Inside I could hear raucous laughter, and wild shrieks.

He knocked, according to a code. Someone was talking, cursing the interruption, and the door creaked open a fraction on its hinges – just enough for me to slam it wide and enter. Inside everything was squalid: naked young girls in opium drowses lay in desultory poses on couches or on the floor, and young men in groups shouted aggressively in triumph as they played euphoric games of *senet*, or traded jokes and insults. But as soon as the men saw me, they leapt to their feet, jeering provocatively, making threatening gestures with their knives, and pornographic ones with their fists and tongues, ululating as they approached. Behind them I saw a few small, long-necked jars of opium juice. These lads were the next step up from the boy I was with. All wore the arrow amulet on leather necklaces. All wore their hair braided in the same style. I held the dagger close to the boy's throat.

Suddenly he was angry and vicious, knowing he had been badly shamed, and fearing his life was worth even less than mine to his gang. A couple of the larger, more senior lads stepped forward, their ostentatious knives drawn.

'Gentlemen, I know this visit is unannounced, but I want to speak to your glorious leader. About this . . .'

And I held up a papyrus bearing the sign of the black star. They stared at it. One grabbed it from my hand, his eyes glittering.

'Where did you get this?' he demanded.

'From the mouth of a dead dealer,' I said. 'We both know what it's about, and I've got information. But I'll only talk to your leader.'

I was blindfolded, and made to wait on a low stool. I listened to the shouts and arguments, and the taunts that came my way. But none of the lads harmed me. Finally I was yanked to my feet, and we set off. Three of them pushed me roughly through passageways and side streets, accompanied by the boy. I could hear the business of the city going on in the distance, and I knew we had moved out of the slum, into a better area. Whenever anyone approached they were warned away. Eventually we arrived at our destination. I was ushered inside. The air was cool, and smelt clean, and I heard the sound of water, and splashing, and the giggling, seductive laughter of girls. The blindfold was removed.

I was in a bathhouse, in one of the private chambers set out with couches for resting. Before me stood a Nubian man, tall and slim. He gazed at me. His stony eyes were alert with intelligence. He wore many gold necklaces, and bangles. He cracked his neck dramatically, and sauntered over to assess me more closely, running his long, ostentatiously serrated gold dagger around me, as if I were a slave he might acquire or destroy.

'Who brought this person uninvited into our place?' he asked quietly.

75

The Nubian boy was terrified. He looked down. The man raised his chin, almost tenderly.

'You made a mistake, Dedu. A bad mistake. You've betrayed us all. Do you understand that?'

The boy nodded slowly. His lower lip was trembling now.

'Please . . .' he whispered.

'Please what?' said the man.

'Please, my lord. Don't kill me.'

The man pondered, watching the boy.

'Wait there,' he said. 'Think about your error.'

The boy nodded and bowed humbly. I didn't have time to feel sorry for him.

Then the gang leader turned to me.

'Normally, I only see Medjay officers by appointment, by night. Is this visit for business, or pleasure?' he asked.

'Something of both,' I responded.

He chuckled, playing with his knife, executing complex little moves he'd honed for performance and intimidation.

'You've got a lot of audacity coming in here like this. Now I have to decide whether to kill you or listen to you. I think I'll listen to you, and then kill you afterwards. You'd better have a good story. Who knows? It might even prolong your life – for a while.'

He threw out the men who had brought me and the pretty young girls who lay about on the couches. Then, when they had all sauntered or scurried away, and only he, Dedu and two bodyguards remained, he offered me a low stool, with exaggerated politeness.

'I'll stand. I've come to discuss this.'

I held out the papyrus. He glanced at it, nonchalant.

'So what?'

'I found it in the mouth of my closest friend. His head had been separated from his body.'

'Ah, your closest friend.' He grunted with sarcastic sympathy.

'Alas, death is everywhere. The God Seth, Lord of Chaos and Confusion, is surely walking the streets of this city once more. Now he does not even spare the fine law-enforcing officers of the Medjay. What are things coming to? And what is it you want from me?'

'I'm sure you are also familiar with this symbol. It has been found in the mouths of others – dead young dealers who were, I'm sure, in your employment.'

'And so?'

'And so we have something in common,' I said.

Suddenly his knife slammed into the wall, just a hair's breadth from my face, near my eye, and juddered there. I stared at him, unmoved.

'You and I have nothing in common. And I still don't know why you are here. I think, and I can find no answer. You had better help me out, quickly,' he said.

'You, I assume, want to know who has been slaughtering your boys, and taking away your business.'

'And what do you want?' he asked.

'I want to know who killed my friend. And I want to kill him.'

He nodded, delighted by this.

'Ah, revenge, it is so beautiful,' he said. 'But my question is this: *what can you do for me that I can't do for myself?*'

'A deal. Mutual benefit. We share all our knowledge. I'm a Medjay detective. This gives me authority, and it grants me access to places you could never reach. However, you will back me up. You will tell me what you know about this new gang. We'll combine intelligence. You provide the force, if and when the time comes. And then you can take your revenge. But the crucial clause is this: the killer of my friend is mine to do with as I choose.'

He put the tips of his fingers carefully together and smiled.

'You think this is funny?' I said. 'You think I'm here to amuse myself?'

He nodded, as if somehow impressed by my reckless behaviour.

'You are truly angry, my friend, and I admire your thirst for revenge. But perhaps you did not think carefully enough about coming here. Perhaps you didn't think about *respect*.'

'I thought carefully. You know who I am. You could easily kill me if you wanted. So why else would I take this kind of risk unless I was – *sincere*?' I replied.

He chuckled at the word, repeating it to himself as if it were the punchline of a joke. Then he reached for a jug of wine, and poured us each a measure.

'Sit down, my sincere friend,' he said, in a warmer tone. 'Let me tell you about myself.'

And so it was I ended up listening to one of the most notorious and ruthless bosses of the city's cartels. I found him to be a hard, intelligent businessman, with an astute sense of theatre; his own grand style of violence he deemed a necessary part of business. It was an expression of power, and a demand for respect. Of course, he was prepared to use it whenever it suited him, which was often; but he was no psychopath. In fact, he saw himself as a benefactor, for the men under his control were young, and otherwise hopeless, and he believed he was shaping their lawlessness to more useful ends. The vast profits of his trade he saw as a reasonable redistribution of wealth. He was himself simply profiting like a businessman from a new market of consumers – the affluent young of Egypt, who could afford the luxury of opium, and then, when pleasure turned to addiction, who could maintain that, too. He had even devised a special deal; the first hit was free. Thereafter, they bought from him. He had no concern for their welfare; in the direct terms of his morality, that was their responsibility.

I began to realize this was a man who believed his actions were reasonable and principled; he saw his cartel as a family, or a kind of brigade, and its rules were based not on violence, but on trust. Most of the kids who came to him were orphaned or from homes so broken by poverty and violence they were better off without them. He gave them something to do, something to define themselves against, and a strict routine with tangible rewards. Most strangely, perhaps, he was proud of the city, and of his position.

As a – now – former Medjay officer, I belonged on the opposite side of everything he stood for, and everything he said. And yet I found myself unable, at times, to challenge the truth of his arguments. But in any case, it was not in my interest to question him further about the less appetizing aspects of his apparently benign underworld tyranny. I only needed to know what he could tell me about the Black Star Gang.

'They are a mystery, and they are a big problem. The supply of opium is limited, and hard to obtain, and therefore of great value; and so all the Theban gangs have always fought over it. It has been notoriously unreliable. Of course it is smuggled up the Great River, by boat. It is not so difficult to bribe the right men to smuggle the shipments through the port. And the captains take their share willingly. Sometimes the quantities are excellent – three or more shipments in one month. But at times they have dwindled to nothing. Some of us tried to set up better, more consistent supply lines, but it was impossible. The distances were too great. The contacts were obscure. The jars are heavy, and the opium juice is inconvenient to transport. It is a strange world out there, beyond our borders, and mostly our dealers and negotiators do not return.'

'And now?' I asked.

'Now, suddenly, the gang war in the city has exploded again. At first we suspected each other. But soon even the most adamant of my rivals recognized this was the work of a different group. They are nothing like us.'

'Tell me what you know.'

He sighed, and began to pace the chamber.

'These killers are like the spirits of the dead. They travel in silence. They destroy everything. They go where they will . . . and no one escapes or survives,' he said simply.

'But how do they do that?' I wondered.

He shrugged.

'It is their style. It's very elegant. And you know, unlike the rest of us, they don't diversify at all. Gambling, prostitution, illegal smuggling of rare goods, kidnapping – these are all potentially lucrative areas. But as far as I know, they have shown no interest in any of this—'

'How do they distribute the opium? It's one thing to import it, and to destroy the competition. It's another to set up a new distribution system of dealers,' I said.

He opened his hands wide in agreement.

'I have no idea. I am hoping you will tell me. Perhaps, when they have wiped out the rest of the opposition, they will offer us a distribution deal. No doubt the terms will not be very acceptable.'

He gazed at me, then leaned back, and roared with laughter.

'You know something; I feel I could almost like you. You must have some balls, coming in here and talking to me like this.'

I ignored him.

'Is there anything else you can tell me? The smallest detail might be useful,' I said.

He pondered the papyrus and the black star.

'Here in Thebes we are at the end of a long process, a long journey, a chain of many connected businesses. This has never been efficient, but it was always necessary. But it seems to me somehow this gang must have solved that problem. I don't know how, but I believe they control the whole process from supply to delivery. Perhaps you should think about that. Think about where the chain begins, as well as where it ends.'

'And where is that?'

He smiled.

'North.'

'Everyone knows the opium crop is grown in the badlands between Egypt and the Hittite Empire. So perhaps Canaan? Amurru? Qadesh?' I said, thinking of the territories that Egypt had struggled to control during the long stalemate of the Hittite wars.

'I will repeat to you one word, which I hear, coming down to me from far, far away.'

He beckoned me closer.

'*Obsidian*. It is—'

'I know what obsidian is. It is the material of looking glasses, and our sharpest knives.' I interrupted.

Then I remembered the masterful butchery of the decapitations. What if the killer had used an obsidian knife?

'Obsidian is a *name*,' he said quietly. I looked at him, hoping for more.

The man stood up. Something in his gaunt face had suddenly changed. He was dangerous again.

'You should go now. But I will be watching you. So don't think you can just walk away from this. Do your part. Or else I will show you what happened to our boys could happen to you, too.'

And with that, he screwed up the papyrus with the black star, grinned and swallowed it. And then swiftly he turned, and slashed his knife across the throat of Dedu, the waiting Nubian boy. Dedu gurgled on his own blood, and then his body collapsed at my feet.

The Nubian wiped his knife over my cheeks so that the hot blood trickled down.

'You are already deep in blood. Remember that.'

11

I had never seen Nakht lost for speech. I had just finished recounting the facts of Khety's death. He embraced me lightly, and patted me on the shoulder – which surprised me, for he was not given to displays of emotion or intimacy, and he rarely tolerated physical contact. We stood like that, uncertainly, for a moment, and then moved apart, awkwardly. We were in the reception chamber on the first floor of the mansion. It gave on to the courtyard, where his caged birds trilled and water trickled along the crisscross of stone channels that fed the plants.

'At the times when we most need language to express our feelings, it fails us,' he said.

'Silence is fine,' I replied, curtly. 'What is there to say?'

He glanced at me, but I was in no mood to apologize or modify my behaviour. He went to a tray, and poured us wine into two handsome goblets. He offered me a place on the inlaid couch, and we sat.

'I suspect you are intent upon some sort of revenge, in response to this dreadful tragedy?'

'And?' I said.

'Let me counsel you. In moments such as this, we are inclined to allow the animal aspect of our natures to take control. It is a mistake.'

'Why?' I demanded.

'Because revenge can destroy a man as surely as the plague. It seems like a god, so pure and true, and full of its sense of justice and entitlement. But it is truly a monster. It feeds perpetually upon its own pain, and upon any pain it can find. And it can never be satisfied until everything has been destroyed utterly.'

'And how would you know?' I snapped.

There was a nasty moment of silence between us. His topaz eyes gazed at me, detached. Sometimes arguing with him was like trying to punch water. It made no difference. And he knew I wanted a fight, and he was not going to give it to me.

'Death makes us strangers to ourselves,' he offered, by way of reconciliation.

He rose, and walked away, to look out of the doorway at the beautiful private world of his home.

'You are right, of course; I know little of grief. I have been fortunate in that respect. Fate has been kind to me. One cannot trust it, of course. We are all vulnerable to misfortune,' he said.

'This was not misfortune. It was murder. And I'm going to track them down and then—'

'Yes, and then what?' Nakht interrupted, sitting down beside me again. 'I suppose you thought I would support and encourage you in your righteous revenge? Now that tragedy has struck you personally, in an instant you forget all your values, and indulge yourself in the barbarity of blood,' he continued, gazing at me, unblinking, with his hawk's eyes.

I had had enough. I drained the wine, then rose and walked to the door, to leave. He followed me, and gently placed his hand on my shoulder to stop me.

'Please sit down, my friend. I'm truly sorry for your loss. I understand. You are trying to make his death into something meaningful. That is right and proper. But you must focus your anger and grief better.'

'How?' I said, desperately.

'Do not indulge yourself in a self-pitying, self-gratifying revenge. More than likely you would simply end up dead as well. And think, too, about the cost of your actions to those who love you dearly. I, for one, could not bear to lose you,' he said.

I remained standing, silent, baffled by the chaos of my feelings and the pain that found me everywhere.

Nakht calmly led me back to the couch, and I sat down again, like a child.

'There is another way to think about this as well,' he added.

'And what's that?'

'You are lucky indeed to have had such a friend, to mourn his loss so deeply. Would he want you to indulge yourself in this display of blame and revenge? I doubt it,' he said.

I didn't want to modify the intensity of my bitterness. I didn't want to listen to these philosophical arguments. He saw my frustration, and continued: 'I hope that were I to die, you would do the same for me. You would make my death meaningful by remembering me. By taking me to the tomb in honour and love. That is what the dead ask of their friends,' he said.

As we sat together, in the sunlight that slanted into the room, I thought about his words. For a moment, it even seemed possible. I swore then that if I returned to Thebes alive, I would lay Khety to rest in his tomb with my own hands, with all the rites. But first I would have my revenge.

'When do we leave for the Hittite capital?' I asked.

Nakht glanced at me warily.

'Under the circumstances, I doubt you are fully equipped to deal with the severe demands of the mission,' he said.

But I had to persuade him of my fitness to undertake the quest. It now offered me an exceptional chance to investigate the start of the opium trade in the north, and then to trace it back to Thebes, and perhaps to 'Obsidian' himself. Something told me I would never find him if I stayed in the city. I would have to track him in the sands of the wastelands beyond Egypt's borders. But I would find him.

'Only yesterday the Queen commanded me to attend you as your bodyguard, and I will obey. You also gave me strong inducements and incentives. And you promised me my family would be safe in your house. Is it not better that I leave Thebes? If I stayed, I would have no peace until I found Khety's killer.'

His topaz eyes considered me.

'Our mission is of vital national importance. Nothing can be allowed to compromise the achievement of our goals,' he said. 'I will not tolerate anything less than your complete commitment. If at any time I consider your emotional state to be a problem, I will send you home immediately. No one is irreplaceable. Not even you. Is that understood?'

'I understand,' I replied.

I felt a shadow pass between us. For a long moment I thought he was going to refuse me. But then he rose and embraced me formally, briefly, and without great warmth.

'Then you had better tell Tanefert and the children. We leave tomorrow.'

I walked up the lane to the gate of my house. I nodded respect-fully to the little statuette of the household God in his niche, and for once asked for his blessing. Inside, the girls were sitting together on the floor, Sekhmet working on a papyrus roll, studying medicine, writing fluidly, the others trying to copy her with their own brushes. As soon as I walked in they ran over, and threw themselves around me, crying for Khety. Tanefert must have told them. I smoothed their hair, and dried their tears.

'I'm so sorry,' I said.

They nodded, and sniffed, and it was a relief to comfort them and share their sorrow.

'Come, let us eat dinner together,' I said.

I made an effort to talk, and not to fall into the silence of grief about Khety's death. While the girls cleaned the dishes in the yard, I beckoned Tanefert into our sleeping room. The girls looked at us curiously, knowing something was up, so I waved them away, and drew the curtain across to give us some privacy. Tanefert assumed I needed to talk to her about Khety.

'How are you, my love?' she asked, putting her arms around me.

I kissed her. She gazed at my face. And then she pulled away slightly.

'Something else has happened, hasn't it?' she asked.

I hesitated. I had to speak now.

'I have been dismissed from the Medjay.'

Her expression darkened with despair, and she put her face into her hands.

'Oh no . . .'

'But I've had a new offer of work. It's a very good offer,' I began, placing the little bag of gold in her hands.

She fixed me with one of her famous stares.

'If it were good news, you would not need to talk like this, nor would you bribe me with gold,' she countered. 'Where did you get this? And what have you done to earn it?'

'Let me finish,' I replied. She sighed, and nodded.

'Nakht has offered me work. Not just as a bodyguard. Not only will I be handsomely rewarded with more gold, but he has also promised me something much more important. He will promote me. If we are successful, I will take over Nebamun's post. I would be Chief of the Medjay.'

Her eyes were taking everything in, every half-truth, every nuance, every uncertain justification and assertion in my voice.

'Nakht is a very powerful man, but such a promise must carry with it a heavy price,' she said.

'Yes.'

'So tell me,' she urged. 'I can't stand it when you don't tell me everything.'

'I must accompany him on a long journey. And I cannot tell you where I am going, or when I will be back.'

Her eyes were blazing. I thought she was going to slap me.

'You promised me you would never leave us again. You promised!'

And then she threw the bag of gold down, walked out of the room, and disappeared into the yard.

I picked up the bag of gold and placed it carefully on the couch. My world had collapsed in a day. I went into the kitchen, where the girls and Amenmose were waiting, agog.

'What's wrong?' asked Sekhmet.

'Stop asking questions,' I snapped, and sat down at the end of the table. Sekhmet was shocked into silence. Amenmose's lower lip was quivering, a prelude to a drama of tears and recriminations. I whisked him into my lap and kissed his face.

'Come here. Don't cry. I need you all to help me.'

My son considered his options, and then nodded, deciding curiosity was better than crying.

The others gathered closer.

'Your Uncle Nakht and I have to go away on a long journey, and while I'm away I need you to take great care of your mother.'

The two younger girls instantly set up a howl of grief, begging me not to leave them. Only Sekhmet reacted differently.

'Where are you going, Father?' she asked.

'I can't tell you exactly. But we're going all the way to the northern sea, and then even further north.'

Her eyes widened.

'If you are going with Uncle Nakht, then you must be going on very important official business,' she said. 'Is it to do with the wars?'

'I can't tell you. But it's very important and secret. So you must not tell anyone. Do you promise?' She nodded, her eyes shining, excited to be a conspirator in the great adventure. I put my arm around her, held her close, and kissed her brow.

'Clever girl. I need you to look after your sisters, and your brother, and your mother.'

She nodded. 'I'm an adult now, Father. You can rely on me.'

'I know I can.' I stroked her hair. I adored her self-belief.

'No wonder Mother didn't take this well,' she said. 'You did promise never to go away again.' And she glanced at me side-ways.

'I did promise. And I wouldn't break that promise unless it was extremely important for me to do so. There is more at stake than I can explain. But I want the world to be safe for you. And that's why I'm going.'

'I know, Father,' she replied. 'I'm just frightened something bad will happen to you. I would want to die, too, if it did.'

To disguise my sudden distress at her words, I turned quickly back to the other girls, who had easily abandoned their grief as they followed my conversation with Sekhmet.

'Now, the other news is good news. Nakht has invited you all to live in his mansion during the whole time of my journey. How does that sound?'

While the four of them jumped up and down in enthusiastic joy, and ran around the kitchen in their delight at this prospect of luxurious accommodation, I went outside, and found Tanefert sitting under the fig tree in the dark. I plucked a ripe fruit from the tree, and offered it to her; she ignored me. We sat in silence for a little. I rolled the useless treat in my hand.

'I'm sorry,' was all I could find to say.

She scoffed: '*Sorry* is easy. It's just a word. You've already made your mind up. So there's no point in talking more,' she said, and rose to walk away from me.

I reached out and gripped her hand. She struggled to free herself, but I would not let her go.

'You're hurting me,' she said.

'Don't just – walk away. *Talk to me*,' I said. I kissed her hand, hoping my feelings would show themselves in this way, when words failed me.

'I'm so frightened,' she said, after a while. 'Some days it feels as if the world is falling apart. And I don't know how to hold it all together for us.'

'Everything will be fine,' I answered, uselessly.

'What will I tell the children if you never return? What will I tell myself?'

'I will return, I promise you that,' I said. 'And then everything will change. Everything will get better again.'

'I know you would only do this if you thought you were doing the best for us all. But sometimes you get obsessed with an idea, and you forget about us. I would much rather have a living husband with no job and no gold than a dead one. I don't care how much Nakht has offered, your life simply isn't worth the risk. And I know it must be dangerous, because why else would you have to go?'

'I have no choice,' I replied. It felt like the most honest thing I had said.

'You always have a choice,' she insisted. '*Always*. And you shouldn't make decisions like this, not now, not when you're grieving. I know you, my husband. You are being driven by rage and guilt. But Khety's death was not your fault.'

'Yes it was.'

She looked at me unflinchingly. 'And so you put your rage and your revenge before your family?'

She had spoken the truth. I felt the cold blade of guilt slip into my heart. I wanted to tell her I had changed my mind. But something else would not let me. I forced myself to keep going.

'I promise you I will return within three months. And then everything will be well.'

She was silent for a long moment.

'When must you go?' she asked, eventually, in a strange voice.

'Tomorrow morning,' I replied.

'Tomorrow?'

She was incredulous.

'We are your *family*. And you have chosen against us. I do not know how I will forgive you.'

And she walked away into the house, leaving me in the dark. I threw the fig into the shadows.

PART TWO

*This northern boundary is as far as that inverted water
which goes downstream in going upstream . . .*

Tombos stele of Tutmosis I

12

Ra rose above the dark horizon, and the Great River instantly caught the glory of the first light on its vast, shadowy surface, and glittered into splendid life.

I stood on the ship's deck and gazed out at Thebes, waking to another day of heat and work. I looked at the crowded docks; at the high temple walls, and the long, fluttering flags on their poles; at the districts of rich villas; and across the Great River at the Malkata Palace itself, where the Queen would be awake, and perhaps praying to Amun, God of Thebes, the Hidden One, for the success of our venture. I would not see my city again for many months. If we failed, then perhaps I would never return. Strangely, I found I no longer had strong feelings about that turn of events, or rather, I felt numb at the possibility of my own death. I thought of our hieroglyph for the word 'expedition': a kneeling man holding a bow, followed by the sign for a boat. I felt like that man, only my weapon was a dagger. I touched its handle; I would keep it tied across my chest at all times, in readiness.

I looked down the elegant curve of the wooden gunwales that ran the long length of the ship. The Eye of Horus was painted boldly on either side of the prow, offering the protection of the God of the Sky, together with falcons on pedestals. Stylized plants painted in interlocking patterns ran entwined along the length of the hull, together with long, bold lines in red and blue, to the high stern where the Goddess Maat, Keeper of Justice and Harmony, was depicted kneeling with her wings open beneath the helmsman's platform. The spacious cabin at the centre of the ship was decorated with a chequerboard pattern in black and white. The great timbers of the ship's keel, ribs and crossbeams and decking were strong and clean. It was a good ship, and along with my dagger, it gave me comfort.

Nakht and his manservant Minmose were supervising the delivery and placement within the cabin of his sealed travelling trunks, which I assumed contained the tablets of the secret letters from the Queen to the King of the Hittites, as well as diplomatic gifts of gold, and the necessary finances, documents and permissions for our journey. There was suddenly a clatter of hooves on the quay stones, and from out of the dawn shadows a splendid chariot drew up. Nakht hurried ashore to greet the arrival: a tall, dignified foreigner, in an unusual, dark embroidered cloak of fine wool, accompanied by a small contingent of troops. The party hurried on to the ship, and to the privacy of their cabin, as if anxious not to be seen. I understood that, for this was the Hittite ambassador, Hattusa and his retinue, returning with us to their native land.

The sailors made their last preparations for departure. The blades of the two great steering oars, painted with blue and white lotus flowers, and more *udjat* eyes, were carried from the roof of the cabin, where they were stored when not in use, to the stern, where they were placed into the leather loops, and lashed to the vertical stanchions that would hold them during the voyage north.

The central mast towered up out of the cabin; its sails would remain furled for the journey north, as the river's current would do all the work. The sailors checked the complex network of rigging, making sure it was tied neat and close. And then, with a cry of command from the captain, all those not travelling hurried ashore, the rowers on the deck below took up their chant, and we slowly sailed out of the dock, past the hundreds of other ships. We towered over the fishermens' skiffs returning from the night fishing. They parted to make way like schools of little fish. Then the river caught us in its firm, powerful grasp and drew us swiftly north, away from the city, as if it shared our sense of urgency. Although I almost never pray, I found myself whispering a prayer, like a dead man remembering the necessary spells for survival in the darkness of the Otherworld.

I had said my farewells to the children on the previous night. I had wanted to slip away from the house as early as possible, to avoid a dramatic or tearful farewell. Tanefert had maintained her angry distance all through the evening and the night. We lay apart, awake and unable to speak. I turned to look at her face in the shadows, but she kept her eyes firmly closed. I whispered her name, but she simply turned away, and curled into herself.

This morning, at the last moment, after I had said goodbye to Thoth, running my hands over his brown mane and talking to him quietly, and imagining he truly understood my orders to guard my family, I had passed his lead to my wife, and we had stood in silence, knowing we had reached the point of no return. Even then, she refused to allow me to take her in my arms. I kissed her quickly on the head, telling her that she was the love of my life. She glanced at me as if this were a bitter truth. I was desperate for some sign of affection from her; but she was locked in her own grief, and could not give it. For a moment I almost fell to my knees and told her I would not leave, I would not abandon her, and our home. But I steeled myself, and as I turned to the door, I swore I felt my heart tear in two.

I walked away down the dusty street, in the chill dark before dawn. When I turned back, I wanted her to be standing in the gateway to the yard, holding the oil lamp in her outstretched palm, watching me disappear into the gloom. I wanted the children to slip into place next to her, one by one, each holding their own oil lamps like tiny stars in the darkness. I wanted them to put their arms round each other, shivering, and wave and wave. But the door remained closed in shadows. I looked back for the last time, and waved even though there was no one there to receive my gesture, then turned the last corner. And then, despite everything, I admit I felt a strange measure of relief, to be finally on my quest, and to have committed myself single-mindedly to its pursuit, no matter what the cost.

Nakht invited Simut and me to pay our respects to Ambassador Hattusa in the cabin. He wore his greying hair long, and he was clean-shaven, like all Hittites. His face was haughty, and his blue eyes keen as a jackal's. He carried himself with immense dignity.

'My lord,' I offered, bowing low.

'Simut is Commander of the Palace Guard. Rahotep is my personal guard. He is trusted by the royal family. The Queen herself commanded his presence on this mission,' said Nakht, by way of introduction.

Hattusa examined me minutely, as if for flaws, then nodded, apparently adequately satisfied.

'I gather the royal envoy has confided in you the true nature of our quest,' he said quietly, in flawless Egyptian.

'He has,' replied Simut.

'And he has made it clear that secrecy is imperative?'

'Yes, my lord,' said Simut.

Hattusa glanced at me expectantly.

'Yes, my lord,' I replied.

'Let me be clear. The safety of the royal envoy is your absolute and only priority. Without him, this mission will fail. He alone can speak for the Queen of Egypt. I expect you to give your life for his, if necessary. Is that clear?'

'Perfectly, my lord,' I said.

He nodded, dismissing us, and gestured to Nakht.

'Come, honourable friend, let us retire. We have much to discuss,' he said. Nakht bowed, and we took our cue and left the cool shade of the cabin, followed by Hattusa's two bodyguards, who assumed sentry duty on either side of the entrance.

Simut and I stood at the prow of the ship, looking ahead at the wide, shining expanse of the Great River, and out across the green and yellow glory of the cultivation.

'These ambassadors are all the same. They have the eyes of Anubis. And they make me feel like a servant. Like a *shabti* in a tomb. "Here I am. I will do it!"' I said, in the formula of the little funeral figures buried with their dead masters.

Simut laughed.

'You get used to it. It's all part of the way of things. They are creatures of their class, and they have certain expectations,' he said. 'But it's true, they often seem rather bloodless.'

'Do you trust him?' I asked.

'Of course not, he is a Hittite. I would no more trust a scorpion.'

He glanced at the Hittite bodyguards with a confident measure of contempt. They ignored him. Simut's own guards were preoccupied with their preparations a little way further down the deck, in the shade of their open shelter.

'I suppose this proposal could look like a golden trap to the Hittite King,' I said. 'I suppose Hattusa must have needed assurances that, once here in Thebes, the Hittite Prince won't simply be sidelined, or assassinated.'

'Well, he'd be right to be concerned about that. But they must have come to terms, for here we are, at the beginning of our great journey. I must admit, never did I think I would find myself on a boat bound for the capital of our enemies.'

'Nor I,' I answered.

We gazed up the river, looking north.

'What do you know of the Hittites and their land?' I asked.

'They say they have a thousand Gods. They say their chief God is the God of Storms. They say they have many laws, and that none are put to death, even for murder . . .' said Simut.

'They probably also say they mate with donkeys, and eat their own children,' I replied, joking.

'Hittites are capable of anything,' he replied, without irony, and spat into the deep green waters passing below us.

The Hittite guards kept themselves apart, preparing and eating their food separately, and sleeping outside the cabin where the ambassador was accommodated. Nakht, Simut and I also took our meals apart from the twelve Egyptian guards – by their choice, rather than ours. They were fit, highly disciplined, well-equipped with high-quality scimitars, spears, and bows and arrows, and silent, as if words alone could betray them. They carried a particular atmosphere of intensity and concentration, and Simut commanded them with an absolute authority. He advised me not to try to engage them in conversation, for that was counter to their training; and indeed they even avoided eye contact.

With nothing else to occupy me, apart from regular tours of the ship, and keeping an eye on the shoreline to make sure there were no assassins hidden with bows and arrows in the fields or the trees by the water's edge, I spent the first days of the journey watching the Great River. Its brooding waters suited my dark mood, and I observed how its surface turned in an endless reflective embrace of light and darkness, curling into and out of itself, gathering reflections of the unchanging sky like strange, distant memories. Sometimes the waters flowed in a lucid suspension, then hesitated and argued in knots and curlicues, until they resolved and continued calmly onwards. I fancied the river was trying to describe itself, and the world it reflected, ceaselessly. And the little dramas of human life – dots and dashes of colour and movement, of poor labouring women in linen clothing, and children playing in the mud, and birds scattered across the sky, and crocodiles waiting in the papyrus marshes – were its passing daydream. But as I watched all of this, I thought mostly of the dead. I saw their cold, disappointed faces turning up towards me in the water – the faces of the dead Nubian boys, and of my friend Khety. I saw my father, too, and only he had the expression of implacable absence held by the peaceful dead. But I could not see anywhere in the changing waters the face of the man I would kill. And that tormented me.

Five days after our departure, we sailed past the unseen ancient pyramids and monuments of the high plateau, towards Memphis, the army city. The river was suddenly busy again, and the shoreline crowded with little mud-brick houses; and then, in the distance, among the hundreds of ships with their sails open to the north wind, we caught our first glimpse of the vast port of the great capital – Horemheb's city, and therefore highly dangerous for us. Majestic war vessels with the Eye of Horus painted boldly on their prows, and with their sails still open to the north wind which had carried them home, slowly negotiated their paths into the immense docks. From our deck, Simut and I watched as hundreds of shackled captives were marched off each boat and forced to their knees in positions of abject submission and trunks of war booty were unloaded on to the quayside. Thousands of soldiers disembarked and were ordered in their battalions towards the distant buildings; meanwhile thousands more stood waiting to board those ships which had been repaired, cleaned and re-stocked, and were bound for further periods of service in the wars.

'They belong to the Ptah division,' said Simut, nodding at a great assembly of soldiers standing in precise, disciplined lines.

I gazed at the vast spectacle of the modern machinery of war. It left me feeling cold and powerless.

'If Horemheb can muster such forces, what hope is there for the future, even if we are able to return the Hittite Prince to Thebes?' I said, remembering what Nakht had told me about the general's divisions.

Simut shrugged.

'You're right. But his success cannot be based upon force alone. That might enable him to grasp power, but it will not necessarily help him to maintain civil authority. And he would still have to do a deal with the priests, for they own everything . . .'

'Do you think Horemheb's here, in Memphis?' I said.

Simut shook his head.

'The campaign season will soon be ending. He will be in the northern lands, commanding his troops.' He hesitated. 'But he'll still know everything that's happening here, and in Thebes. He overhauled the military messenger system – now he can receive up to date news from the city in only a few days.'

'If he has eyes and ears everywhere, then that's bad for us. If he knows about this mission, then he'll simply stop us. He'll kill us all,' I said.

'Yes. But luckily he's not the only one with the benefit of intelligence,' he replied.

'What do you mean?'

He glanced at me, and lowered his voice.

'Come on, Rahotep. How do you think Royal Envoy Nakht gets his information about events in the north, and in the war? The army has its intelligence, and the palace has its own, too. The days when an invasion or an attack took place and no one heard about it for months are long gone. This war's all about speed and information, and you can be sure Nakht has a very efficient system. The problem is, each system is always trying to infiltrate the other. And there's always the danger of spies.'

'But surely not in our camp?' I said.

'I hope not. My guards have been vetted. Every crew member on this ship has been vetted. I know everything about them: I know what they eat, who they love, who they sleep with, and what they're afraid of. There's no question of their loyalty.'

'But what about the others? There must be other palace people back in Thebes who know about our mission. The presence of the Hittite ambassador at the palace alone will have stirred all sorts of speculations.'

'Possibly,' Simut said. 'But his presence has been very low-key, and the official reason for his visit was given as war negotiations. We have to assume Nakht has thought of all of this, and taken the necessary precautions.'

Later that day, we passed close to Heliopolis, the city of the Sun, where the most ancient temples of the Two Lands stood. It was known as a city of mystery and wonder, but nothing I had heard could have prepared me for the dazzling vision that came into view: in the distance, beyond the cultivation, in the harsh desert to the east, the blazing electrum-tips of innumerable black granite obelisks shone incandescently brighter than Ra, the Sun itself. I was witnessing the dazzling light into which no man could look without blinding himself. Hattusa and Nakht stood with us at the ship's gunwale, in awe, shading their eyes. Nakht lectured us about the city, its infinite wealth, and its five vast and ancient temples of the Sun, to which the kings of our own dynasty – including Akhenaten himself – had added their own monumental constructions, in honour of the great Lord of the Sun. I think of our Temple of Karnak as the greatest in the world; but Nakht assured us the temples of Heliopolis were twice as large.

'One temple has a floor so perfect, the stones so polished by time, that the night sky is clearly reflected in it, as if it were water. I assume you both know the origins of Egypt's great theology?' he asked airily. We both shook our heads like admonished school-boys. He tutted.

'Atum, Creator of the Universe, was self-created, self-begotten, but alone in his universe. He therefore created the Nine Gods, the Ennead, who embodied the sources and the great forces that make up this world and the Otherworld. He ordered that each and every king must rule through the just and rightful ordering of those forces. One of the temples contains a pillar called the Benben, which offers back to the sky the Stone of Creation. It is the dark seed of all existence. It is nothing less than a star that fell to earth. And it is also within the sacred precinct that the grey bird – which, as I am sure you know, is depicted in our Book of the Dead as the heron, because it is the manifestation of both Ra and Osiris – returns, and is reborn from his ashes as a swallow, singing on the stone at dawn, according to the calendar of Sirius, renewing the year and the world, and ushering in a new era with its song.'

'When is the bird next due to grace you with its presence?' asked Hattusa, and I could not tell whether his tone was serious or ironic.

'Alas, that is secret knowledge,' replied Nakht. 'Of course, we might say its return soon would be greatly desired. The priests of Heliopolis can calculate and predict the rising and setting of the great stars. They maintain the sacred calendar of the universe. One could say they control time itself. But that is all secret knowledge . . .'

'But surely the great and learned Nakht is an adept of this knowledge?' asked Hattusa, this time with more warmth in his voice.

'Alas, no. It is an old dream of mine to study here. But the demands of the world have not permitted me the opportunity. Many come seeking the knowledge and wisdom of the heavenly bodies, and what we call the geometry of sacred time.' Nakht paused, and gazed at the distant, dazzling towers. 'It is said that Thoth himself left here a secret book containing spells to charm the sky, the earth, the Otherworld, the mountains and the waters. It is said there are spells to enable man to understand the speech of the birds. And it is said the most secret of all the spells brings forth a vision of the living and the dead, with the great God appearing with the Nine Gods, and the new moon in his hand.'

'And where is this marvellous book to be found, and who may read its secrets?' asked Hattusa.

Nakht smiled, and quoted:

'In the middle of the water is a box of iron. In the box of iron is a box of copper, and within that a box of juniper wood; within that a box of ivory and ebony, and within that a box of silver. Within that is a box of gold, and within that is the book. But the box is full of scorpions, and wound around the box forever is a great serpent. And even if a man opens all the boxes, and destroys the scorpions, and kills the serpent, and reads the book and learns its wisdom – even so, Thoth also laid a curse on his own book, and promised death to the reader.'

Only the sound of the keel slicing through the water followed these extraordinary words. Nakht had spoken with a strange melancholy. Hattusa broke the silence.

'That is most interesting. But I believe this is not the time to think of secret books and curses. Surely there are enough serpents and scorpions already around us in these strange and changing days. Let us conclude our great business first, and then we may speak of these other, more wonderful mysteries.'

I paced the deck. Hour after hour I had nothing to do but go over and over everything, feeling like a trapped dog, and as I did so, I realized I agreed with Hattusa's words. The demons of this world were my enemy – the ones in the next could wait. Nakht's curiosity about the next world was foolish, and I felt a strange anger towards him gripping me. Of course he was my master, and I his servant, now. But I kept myself apart from him as much as my duties allowed, and he must have noticed, for he made no effort to resolve the new silence between us.

And as I watched, the landscape itself was changing, too: the Great River had begun to divide up into its five branches, from which the many smaller branches subdivided into the fertile fields and vast marshes of the delta. The ancient dividing line between the Black Land of the valley and the Red of the desert, which draws the great division of life and death, had vanished; the distinction between land and water had become blurred. Beyond this outpost lay the sea, that mysterious frontier where the Two Lands of Egypt end, and all that is not Egypt begins. I was looking forward to crossing it.

13

The next day we reached Bubastis, the trading and temple capital of the eighteenth *nome* of Lower Egypt – famed for its markets and for its worship of Bast, the Cat Goddess – as a result of which more cats were buried there than anywhere else in the Two Lands. Its position between our great Egyptian cities to the south, and the north-eastern trade routes into Canaan, Qadesh and Byblos, and then the remote empires of Babylonia and Mittani, had made it a key trading post.

I was impatient for the feel of solid ground beneath my feet again. But Bubastis only amplified the sensations of strangeness that had begun to haunt me, and which I had been unable to brush aside. Despite the fame of the grand centre of the city, what I could see of the place was overwhelmingly awful: improvised out of mud and water and sun, and dominated by a terrible damp heat that clung at our skins. The docks smelt of decay and filth. Commodities lay piled up in great heaps of confusion and noise; thousands of indistinguishable labourers and dock-workers merged together into one seething mass of humanity, toiling and shouting in the oppressive heat. And the flies and mosquitoes! Nakht insisted we each carried heads of fresh garlic to chew continuously as a remedy against the fever sickness. But their ceaseless buzzing and aggressive attentions irritated me intensely, giving me no peace; and I was forever swatting away at them, and slapping myself like a lunatic.

I asked Nakht for permission to take a tour of the town. Assuming I wished to visit the city's sights, he agreed, saying Bubastis had 'many temples and monuments of interest', and he looked forward to my account over dinner. I did not tell him I had no interest whatsoever in temples and monuments. If opium jars were being imported into Thebes via the Great River, they would almost certainly not be brought ashore to be secretly traded in Memphis, because it was the most secure, and carefully controlled, military city in Egypt. It would make more sense to trade and transfer them here, to smaller ships among whose consignments the jars could be hidden. I decided I would see what I could find. But as I was preparing to set off, Simut appeared and asked if he could join me. I tried to refuse, but he smiled, and accompanied me anyway.

Leaving the ship, we descended into the chaos of the docks. Instantly, my skin burst with perspiration. We commandeered the best transport we could find to carry us into the city: a poor chariot of crudely hewn wood, undecorated, and without any suspension, driven by a toothless and incomprehensible local man. He stared at us in wonder and joy, as if we were visiting gods come to be fleeced on earth by him. We set off towards the dock gate, our bones grinding in their sockets with every jolt, while the man screamed vile curses in his unfathomable accent at the crowds.

As soon as we passed through the great gate of the docks, a vast, pathetic crowd of supplicants and beggars, young and old, raised a well-practised wail of hope and despair, clamouring for our attention and pity. Desperate and mostly unlovely young girls and boys smiled winningly, offering themselves to us; weeping mothers held up scrawny, mewling infants; deliberately crippled children begged for charity with rehearsed smiles and tears, crying out for pity, for the Gods' sake. They were all beaten back by the dock guards, who casually set about them with their truncheons, and we quickly moved ahead.

The city's main street ran into the baking, shimmering distance. Through the humid air, we could see the walls of a large, square temple rising above the grander houses that surrounded it. The green tops of trees appeared above the enclosure walls – a welcome sight amid the dry dirt. But I ordered the driver to turn away in the direction of the less salubrious quarters of the city. He grinned at me, spat in surprise, and headed down a dusty, narrow street, which led to the poor districts crowding the water's edge. Hovels packed its sides in dark piles of crumbling, unstable mud-brick several floors high, most indistinguishable from the decomposing heaps of ordure and junk that lay everywhere, playgrounds for filthy children, feral cats, wild dogs and vicious birds.

'I thought you wanted to see the sights?' said Simut.

'I do. I thought we'd take the scenic route.'

He glanced at me suspiciously.

'What are you up to, Rahotep?' he asked.

'Just satisfying a private curiosity,' I replied.

Narrow alleyways ran off into dark warrens and grim tenements. Tiny dark stores sold vegetables in piles on woven mats – but these were not the beautiful fruits we were used to in Thebes. These were the cheapest leftovers, most already bruised or rotting under a cloud of flies, unfit for sale in the central markets of the great cities. And every other shop front and narrow passageway offered young, human flesh. Countless young girls displayed themselves to us, calling offers and imprecations, and, when we passed without responding, they cried after us the filthiest, most inventively abusive insults I have ever heard, mostly about the superiority of dogs over Simut and myself as potential lovers.

Simut shouted over the noise of the street, and the creaking of the cart: 'I heard this place was called the Way of Shame. Now I know why! I suppose most of them come from small delta villages, and end up in this fly-ridden dump for the rest of their lives.'

'Most of them have been abandoned by their families, and here they are, selling the only thing they have left . . .' I replied.

In our fine linens we were an unusual sight in this ghetto; children chased after us, shouting and yelling expletives, and women's voices, rough and caustic, called out to each other from hovel to hovel, laughing and mocking. We drove on, and I saw no sign of what I was looking for, until suddenly I glimpsed something near a tavern. I commanded the driver to stop. Instantly more young women and girls crowded around us, offering their naked breasts with exaggerated smiles of seduction, which only served to display the rotten teeth in their mouths. Many of them bore the black spots and marks of the diseases of their trade. Simut shouted at them, but the women were not afraid; they just laughed louder, pushing their bodies even more ostentatiously forward, playful but forceful.

'We can't stop here!' said Simut.

'Wait in the chariot. I won't be long,' I replied.

'I think we should go back right now,' he replied, gripping my arm.

'Just give me a moment,' I said, and jumped down from the chariot. Simut jumped down after me.

'I'm coming with you. But I don't like this . . .' he said.

We entered the tavern. I looked around, but the young man

with the dazed eyes and languid movement, who had caught my attention as he entered from the street, was nowhere to be seen. The proprietor, a vast man in filthy linens, couldn't believe his luck; he shambled forward to greet us, bowing subserviently and yelling at his tiny wife to bring beer. The place was a dump. The few crude benches and stools had been broken and mended many times over, the floor was filthy with bits of food and duck-shit trodden into the muck, and the clientele were a motley band of low-ranked sailors and dock-workers; a few Egyptian, but most Nubian or Syrian. Young women called from the staircase leading up to the brothel on the first floor. Simut surveyed the surroundings with utter contempt.

The proprietor kicked two mangy cats off a bench, and bade us be seated. He set out two chipped bowls of beer and a dish of bread and chickpeas. The whole place watched as expectantly as an audience at a performance as we received these offerings. The beer was thick and cloudy, and the bread and chickpeas full of grit from the crumbling grindstones.

'This is not what we want,' I said. 'We are looking for other pleasures . . .'

He scowled sourly, but when he grasped my meaning, his jowly face lifted itself into an ugly grin. He jerked his thumb up at the ceiling.

'Only the best for you, sir. Only the best. Go on up, please . . .'

'If I wanted a woman, I wouldn't come here . . .' I muttered into his filthy ear.

His eyes narrowed. He considered us both, and then nodded, throwing his filthy cloth over his shoulder, and indicating we should follow.

'It's definitely time we left,' said Simut, getting up to leave.

'Not yet. Wait here,' I replied.

'Have you lost your mind?' he hissed.

*

I followed the landlord down a fetid corridor, which gave on to an even filthier yard, where a few miserable ducks, tied together by their feet, huddled in the shade, and then, via a broken doorway, into a dank lane. Human ordure ran along a channel in the middle, and naked children splashed around in the mud and mess. He knocked on the lintel of a doorway opposite. The ragged cloth that served as a curtain was drawn back, and the landlord shrugged with barely disguised contempt and proposed I should enter. By the dim and dusty light filtering in through the shadows, I saw men and women lying together, in a kind of stagnant disarray. Most had their eyes closed, dreaming deeply. The place smelled of sweetness and corruption. The languid man I had noticed earlier was just settling into the bliss of his latest fix. A thin young man, all skin and bone, his weak face pitted with spots, beckoned me further inside with a gap-toothed grin, showing me jars in the shape of the poppy seed that contained the opium itself, and nodding enthusiastically.

'Here is plenty for you, all excellent quality. Come . . .'

I pulled him aside so that his back was to the wall, and I was close to his face.

'Where do you get it? Who is your supplier?'

He scowled.

'Why do you care, as long as you can buy?'

'That's my business. Answer the question.'

He turned away, and I saw him reach for his little flint knife. I grabbed his arm, shook the knife from his hand, and held my dagger's blade to his sallow cheek.

'Call that a knife? This is a knife.'

He glanced down at the clean blade of polished bronze. Perspiration beaded his dirty brow.

'Answer the question, and then perhaps I won't cut your nose off.'

His eyes were mean and vicious, so I sliced into the skin of his cheek, just a little. Some of the clientele gazed at us without moving.

'I get it from the docks!' He winced.

'Where in the docks?'

He was too slow answering, so I jabbed the knife deeper. A line of blood appeared and began to trickle down his scrawny chin. He would have a scar to remember me by.

'From the ships . . .'

I changed the position of the blade to draw a different cut across his face. Another line of blood began to follow the first, dripping off his chin on to the floor in slow drops.

'I don't have all day.'

'From a man . . .'

'What is his name?'

'I don't know!'

'Where can I find him?'

'You can't. I don't find him. He finds me.'

'When? How? What's his name?'

'I don't know, I don't know! He makes a delivery via an intermediary, and he takes the payment . . . I never know when they're coming—'

'When did they last come?'

There was no answer, so I made another cruel downward cut with the knife, and more blood flowed.

'Yesterday!' he shouted, struggling.

Suddenly, a black storm blew up inside me. I punched him hard, and he fell backwards among his clientele, who murmured gently in their trances, and peered at the commotion. Two strangers pushed through the filthy curtain, and came at me. I had my knife poised to slash at them, but one of them kicked my feet from under me, my dagger went spinning away across the floor, and I sprawled among the muttering clientele. When

I looked up, the other thug had his own blade – a long, curved scimitar – poised. He grinned toothlessly. My hand gripped the leg of a stool, and I threw it with all my strength. But the thug ducked, and the stool slammed into the wall behind him. The man whose face I had cut was leering, encouraging the two thugs to kill me. They came for me; but suddenly a jar shattered over the skull of the one with the scimitar, and he crashed to the floor; the other turned, and I saw Simut slam him hard in the face with the heel of his hand, shattering his nose. He slumped to his knees, holding his face, blood dripping down his chest. I snatched up my dagger and Simut dragged me away towards the door. The evil little guy I'd cut was cowering in a corner.

'Leave him!' shouted Simut.

But I gripped him tightly by the throat.

'Tell him Rahotep is looking for him. Tell him to come and find me. If he dares! Understand?' I said.

He nodded, terrified, unable to breathe.

And then Simut was pulling me away, into the filthy lane, and back into the crowded streets. He was furious.

'Whatever you were doing in there, it's got nothing to do with our mission. It's unacceptable!'

'It's none of your business,' I snapped.

'It's all of our business! What do you think this mission is? Some sort of opportunity for you to conduct a personal vendetta?'

I stared at him.

'Nakht told you, didn't he?'

'Of course he did. Your emotional state was considered a liability to the mission. But it was Nakht who said he would take personal responsibility for your behaviour. And now you've let him down.'

'Don't tell him,' I said.

'I have a duty to tell him,' he replied.

We rode on in silence, until we arrived back at the boat. I was about to jump off, but Simut grabbed my arm again.

'Listen to me, my friend. I know how you're feeling. Everything's unreal except your grief and hatred. You want revenge. But this mission matters more than anything else. And remember – whatever you do, you can't bring Khety back.'

'Why do people keep telling me that?' I said, shaking him off.

'Because it's true,' he replied.

The wind of rage died away suddenly. I felt tired. Simut let go of my arm.

'Every night, when I lie down to sleep, I see his face,' I said.

'I won't patronize you by telling you time heals,' he replied. 'And I won't say anything to Nakht. But please, my friend, take my advice. Focus on the mission. If we fail, then I fear the End of Days is upon us.'

Later that night, when I finally drifted off to sleep, I dreamt a thin cord, clotted with blood, had been stitched into my mouth and tongue, and then down my throat, into my heart, where a thick black knot held it tight. And the knot was feeding on my heart's black blood, and growing bigger. And no matter how hard I pulled, no matter how much agony I tolerated as I pulled, I could not loosen that knot. I woke suddenly, with a brief cry, sweating, my heart racing. A feeling of insistent irritation seemed to have taken over my limbs, and I could not keep still. My fists were clenched. My jaw muscles were tight. My shoulders ached. I felt a tension in my skin, as before a sandstorm. The ship felt like a trap. I couldn't breathe. I had to move.

A half-moon shone down on the docks and the ships. Two palace guards stood watch.

'I need to conduct a security tour of the docks . . .' I said to them.

'No one is allowed off the ship after dark,' said the first, firmly and without any finesse of respect or politeness.

'And I'm telling you I'm not happy to sleep until I've satisfied myself there's no threat out there in the docks.'

'Our orders are clear—' said the other.

'And so are mine. The royal envoy's safety is my responsibility, and I'll answer only to him. Do you really want to wake him up over something as trivial as this?'

The two guards exchanged glances.

I quickly slipped past them before they could say anything more. Once on solid ground, I jogged quickly away into the shadows. On the far side of the high mud-brick walls that surrounded the docks, I could hear the late-night noises of the boisterous taverns and brothels of the town. Lamps were still burning in a few of the ships' cabins up and down the wharves; night guards were stationed at the main – and only – entrance gate. Mosquitoes buzzed constantly in my ear. I slapped them away. Waving, and munching on my garlic, I loped silently over to the long, low storage depots, which cast strange shadows in the moonlight. Keeping within them, I moved from entry to entry – but they were all locked; the seal on each one was freshly made, bearing the marks of the owner. I hesitated, unwilling to leave traces of myself, but unable to control my curiosity.

The seal broke under my hands, I swiftly untied the cords and opened the doors. Inside all was dark and still. I could just make out mounds of materials, under protective sheets. These would be embargoed goods – gold, ivory, ebony or alabaster – which Egypt trades for the things it needs – silver, copper, cedar, lapis lazuli, unguents, horses and so on – from the northern lands. They would be awaiting recording, taxation and permissions before passing into or out of Egypt. I went quickly through the piles, but there was nothing but rough-hewn blocks of alabaster there. No sign of anything less legal.

Even if I worked all night, it would be impossible to search every warehouse. Away from the ship, the irritation in my limbs had calmed, but I felt reluctant to return at once. My mind was still buzzing, and I knew I would not sleep. So I continued down the wharf, away from the gatehouse. It was now so quiet I could hear the occasional catfish flopping in the river, and the far, brief cry of a hunted animal out on the marshes. I walked as far as the northern end of the docks, only to find my way blocked by a high wall. I could see no entrance gate, or doorway. I followed the course of the wall to the very edge of the dock, where it met the river. It then continued out on to the water, supported by wooden foundations set in the river mud. I looked around for something to stand on, so that I could see over the top of the wall. I found a large, empty storage jar, and with some effort managed to roll it into position next to the wall in relative silence. I climbed on top and found I could just reach the parapet with my fingertips. I was not as fit as I used to be, and I struggled to pull myself up, using my feet to push and scramble for support.

A pair of soldiers on watch were standing right below me. I saw a large open enclosure; here were more storehouses, all dark and shut, but in one there was an open door to what looked like offices and dormitories. A military ship was moored at the jetty. By the light of the moon, a small team of soldiers was unloading long boxes made of crude wooden planks, two men to each one. They looked like crude coffins. The soldiers carried no standards, and so I could not tell which division they belonged to. The two soldiers beneath me walked away along the dock, watching the process carefully. They seemed to be in charge. They had their backs to the moon, their faces were only shadows. When one of them turned to speak to the other, for a moment I caught a glimpse of his profile. But as he turned, I ducked down quickly, for he would have stared straight at me – and I would have been picked out clearly by the moonlight.

I walked back quickly to the ship, wondering exactly what I had seen on the far side of that wall.

14

I could not sleep for what remained of that night. The half-moon hung low in the sky like a white ship's hull in an ocean of stars. At last the air was fresh and cool. The incessant irritation of the mosquitoes had finally died away. Before dawn, our ship departed and sailed silently down the river, until Bubastis and its miseries disappeared behind us. I stood at the prow of the ship facing into the darkness, gazing at the glory of the late stars; and suddenly, inexplicably, my spirits lifted.

Everyone rose early. Just before dawn, Simut called me to a meeting in Nakht's cabin. As soon as I entered, I knew he had kept his promise and said nothing about our little adventure, for Nakht greeted me calmly. I nodded respectfully to Ambassador Hattusa. His two bodyguards stood behind him, as always, loyal as shadows.

'The ambassador and I have concluded we will take the land route north, rather than the sea route along the coast. There are no ports or natural harbours to put in along the southerly stretches of the coast of Canaan; also, the danger of storms and tides, and of pirates, is too great to risk. The Way of Horus, however, is always busy, and we will not stand out among the merchants, caravans of goods and people, and military convoys. All along the route the way stations and Egyptian garrisons will provide us with security, accommodation and food each night,' said Nakht.

Simut and I nodded. It was much the best plan.

'We need to accomplish this part of our journey as quickly as possible, so as to arrive in the port city of Ugarit in the Kingdom of Amurru within twenty days. As you will know, Ugarit is loyal to neither Egypt nor Hatti, so we must take great care. But we have a good contact in the city, a merchant of Egyptian birth, who will provide secure accommodation. The ambassador also has his own connections in the city, and will be accommodated by them. From Ugarit a ship will be commissioned to carry us to the south coast of Hatti. From there we will proceed overland towards the Hittite capital of Hattusa.'

The ambassador assented with a brief nod of his proud head, and took up where Nakht left off: 'Security for Egyptian travellers becomes far less reliable in the far north, of course, but it is written in our laws that safety must be guaranteed by towns and districts to merchants, envoys and their entourages – on pain of punishment by law. However, we must also consider the other danger ahead of us: the chance of random attacks by bandits, who could rob us of the precious gold you carry as a royal gift for my lord, the Hittite King. I cannot be responsible for such eventualities,' he said.

'My men have been trained to respond to them with force,' replied Simut.

'And what of General Horemheb?' asked Hattusa. 'I am well aware of the threat he poses as we travel through the regions of the wars.'

'He is unaware of us,' replied Nakht quickly. 'I have excellent, up to date intelligence.'

'I hope your intelligence is reliable,' replied the ambassador. 'It would be highly damaging if the letters from your Queen were to fall into the wrong hands.'

Nakht nodded.

'Such an eventuality has been considered, and all possible precautions have been taken against it,' he said.

There followed a moment of tense silence.

'You and your guards will be under my command when we enter Hittite territory,' said Hattusa imperiously.

Simut glanced at Nakht, who nodded discreetly.

'Yes, my lord,' he replied. I could tell he wasn't happy about that.

It was still dark when we finally disembarked from the ship at Avaris, the easternmost town on the border of Egypt and the unknown. Once upon a time this had been a great port; but it had fallen into near-dereliction as the docks of Memphis grew in stature and importance. In recent years, however, Horemheb had made it once again a key port for the military, and for this reason we had avoided it for as long as possible, and would leave it immediately.

Even though it was not yet light, the place was alive with activity. The ruins of the old citadel had been turned into vast storage areas and warehouses. Teams of builders and labourers were already working in the cool, moonlit hours of late darkness on a vast new structure of offices and accommodation for the army. Battalions of infantry soldiers were housed in camps, and there were rows of stables for the horses of the elite chariotry. Caravans of merchants and goods from the north waited impatiently to board their ships home with relief and delight; while, travelling in the other direction, hundreds of other merchants on business outside Egypt were just beginning their great journeys. Everyone's breath plumed in the sweet, cold air. Men yawned widely, rubbed their hands together, and beat their arms against their sides to keep warm as they took refreshments of bread and beer, or bought final necessities at the stalls doing excellent trade all along the open square that marked the start of the Way of Horus. Everyone was taking advantage of these cold early hours, before the heat of the day made progress too uncomfortable. It was a strange sight to see so many carriages and wagons setting off in the moonlight, alongside a few lone riders – commercial, or perhaps military, messengers – on fresh horses setting off swiftly on their private business north.

Our team set off – Nakht, Simut and myself on horseback. Like any other affluent merchant, Ambassador Hattusa travelled in a shaded palanquin. Chariots carried our necessities, guarded by Simut's men, who jogged easily alongside as if they undertook such exertions every day, their shields over their shoulders, their weapons in their hands, like the other teams of commercial bodyguards. Quickly, the chaos and activity of Avaris disappeared behind us, and all around the green cultivation lay in shadows and vast silence. The stars soon began to fade and the sky was just beginning to change from black to blue when, suddenly, the cultivation all around us ended, and the desert began. As dawn broke, and Ra rose above the horizon, returning light and life to the world, I saw rolling into the distance the famous Way of Horus, its red earth trodden down into a hard, wide, reliable surface by the feet of the countless men and soldiers who had marched it since the long-ago days of the King Tuthmosis I. This was the moment of no return; from here onwards, we crossed the border of the Two Lands into the lands of the Levant. Despite the anxieties of the journey, we were all suddenly alert. Nakht waved his hand in the air, and with the assent of Ambassador Hattusa, we began the next stage of our journey on into the heart of the unknown.

*

'What is in your satchel?' I asked Nakht, after we had ridden for some time. The sun had risen quickly on our right, and the cold of the night had vanished immediately from the air. It was already hot.

'Important letters and documents,' he replied. 'If anything goes wrong, I will destroy them before they can be seized.'

'Can I see one?' I asked.

He showed me a small clay tablet, covered with tiny, incomprehensible angled marks.

'What sort of documents are they?'

'Diplomatic letters, and so on. But most importantly, the private letter from the Queen herself, addressed to Suppiluliuma, the King of the Hittites, remains securely locked in my trunk.'

He paused, and added confidentially, 'I composed it myself, on her behalf . . .'

'You write letters for the Queen of Egypt?'

He nodded, acknowledging my admiration.

'In these strange marks?' I asked.

'Those strange marks, as you call them, are Akkadian. It has been the lingua franca of the world for as long as anyone can recall. The Babylonians and the Assyrians both spoke it, variously. But now it is mostly a written language, used by high-level officials in international exchanges regarding politics and diplomacy between the Great Empires.'

'Why isn't Egyptian used? Isn't it the greatest of the languages?' I said.

I knew Nakht would enjoy the chance to expostulate on this subject.

'Egyptian is the most complex and subtle of all modern languages, but despite its obvious superiority, it would not be politic to impose it upon everyone, or indeed to have it become widely known outside the Two Lands. Akkadian is useful for a number of reasons. Firstly it means all diplomatic exchange has to be conducted in a mutually foreign tongue. The advantages of this are obvious – neutrality of expression, minimal ambivalence, equality of articulation, and an absence of confusing metaphor or hidden meaning. And the formality is recognized and understood everywhere. Kings, no matter how much they despise each other, are always "brothers". The royal household is the "house". Empires are big "families", with the rivalries, jealousies and warm concord common to all ordinary families. Negotiations, treaties, marriage arrangements, exchange of gifts and services, are all managed in this apparently simple metaphor of familial relationship. And, of course, it is a guarantee of status: those lands and so-called kings who cannot communicate in Akkadian simply forfeit the right to join in the company of those who can. They are, literally, barbarians.'

I thought about that.

'So I suppose it functions like a code, for you must be highly educated to be able to decipher it,' I suggested. 'And without this old language, which no one speaks any more, there might be no stability, and no order in our international affairs?'

Nakht smiled.

'Exactly so. Although I sometimes wonder whether language alone is powerful enough to vanquish Seth and his forces of disruption. But that is the dilemma of the world today. The enlightenment against the dark forces of chaos . . .'

'Is it so clear?' I asked. 'Can human affairs be divided so simply? Is there not a realm between those two absolutes, where in truth we all live?'

'Our times are a struggle between the light of Osiris and the darkness of Seth,' he replied, quietly and with absolute conviction. 'How are you feeling these days?' he added, suddenly solicitous.

'I feel grief. But the rage for revenge has gone,' I lied.

'It is just as well. Revenge only destroys the revenger. That is its tragedy,' he said.

We lapsed into silence. The only sounds were the breeze rustling the scrub and the gritty sand, the clanking of our wagons, and the repetitive clip-clop of our horses. The way wound ahead into the shimmering heat of distance, dotted here and there with tiny figures of travellers, and their diminished shadows. I wondered again how quantities of opium could possibly be transported across these vast distances.

'It is extraordinary to think of the complex system of trade routes which reach from Egypt to the furthest parts of this world,' I said. 'And how vital they are to our modern way of life, now.'

He glanced at me, wondering about this change of subject.

'I know you very well, my friend, so rather than speculating hazily on the way of the world, why don't you say what is really on your mind?'

'Perhaps you will not like the subject,' I replied.

'If I dislike the subject, I will not feel the need to answer you,' he said coolly.

'Well, I suppose all these busy and profitable routes of trade and high-level communication must also permit the exchange of other, more clandestine or illegitimate businesses and goods,' I said.

'I fail to see where this is leading,' he said quietly.

'The value of anything depends upon demand, and if it is illegal or subject to taxation then even more so. So, take opium as an example. There is a proper and legal trade for the medical profession and the temples. But there is also now a new trade that makes fortunes, perpetuates violence and creates disorder in the cities – a black market, so to speak. What if someone has seen this as a huge business opportunity, and taken advantage of it?'

'Perhaps they have,' replied Nakht. 'But I am not sure I understand your point . . .'

I drew a deep breath, to focus my thoughts.

'Obviously, to set up a chain of supply over such huge

distances requires a complex system of interdependent parts, that communicate with each other in a reliable but covert manner. Communication and secrecy are the most important and powerful aspects of that system. But it strikes me that that also applies equally to the army – or, for instance, to the palace.'

I let that hang in the air.

'Now, be very careful,' he said, giving nothing away. 'Is this what you have been pondering all this time?'

I nodded.

'I am thinking there must be networks of agents in all the key cities and ports . . . I am thinking the Way of Horus would be the most obvious route for transportation. I am wondering if your intelligence network might not have picked up on some aspects of this . . .'

Nakht stared at me for a strange little moment.

'My friend, I must give you some advice. I hope you will heed it carefully, for it is given with great thought and weight of consideration. It would be wise for you to put away such thoughts. It would be wise never to speak of such things again.' He said these words quietly but very clearly.

But then his expression changed from coldness to a dawning wonder. He was gazing ahead, a look of open amazement now on his face, the way he used to look when he was younger, before he became the royal envoy, before he became a great man of the world. I turned to look in the same direction and my eyes were dazzled by a great and glorious brilliance. *The sea.*

I know the sea is made of water, but surely it is made of light, too; for it danced with brilliance, turning one sun into thousands of points of sparkling, ever-changing light. We stood together, our hands shading our eyes as they feasted upon the wonderful vision. I wanted to remember everything, to tell my family what I had seen and felt: the tang of salt in the air, and on my skin; the compelling repetition of the gentle waves that arrived, scrambling

124

up the shore, and then failing, falling back, over and over. And above all the dazzle of light, a wild shower of daylight stars, like a god revealing himself to this world.

Simut and I approached the water's edge. We kicked off our dusty sandals like children, and let the water wash over our dirty feet. It was such a curious sensation! Both deliciously cool, and enlivening. The guards remained standing on a low bluff of sand, staring away, as if pretending to be disinterested – although they, too, must have greatly desired to join us.

Nakht at first refused to approach the waters, but I would not allow him to desist; so I playfully encouraged him, and he finally relented, hesitating as the waves slapped gently, coolly, at his ankles. And so we stood there, in the dazzling morning sun, the three of us, the Royal Envoy to All Foreign Lands, the Commander of the Palace Guard, and myself, Rahotep, Seeker of Mysteries become bodyguard to the royal envoy, laughing with pleasure, up to our knees in the incandescent sparkle of the sea.

15

We quickly accustomed ourselves to the repetitive rhythm and routine that was necessary for covering the great distances involved. We rose in the dark, travelled under the late stars, and reached the next way station, with its supplies and security, before the sun reached its zenith, to eat, rest and – where there was a water tank – wash. Pairs of young soldiers, lounging in the shade of their little huts, and army units near the villages and towns also guarded the way. Nakht's documentation always carried us immediately through these checkpoints; as soon as they saw it, we were waved on with a brief salute of respect. I remained close to him at all times, scanning the landscape and the horizon for any signs of danger, conscious of my responsibility for his safety.

It was the harvest season; local farmers sold baskets of olives, grapes and pistachios, as well as mounds of wheat and barley at the side of the road. We were well-attended and fed with friendliness and respect. By midday the air grew impossibly hot, but a wind from the sea in the evenings – and a vivid breeze from the highlands at night – cooled the air wonderfully. I felt both exhausted and light, and I slept strangely, with powerful dreams that left a strange sad taste in my mouth. I woke often, because we were always alert. I remembered my family, and my home, and my heart ached for them; but they also seemed small and distant. Often, as I looked ahead into the distances yet to be conquered, or behind along the way we had travelled, the air shimmered with mirages. Out of these, caravans and horse riders arose to meet us, greeting us cautiously, and then continued on south. A strange sensation of unreality gradually took hold of me; I felt the darkness in my blood changing into something lighter, as if every step away from Egypt was turning me into a different man. Into a stranger; a man without a home.

We were soon travelling through a much less hospitable, much more remote, part of northern Canaan; here the few villages that served the Way of Horus were poor and squalid. The great fertile agrarian hinterland to the east had given way to barren highlands, grey and green and white, that encroached close to our path. Beyond them, in the clear distance, I glimpsed mountains far greater than any I had ever seen in Egypt. Instead of farmers, we mostly encountered shepherds and their straggling herds of goats, grazing on the sparse scrub that now covered the landscape. And as we passed through the increasingly impoverished villages, I noticed glances of undisguised unfriendliness, and the abusive chatter of unseen children in a language we could not understand. Sometimes stones from unseen assailants would land near us from a hideout of rocks or grasses.

And as we continued onwards I began to be haunted by the skin-crawling instinct that we were being followed, traced by unseen figures hiding just out of sight. Every gnarled tree, every rock, every derelict hovel seemed to suggest danger; my dagger was constantly in my hand. I might have thought myself paranoid, had I not also noticed the same tension in our guards; they, too, held their weapons ready, and their arrows primed in their bows. Hattusa's two bodyguards never left his side, and I was Nakht's shadow. So a few days later, when the next way station, with its familiar square mud-brick walls, and central lookout tower, finally rose up out of another of the mirages and became real, we were all quietly relieved.

But as we entered through the big wooden doorway, under the crenellated walls, and came into the courtyard, expecting a respectful welcome and some measure of comfortable accommodation, we found the crude wooden furniture had been smashed and broken up; most of it had been burned on a fire which had gone out some time before, leaving ashes that drifted around. A few untethered goats helped themselves to whatever they could find, and the floor was scattered with goat-shit. But most surprisingly of all, the place was full of native people: poor, evidently hungry herders and their families, huddled silently in the shade, gazing at us with fearful eyes.

Nakht was furious.

'What has happened here? This is a disgrace. Find the captain.'

I found him in his stifling little chamber. He was drunk, curled up in the corner, his head crooked to one side, his mouth wide open, his hands clasped together like a child. His heavy linen head-dress, which should have served as his helmet, had fallen askew, revealing his bushy hair. A tame little jackal was waiting patiently at his feet, guarding him; it snapped at me as I approached. This woke the captain, who peered at me with bloodshot, bleary eyes. Suddenly he threw his arms around me, blubbing like a baby. I could hardly make sense of his words, but it was clear he was overjoyed to see me.

'Forgive me,' he said, eventually, wiping his tears. 'It has been such a long time since I saw a friendly Egyptian face. A true face from home.'

'I think you'd better be ready to explain yourself to some less friendly Egyptian faces,' I said.

I hauled him into the courtyard, where he stood swaying and rubbing his eyes at the sight of Nakht glaring at him.

'Ambassador, please forgive these appalling circumstances. If you will be patient, I will have everything quickly organized for your comfort,' Nakht said to Hattusa.

'I certainly hope so. This is not what one expects of an Egyptian military garrison,' replied Hattusa, and he retired angrily to the shade, to wait.

Nakht took the captain inside for a dressing-down, while Simut and his men set about imposing some sort of order on the chaos, commanding the extended local families to leave – which they did with extreme reluctance, wailing, pleading and remonstrating in their strange language.

'I would have thought a place this far north would definitely have a proper set of guards, not just one drunken captain left to cope on his own. There isn't even a mule to carry supplies. It's as if the whole place has been abandoned,' said Simut.

'Haven't you noticed? These people are terrified of what's outside these walls,' I replied.

'Perhaps they're only afraid of missing out on the free food and water,' he countered, as he watched his men round up the last stragglers, and shoo an elderly couple away.

'No, there's something else,' I said. 'They're nomadic herders. They would only take shelter here out of fear for their lives.'

'So what are you suggesting?' he asked.

'I don't know. But I think we should question the captain. And we should make sure all your men are on guard all through the rest period.'

Nakht and Ambassador Hattusa ate and rested in a chamber we cleared for them, arranging the travelling furniture as well as possible. Simut and I settled down outside in the courtyard to a meal of bread and goat-meat stew prepared by a mad old woman in the garrison kitchen who had adamantly refused to leave her pots and fires, insisting in her own toothless tongue on her right to remain. As we were eating our way through the bony meal, and discussing the strange state of affairs there, the captain himself appeared. He had the grace to look ashamed of himself, and had made some effort to smarten up. His heavy linen headdress was now set correctly on his head.

I invited him to join us, and he sat down gratefully, cross-legged, next to me. He looked hugely hungover, but when he saw the wine jug – for Nakht had brought with him what he called 'a modest sufficiency' to share among us on the journey – his eyes brightened, and a big smile graced his stubbled face. To Simut's annoyance, I poured him a generous measure in one of the crude, cracked mugs which were all the station could offer.

'Life, prosperity, health! To the King!'

The captain saluted, and then drank the wine, closing his eyes with pleasure.

'Do you know, to taste fine Egyptian wine, in the company of fine Egyptian men like yourselves, is a pleasure I thought I had lost for ever,' he said, mournfully.

I thought for a moment he was going to cry, and indeed tears had begun to spring once more to his eyes.

'This wine tastes of home. I salute you, comrades. You have brought me joy. Yes. Joy abounding . . .'

And he nodded, drank deeply to confirm the deep truth of his statement, and then attended hungrily to his food.

'How long have you been in charge of this garrison?' I asked him.

'Six years,' he replied, his face falling deeper into depression. 'Six long, hard, lonely years. It feels like an eternity. But this is the fate of soldiers like myself. A long tour of duty in a miserable dump like this is the only way up the ladder of promotion. When I get back to Memphis, I'll be set up for life. In return for this hopeless existence, I've been promised a quiet post in one of the division headquarters. Weaponry, I hope. Yes, I like weaponry . . . And then I'll find a wife. And have a family. Before it's too late . . .'

'Tell us how it has been for you here,' I asked.

He looked at me, as if surprised I should even care. His eyes were crazed, glassy like the glaze on a cheap dish.

'I have been dwelling in Damnationville!' he cried. 'I've had no support, no company, no supplies, no letters; and although I've received promises of these things, nothing has arrived. Nothing. Not even messages. The supplies I brought with me are long gone; and there aren't even any mules, they've all been stolen or eaten. So I spend the day observing the birds, and fishing, and watching the way, and all the while suffering such terrible homesickness . . .'

Simut and I glanced at each other.

Quietly, Simut asked: 'I find it hard to believe the army of General Horemheb would simply abandon you to this situation. Where are the other men? Where are your fellow soldiers?'

'Gone!' cried the captain. 'Probably dead,' he added, nodding his head. 'After they deserted, they most likely didn't make it. They'll be nothing but bones by now.'

'And what of their replacements? Surely this post has strategic value?' asked Simut.

'Strategic value? Of course it has strategic value! But I've been abandoned! No one comes here, other than the one platoon, once in a while, and they share nothing of their own, even though they are plentifully supplied with excellent food and wine, and then they leave, without saying a word. They never invite me to drink or eat with them. No, they don't even spare me a kind word.'

'Which platoon are you talking about?' I asked.

131

Suddenly the captain looked as if he regretted his words. He pushed his mug forward for more wine, which I refused to give him until he answered my question.

'I cannot say,' he said warily. 'I cannot remember.'

'You will remember if you wish to drink more of the taste of home,' I replied.

He scowled, caught out.

'They are a platoon from the Seth division.'

Simut and I glanced at each other. The Seth division was from the delta. They were known to be fiercely loyal to General Horemheb. The captain nodded expectantly. I poured him wine.

'I shouldn't be talking so much. They made me swear never to speak of them, but I've no one else to talk to, except that mad old bitch in the kitchen, and neither of us has a clue what the other's saying.'

Simut was suddenly angry.

'You are a soldier of the Egyptian army, and a representative of the powers of the King of Egypt. Why have you allowed this place to fall into such a mess? Where is your sense of duty? You are a disgrace to your uniform!'

The captain rose to his feet, reluctantly, and with the last of his pride he smoothed out his creased, food-stained kilt and tunic.

'You are right, sir. But I am alone here. I live in fear. I have nothing to depend on. Every night I pray to the Gods to guard me, so that I may live to see Ra rise upon another day.'

'Why are you afraid?' I asked quickly. 'Why were all those herders afraid?'

'They are everywhere,' he answered. 'They attack by night. They destroy everything. They spare no one.'

'Who do?' I said.

'*The Apiru!*' he whispered furtively.

I confess a shiver ran down my spine at the mention of this

notorious name. And yet I might have laughed at the absurdity of his manner.

'The Apiru were wiped out years ago,' said Simut contemptuously.

'Perhaps,' replied the captain. 'But I can assure you they are very much alive again.'

He turned to go, but I still had one question.

'Why did this platoon from the Seth division swear you to secrecy?'

'I don't know,' he said. 'They promised I would be killed if I spoke of them. But you won't say anything, will you?'

'No,' I replied. 'I won't say anything.'

Simut and I retired to our pallets for the afternoon's rest.

'Do you think he was talking nonsense?' I said.

'He's a drunk, he's failed in his duty, he's no idea what's going on. Why would I take such a man's absurd claims seriously?' Simut said. But he looked distinctly anxious.

'But what if he's right? That would explain why the herders were afraid to leave. And a merchant's caravan like ours is a prime target for the Apiru,' I said.

'Even if he's right, they'd be no match for my guards. The Apiru were only ever a bunch of disaffected bandits. And their hunting grounds were known to be far away to the north-east.'

And he went outside to check on his men.

I lay back, my hands behind my head, thinking. The Apiru's reputation as a wild band of notorious killers had once spread far and wide. It was said they roved across the Levant, plundering, massacring and destroying villages and small towns. Marginal, lawless people, without ethnic or religious affiliation, they were mostly escaped convicts, slaves and horse-thieves who had formed into bands of mercenaries, often for hire by small-scale despots and chieftains in petty local wars. They were known to have caused chaos and bloodshed in Canaan, especially in Byblos and Megiddo, and the other cities of the Levant coast during the time of Akhenaten. But Simut was right: that was years ago, and they were said to have destroyed themselves through internal power struggles. And so no one took them seriously any more.

I pulled the remaining papyrus from my leather bag, and stared at it. The black star; the star of chaos, of nothingness, of disorder and disaster. It was not an Egyptian sign. And it made no sense to connect it to the Apiru, if they still existed, for they were known only to range in the badlands of the north-east. The killers of the new Thebes cartel were, from what I could tell, highly trained. I wondered about the platoon from the Seth division, and their cargo. Were they perhaps Horemheb's private division? Were they part of his intelligence network? But if so, why would they habitually travel along a route if they knew it to be vulnerable to attack from a band of mercenaries? Something was not making sense. And it would not let me sleep.

16

We continued northwards for eight more days. The way became emptier and more haunted than ever. The captain's words about the Apiru had had a strange effect. We did not believe in them, and yet now we imagined bandits tracking us, even though they were nowhere to be seen. We had relayed the captain's information to Nakht, and he had noted it, but said the idea that the Apiru had re-formed was not credible. Nevertheless, Simut and I found ourselves glancing over our shoulders, and paying greater attention to the rocks on the scrubby hillsides, the remote shacks, and the turns in the way where danger might lurk; we avoided villages, sleeping under the sky, in whatever shade we could find by day, while the guards took turns to watch, poised in the heat.

During these days we crossed the border into the Kingdom of Amurru. We were halted by young Amurru guards, desperately bored, lounging in the shade of their reed hut. When they saw us, they leapt up, shouting and brandishing their poor weapons in aggressive excitement, thinking they could have some fun tormenting a lone caravan of Egyptian merchants. But Nakht spoke to them forcefully in their own language, ordering them to show respect to Egyptian merchants. Then he sweetened the exchange with a small bribe, and they suddenly grinned amiably and fell back like obedient dogs, and we passed on.

We approached the huge walls and gatehouses of the great port of Ugarit with considerable relief at completing this strange part of our journey successfully, as well as astonishment at the spectacle of this famous city, where, as they say, all roads meet. After so many days in the isolation of the wild lands, the sights and sounds of crowded streets and crammed markets came as a delight, and I absorbed everything: from the different faces and dresses, to the strange statues of their God, Baal, and the incomprehensible sounds of their language. I saw people from many different empires and kingdoms, all in their native costumes, all there on business, for Ugarit is the greatest emporium of the world because of its prosperous position between the great sea and the trade routes that run alongside the two great rivers of this world – the Tigris and the Euphrates – as well as south towards Egypt.

The ambassador had arranged accommodation for himself at the palace of the Hittite embassy in the city, and he took his leave of us, agreeing to meet again at the docks in two days' time. We were lodged in the city home of Nakht's 'contact' – Paser, an Egyptian merchant. Bright and alert, with bold features, a neat physique, and the excellent, casual manners of a successful businessman whose charm was underwritten by determination, he greeted us with hospitable warmth, and treated Nakht with flattering, respectful attention. He spoke Egyptian with a curious accent, as if, despite his fluency, he was not truly a native speaker. On the other hand, he seemed delighted to be talking in a language he clearly loved. He had lived outside Egypt for most of his life, having been raised in Ugarit, and he had inherited a substantial trading company from his father. I imagined he was a man who knew how to get what he wanted, in the nicest possible way – and if not, by some other method.

He welcomed us inside the courtyard of his substantial house. The wooden gates were swiftly closed and barred behind us, and the noise of the city on the far side of the high walls suddenly died, to be replaced by the luxury of quietness. 'Safe and sound,' he said, with a slightly enigmatic smile.

Servants showed us to our quarters. Nakht had his own large sleeping room, Simut and I would share another, adjacent, and the guards would sleep on pallets in the passageways and under the roof that ran along one side of the courtyard. We enjoyed the luxury of a bathroom after a long and arduous journey. I washed in clean, cool water, and after Paser's barber had attended to both Simut and myself, we looked like new men in the polished bronze of his mirror.

Dressed in fresh linens, I came down the stairs to wait upon Nakht and Paser. As I made my way along the passageway to the reception room, I noticed a chamber, with many wine jars stacked in rows in the cool shadows – for wine was Paser's business, as he had explained, and I intended to interrogate him about the famous Ugarit vintages. Quietly, I entered and examined the jar stoppers for marks – normally one would find an indication of the regnal year, the name of the estate, the type of the wine, the name of the vintner, and the quality of the contents. But some of these were unmarked. Perhaps they had not yet all been inspected. I could hear Nakht and Paser murmuring in low conversation in the chamber next door. Curious, feeling like a spy, I listened.

'I will need your report immediately,' said Nakht.

'Alas, you will not be pleased,' said Paser. 'Our former friend has been up to his old tricks.'

'As I feared,' Nakht replied. 'I think we should now share this information with my men.'

'I assume they are entirely trustworthy,' said Paser.

'Absolutely,' said Nakht.

But then I heard Simut descending the stairs behind me; he would surely catch me listening. So I left the wine cellar, and joined him as he arrived at the foot of the stairs. We entered the chamber together, and stood to attention. The two men were sitting on low benches opposite each other.

'Gentlemen, please join us,' said Nakht.

'I think it is time for a glass of something,' said Paser.

'Rahotep is a connoisseur of wine,' said Nakht.

'Indeed?' said Paser. 'Then perhaps you would be interested in our Ugarit wine. It can be rather good.'

'So I hear,' I replied. 'In fact, I took the liberty of looking through your cellar,' I said.

Paser glanced at Nakht. He walked over to a tray set out with jugs and goblets.

'You are welcome to look at anything that interests you,' he said casually, and offered me a beautifully wrought silver goblet. I sniffed the wine carefully, swirling it around to release more of the bouquet. Paser was watching me. I took a small sip.

'It is drinkable. But may I be honest?'

Paser nodded.

'There is a lack of depth, there is little subtlety. I suspect it is blended,' I said.

Nakht looked alarmed by my candour, but Paser was very pleased.

'You are right. It is a secondary wine. A merrymaking wine, at best. You have passed the first test. Now, try this.'

He poured from a different jug. This time I was astonished – this wine had remarkable melancholy depth and complexity – it married sorrow and beauty in its dark richness.

'That is absolutely sublime,' I said, amazed. 'Where is it from?'

Paser smiled.

'It is also a native wine. But a rather special one! Come, you must be famished,' he said, ordering the servants to bring food on trays. Paser sat next to me as we ate.

'Egyptian wines are of course excellent, especially those from the oases of Kharga and Dakhla. But those from Ugarit are the finest in the world, and of course the vines are also the oldest. And despite the constant state of conflict in this area, there is a large clientele in Memphis and Thebes who are willing to pay the highest prices for the wines' rarity, and delicate sophistication.'

'Hence your thriving business,' I replied. 'I suppose your cellar here is for your private use . . .'

'It is really my library of wine, if I can put it like that. The main warehouse is by the docks,' he replied. 'I must attend to my worldly business there tomorrow. I hope you will be comfortable, meanwhile, in the house.'

I decided to take my chance.

'I would be most interested to visit your warehouses, before we depart. Would that be possible?'

Paser turned to Nakht, who considered, and then nodded.

'I will work in my chamber tomorrow. So I can spare Rahotep for a short while in the morning,' Nakht said. 'But now, we must attend to business. Please dismiss the servants, and make sure we are alone and not to be disturbed.'

When this was accomplished, Paser began to speak.

'The royal envoy has asked me to deliver my report on the current state of affairs in this city, and in the kingdom. But in order to do this, I must digress. History is important, gentlemen . . .'

'I am woefully ignorant of history—' I replied.

'Please be brief,' interrupted Nakht, and Paser nodded.

'We must step back a little to the reign of King Akhenaten. Back then, the King of Amurru was named Abdi-Ashirta. He was a notorious troublemaker, intent only upon creating calamity and friction with his neighbours. In particular, he coveted the territory of Byblos, to the south, and so he repeatedly attacked and antagonized the king of that territory, Rib-Hada, who was a loyal servant of Egypt. Rib-Hada wrote many pitiful letters of complaint to King Akhenaten, but answer came there none. Finally, Akhenaten, apparently concerned about any weakening of Egyptian authority in the area, summoned Abdi-Ashirta to court. He came, but whatever he said did not please Akhenaten, and he was imprisoned, and finally executed.'

'And then everything returned to normal?' I asked.

'Well. Byblos was loyally grateful for its peace, Rib-Hada stopped writing letters of complaint, and above all Egyptian authority was confirmed. Calm returned to the Levant. For a while . . .' said Paser.

'But that's not the end of the story?' I said.

'Unfortunately not,' replied Paser. 'Conflict is the normal state of affairs in this part of the world. Abdi-Ashirta had a son. His name was Aziru. It turned out this son was an even more talented and committed troublemaker than his father. When he came of age, he picked up where his father had left off, and continued to gnaw off chunks of Byblos, taking control of various nearby towns, and the city of Sumur. His ambition was to extend the boundaries of Amurru up and down the coastline. Cue yet more letters from Rib-Hada to Egypt, containing dire warnings of peril and destruction, and pleas for arms and protection – none of which came. Then Aziru somehow engineered a palace coup in Byblos, and Rib-Hada was exiled from his own city, and finally assassinated by his own brother.'

'And that was the end of Rib-Hada,' said Nakht, calmly. 'But it was only the beginning of the inglorious career of Aziru of Amurru.'

'I suppose if my father was executed, revenge would be on my mind,' I said.

Nakht frowned at me.

'Conciliation and the proper respect of a vassal towards his king should have been on his mind,' he said tersely.

'So what happened next?' I asked.

'Akhenaten summoned Aziru to court. But this time, with a view to his own survival, he refused to come. Instead he sent a letter, saying he would only attend the King if his life was guaranteed,' said Paser.

'Didn't want to end up like his father . . .' interjected Simut.

'Sensible enough from his point of view,' I suggested.

Once again, Nakht looked annoyed.

'Aziru was given assurances, and eventually he came to Egypt. He was detained for one year at the court,' said Paser.

'And that is when I first met him,' said Nakht, quietly, as if playing an unexpected move in a game of *senet*.

'And what was your impression of this infamous trouble-maker?' I said.

'Ambitious, mercurial, avaricious, intensely vain and, I perceived, entirely without human empathy. However, I was also struck by his strategic intelligence. He was brighter than his father. More astute, politically,' said Nakht.

'Would I be right in thinking he was offered a deal he could not refuse?' I asked.

'Aziru was allowed to return to Amurru on the condition that he remained loyal to Egypt, and reported back to us with intelligence on the Hittites and the movements of their divisions, their politics and so forth. In return he was allowed a certain leeway to conduct his expansionist policies, but only within agreed limits. In addition, he was offered funds to employ scouts and spies, as an inducement to loyalty. It seemed a good arrangement,' said Nakht.

He glanced at Paser.

'I'm assuming from your look he's no longer doing as he was told,' I said.

Nakht nodded to Paser to continue the story.

'First he began to take a small cut of all commodities passing through Ugarit on their way to Egypt. A kind of unofficial tax – which, given the scale of trade that passes through this city every day, was quickly a very significant amount. His strategy was obvious – he was enriching his own treasury, building up a kind of war chest. This alone was of concern to Egypt. We also had anxieties about his relationship with the Hittites. There were suggestions he was building a new alliance with our enemies. And then, recently, the reports stopped coming in. He vanished. We lost track of him completely,' said Paser.

The room was suddenly silent.

'Amurru is the most important buffer state between Egypt and the Hittites, and that is why, strategically, we have made great efforts to influence what we could not overtly control. But our position here can no longer be considered secure. Recent intelligence suggests Aziru is in Hattusa. I suspect he is negotiating with our enemies. It is likely he has changed allegiance,' said Nakht carefully.

'Because, after all, his enemy's enemy is his friend,' I suggested.

'Exactly,' replied Nakht, glancing at me.

We all thought about the implications of this revelation.

'So let me see if I understand. We are about to enter the capital of our enemies, with a highly secret proposal of marriage, on which the future of Egypt depends, and Aziru the traitor is perhaps there ahead of us, preparing his own warm welcome,' I said.

'That appears to be so,' said Nakht.

Simut and I looked at each other. This was bad news indeed.

'Shall I continue?' Paser asked Nakht.

'Please do,' he answered.

Paser refilled our goblets.

'I have unconfirmed reports of a series of unprovoked attacks on villages and towns well beyond the borders of Ugarit. These attacks are notable for their apparently random nature, and the extreme barbarity of their violence,' said Paser.

'The Apiru,' I said.

Paser looked surprised.

'You are right. It seems the Apiru, who were destroyed, root and branch, years ago, have recently re-formed, under a new leadership, and a new name,' conceded Paser.

Simut and I glanced at each other, remembering the captain's fear. Nakht looked discomfitted.

'And what is their name now?' I asked.

'The Army of Chaos,' he replied.

I stared into my goblet of wine.

'What sort of army are we talking about here?' asked Simut.

'We're talking about whole villages hacked to death. We're talking about torture, about children made to execute their parents, and blind their own siblings. We're talking about families burned alive in their homes. We're talking about young men dragged to pieces behind galloping horses . . . And as for what they do to young girls, I won't describe it,' said Paser.

We sat in silence, the food untouched before us.

'That doesn't sound like unconfirmed reports to me. That sounds like eyewitness accounts,' I said.

'Therefore we have not one but two areas of pressing concern,' continued Paser. 'Firstly, Aziru's destabilizing presence and influence in the Hittite capital. And secondly, the threat of the Army of Chaos, for the security of the return journey. And in the long term, for the security of the region.'

'But what if there is a connection between Aziru and the Army of Chaos?' I said. 'You already told us he has a history of expansionist ambition. Wouldn't it be to Aziru's advantage to encourage these attacks, and then send in his own troops to offer "security" to the devastated towns, and so occupy them as if legitimately?'

Nakht and Paser exchanged glances.

'That is indeed what we fear,' said Paser. 'If you are right, then it would be the worst of all possible worlds.'

17

The morning sun shone down on the busy streets as Paser and I made our way to his warehouse near the docks. After the previous night's conversation, my thoughts were as dark as the day was glorious. I felt sure there was a connection between the Army of Chaos and the gang in Thebes. And yet how could a band of itinerant barbarians, who operated in the wastelands of the Levant, have any power or presence in such a faraway city? And if so, how was Aziru part of the mystery? Paser, however, seemed determined not to talk about such matters. Instead, he wanted to discuss wine.

'There are three essential elements in wine – the power of the sun, the availability of good water, and the flavours of the earth – all of which combine magically within the grape itself. The properties unique to each vineyard will be intangibly present in the final character of the wine, together with the infinite varieties of time, weather, and so forth. Here in Ugarit we have gentle rains, and morning mists, to irrigate the vines. Some say the dews are the secret of the wine's flavour. Others say it is something to do with the evening shadows that are mysteriously gathered into the black of the grapes. But I say it is the soil itself; it is rich but light, with astonishing dry tones of minerals from the rocks and the underground waters. And the result? Wines that are romantic, with a voluptuous perfume, an indefinable sweetness, and a depth so strong and true . . .' He stopped suddenly in the street, threw open his arms and declaimed: '"Day long they pour the wine! Wine fit for kings! Wine sweet and abundant!"'

He smiled apologetically. 'Lines from an old poem! Forgive me, I sound like a fool when I discuss wine . . .'

'There's no finer subject,' I replied.

'Except love, of course. Which is almost the same thing. But wine is better, because you can bottle it!'

He laughed again, and put his arm through mine, and we walked on.

'Nakht is a great man, with a formidable intellect, but I can see he appreciates wine without really *loving* it. In fact, it has just come to me: he is like a lover whose hands are tied behind his back. He can see, but not touch. But I saw your face. You looked as if you were in a state of rapture! And that is the sign of a true devotee . . .' he said.

'It was among the finest wines I have ever had the fortune to taste. But you, as a merchant, must have tasted some legendary ones . . .' I replied.

'Yes, indeed. The Star of Horus on the Height of the Heaven must surely rank as the greatest, and the most ancient of our home-grown vintages.'

I had heard of it, but the cost of a jar was legendarily exorbitant. Only kings and nobles could afford such rarities.

'And perhaps you have tried a Chassut Red?' I asked.

He smiled and clapped his hands.

'Only once! They say the Chassuts are not ready to drink until

146

they have aged a hundred years. And I can personally confirm that opinion. It is worth the wait!'

I was about to ask more, but the grand street, lined with shady shops where merchants invited passers-by to examine their wares, suddenly opened up to reveal a vast panorama: the harbour and market of Ugarit. Uncountable numbers of ships were moored at the long lines of the timber wharves; others negotiated their passage in and out of the densely crowded waters. Hundreds of sails fluttered and unfurled in the breeze. The harbour waters, tamed by the stone arms of the sea walls, glittered and shimmered in the clear morning light. Directly in front of us the great market spread out, occupying all of the vast open space before the docks.

'It's quite a sight, eh?' said Paser, once more taking my arm, and leading me down into the chaos of the market. Thousands of stalls were set up under shades, and customers, browsers, merchants, and mules and porters carrying goods, all struggled together, shouting insults, imprecations, advice and unbeatable offers. We passed stalls selling beer, and others selling oils, grapes and figs, and then magnificent silverwork.

'Ashkelon silver. Very fine work,' said Paser, pointing. 'You should buy something to take home for your wife!'

Instantly the silver merchant came forward, bowing and smiling, greeting Paser, and engaging him in conversation. But I shook my head, not having the funds or the heart for such a transaction. With a casual wave of his imperious hand, Paser passed on, and the merchant sank back into the shadows, his smile immediately vanishing at the lost sale.

'Here is the precious stones market. Lapis lazuli, gold, amethyst, jasper, turquoise? Yours for the taking, and much cheaper here than at home in Egypt. Finger-rings, earrings, bracelets wrought by the finest Minoan craftsmen, for your daughters, perhaps? Over there, to the left, is the olive oil and wine – see, they are unloading a fresh consignment from Crete. They have the most beautiful vessels! Over there, the perfumes, and beyond the wools and linens, mostly from Egypt, of course, highly expensive, and very much in demand among the new class of affluent families . . .'

I shaded my eyes. Further away, closer to the waterfront, I noticed long, low depots teeming with men and carts.

'And those?'

'Those are storage for the consignments of raw materials – tin, copper, cedar, lead and bronze. Those merchants have standing orders from all across the world, from royal and noble families. The caravans have long been contracted, and they will soon begin their long journeys to their far destinations.'

He gazed with worldly satisfaction at the panorama of the emporium before us, then nodded ahead, as we approached a corral of horses, steaming in the heat of the sun. Merchants in long woollen cloaks were carefully scrutinizing the fine, dignified, nervous animals.

Paser leaned into me and said, 'Those are Hittite merchants. They buy all the best horses for their infantry.'

'Do Hittite and Egyptian merchants trade together? Despite the wars?' I asked.

'My dear friend, the world is really one vast marketplace. No one cares where a man is from as long as he has gold in his pocket, or something you want. And the remarkable thing is this: the wars have only encouraged demand, trade has actually *boomed* in these difficult years. The ships are full, everyone is happy. War and politics are irrelevant, unless the great flow of trade is disturbed.'

'And what are the ships full of?' I asked.

'Everything this world has to offer. Silver and copper, glass and bronze, lapis lazuli and gold, oils, perfumes, animal skins, live animals, potions, dyes, cedar, slaves, women, children . . .' he said, listing them casually.

'And opium?'

'Why do you ask?' he said cautiously.

'Curiosity,' I replied.

But Paser was not satisfied with this answer. He pulled me suddenly aside.

'I like you, Rahotep, so I will be open with you. Nakht has already told me about your private loss. I was sorry to hear of it.'

'I appreciate your words. I lost a great friend. His name was Khety. He was a fine Medjay officer investigating a new opium gang. Until he was brutally murdered,' I said. Even saying those few words stirred the blackness in my blood again.

Paser nodded sympathetically.

'We live in a dark time. But I must tell you Nakht has instructed me not, under any circumstances, to discuss any matters connected to this with you.'

I took out the papyrus with the black star from my leather satchel, and showed it to Paser.

'Does this mean anything?' I asked.

He gazed at it in astonishment.

'Where did you get it?' he asked.

'From inside the mouth of my murdered friend,' I replied. 'It was left as a sign by his executioner after he cut off his head. I see you recognize it.'

Paser nodded slowly.

'It is the sign of the Army of Chaos,' he replied.

At last. Paser had confirmed what I had suspected. There *was* a connection between the Theban gang and the merciless brutes of the Army of Chaos.

'How could the Army of Chaos have any connection with a high-level opium gang in Thebes?' I asked, my mouth dry.

Paser patted his now-sweating brow with an embroidered cloth.

'I see what sort of man you are, Rahotep. You are honourable. That is a rare virtue in this corrupt and terrible world of ours. But it is also a risky one. You must be very careful.'

'All I know is I will not stand by and let the things I love be destroyed. There has to be justice,' I replied. 'If there is no justice, then what will become of us all?'

Paser nodded and patted my hand.

'Justice! That is a word one does not hear much these days.'

He seemed breathless. I was determined to keep him talking.

'Shall we continue?' I suggested. He nodded.

'I asked you about opium because I believe there is a black market trading in it, which is connected to the new kind of gang in Thebes,' I said. 'You have confirmed the black star is the sign of the Army of Chaos. Now I need to know how they transport the opium, where they get it, and how it is sold into Egypt.'

Paser stopped dead in his tracks.

'Let me warn you, Rahotep, friend to friend. Opium is the worst of trades, and the most violent. No one who enters it lives long.'

'As my friend Khety discovered to his cost. Do you know how they butchered him?' I asked. My hands were suddenly sweaty and shaking. I wiped them against my robe.

'I do not, nor do I wish to hear it,' he replied.

We arrived at the sea wall itself and climbed the hewn steps, smoothed by innumerable feet over the ages, in silence, until we stood, shading our eyes, admiring the beauty of the coastline, green with trees and fields, grey where it was rocky, and beyond it the great spectacle of the open, ever-changing sea.

'I will not seek revenge for Khety's death while on this journey. I know I have my job to do. But I have to *know*. If I don't know, I can't live with myself,' I said.

Paser glanced at me and sighed.

'I will tell you something, but it must remain absolutely between ourselves. Is that understood?'

'Absolutely,' I promised.

'Everything is upside down in these strange days. Everything is in flux, and that is good for those who would do evil, and make their fortunes from chaos. These long wars have had strange consequences: they have created unreliable borders; they have allowed local conflicts to develop into shifting and unreliable allegiances that in turn have adversely affected the great empires. The balance of power is no longer certain. Chieftains are able to play off kings for their allegiance. No matter what they promise and swear about loyalty and long-established political alliances and so on, every one of them is motivated by selfish imperatives; and in the case of the small kingdoms that means not only taking every advantage of the usual markets of international trade, but also of the opportunities of the black market. Do you understand?' he said.

I nodded. 'The wars have opened up the black markets to the gangs, and now they have power, while Egypt is losing control . . .' I said.

'Quite so. And in addition, Egypt has become arrogant. It has assumed its absolute superiority without doing the necessary political work to ensure its respect in the world. It has committed injustices against the peoples of this region. It has too often ignored its vassals and its allies, and where it has not ignored them it has treated them with contempt. I say this as a loyal Egyptian, but I see the negative consequences everywhere here, on the ground.'

Paser leaned in closer to me.

'Of course, no one wants to hear this. Not even Nakht. But I fear Egypt sowing the seeds of its own disaster. This war has produced the best possible conditions for the success of a different kind of crime: one that extends beyond these newly permeable borders. The black market is now bigger and more powerful than it has ever been. In its scale and its scope it could one day even challenge the financial might of Egypt herself. So you see, your question goes to the heart of the matter.'

I thought about this.

151

'And opium has become one of the most lucrative of all the black market commodities?'

He looked around and waited until a group of strolling sight-seers had passed, so that no one might overhear us.

'It is *the* most lucrative. And therefore the most dangerous.'

'Is it for sale, here?'

'Of course it is. But I trust you are not so naive as to think you can single-handedly trace it to its source, and destroy it. It is a many-headed serpent. Certainly, you might find it here, being offered to you by a child on the street. That boy is only the lowest-level seller. You would most likely not find the man behind the deal, but if you did you would certainly not find the man behind that man, and so on, and so on. These men are not merchants. These are not domestic, petty criminals. We Egyptians are a people who admire order. We worship the Goddess Maat, Keeper of Justice and Harmony – in the seasons, the stars, and the relations between the Gods and mortals! But she is not the only God of power. There is Seth, God of Chaos and Confusion, patron of deserts and wild places, abhorred creature, part-dog, part-donkey, with his forked tail, he who confronts and blinds Horus, he who murdered Osiris himself, he who would be ruler of the Earth!'

He wiped his brow, and laughed a little.

'I thought we were talking of men, not Gods,' I said.

'Indeed. But I will tell you something. I have my ear to the ground, and there are those who are saying Seth is here again, walking unseen among the living. They say his time has come again. They say there is a man come forth in our day who will be Seth the Destroyer.'

He shrugged.

'It does not take a seer to imagine who might be the first candidate for such a role. I imagine Aziru, from what you said last night, would relish it,' I said. 'Does this mysterious man have a name?'

'If he does, I do not know it,' replied Paser, carefully.

'Have you heard the name Obsidian at any point?'

Paser glanced at me.

'No, I have not. Why do you ask?'

'Because I have heard this name spoken in connection with the opium trade in Thebes.'

The shouts and noise of the marketplace below us suddenly seemed far away.

'My friend Khety was killed by a mysterious new cartel in Thebes. Now you have confirmed that the papyrus left in his mouth is the sign of the Army of Chaos. And they probably have a connection with Aziru, who is, most likely, allied with the Hittites. Does there not seem to you to be a chain of connections between my beheaded friend in Thebes and where we are standing now?'

Paser blew out his cheeks, as if he was about to say something, but chose to remain silent. We gazed out in silence at the incongruously glorious vision of glittering water, of beautiful, busy ships, and the great panorama of the trade of the world. I turned around to gaze at the vast city. The mountains in the far distance were capped with dazzling snow. I tried another tack.

'Let's assume the supply chain runs along the course of the Great River, and along the trade routes, via Bubastis and the other eastern delta towns. Let's suppose local officials, motivated by greed or fear, each take their place in the process, to maximize efficiency and minimize risk. Let's imagine the chain ranges from low-level street dealers, through the gangs, and the middlemen, up to the top level: gangsters whose corrupt influence reaches into the heart of the empire's power. But it all starts with the crop. Where does it come from? Where is it grown? And how could such quantities be smuggled all the way to Egypt's cities, even if corruption were able to control everything?'

Paser nodded at the forbidding range of mountains in the distance.

'Beyond those mountains, to the south-east, are remote, high valleys – wild, barbaric, extremely dangerous places. Hidden away inaccessibly, the highest, most remote valley is secret, and closely guarded. No one who goes there ever returns. They say it is long and narrow, green and lush in the south, drier and harsher in the north. The summers are long and dry. And they say it is a perfect paradise, for any seed you drop on the earth will grow . . .' he said.

'So that is where your glorious wine comes from?' I said. Paser nodded. But then I realized the other connection. 'And it is also the perfect land for the cultivation of opium.'

'I did not say so,' he replied. 'And you must not let the royal envoy know we have talked about anything but wine. Wine is safe, at least.'

'Our conversation is private. But if it is so dangerous there, how do you acquire that glorious wine?' I asked.

'Almost all of the wine I acquire and sell comes from this side of the mountains. But very occasionally a consignment from that valley comes on to the market, privately. I know how to acquire it, of course for a very high price, for my most discerning customers.'

'And have you been there yourself?'

He laughed briefly.

'Of course not! Do you think I do not value my life?'

'But if I wanted to go there, do you have contacts who could guide me?' I asked.

His hands flew up in frustration. I had pushed him too far.

'Have you listened to a single word I have said? You must swear to me to put aside all such thoughts! You could never survive there. It is a place of terrible poverty and extreme tribal violence.' He was sweating hard now. 'I will tell you a story. They say the reason the wine is so perfect, so dark and complex, is because the vines are fed with human *blood*. The gang that runs this garden paradise is the Army of Chaos. That valley is their homeland.'

154

PART THREE

May you flow forth who comes in darkness and enters furtively . . .

Spell for the protection of a child

18

We sailed out of the harbour of Ugarit aboard a Hittite merchant vessel fully loaded with Egyptian grain, and turned north once more. The sparse coastline of the land to our east remained always in view, because, for all sailors, the open seas of this voyage were notorious for their perils: pirates from the island of Alishiya, who could ram, board, rob and murder; and perhaps even worse, sudden disastrous storms that could wreck a ship in moments. But we were lucky with the weather, for the sky remained clear and the wind reliably strong. However, the boat struggled with the contradictory waves, and the rolling rise and fall affected everyone; for the first few days I felt sick, and could only find relief on deck, in the open air, with my eyes set upon the horizon. Nakht suffered greatly; he remained confined to his pallet in the airless cabin of the ship, where he lay sweating, unable to eat or move, his eyes closed, in silent surrender to the unrelenting power of the waters.

But under the protection of Ra, after four days at sea, we

safely reached the port of Ura in sparkling sunlight. A wide green plain spread around the port and its extensive domains. Not even pausing for one night of rest, we set off immediately in a long caravan towards the Hittite heartlands. Ambassador Hattusa took command of the journey from this point; he seemed impatient to return to his home again.

We passed through small, carefully cultivated fields and meadows; I saw several kinds of wheat and barley, together with beans and peas, carrots, leeks, garlic and herbs. Their olive trees were gnarled with age, and their neat orchards dense with unfamiliar fruits. Every house or shack raised its own pig, hens, sheep, goats and, perhaps, if they were unusually affluent, a cow. Smiling children came to barter respectfully, with figs and apricots, pomegranates, tamarisk, honey and cheeses. We replenished the food cart for the journey ahead.

Then we left this verdant plain behind us, and began to trek up winding routes of grey, dusty, well-maintained tracks that rose through stony valleys. Dense stands of thin silver trees with rustling green leaves in the shape of hearts grew beside rushing waters, which tumbled down impassable crevasses. By bridges and at crossroads, we came upon little shrines to the deities of the place: crudely carved statues of shapeless females, which Nakht pronounced fertility Goddesses, and offerings of wild flowers left in cracked jars. As we ascended higher, strange mists gathered and drifted among the sharp green angles of the forests, resolved into sudden, light rains that refreshed our faces, then vanished again into sunlight. When we rested, we gazed back down at the vast empty valleys below us – wildernesses of forest and rock and barren brown land, under blue skies and drifting temples of pure white clouds.

Finally, after three days of climbing, we found ourselves on a high, windswept plateau. It was liberally scattered, as if by a careless builder-god, with handfuls of huge, spare rocks and the rubble of innumerable leftover stones. Richly scented, woody herbs grew in every nook and cranny in dense, thorny bushes, throwing up intensely bright red and white blooms on bristling stems; unseen streams argued their way through narrow declivities, and the muscular, buffeting wind carried a sharp, chilling freshness. We camped for the night near an escarpment, and in the grey light of the next day's dawn we stood together, gazing in astonishment at an ocean of fog and mist that had risen up in silence in the darkness, and now covered the world below; it moved slowly in massive divisions that swept over our heads, but had no power to harm us at all. I looked at us: a band of weary Egyptian travellers, strangers in a strange world.

We moved on into a lost, high land, yellow and brown and grey under blue skies, where the wind swept its great hands over and through the wild grasses in huge waves. We passed large flocks of sheep and herds of cattle being driven to the higher pastures by shepherds, their wrinkled faces tanned by the sun and wind; they whistled to their capable, intelligent dogs, who accomplished dizzyingly complex manoeuvres to corral the animals. We passed outcrops of red and grey rocks jutting out of green slanting fields; and we paused to stare at misty valleys falling away to the left or the right, into sunlight or shade. Wild horses, nut-brown and silver-grey, grazed on the gold and silver grasses, flicking their tails and ignoring us unless we came too close – and then they cantered away, kicking and tossing their manes, and rising up on their hind legs. We came upon a lake of dark, cold water, still as a bronze mirror, cupped in the huge rocky hand of a mountain God, his head far, far away in the sky, crowned with the whiteness of snow.

And then, one afternoon, as we crossed a vast dry plain of gold grasses, up ahead through the heat haze we saw a strange cloud of dust; Hattusa raised his hand and pointed. His bodyguards cantered forwards, away around a curve in the way, and disappeared. We waited in silence. Simut and his guards were on alert, and swiftly took up positions, their weapons flashing in the sunlight. I stood close to Nakht, my dagger and a long spear ready in my hands. We listened intently; we heard the whispering of the wind through the sea of grasses, and the singing of unseen tiny birds, high in the clear sky. But there was something else too: a faint, distant murmur, as of many animals, sighing and moving.

Then the Hittite guards reappeared, and signalled us forward. Simut's guards maintained their alert, and I insisted on riding before Nakht. But as we rounded the corner, instead of a long train of animals on their way to pasture, we saw a multitude of the most dismal, desolate people: long columns of foreign captives, men, women and children, taken from plundered and besieged towns and cities, and now being driven like cattle to Hattusa. They stumbled, groaned and shuffled, goaded and pushed ever onwards by Hittite soldiers.

'These are booty people,' said Nakht, quietly. 'They are being taken to a life of indentured labour in the Hittite homeland.'

'If they survive,' I added.

Even as we passed, an emaciated woman collapsed, and was simply left where she fell, as carrion for the menacing dark hawks that continually hovered and swooped in the blue sky. The booty people turned away from us instinctively; none were permitted to look in our direction. I glanced at Hattusa, who rode ahead, apparently impervious to this spectacle of misery.

'What sort of people treat their prisoners in this way?' I said quietly to Nakht.

'With so many able-bodied men at the wars, they are always short of manual labourers. These people will live out their lives as best they can,' he replied.

'But there's something inhuman about this – look at them. They're less than animals.'

'We are not here to criticize the practices of the Hittites,' he replied. 'But I admit, the sight is distressing. The Hittites are not perhaps as advanced as we are in their treatment of slaves.'

Suddenly, one of the captives surged out of the column of men, and caught my foot in his grasp. He was younger than I, and something about his features, and his black hair, however dirty with dust, reminded me of Khety. I realized his eyes were the same colour as Khety's, and they were staring at me desperately. He uttered some words in a language I could not understand, but I knew they were pleas for help. He gripped my leg again, as if to pull me from my horse. Instinctively, in shock, and determined to protect Nakht against any danger, I kicked back against him, but he held on with the strength of despair. All at once, he was enraged, calling upon the other men close to him to join him; but to his despair they merely gazed on in a kind of apathy. A young woman, presumably his wife, clutching a bundle that must have held a baby, began to scream; and then very quickly his captors closed in on him, and one clubbed the man's skull, and he loosened his grip, and with a low moan fell away from me, into the dust.

'Don't look back,' commanded Nakht, but I felt that man's desperate eyes on me every step of the way. What could I have done? I asked myself, over and over. I told myself, nothing. And yet he haunted me, and his face blurred with Khety's. I could have saved Khety, too, if I had listened to him more carefully.

The landscape ahead seemed to mirror my dark mood, for the open plateau now gave way to dense, endless forests of dark trees with sharp, viridian needles. Their strange angular shadows fell across the way, creating worrying unseen hiding places, where birds and creatures rustled, and sudden crickets let off their alarms. Everything made me nervous now; such forests could easily disguise bandits or enemies waiting in ambush. And then, one morning, as we rode, suddenly we were surrounded by a group

161

of men on horseback. They appeared out of the forests, before and then behind us, shouting orders in an incomprehensible language. Simut's guards immediately deployed into a defensive cordon around Nakht, and I raised my spear in readiness. My heart was beating fast. I looked around for any possible route of escape, but all I saw were the impossible depths of the dark trees.

But the ambassador called out in his own language, and raised his hand in salute, and the leading horseman of the group responded with the same gesture. Then the ambassador turned to Nakht.

'There is no need for alarm. These are Hittite soldiers. They were just doing their job, and we appeared unexpectedly. They will accompany us the rest of the way. Tell your men to stand down.'

All the Hittite soldiers wore conical leather helmets with ear-flaps, and leather shoes with curled-up toes; and they carried spears, scimitars and hide-covered shields. Their black hair was worn long, and was as glossy and well-combed as a woman's. And they were clean-shaven, too. Their sharp eyes flickered over us, curious and hostile. They quickly fell in before and behind our company, and we moved past a wooden watchtower, its guards regarding us carefully, and on through the endless, dark forest of the Hittite homeland, towards their capital.

Finally, towards the evening of the following day, covered in dust, weathered by the harsh light and the buffeting wind of the high world we had traversed, we saw the dark green forests unexpectedly give way to open, rolling land bathed in sunlight; in the distance were the pale-yellow mud-brick towers and the tall city walls of Hattusa. It was built on long green hillsides, surrounding an impressive summit of rock that rose high above everything else in the landscape.

As we came closer to the city, workmen carrying long, lightly

162

coloured stripped timbers on their shoulders paused to watch us, and gangs of foreign labourers – just like those we had passed on the way – roped together, toiled in the fields. But something was wrong with them; they held on to each other, and seemed uncertain of the world around them. And then I realized: most of them had been blinded – even the children. They moved like lost, hopeless people, going about their interminable labour.

'What has happened to them? Why are these people blinded?' I asked.

Hattusa was not impressed by my reaction. 'To stop them fleeing for their homelands,' he replied, as if it were the most obvious thing in the world. 'And what do they need sight for now? They can labour perfectly well without it.'

And he turned his haughty face to the towers of Hattusa.

'Welcome to my city,' he said proudly.

19

Lions leapt out at us from the light stone of the city's great gateway, set into the towering walls; these were not lions of terror and war, but of pride, magnanimity and courage. We clattered through the gate, past the guards of the watchtowers, through a long, dark, high triangular tunnel that led under the massive ramparts – and finally entered the capital of our arch-enemies.

Once inside, we ascended a stone-paved, stepped ceremonial way that wound past small dark temples, low warehouses, and what seemed like sizeable underground grain siloes, beside extensive offices and elite dwellings. Hattusa pointed out the impressive engineering of the terraces and the viaducts that audaciously spanned the crevasses surrounding the citadel rock.

'This is the Upper City. Here are all the offices on which the palace of the King depends.' Hattusa nodded at the prominent acropolis above us, clearly separated from the rest of the city by its grand elevation, and by more encircling, protecting high stone walls.

'If we have leisure I will be glad to give you a tour of the greatest of them, the Temple of the Storm God. That is a wonder you must see,' he added, pointing at a vast building, its great walls covered with carvings and reliefs of lions and sphinxes fashioned from a dark-green stone the colour of deep water.

'I would much appreciate the opportunity to admire it,' answered Nakht.

As we made our way up and up, groups of Hittite men in fine woollen robes stared at us. Some nodded respectfully to the ambassador, and exchanged earnest greetings of welcome; but most turned aside so as not to look upon us, and a few even spat ostentatiously on the ground as we passed.

The ambassador showed us our accommodation, in a timber and mud-brick dwelling decorated with simple friezes.

'These are your quarters. They are simple, in the Hittite fashion. But I hope you'll be comfortable here. So, please rest, and wash, and refresh yourselves. Tonight there will be an official banquet, and then tomorrow morning, the King has granted us an audience. I hope it will be the first step in the successful resolution to our project. If you need anything at all, before then, I am at your service. The servants will assist you. Guards have been posted, but please be assured, they are there for your protection. You are not their prisoners. Meanwhile, I must return to my home, and then attend the King himself. I have been away for a long time. Perhaps my wife has finally noticed my absence!'

We waited until the guards had closed the wooden doors to the outside world, and Simut had ordered his guards to take up their own positions; and then we set to talking.

'Is this strange place really the capital of our great enemy? Compared with Thebes or Memphis, it seems primitive!' said Simut.

'The old city was sacked and almost destroyed by fire, before the reign of the present King's father,' said Nakht. 'So this is a relatively new city, and from that perspective, it's more impressive. All the same, I'd assume the Hittite King has been greatly preoccupied with his military campaigns, at the expense of any magnificent building projects. This is not what I expected at all. It's all very interesting . . .'

Simut raised his eyebrows at me, in mockery of Nakht's high-handed tone.

'This is a strange land in every way. And yet they seem to have created an empire to rival our own in just two or three generations. How have they done it? It would seem impossible,' he said.

'Do not be deceived. For all their foreign triumphs, the Hittite empire is young, unstable and underdeveloped. They are surrounded by domestic enemies to the north and west, and have therefore to fight wars and defend borders on several fronts simultaneously. They lack reliable supplies of grain sufficient to feed their population, and so they are dependent on the international market – and as you see, transportation from the ports is a serious problem, for they have no great river,' replied Nakht.

'And yet despite those disadvantages, they have conquered the empire of Mittani, absorbed its territory into their own, and subjugated the great cities of Carchemish and Ugarit, making them vassals,' I said.

'And that is what I find alarming,' said Simut, removing his sandals and lowering his feet into a bowl of cool water with a sigh. 'Because if a young, fairly primitive kingdom, with few resources, and no natural geographical advantages – not even a decent river to call its own – can destroy Mittani, and then seriously challenge Egypt itself for supremacy, what does that tell you about the way the future may turn out?'

Nakht nodded, absorbed by these words.

'Egypt can no longer live on past glories. We must set the terms of the present, in order to conquer and possess the future.' He broke the seal on his official trunk, and opened the lid. 'So let us focus on our task at hand. It will certainly make all the difference to the future,' he said, very carefully producing from his bag the official diplomatic tablets from the Queen herself, wrapped in fine linen. 'These are the keys to that future,' he said. And then he broke the seal on another, heavier trunk. 'And these are the gifts which will sweeten the marriage proposal,' he said. Inside was a collection of magnificent gold objects – plates, goblets and statuettes. 'All men love gold. And they will do anything to possess it.'

He gazed at the objects, his face strangely lit.

20

That evening, as the sun was setting, casting long shadows everywhere, we were accompanied by the ambassador and twelve palace guards up through the densely built temple quarter, towards a stone viaduct spanning the rocky gorge that ran east to west between the Upper City and the royal citadel. As we crossed this, we paused to admire the panorama that spread before us to the south, east and west. The ambassador pointed out the sights.

'There to your left is the sacred pool where our priests must wash before serving in the temples. As you can see, the temple city spreads south, with the great processionals leading away towards the Lion Gate in the south-west, the King's Gate to the south-east, and the Sphinx Gate to the south.'

I gazed beyond the walls and gate-towers that surrounded the city, to the landscape that stretched into the distance. A chilly breeze swept in from far across the high plateau and the forests, carrying scents of pine, thyme and rosemary, and the sounds of the far bells of many herds of goats, sheep and cattle being corralled in the last of the light. The sun's low-angled rays picked out the details of the shacks of the town beyond the walls, and the dense orchards and woods that surrounded everything. I caught the bitter scent of woodsmoke drifting from domestic fires below, and winding upwards into the clear, pure air. Small birds, their tails fletched like arrows, dived and swooped over our heads, crying and wheeling in brilliantly choreographed flocks. And in the midst of this strange beauty, I felt a stab of memory – guilt at Khety's murder, and guilt at the abandonment of my family, so far away. I thought of my wife taking all the responsibilities of the family, and sleeping alone, uncertain whether she would ever see me again. Can love communicate over great distance? I could only hope so.

'The city gates are being closed for the night. The guards will bolt them now, and the officer of the gates will seal them personally. Night guards sleep in the gatehouses. The city is impregnable. And in the morning, sentries on the walls will scan the horizon. And only when they are satisfied that all is well will the gates be opened once more . . .' said the ambassador.

'So now we are locked inside the city of our great enemies!' whispered Simut to me.

'I know. We're surrounded, and to be honest I am not sure what it is that prevents them from killing us all.'

'We are here under the official protection of their King. That carries great weight,' he replied.

I kept my hand on my dagger, and remained close to Nakht. As we continued across the viaduct, I whispered to him: 'What does Aziru look like?'

'He is distinguished by his red hair. But if he is here in the city I don't think he will be so careless as to show himself yet,' he replied.

We arrived at the gatehouse at the far end, set in high, thick stone walls, where a different set of royal guards waited for us,

169

spears in hand. Their hair was long, and they wore striking tunics, decorated around the neck and the hems with repeating motifs in blue and red. Carved into the stone above the gate was a large double-headed eagle, its arrogant wings spread wide.

'That's the symbol of the Hittite army,' said Simut quietly. I liked it far less than the brave, welcoming lions of the city's gate.

'And these are the notorious Golden Spearmen, the most elite palace guard,' added Nakht. 'Please keep your eyes open, gentlemen. It would be a pity for me to become the victim of an assassination, especially now, after we have come so far.'

The interior of the palace was spectacularly lit by many torches that burned smokily. But a heavy gloom dominated. At the end of a long, high passageway, carved wooden doors were open; and through these we were ushered into a ceremonial hall, where a large crowd of Hittite nobles had gathered. They were all ostentatiously armed. As we entered, the roar of talk stopped, and all eyes turned on us. In silence, they watched Nakht as he worked his way slowly and respectfully along a line of waiting, hostile dignitaries, while Simut and I remained on either side of him as his loyal retinue. I glanced at the crowd, looking for a man with red hair.

Nakht was invited to sit at a long wooden table, in a high-backed, carved wooden chair. The ambassador sat opposite, and around him the other chiefs ranged themselves: the Chief Steward, brother to the King, who preserved a haughty distance; then the Chief of the Royal Guards; the Chief of the Royal Table; the Chief of the Scribes; the Chief of the Bodyguards; and many others who were the elite of the Hittite world. At the head of the table on a dais was an imposing throne, but it was empty.

'The Hittite King is not gracing us with his presence,' I whispered to Simut.

'No, nor any member of the royal family,' he replied. 'In any case, the atmosphere is not welcoming . . .'

A hundred Hittite nobles and magnates stared at us coldly, in the flickering light of the torches. Nakht looked surrounded and outnumbered by the enemy at their dinner table; they were poised in silence, as if ready to pounce and eat him alive. But somehow he managed to seem calm, composed and unafraid.

With a clap of his hands, the Chief Steward summoned the food for the banquet; servants entered from side doors, carrying platters of crudely roasted meats, breads, roasted vegetables and piles of richly coloured fruits. Instantly the atmosphere improved – I suppose the prospect of dinner improves the mood of even the most mortal of enemies. Behind each seated dignitary stood a food-taster, and suddenly I realized I would have to stand in as Nakht's. I was starving, and the scents of the rich meats were wonderful. I sampled each dish quickly, my fear conflicting with my appetite. Once it was clear I – and all the other food-tasters – had survived, everyone set to feasting. Nakht began an earnest, awkward discussion with the Chief Steward, their heads nodding as they went through the rituals and motions of politeness. It seemed the banquet was going to plan.

Until suddenly there was an unexpected blast from the trumpets, announcing the entrance of a dignitary who – judging from the aghast looks on the Hittite nobles' faces – was clearly unexpected. A young man, richly attired, wearing an excess of gold chains around his neck, his long, straight black hair falling about his sharp features, entered. He was accompanied by a band of arrogant, noisy young nobles, who clearly scorned the older generation gathered in the great hall. At an urgent signal from the Chief Steward, everyone stood up, their chairs scraping on the flagstones, their heads bowed. The Prince, followed by his aggressive young companions, casually strode along the length of the banquet table, taking in the gathering and relishing the nobles' discomfort. He reached the throne, stroked its arms, and leaned against it. But he did not sit in it. Instead, he nodded nonchalantly at his uncle, the Chief Steward at Hattusa, then at the Chief of the Bodyguards and the other chiefs. And finally he scrutinized Nakht, who had bowed his head respectfully. The hall was absolutely silent.

'Remarkable. I return to find an Egyptian, the royal envoy of our great enemy no less, is dining at the high table of my father, the King. What on earth can he be doing here? Have the Egyptians conceded defeat? *Have they come to beg for mercy?*' he said. His voice was ugly with sarcasm. His companions tittered. Hattusa mustered his dignity and bowed.

'I present the Royal Envoy Nakht of Thebes, representing our Brother Ay, King of Egypt, to the Crown Prince Arnuwanda, son of the Sun of our Land.'

Nakht bowed with great care, but the Crown Prince barely even nodded.

'I was not aware of plans for your visit, Royal Envoy, otherwise I can assure you I would have insisted on being present to behold our enemy enter under the battlements of the city of my father.'

Hattusa looked askance, and cleared his throat.

'We were not aware of your presence in the city, sir. You were known to be away, at the wars, with your battalion. Otherwise, your royal presence would have been first in our thoughts.'

The Crown Prince studied him, reaching out for a bunch of grapes, and began to stroll around, eating them slowly.

'Welcome home, Ambassador. How did you fare in the famously treacherous court of the Egyptian King? And why have you invited this Egyptian to dinner? I would have preferred it if you had returned with his head only . . .'

His friends laughed loudly. The ambassador glanced at the Chief Steward, in a silent plea for assistance.

'The King himself has invited the Royal Envoy Nakht. There will be an audience tomorrow. No doubt he will insist upon your presence – now that you are known to be here,' replied the Chief Steward.

The Crown Prince seemed to respect his uncle's authority. He nodded curtly, but continued to eat his grapes, one by one.

'I will insist upon it myself. I am fascinated to hear the contents of the letters of the aged and infirm King Ay, who we hear is a very decrepit shadow of a man, fit only for his tomb. Or perhaps the ambassador brings news that the Egyptian King is already dead, and so, in despair and weakness, the Royal Envoy has come to press for peace. Which we will never grant!'

His companions cheered, and the crowd in the chamber set about laughing dutifully, as seemed necessary. In the silence that followed, Nakht had to respond.

'Peace would be valuable to both our great empires,' he replied carefully.

But now some of the nobles were booing. The Crown Prince grasped his advantage.

'Peace is a word spoken only by cowards, the vanquished and the weak! We are Hittites. We yearn for a war of such glory that it will bury all Egypt in its great calamity for thousands of years!'

The young men, and others in the hall, shouted their agreement. Nakht seemed to be losing control of the situation.

'Egypt has come to speak to our brother, the Sun, the King of the Hittites, whom we respect as our equal, in war and in peace. We have come to remind ourselves of our good relations. May all go well with him, and with us,' he cried out, in the careful formulas of international diplomacy.

The crowd laughed scornfully at this, and the Crown Prince made the most of it, turning to his audience, his eyebrows raised in scorn like a comic actor. Hattusa looked deeply embarrassed.

'Good relations? Is it not wonderful to behold, nobles! Egypt has come crawling across the world to us! Indeed, may all go well with you, but you are no brother of ours,' replied the Crown Prince in an ironic tone. 'Until tomorrow, as a Hittite guest you shall be duly honoured. But as our enemy, know this: whatever golden words you pour into the ear of my father the King, the Hittites will never accept peace. We have conquered three empires in one generation. And we have hardly begun, for soon we will conquer Egypt, and your monuments will be as ruins, and all your carved names will be destroyed, and your glories will be dust. Your Gods will despair and abandon your temples and your lands, and we will trample you and smite you to death in your own palaces. So much for good relations!'

The young men now gathered around Nakht and roared their approval directly into his face. It was astoundingly disrespectful. Nakht met this hostility with implacable diplomatic manners.

'We hear the words of the Prince of the Hittites, and remember them well. We bring good wishes and gifts of gold from our great King. We bring respect for the glories of the Hittites. We bring the wisdom of honour to our discussions. We remember your father's great work in creating the treaties that once bound us in amity, and may do so again, to our mutual advantage.'

The Crown Prince gazed back at Nakht, his lip curled in contempt. Then he turned to the Chief Steward.

'Uncle, I would speak with you later, perhaps once you have concluded this – feast of cowards.'

His uncle nodded, and the Crown Prince, ignoring Nakht, walked swiftly out of the chamber, followed by his retinue of aggressive young nobles. The delicate atmosphere of the occasion had been shattered. Nakht did not resume his seat.

The Chief Steward spoke quickly, seeking to redress the harm that had been done.

'On behalf of our King, may I express our honour at your presence. The Crown Prince seems not to have been informed of your arrival. He is therefore dismayed, and unprepared. Hence his speech . . .'

'We are honoured by his royal presence. Nevertheless we note his words carefully,' said Nakht precisely.

'His words were hasty,' offered the Chief Steward.

'His words were extremely insulting to the King of Egypt,' replied Nakht uncompromisingly.

I noticed the Chief of the Royal Guards looked at some of his colleagues at this moment, as if silently dissenting from this attempt at diplomatic reconciliation. It seemed clear now that any offer Nakht might make of a peaceful resolution to the wars would be met with huge internal political hostility. I wondered whether Hattusa and Nakht had anticipated this.

'We will retire now. Tomorrow is an important day,' said Nakht.

There was a flurry of activity, everyone stood up, and suddenly we were following Nakht out of the chamber. Simut's guards fell into position. Weapons were poised; at any moment they might be used. I quickly surveyed the hostile crowd. And then I sensed something that made me look up: I glimpsed a man staring at Nakht, through the crowds, from the far side of the chamber. His face bore the features and the colouring of a Levantine. He wore a conical hat. I was struck by the intensity of his gaze. As I stared at him, he noticed me, too – but then a crowd of Hittite nobles walked between us, and we passed through the doors and into the passageway, and into the shadows of the palace, and he was gone.

I mentioned the man later to Nakht, as we prepared to take our first night of rest in the city.

'Give me an exact description,' demanded Nakht.

I did so. Nakht listened very carefully.

'I'm sure he was not a Hittite,' I added.

A little furrow of worry appeared on Nakht's brow.

'Did you also see him?' he asked Simut, who shook his head.

'I did not. But I saw a great deal I did not like or trust. The Crown Prince was open in his threats.'

175

'We are in the heart of our enemy's land. Many here will have fought against Egypt, or lost brothers and fathers in the wars. Many will hold a deeply entrenched hatred of us, their mortal enemy,' said Nakht. 'It is to be expected.' But he suddenly seemed uncertain, as if the events of the evening had shaken his confidence. He turned to me quietly: 'Keep an eye out for that man, and tell me if you notice him again. We can't be too careful. Tomorrow is our only chance to persuade the King of our proposal, and I have no doubt if Aziru is here he will be working behind the scenes to destroy any chance of a peaceful settlement between the two empires. As we saw tonight, even within the Hittite royal family, there is great internal dissent . . .'

'How many princes are there in the royal family?' I asked, to restore us to the solid ground of facts.

'Five. There is Arnuwanda, who we met tonight: he is heir to the throne. Then there is Telepinu, who has been instated by his father as Viceroy of Aleppo, and made Priest of Kizzuwanta, which is an extremely important position; and Piyassili, who is now Viceroy of Carchemish; then Zannanza, and finally Mursilis, who is still underage,' he said.

'So the Hittite King has been as lucky with his sons as the Queen has been unlucky in her own offspring,' I said. 'How strange that the destiny of empires comes down to the fruit of a woman's womb.'

Nakht nodded.

'Indeed. But there is another dimension to the Hittites' own problems of succession: having loyally provided him with five sons, the Queen Henti has recently been banished by the King, and in her place he has married the daughter of the King of Babylon. Her name is Tawananna.'

'So I assume she isn't very popular with the sons . . .' I suggested.

'It makes for an additional complexity in the political situation between the father and the sons, and perhaps what we witnessed tonight is testimony to that tension – something which we must take advantage of. Families are so strange and unaccountable, one sometimes wonders why people actually have them . . .' he added. I saw he was only half-joking.

'All families are complicated. But royal families are surely the most complex of all – for they squabble over power and gold and revenge, not just over who has the last bowl of soup . . .' I suggested.

'No matter how poor a man may be, if he has family he is rich,' Nakht quoted the old proverb back at me. 'As you know.'

Then he lay down on his couch, and prepared himself to sleep, as if nothing were the matter, as if he were not carrying such a great weight of responsibility upon his narrow shoulders.

'How can you just sleep like that, when you know tomorrow you hold the destiny of our land in your hands?' I said, in amazement.

'No great task was ever undertaken without a good night's sleep. Wars are lost through weariness and won after a good night of rest. I have prepared as thoroughly as possible. Nothing has been left to chance. I know what I have to do. Lying here awake all night worrying, and waking up tomorrow, before dawn, with red eyes and nothing in my brain will hardly help our cause. So if you don't mind, please would you provide me with the silence necessary to allow me to get some rest? Good night.'

And he closed his eyes firmly. Simut and I tiptoed around him, and went outside to check his guards were in position for the night watch. We could trust no one here but ourselves, and as the Crown Prince's behaviour had confirmed, we were unwelcome guests for many of the Hittites. We knew at any moment we might be attacked. Outside the entrance to the building, Hittite guards had also been posted. They stared at us, and our own Egyptian guards, with antipathy.

I glanced up at the night sky, full of stars, and a new moon's crescent, which had slipped into the corner of the vast heavens.

'Well, here we are,' I said to Simut.

He nodded. 'And I'm already looking forward to going home. This place gives me the creeps.'

'Me, too. For some reason I keep thinking of snakes.'

He laughed.

'It's a palace. All palaces are full of ambitious men, women and children who'd eat each other alive for advancement. They're all supposed to be the elite, but they clamber over each other, and behave with a viciousness and cruelty that would shock a dumb animal. That Crown Prince is a nasty piece of work. He's no friend of ours.'

'He'd love to see our Egyptian heads impaled on the city walls,' I replied. And I thought about the strange Levantine I had seen, and his twisted face.

Simut decided to stay up with his guards for some of the night watch, so I returned to our chamber. Nakht was already breathing lightly, like a child. I gazed at his elegant head resting on its sleeping stand, and at the fine, delicate features of his face. I couldn't tell if he was truly asleep or not. This journey had made me realize I did not know this man, my old friend, as well as I thought. We had been close for so many years. But even now, I never could be quite sure what was happening behind those hazel, hawk-like eyes, now closed in sleep. His face was a mask of calmness.

I sniffed the flask of water, to check it for poisons. It seemed fine and clear, so I drank a draught. It didn't kill me at once, anyway. And I soon fell asleep, into a deep dream of high places, and drifting mists, and my family calling to me from very far away . . .

21

We were made to wait, and we were not alone. In the stifling antechamber a crowd of petitioners, bureaucrats, army officers, rich merchants, magnates and vassal rulers had come to pay their respects and to report on their territories. Every time a new person and his retinue appeared, everyone looked up to see whether they should rise, out of respect, or remain seated, out of pride. When we had entered, we had been assessed and then deliberately slighted. No one had stood up. The ambassador was embarrassed, but Nakht refused to allow the slight to offend him, nor the greater one of the long wait – even when the morning sun approached its zenith, and the air crackled with the day's heat and the whir of crickets, and we had been waiting on the King for many hours, and had seen almost all others pass before us into his presence.

'This is nothing,' he said. 'Sometimes envoys and ambassadors are made to wait for days, even weeks, for a royal audience. And as for messengers, most of them are lucky if they only have to wait a year for a reply to carry home.'

And he returned to his private contemplations. But suddenly, when I had begun to think we would indeed have to wait a year ourselves, the doors of the antechamber creaked open, and we were summoned.

The palace guards escorted us in a grim silence through several colonnaded courts, each larger and more impressive than the preceding one, and then up a wide flight of stairs to a higher floor, which opened into a vast terrace containing a spacious courtyard surrounded by a large, elegant colonnade. We were shown to bowls of clean water, and then our hands and feet were scrupulously washed by royal attendants. The pungent scent of branches of burning herbs haunted the air. Finally, we were led to magnificent doors, carved with the royal symbol of the lion and covered in gold leaf. There was absolute silence. Hattusa nodded to a royal herald, who knocked three times with his ceremonial mace on the door, and we were admitted.

We found ourselves in a beautiful shaded hall. Open arches along three sides gently admitted light and a warm breeze. Countless pillars, of great elegance, held up the high ceiling. At the far end of this hall, a group of men stood in the shade. The ambassador formally led us towards them; some I knew from last night, including the Crown Prince, who once again affected barely to acknowledge Nakht, and his uncle, the Chief Steward, who was politely respectful. Others were introduced: Hazannu, Mayor of the City; Zida, Chief Minister, and several other political advisers who formed the royal cabinet; but there was still no sign of the King. Simut's guards carried our trunk of gold treasure, and laid it down before the royal throne.

We stood awaiting His Majesty in a line, in uncomfortable silence; until at last the royal herald grandly announced his imminent appearance, and suddenly, through a double doorway that must have led further into the private royal apartments, he appeared, as if in a great hurry, giving an impression of imperative, impatient energy. Everyone quickly got down on their knees, and bowed low.

When we were eventually permitted to rise, I found myself glancing cautiously at a man of no great height, but solidly built, scrupulously and unostentatiously dressed, with an air of barely subdued temper mixed with melancholy, and blue-grey eyes of penetrating, alarming astuteness. He sat down and gazed balefully and contemptuously at the company, drumming his ringed fingers on the arms of his throne. Suddenly, he barked something in his own language. One of the servants, quivering with fear, came forward and bowed before him. The King shouted a command, and then the servant bowed once more, turned, walked quickly to the far end of the chamber, and, without hesitating, threw himself off the edge into the void below.

'I command every living creature in this world, and I command death. Remember that,' said the Hittite King, in badly accented Egyptian, directly to Nakht.

Then he nodded brusquely to Hattusa, who began to deliver a speech in Hittite. I understood nothing, but I could see the King was affecting not to listen – or at least not to give away any response at all. Hattusa then invited Nakht to come forward. I confess that, for the first time, I am sure I saw my friend's hands shaking with nerves. But when he spoke, his voice was calm and clear. And he spoke in Akkadian, the old, formal, otherwise unused language of all international diplomacy, as if it were his native tongue. Hattusa translated sentence by sentence into the Hittite tongue, and the King listened carefully, all the time refusing to respect or honour Nakht by looking at him. The other ministers and officials also listened, their eyes to the floor, each one carefully not giving away any response. Finally, Nakht bowed, and opened the trunk to reveal the gifts of gold. The Hittite King affected not even to glance at the contents. Instead, he sat forward impatiently, and spoke rapidly in Hittite. Hattusa in turn translated for Nakht, directly into Egyptian.

'He commands us to speak in Egyptian and Hittite. He says it is better. Let brother speak to brother in his own true tongue.'

Nakht bowed. 'We are graced by the King's wisdom.'

Hattusa translated that, too, and the King waved away Nakht's praise, and began a long, authoritative speech, starting assertively and ending by shouting. The ambassador took a deep breath, and translated the tirade formally, and evenly. This bellicose manner was for show, and underneath it something subtler was taking place.

'The King, Son of the Sun, sends his best wishes back to his dear sister, the Queen of Egypt. He thanks her for her small gifts. He thanks her for her concern for his health, which, as you can see, is perfect. He wishes the same for her. Life, prosperity and health to the King and Queen of Egypt! He thanks the Queen for her surprising proposal. But he asks how she thinks it possible that a Hittite prince could possibly be spared to supply the desperate needs of the Egyptian throne. And why the King, the Son of the Sun, should send one of his own sons as a hostage to the court of Egypt? You will not make him King!'

The King and his courtiers watched carefully as Hattusa spoke, gauging Nakht's response. Nakht nodded as if he expected this, and quickly replied, showing the King the tablet on which the Queen's message had been inscribed, and daring to address the King more directly.

'My lord, Son of the Sun, here are the private words the Queen of Egypt sends to you through me, her loyal and unworthy servant: "If we had a son of the great King Tutankhamun, we would not come to you asking for one of your princes. I will be solitary. I will be alone. I seek one of your princes to become King, and a husband. I have come to you, and to no other land."'

Nakht offered the tablet, but the King refused to take it.

Nakht continued, speaking directly: 'We would honour our glorious alliance with guarantees of the Prince's security. This, the Queen vows. She begs instead your indulgence to consider the advantages for both our great empires of a more brotherly and loving friendship.'

He paused, and the ambassador translated fluently. The Crown Prince quickly interrupted.

'No, no, no, Royal Envoy of the Egyptians. We are not so foolish. My brothers are viceroys in Aleppo and Carchemish, we control those territories, and from there we will conquer all the lands of Egypt . . .'

But the King brusquely gestured to him to be silent. The Crown Prince scowled but retreated.

Nakht continued: 'In the spirit of the brotherly respect that holds firm between great equals, let us consider the truth of things. The wars between us are no longer beneficial to either of our lands. The only beneficiaries of the conflict are the lesser states that lie between us. Can either of us trust their loyalty? Never. They lie and cheat like thieves in order to win their advantage, and to stir up enmity between each other, and between the great brothers. It costs both Egypt and Hatti many divisions to maintain order among such chaos. But a treaty of peace would bring those territories under the feet of the Queen of Egypt, and the feet of the great King of the Hittites.'

Some of the ministers conferred among themselves briefly. But the Crown Prince was looking thunderous now.

He rose and shouted: 'You speak words of peace, but Egypt has repeatedly launched unprovoked attacks against Hittite allies and subject cities. You attacked Qadesh! You did evil to the Hittites . . .' he cried.

'Yes, sire. And then Hatti violated the treaty and attacked us in turn. You besieged Carchemish! What is the purpose of this aggression? If this were the relationship between two brothers, would we not call it wasteful of love, and wasteful of trust?' responded Nakht, with a new tone of authority.

The King was listening carefully now. Nakht pushed home his argument.

'War between Hatti and Egypt is a costly and wasteful business. We are proud empires. And yet why must each of us commit so much to gain so little? Only peace reaps the profit of time. Why should there not be a glorious and respectful peace between our brotherly lands? Why should we not join forces, as brothers, to quell the foolish disturbances, and the anarchic forces of chaos, that trouble us both in the lands that lie between us? Let it be known before all here: I speak of Amurru, and its so-called King Aziru, and the band of vile malcontents he has allowed, with great contempt for both our empires, to ravage the lands that should offer up in tribute the best of their bounty – of grain, of timbers, of wines and oils – to us. Why are these things squandered amongst criminals, when we could share them together, in celebration?'

This radical speech caused a ripple of whispered discussion among the advisers, and even the King shifted on his throne. The Crown Prince approached Nakht. I thought he was going to strike him.

'Aziru, who was once the subject of Egypt, is now a loyal ally of the Hittite King, and a loyal enemy of Egypt. You clearly do not know this,' he said.

Nakht stared back at him.

'I am Royal Envoy to All the Foreign Lands. I know very well the tricks of Aziru, here in this great city. Let all present know, I speak the truth. I stand by my words. Aziru is a serpent. He will strike and poison any who trust him.'

'My royal Father, we have heard enough! Let us take this man, this envoy, to the place of execution, and let us show the world our contempt for our enemies!' shouted the Crown Prince in reply.

The King gazed at both Nakht and the Crown Prince. But

then, to my intense relief, he motioned Nakht to continue. The Crown Prince was apoplectic, but silenced by the authority of his father.

'Egypt respects Hatti. The King is a great warrior, a hero-king, and a God. His glory is known everywhere. He has conquered empires and great cities. Let him now consider an even greater victory: that of a peaceful alliance, of mutual benefit, bringing forth a new age of order and triumph. Let diplomacy and love achieve more than force of arms ever could! Let us conclude a new treaty. Let our two empires be joined in *marriage*,' cried Nakht, with a rhetorical theatricality I had never suspected might lie within his character.

Silence dominated the great hall. Nakht had spoken brilliantly, and I could see some of the Hittite courtiers were engaged by his proposal. The King studied him, and then spoke, with Hattusa translating.

'We have heard the words of our sister, the Queen of Egypt. We will give them consideration. Remain in our city, under our protection, until we call for you again.'

Nakht and Hattusa bowed low, and then the King hurried back into the private royal apartments as swiftly as he had come, followed by servants carrying the trunks full of gold. Some of his ministers stared at us with open antagonism – as did the Crown Prince. Others gave nothing away. We backed out of the pillared hall, bowing as we went. We could hear the furious argument that broke out between the Hittites who remained behind even before the great doors closed.

22

Now that the audience was over, Nakht could not contain his anxiety. He paced back and forth in the antechamber, trying to catch his breath, like a man who had just run a race and didn't know whether or not he had won. The ambassador, too, was nervous.

'I think that went very well. I think you did *extremely* well.'

'But was it good enough?' asked Nakht.

'We shall see, we shall see. But the offer is there, on the table. It is a very fair offer. No one could mistake the integrity, or the value of it, for both sides,' said the ambassador.

Nakht shook his head.

'The Crown Prince, for one, is never going to be persuaded. He has another agenda. And there is an old admiration and appetite for war within both our cultures, which interprets peace as weakness . . .'

'You are right about that. As for the Crown Prince, he will do everything and anything necessary to protect his inheritance of

186

the throne, and the continuation of the war. He has the most to lose through a marriage alliance,' agreed Hattusa.

But as we prepared to make our way out of the palace, the ambassador was suddenly accosted by a messenger, who whispered urgently to him.

'We have been asked to attend an urgent meeting with the King's brother, the Chief Steward,' he explained. 'Immediately.'

'Excellent,' said Nakht, rubbing his hands together. 'The wheels are already in motion.'

We were swiftly escorted through the palace to a private apartment, where the Chief Steward was waiting, together with several other nobles from the audience.

'We wish to discuss your proposal in more detail. We have some questions,' he said quickly.

'We note the absence of the Crown Prince from this meeting,' replied Nakht.

'This conversation is private. It has not happened. Nothing has been spoken. No scribe will make a record. Is that understood and agreed?' said the Chief Steward.

Nakht inclined his head. I could tell he was pleased, and was feeling in control of the situation.

'The King is disposed to consider your proposal further. At first this marriage seemed a sign of Egypt's absurd desperation, and he would have dismissed it without thought, had not your speech contained other points of interest. But many questions remain. For instance, if we were to concede, and supply Egypt with the prince your Queen so obviously needs, how will the nobles of Egypt react to a Hittite prince on the throne? Surely he would be merely a puppet, and one could imagine his usefulness could easily be – outgrown. What would happen then?'

'He would be welcomed for these reasons: firstly, he will take his place in the greatest dynasty Egypt has ever known. He will join a Queen who is admired and loved, and who commands the affection of all her subjects . . .'

The Chief Steward shook his head. 'Let us be candid. Your Queen is desperate. She will soon have no husband. She has no child. She is confronted by an avaricious priesthood, and a rebellious army whose general has made no secret of his claim to the crowns. She is playing her last throw of the dice, and we are not so stupid as not to know this. That is why you are here.'

'Of course, you are right,' admitted Nakht, to my surprise, but then he continued: 'But one must always seek a way to turn a crisis into a success, don't you agree? I'm sure this is a general rule of politics here as well. You have a King whose recent marriage has caused great disagreement among his own family. The Princes are antagonized. Their mother has been banished. She, too, has her supporters. There is considerable dissent within the Hittite court about this. The mother of the Princes was extremely popular. In addition, your recent harvests have been poor. Your people are hungry, and your troops, when they return, will need to be paid and fed. All kings know they have to make difficult choices, especially when faced with internal dissent; usually, they organize a marriage, or find a useful war. Well, the war is no longer useful, and the marriage has only made things worse . . .'

The Chief Steward stared at him, then glanced at his colleagues, who conferred among themselves in their own language. Nakht waited calmly.

'There may be room for a mutually beneficial solution to both of our internal political dilemmas. However, you get both domestic and international stability from this. What do we get?'

'You get a Prince on the throne of your arch-enemy, Egypt, which you present publicly as a diplomatic triumph, tied up with an excellent new economic treaty. You get peace in the Levant, which means we negotiate a division of the existing minor powers, a fair share of the spoils, and a balance of power which will allow you to expand further to the east, as I understand is your intention, following your alliance with Babylon. You cancel at a stroke the justification for the Crown Prince's belligerent attitude to foreign affairs, and you focus his youthful energies more wisely on other areas of concern,' said Nakht confidently.

'Such as?'

'Freed from the vast burden of our wars, your armed forces can be settled along your domestic borders, where, I understand, they are needed imperatively. After all, they cannot be everywhere at once. Your local enemies must know this. I believe there have been a number of aggressive sorties and attacks recently . . .' he added, for effect.

I could feel the negotiation going Nakht's way, but the Chief Steward followed up swiftly.

'Egypt and Hatti are the only two truly great empires in the world. But look at it from our point of view. Mittani we have conquered. Babylon we have conquered. Byblos, which is yours, has struggled and may fall. Ugarit is now loyal to us. Qadesh you have lost. Carchemish is ours. The game is in our favour. We hold more pieces than you.'

'For now,' conceded Nakht. 'But Assyria remains a thorn in your side, and it will not rest until it has won Mittani. Arzawa is inclined to us. Alashiya will always remain our trading partner. But above all, you are almost entirely dependent on the import of Egyptian wheat. What would you do without it? One bad harvest, one harsh winter, and your people would starve. If you refuse us what we propose now, we might stop all grain trading in the future. You could not expect sympathy if General Horemheb were to take power in Egypt.'

Nakht watched as that sank in. He knew he had won that round. So he straightened his robes, and then introduced another subject.

'And what of Aziru of Amurru?' he continued.

'He is loyal to Hatti,' replied the Chief Steward awkwardly.

'Be careful, brother. How can such a treacherous creature as Aziru be considered loyal? You are aware of his connection to the Army of Chaos? His alliance with you is false and unreliable, and yet you protect him – or at least your Crown Prince does. Dangerous petty tyrants like him create the conditions in which anarchy flourishes. Do not be beguiled by him. It is in both our interests to subjugate him, and his forces, and bring stability to the region – a stability we jointly monitor and control, through the agreed appointment of vassal kings, which we instate, supported by loyal garrisons and forces.'

The Chief Steward gave nothing away.

'We have no contact with the Army of Chaos.'

'Of course not,' agreed Nakht, diplomatically. 'Not officially, anyway. But let us be candid – we are aware of Aziru's contacts with the Army of Chaos, and of his negotiations with some inside the Hittite administration. We are aware of his change of loyalty. We have much experience of this snake, and we warn you, brother, to take care lest you are bitten and poisoned in turn.'

The Chief Steward shook his head.

'This is a matter of internal policy. It cannot concern Egypt.'

'It deeply concerns Egypt. It must form part of our agreement. Aziru must be dealt with, in such a way that he will trouble none of us any further. By that, I mean definitively. That is something you could help us with. I have not said that, of course.'

The chamber was silent. No one could be in any doubt as to the meaning of Nakht's words.

'We must consider further. You have brought an unexpected new element into the proposal. There are – implications,' said the King's brother.

'I quite understand. These things are complex. There are always competing loyalties. There are always risks,' replied Nakht. 'But there are great gains to be made by compromise. I would

190

remind you, gentlemen, that the opportunity for change comes only once. It must be grasped confidently.'

The Chief Steward stood up, and Nakht followed suit.

'You and your retinue will remain under guard, here within the walls of the palace – for your own security, of course. But the King also wishes you to witness and admire the marvels and wonders of his city, so you can tell your people of his great achievements. The ambassador here will escort you. I will of course report privately to the King immediately, but I cannot say when he might have the leisure to consider all of this further. No decisions have been made.'

'No doubt he has many pressing concerns to attend to. But I would remind you: every day is important. Let us not hesitate. Those who would destroy our proposal for peace and stability are gathered around. They are here, in this city. We know this. We must not give them time to strike.'

The Chief Steward considered him.

'Then is it well you are here in the city for our great festival to celebrate the bounty of the harvest, which begins tomorrow. We call it the Festival of Haste.' And he smiled at the irony.

23

The next morning we set out into the Upper City, accompanied by Simut's and the Hittite guards. The ambassador and Nakht conferred together, while Simut and I concentrated on making sure nothing went wrong, as we made our way through hostile crowds of Hittite men. Finally we reached a wide limestone-paved street between two large complexes of buildings. Two monumental pylons built of enormous blocks of stone faced each other, flanked by sentry rooms. This was the entrance to the Sanctuary of the Storm God.

At a gesture to the guards from the ambassador, we were allowed to pass under the pylons, into the sudden cool of the shadows. We came out into an open area, with offices and narrow storage rooms full of large jars on either side on the ground level, and stairs leading up to more offices on the upper floor. This in turn gave way to an enormous paved courtyard, within which the temple itself stood.

Whereas our temples are ancient, and every surface of their

massive structures is covered with hieroglyphs and reliefs, here the decoration and carving in the stone friezes was sparse and basic, and portrayed the Hittite Gods, who were of modest stature. They wore pointed hats with little horns attached, and slippers curled up at the toes, and carried axes – but this was not my image of a powerful God of Storms. All around us, Hittite priests, dressed in the strangest clothes – long robes, shoes with upturned toes and skullcaps – and carrying staffs that curved upwards in spirals, went about their business, with a pomp not unlike that of our own priests.

'On the northern side is the House of Purification, where all worshippers must wash themselves before entering the temple itself. The King enters through the nearby gate, crosses the courtyard, purifies his hands, and then enters the shrine to enact the rites,' said Hattusa.

'Fascinating. May we enter?' asked Nakht, his eyes glittering with curiosity.

'Not into the shrine itself, of course. But come with me . . .'

Hattusa led us around to a portico, and we passed through that into an inner courtyard. In front of us were two doorways set into decorated stone walls. Priests coming and going looked askance at us, disconcerted by our presence in their sacred temple.

'This is as near as I can allow you to the sanctuaries themselves,' said Hattusa quietly. 'Any closer, and we would commit an act of desecration. But in the right-hand room stands the statue of Arinna, the Sun Goddess, Queen of Heaven and Earth, Queen of the Land of Hatti. And in the left, that of the Storm God. Unlike your sacred shrines, which are dark, ours are full of light. Each sanctuary has many windows. Our Gods are everywhere. Every rock, every tree, every spring in our land has its God, and here in this temple we serve and worship the greatest of them. And we provide them with food offerings of perfect cleanness, and entertainment. "Are the desires of Gods and men different? In no way! Do their natures differ? In no way!"' he declaimed.

I had the strange sensation that Hattusa was talking slightly nervously to pass the time, as if waiting for something to happen. And then something did. From out of the archway of the Temple of the Sun Goddess emerged a foreign woman of astounding beauty, her head covered with a magnificently embroidered cloth. She was followed by a small retinue of young women. Instantly, Hattusa sank to his knees, his head bowed, and we followed suit.

She spoke to him in the Hittite language. She then turned to gaze imperiously at Nakht. Her face was ravishing but also full of elegant sorrow. She was Babylonian. Hattusa introduced her formally as Queen Tawananna of the Hittites – but she politely interrupted him, and spoke in competent, beautifully accented Egyptian directly to Nakht. I was sure now that this was an 'arranged' meeting.

'Wise old Hattusa, why have you not brought this nobleman into my presence before? One hears so much about the Egyptian Royal Envoy Nakht.'

Nakht bowed.

'And I of Your Highness. It is an honour to be in your presence. The Gods have smiled upon us,' he said.

'May they continue to do so,' she replied.

They regarded each other for a moment, and I saw Hattusa looking at both of them, as if waiting for a play to begin.

'Shall we walk together a little way?' he suggested. They both inclined their heads to offer their assent, and our little group moved back across the huge courtyard. The women kept careful vigil around the Queen. Although there were many priests and servants going about their business, the open air made for a safe place to converse in private for Nakht and the Queen.

'By chance, I was here to perform the rites and to consult the oracles,' she said.

'And may I ask: were the oracles favourable?' Nakht said.

Queen Tawananna spoke more quietly now.

'Both favourable and unfavourable.'

'May I know more?' asked Nakht. 'What exactly did they fore-tell?'

'Negative influences threaten our well-being. There is a shadow. The shadow is angry. The shadow is among us. The sky is dark now, without a moon. But good magic may defeat him. Good magic may reconcile old friends. A large star is predicted in the heavens on a favourable night of blessings.'

Nakht seemed to take this seriously.

'The Gods have spoken. We heed their warnings,' he said.

After a little silence, the Queen spoke again, as if she did not wish this meeting to end yet.

'How is my sister, the Queen Ankhesenamun? I think of her often, and wish her well.'

'Life, prosperity, health to the Queen, she is well. I have been honoured to offer you her expressions of love. She desires your well-being. She desires you to know she is your friend in all things, at all times.'

The Hittite Queen listened carefully.

'I have need of her friendship. I am a stranger in a strange land. I am Queen here, but there are some, even close, who are not friends.'

'We are aware of them,' said Nakht.

She glanced at him, relieved.

'The oracle speaks of a shadow. I am afraid of the dark,' she added.

'May the Gods protect you,' he said. 'We hope to draw the shadow into the light.'

'I am glad to hear it. Send my love to my sister. I will do all I can to help her in her quest. And I hope the same from her.'

'The Queen's gratitude and loyalty to her sister will be bound-less,' offered Nakht and he bowed.

Without looking back, the Hittite Queen and her retinue crossed the courtyard and entered a covered carriage, which jolted away through the gatehouse into the streets, accompanied by a running guard. There was a moment's silence. Hattusa looked at Nakht.

'May all go well, brother,' said Hattusa, as if in response to the strange conversation.

'I have hope,' said Nakht, gazing into the distance where the Queen's carriage was disappearing. 'Truly, may the Gods protect her.'

Hattusa nodded.

'We have done all we can for now. I will accompany you to your quarters, to prepare for the Festival of Haste. And then I must go to my prayers in the sanctuary.'

'No need,' said Nakht. 'Stay here for your prayers. Our quarters are near by, and I have my guards with me.'

Hattusa nodded reluctantly.

'Very well. But take every precaution. The Crown Prince has his allies in the city, and everyone will by now be aware of the nature of our business. We cannot be too careful. The Chief Steward has insisted he accompanies you personally to the Festival of Haste. He will call for you in good time. I will find you there. No doubt you will enjoy the entertainments. There are horse races, foot races, mock battles and the like . . .'

'There is nothing I like better than a mock battle,' said Nakht, politely, and he bowed to Hattusa, who then hurried away into the crowds of the temple.

'We find ourselves in a fascinating situation,' said Nakht quietly to Simut and me as we began the walk back down the countless stone steps of the way.

'The Queen is very much in favour of our proposal, and in sympathy with our own Queen. She understands the value of peace between our empires, and she supports the King in his wish to conclude a treaty. But she finds herself in a difficult position. Both of the older Hittite Princes have their eyes on the succession, but they know that following the traditions of the land, when the King dies, the Queen will inherit his authority for the term of her life. And so she is afraid . . .'

'Of assassination?' I said.

'Exactly. She needs allies at home and abroad, in order to support her authority, and to protect herself in the event of the King's death. And she needs the Princes' powers to be curbed, as much as possible.'

'So her help comes at a price?' I asked. 'She will further our proposal if we commit to supporting her?'

'Yes. But, of course, it is a very good deal,' he replied. 'Our interests match exactly, and she is a far more useful ally on the throne of Hatti than any of the Princes.'

'But then neither of the older Princes would agree to return to Egypt with us, would they?' I asked.

'They would have no choice, if their father ordered it. And to sit on the throne of Egypt is no small thing,' he replied.

'I cannot imagine the Crown Prince acquiescing to that. No matter what his father said. And if I may speak personally, I would not relish the prospect of his presence in the Egyptian royal court,' I offered.

'I think we may be sure that the second eldest, Telepinu, is the most likely candidate,' answered Nakht.

We walked on for a little.

'What was all that about the oracle?' I said quietly.

'I understood her meaning,' he replied.

'You mean about the shadow?'

He nodded.

'Have you seen that man again?' he asked.

'No,' I replied. 'But I find I cannot shake off the feeling that someone is watching us.'

He nodded.

'I agree. We must take every precaution. Aziru is here biding his time. Things are going quite well. But we are not home yet.'

24

We heard them before we saw them; beating drums, rattling tambourines and clashing cymbals announced their approach, and the crowd responded jubilantly, yelling prayers and oaths in their strange language. Nakht, Simut and I waited with the Chief Steward to witness the return of the festival procession to the temple. The King and Queen finally appeared in their chariot. They were both wearing blue robes; the King carried a crook and a silver axe. Dignitaries and priests followed in a long procession through the crowded ways, followed by the entertainment – acrobats flipped over and over, jugglers competed to cast their balls in daringly complex patterns, dancers in bright costumes, accompanied by the wild drums and tambourines of the musicians, performed for the applause of the crowds. And above all of them towered the image of the God himself, carried on an ox-drawn carriage, its axles creaking with the massive weight of the burden; three times as tall as any man, his gold body was densely decorated with jewels, which dazzled in the late light. His appearance encouraged cries of awe, prayers and urgent petitions from the crowds.

The Crown Prince and his entourage were standing close to the temple gateway. I realized his expression had altered. He suddenly looked like a man who had received good news. Several times he glanced over at Nakht, and smiled.

'The Crown Prince has changed his manner,' I whispered to Nakht.

'So I see,' he replied. He was not cheered by the difference.

As the chariot of the King and Queen arrived at the temple entrance, I saw how the Queen cast a quick look at the Crown Prince, an attempt at respectful friendliness, and how he responded by simply turning away.

In the inner courtyard of the temple, tables and benches had been set out for a huge feast. The God was set up at the head of the main table as the guest of honour. The King raised a silver cup in the shape of a bull's head, full of wine, to the God, loudly proclaiming what seemed to be his eternal health, and then he drank deeply. Everyone cheered.

'The King is drinking to the God,' explained the Chief Steward to Nakht, who nodded sagely.

Then a herald announced the feast, and suddenly everyone else rushed to find places to sit. The Chief Steward guided us towards one of the tables near the King's. Servants delivered grilled and roasted meats from sacrificed animals on huge platters, and the King chose the best cuts, glistening with fat, to offer to the God. Then he picked out one of the loaves baked in many shapes of men and animals that had been set before him – this one in the shape of a bird – and broke it into pieces. Once this last rite was completed, the crowd knew they could really start to enjoy themselves, and they set to devouring the food as if they had not eaten for weeks.

Simut and I insisted we stand either side of Nakht while he ate.

'I do not see Ambassador Hattusa,' I said quietly to Nakht.

He nodded.

'Is Ambassador Hattusa not joining us this evening? We were expecting him,' he said to the Chief Steward, sitting opposite him.

'I, too, have noticed his absence,' he replied.

'I trust he is not ill,' said Nakht.

The Chief Steward wiped his lips, clicked his fingers, and a servant hurried over, listened to his instructions, and ran off. Nakht and the Chief Steward exchanged a small glance, but continued to converse about other subjects, with other members of the table. Simut and I whispered briefly behind Nakht's back.

'Why is he not here?' he said.

'I cannot imagine. This is an important event . . . I hope there has been no problem . . .'

After a good period of feasting and drinking, the convivial atmosphere was becoming noticeably raucous. The Crown Prince and his companions in particular were in a riotous mood. Several times I observed how the other guests glanced at them, and commented to each other on their crude behaviour. At one point, the King himself glared at his oldest son; but his look of admonition seemed not to concern the Crown Prince at all. In fact it was almost as if he welcomed it, and was vying with his father.

Suddenly, the King clapped his hands. The daylight was fading, and the evening shadows had begun to lengthen and gather. Servants lit torches around a performance area, and a troupe of dancers ran into the flickering light. They were dressed as leopards and hunters. The Crown Prince and his retinue ambled over, and the other nobles quickly made way to allow him the best view of the show. The dancers bowed low to the God, and then the King. The musicians struck up a strong beat, and the performance, which recreated the drama of a royal hunt, began. The hunters danced their pursuit of the leopards, which ran in wonderfully lifelike, fluid choreography; they evaded their hunters, and then they turned on them, standing on their hind legs with powerful stylized claws raised in magnificent retaliatory attack. The hunters withdrew, in awe of these magnificent creatures. Then archers drew imaginary bows, and fired arrows that split the imaginary hearts of several of the magnificent beasts, and they died and were carried off in glorious style.

The King observed the spectacle carefully, for he was represented in the dance as the chief hunter. One by one, the other hunters and leopards faded away, until only this central figure was left; he now began a complex dance with the last and most powerful of the leopards, the King jousting with his spear, the leopard curling around his attacks, while two younger dancers, representing loyal hunting dogs, tried to attack the leopard's belly and back without success. For a moment, the leopard appeared to be succeeding, and the King dancer himself was suddenly on the defensive, at the mercy of the leopard, poised for the kill – the crowd gasped, and the real King looked deeply dismayed. The Crown Prince, I saw, shared a small smile with his men.

But then the dancer representing the King raised his spear high in the air, and held it very still in a posture of regal dominance and triumph. The leopard, succumbing at last, looked up at the hunter and his poised spear, facing the moment of its own death with dignity; and the crowd roared for the kill, waiting for the King himself, who had risen to his feet, to give the sign of his approval.

But at that moment, from out of the shadows, an object like an uneven, clumsy ball bounced and rolled at speed across the stone slabs of the courtyard, and came to rest before the King. For a moment no one understood. But I did. I had seen this before. The ball was a human head, decapitated, and still dripping with blood. The grave, dead face belonged to Hattusa, the Hittite ambassador.

The King's guards instantly formed a protective shield around the King, their spears pointing into the gathering shadows.

'Make them shut the gates,' I shouted to Nakht.

I grabbed a lit torch from its stand, and ran in the direction from which the decapitated head had been thrown, through the sudden pandemonium of the crowd, paying no attention to the cries of horror and outrage, or to the rush of bodies running away from the scene in confusion and disarray. Simut was just behind me, a torch in one hand, his dagger in the other. We came to the edge of the arena. The shadows deepened into darkness.

'Which way?' said Simut.

I shook my head, staring into the obscurity, scanning the passages, which disappeared in several directions, listening for the faintest sound. And then – was I imagining it? – I could sense something, someone, poised, waiting in the silence, and then moving away into the dark distance. I waved to Simut, and gestured to him to abandon his torch. We made our way stealthily along a shadowy passageway, which opened out into an inner courtyard. Several doorways led off into dark chambers. But only one compelled me. From within I could see the faint flickering of lights. It was a holy sanctuary. We took one side each and approached. We listened. Silence. I nodded to Simut, and we raised our swords.

But suddenly, from behind us, came the noise of many feet pounding on the stones, and a troop of palace guards ran into the courtyard, barring the way into the sanctuary. The captain spoke urgently and forbiddingly in his own language. It was perfectly clear: we were not allowed to enter and desecrate the God's shrine. I yelled into the captain's face in frustration, and he bellowed back, and then before I knew what I was doing, I had raised my fist to strike him. Suddenly spears were pointing directly at my chest, and Simut was dragging my arms to my side, and pulling me away. And then the Crown Prince and his retinue were standing there, staring at me.

'How dare you desecrate the shrine with your filthy foreign presence?' he said, and whacked me hard across the face.

'We were following the killer,' I said, spitting away bloody phlegm.

He hit me again.

'Don't you dare address me. If I had my way you would be cut into more pieces than our dear friend the ambassador.'

And he nodded, and a couple of his men began to punch and kick me as hard as they could. Simut was powerless to help. After a while, the rain of blows ceased. I struggled to breathe. Blood trickled down my chin.

'If I ever hear another word from you, I promise it will be your last. Your royal protection doesn't work with me,' sneered the Crown Prince, pushing his foot down onto the side of my face.

And then Simut and I were shoved back up the passageway by the Crown Prince's retinue.

The ambassador's head lay on the ground, staring in dismay at something far beyond the circle of men gathered around. The King was shouting at the Chief Steward, and Nakht stood in silence beside the Queen. As our little group approached, they looked up.

'These foreigners were about to desecrate the shrine of the God,' said the Crown Prince as he kicked us hard and sent us flying at his father's feet. 'You should arrest them, blind them, and send them to the work gangs. That is where foreign spies belong.'

As he said this he pointedly looked at the Queen. Nakht surveyed our battered state, and quickly intervened on our behalf.

'I beg your pardon, my lord. My men were ignorant. But they are officers of the highest rank. Rahotep is known as the finest

Seeker of Mysteries in all Egypt. His only motivation would be to apprehend the murderer. If you would permit, he may be able to help.'

The King looked me over briefly, then nodded. I wiped the blood from my face and took a better look at the decapitated head. The wound was accomplished with several powerful hacks from an axe – so I knew at once this was not the work of the Theban murderer. I reached out to Hattusa's mouth. There was a shout of outrage from the Crown Prince, but I continued regardless, while the King spoke to him sharply. The jawbones were locking together – he had been dead a little while already. I slowly prised them open enough to insert my fingers into the clammy, cold mouth. I drew out a little scrap of folded papyrus. Without even opening it, I offered it to Nakht, but the Chief Steward snatched it away. He opened it, then, puzzled, he showed it to the King. And I watched carefully as the Crown Prince took it from his father, glanced at it, and returned it to me with a look that told me precisely nothing.

The Hittite King began to shout at me, and Nakht translated quickly.

'He wants to know how you knew this was there, and what it means,' he said. And from his look I knew he was also saying, 'Please be extremely careful how you reply.'

'I didn't know what I would find. I was merely checking the condition of the jaws because that gives an indication of the time of death—'

Nakht interrupted: 'This is not an Egyptian star at all, as you can see. In our hieroglyph a star has five points surrounding a small circle of light. This has eight arrows around a black centre. Perhaps it is a Hittite sign?'

'Of course it is not. This is all nonsense,' interrupted the Crown Prince. He shoved the papyrus aggressively at the Queen. 'But perhaps you recognize this sign, my dear lady? Perhaps it is a Babylonian star. Your people are famous star-watchers, aren't they?'

The Queen glanced at the sign.

'This is not a sign from the zodiac of my people,' she said clearly.

'It is the sign of the Army of Chaos,' I said.

Everyone stared at me, astonished.

'The ambassador has been murdered as a punishment for his association with Egypt and with our mission,' I continued. 'I name Aziru as the suspect.'

The Crown Prince roared with fury, but Nakht followed up quickly: 'Let us be clear. You have a murderer in this city, and he knows about our most private discussions. He is warning you, as well as us.'

The Chief Steward respectfully took the King aside, so that we could not hear the exchange that followed. The Crown Prince confronted Nakht and me.

'You should leave now, before you, too, suffer the same fate,' he said, so only we could hear him. Then he turned to join his father and uncle.

The Queen stood in silence, gazing at the ambassador's head.

'That sign. I have seen it. It is not Babylonian, but for us it represents Ishtar – the Queen of Love and War. But why is it here, like this?' she said quietly to Nakht and me.

Nakht shook his head, deeply alarmed. I was desperate to ask her more, for this was compelling new information about the meaning of the sign. But the King and the Crown Prince were openly arguing now. What was going on, underneath the surface of these events? The Crown Prince was feeling betrayed: his father had exiled his mother, and why would he forgive that? No matter how useful the political argument for the union with the Babylonians might be, blood is blood. But had the Crown Prince ordered this murder? Was he an agent in Hattusa's death?

Or was Aziru acting on his own? It was hard to believe the Crown Prince knew nothing about the murder, for it served his purposes too well. Perhaps that was why he had been so cheerful during the festivities. I glanced at the Queen, who stood like a statue of melancholy among these angry, arguing Hittite men. I wondered how long she could really survive.

Suddenly the guards ran up, pushing two men, bowing in terror, into the presence of the King. I had seen them earlier; they were gatekeepers. They trembled like lambs before slaughter when they saw the head of Hattusa. The Chief Steward began to question them, and immediately they shook their heads, their hands raised to the God, protesting their innocence.

'They claim all who came or went during the feast were permitted and authorized,' translated Nakht.

'Ask them if they saw a man carrying anything – a box or a bag,' I said to him.

He translated quickly, but the gatekeepers only shook their heads.

'Ask them if they saw a man, a Levantine, with red hair, about my height,' I said.

Once more they pleaded their innocence, when suddenly, without warning, the Crown Prince stepped forward and simply thrust his sword into the chest of one of the two men. The man looked aghast and slowly collapsed to his knees. The Crown Prince pulled out his sword. The man clutched uselessly at the torrent of blood, as if to plug a leaking vessel, and then keeled over. The Crown Prince wiped his blade on the dead man's clothes. The second man closed his eyes, and began gibbering and praying for mercy.

'Each man must pay the penalty for failure to protect the King,' said the Crown Prince, preparing to kill again. But the King stepped forward, and with his own sword he executed the second man, who died with a grievous howl that silenced everyone present.

25

I awoke the next morning stiff and aching from the beating administered by the Crown Prince's guards. I was black and blue across my arms and legs, and a dark bruise shadowed my left cheek.

'At least your teeth are still in your head,' quipped Simut as we made our way through the city streets towards the palace, accompanied by our own guards.

'And your head on your shoulders,' added Nakht.

It seemed to me there was a new air of tension on the streets. Now the Hittites deliberately slighted us, turning their backs as we approached. And the Chief Steward, who was waiting for us inside the palace itself, looked deeply uneasy. Their internal security had been tightened for our visit; other than the Hittite palace guards, who surrounded us as soon as we entered, the place seemed deserted.

This time we did not have to wait for an audience with the King. We were immediately led through the dismal, deserted passageways, and swiftly ushered once more into the pillared hall. Once again, the Crown Prince looked pleased with himself, as if he knew something we didn't. I noticed Nakht warily absorbing this, too.

'What is happening?' Nakht asked the Chief Steward quietly.

'I'm afraid I have not been party to the latest discussions with the King. His son has been with him all morning,' he replied nervously.

Quickly the King entered the hall. He spoke rapidly, and the Chief Steward, translating, attempted to keep up.

'We have considered the Great Queen's proposal, and find it to our liking. Let our two great empires be joined as one family by marriage. We will send our son to the Queen, in marriage, to sit upon the throne of Egypt with her. He will be King. The terms of his powers and necessities must be satisfactory. Do not disappoint us.'

He glared at Nakht, and at the Crown Prince himself. Nakht, pleased at this development, stepped forward to respond.

'On behalf of the Queen of Egypt, may I offer our congratulations at this happy news. The Prince will be welcomed and honoured in Egypt as a son, and as King. I lay down my own life as bond for his safety, well-being and contentment. He will be able to call on me, at any time. I am his loyal servant.'

And he bowed respectfully to the Crown Prince.

But the Crown Prince smiled with a strange satisfaction, and slowly shook his head. Too late, Nakht realized he had fallen into a trap. A brief fanfare heralded the arrival of a new character. Absolute silence dominated the hall. And then, someone entered quietly, reluctantly, through the arched doorway to the royal apartments. All eyes fell upon this figure, whose nervousness and anxiety were painfully obvious.

His face was exquisite; his glossy hair fell around his shoulders in lustrous black waves. He held himself proudly and yet vulnerably, with little of the masculine confidence of his brother and father. He was nevertheless amazingly charismatic.

'I am the Prince Zannanza,' he said.

The pillared hall was utterly silent. I watched as Nakht struggled to regain his footing. He had been comprehensively outwitted, for how could he bring back this delicate, gentle man to be the husband of the Queen, and to sit upon the throne of Egypt? It was as if the Hittites had played an enormous, disastrous joke upon us. But what could Nakht say? It was too late. So he bowed to Prince Zannanza.

'The Royal Envoy Nakht presents himself. It will be my great honour to escort you to Egypt on behalf of the Queen, who bids me wish you well.'

Prince Zannanza returned the bow. He glanced at me with bright, intelligent and frightened eyes. Simut and I bowed carefully to him.

'My son will leave for Egypt with you as soon as possible. We remember the urgency of the Queen's request,' said the King. 'Furthermore we will negotiate the terms of a settlement regarding the disputed and troublesome territories that lie between our empires.'

To my surprise, the Crown Prince nodded with agreement at this. Only a few days previously, he had been utterly opposed to an armistice. Now he looked like the architect of this plan. Suddenly the King stood up, and approached Nakht directly, threateningly.

'But hear my words. The Prince Zannanza is your responsibility. You must ensure his safe passage, and his security in Egypt. If any harm should befall him, at any time, know this: our anger will overflow, our wrath will be terrible, and the Hittite army will rise up and destroy Egypt. Tell this also to your Queen, for the life of my son is in her hands.'

Nakht bowed low, and the King departed as suddenly as he had arrived, taking Prince Zannanza with him. Once he had gone, the atmosphere shifted. The Crown Prince, surrounded by his uncle and other ministers, spoke with a new, and utterly untrustworthy, warmth. He was practically dancing with amusement.

'We are *delighted*, Royal Envoy. Surely your mission to Hatti has been a *complete* success. Your Queen will have a marvellous new husband. Egypt will have a marvellous new King. My dear brother has many fine accomplishments. He dances beautifully. He adores music and poetry.'

And then the fake smile passed from his face, replaced by an exultant grin.

'Who could have said such a day would come to pass, when ancient enemies are suddenly united in marriage? Who would have prophesied we would master the Egyptian throne so easily? We must celebrate my dear brother's great good fortune even as we deeply lament his leaving. Our loss, of course, is Egypt's gain. We are sure he will be the *perfect* husband to the Queen of Egypt. May their marriage be blessed with many fine, strong sons who will grow into warrior kings, who will be the fruit of this charming alliance, and the future of a great dynasty.'

He laughed out loud at the huge joke of it all.

'There is peace between our empires,' said Nakht. 'We are satisfied. But what of Aziru?'

The Chief Steward stepped forward, uncomfortably.

'The necessary arrangements have been made,' he said.

'What arrangements?' the Crown Prince asked, uncertainly.

'Alas, little time remains to us to conclude our own arrangements for departure. I will leave your uncle to give you an account of our agreement regarding the troublemaker and tyrant Aziru,' said Nakht, taking the only revenge available to him. And so, having thrown his cat among the ducks, he chose to depart; and we bowed and left them to their arguments.

*

211

Back in our accommodation, Nakht stood very still, trying to come to terms with what had happened. He was holding a drinking bowl, and sipping the water. Suddenly, in a fit of fury, he dashed it against the wall. It shattered into shards. I was shocked; I had never before seen him succumb to such fury. He was always so controlled in his behaviour.

'I am an imbecile. Why did I not foresee this?' he hissed.

'If that delicate boy ever sires a warrior king, I will eat my own sandals,' said Simut unhelpfully.

'It is a calculated and terrible insult,' said Nakht. 'No wonder the Crown Prince was looking pleased with himself. I made a fatal mistake. I underestimated him.'

He began to pace, trying to think his way out of this catastrophe.

'However, we have no choice. We must return home to Egypt with Prince Zannanza, and find a plausible way to present him to the court and the people,' he continued. 'Egypt has suffered greater difficulties. Tutankhamun himself was no warrior king. Nor was his father. Perhaps a quiet, artistic, intellectual Hittite noble on the throne will actually be more acceptable, and indeed desirable, than a foolish, knuckle-brained warrior. Who is to say there will not be heirs? These things can be managed, arranged . . .'

But he did not sound truly convinced of his own arguments.

'Just because he is beautiful does not mean his private desires lie in . . . other directions,' I said. 'And even if they do, who is to say such a man would not make a fine King and still father heirs? The Prince seems to me noble and accomplished, and he must have had to discover the courage to be himself in a land that would hardly value his qualities.'

Nakht absorbed these words quietly. He and I had never discussed the reasons for his not having married and raised a family of his own.

'Indeed, the *Tale of King Neferkare and the Military Commander Sasenet* is a story of just such a secret love,' he said quietly. And then he glanced at me carefully.

There was a moment of silence between the three of us.

'This is all very well, but tales of love will not help us to return the Prince to Egypt without misfortune,' said Simut. 'That in itself will be a dangerous task.'

'The sooner we return to Thebes the better. Time is running out. Who knows what events may have passed in the court? Perhaps Ay is already dead . . .'

'You are both forgetting something. The killer is here. Aziru is the most likely suspect, and he has not been caught,' I said. 'He knows about us. We cannot afford to leave this matter unresolved. We cannot afford to have him shadow us, and then attack again, outside the city, when we do not have the protection of the King.'

Nakht was about to reply when there was a loud knock on the door. It was the Chief Steward returning with the King's instructions for our return.

'The King considers the sea journey from Ura to Ugarit too dangerous. The currents, as you know, flow against the return journey, and risk taking the ship too close to the Alashiyan coastline. Besides, it may be known to foreign spies that you have already travelled that way, and it is bad strategy to repeat your movements,' he said.

'But Ura is a Hittite dominion, and Ugarit is loyal to you, so surely the King can ensure the safety of a convoy through those cities?' said Nakht.

'As you know, the King's second son is Viceroy in Aleppo. Therefore a Hittite military convoy will accompany you to the border town of Sarissa, and beyond to Aleppo. We have garrisons, of course, but it is approaching winter, and our troops will be returning to the homeland. So from there, you will be on your own. But your own army is engaged in the wars there. I believe the divisions have not all retired to Memphis. Therefore you can call upon their support,' replied the Chief Steward.

'My lord, it is well known your eastern borders are insecure, and that the reason the King's second son, the Prince Telepinu, has been sent to Aleppo, is to quell anti-Hittite forces in that area,' said Nakht. 'I mean, of course, the Army of Chaos are known to be active in that territory.'

The Chief Steward looked uncomfortable.

'My lord Envoy, your information is out of date. Hittite authority is well established in the east. Our forts and watchtowers will provide security and accommodation. Our watchmen of the Long Road will be responsible for your safe passage. And surely you must know, according to our laws, all citizens of every locality are held personally responsible for the safe passage of all merchants and dignitaries. If any harm comes to them, then restitution must be made.'

'That will be little satisfaction to us if we are already dead,' replied Nakht.

'Hittite honour is at stake in this. Such a thing is unthinkable,' replied the Chief Steward quickly.

'It is not only thinkable, it is also alarmingly plausible. We could not be more vulnerable, and any ill fortune that might befall us would be simply catastrophic, for both sides. I hope you understand that? I hope you understand my concern about the alarming internal discord within the royal family?'

'The Crown Prince is reconciled. You need have no fear of reprisals,' replied the Chief Steward. 'And we have accomplished an agreement to create the circumstances of peace between our empires.'

'But that will not be confirmed until the marriage is performed, and so everything remains in peril. There is great dissent among you. There is a killer here in your city and it is most likely Aziru himself. Where will he strike next? We are travelling through unstable, dangerous territory. It offers him the perfect opportunity to assassinate us. You can see my point.'

The Chief Steward nodded and shrugged, exasperated. 'I have done my best. These are the commands of the King. For the moment, the Crown Prince has his ear. We must make the best of it.'

Once the Chief Steward had departed, we fell quickly into discussion.

'He's right about not retracing our steps. They will have to guard us all the way through the Hittite lands,' said Simut. 'And then we can travel west, and take a ship south, or join up with the Way of Horus; either will take us quickly back to Egypt.'

'We have no choice. But how can we trust these guards? I fear some further revelation of the Crown Prince's treachery,' said Nakht.

'I would like to point out that the land route takes us into territory where Egypt has no alliances, no forts, and no way stations. We will have to pass through what is essentially the no-man's-land between ourselves and the Hittites. And remember, too: the last thing we need is for Horemheb to discover us. That would be worse than meeting the Army of Chaos!' I said.

'The Way of Horus is probably safest. I will be able to send letters ahead of us. We can pass again for a commercial delegation, provided Prince Zannanza assents. And as for Horemheb, the war is over for this season; the Hittites are retiring to Hattusa. He has no need to waste his time on the front. He has more pressing matters at home. He will need as many of his troops as possible back in Egypt. For obvious reasons.'

We left the city the following afternoon. The future marriage had been announced, and so the processional way was lined with nobles, bureaucrats and dignitaries; our own convoy was surrounded by a troop of Hittite guards, bearing spears and axes. The King rode before us, with the Crown Prince and Prince Zannanza on either side of him. The Queen rode behind them, but at no point did she turn in Nakht's direction. I looked around, searching the countless faces of the crowds, desperate to catch a glimpse of the Levantine face I had seen at the banquet. But there was no sign.

When we reached the Lion Gate, the King publicly embraced Prince Zannanza – but I have rarely seen a colder, less effusive embrace between father and son. Prince Zannanza turned to look back at his home, and he must have known he would never see it again. The Crown Prince slapped him vigorously on the shoulder, and whispered something in his ear that caused Prince Zannanza to stiffen and redden as if he had been cruelly mocked and cursed.

And then, deafened by the cacophony of the fanfares that followed, we were led through the long dark tunnel of the great gate. We emerged into the light. The carved lions leapt from their stone. I looked up at the crenellations of the city walls, which were crowded with people. I searched them for any glimpse of the man I had seen staring at Nakht, or a man with red hair. But there was nothing, and our path was set, our journey was only just beginning. Before us lay the dark forests, and the long, dangerous road home.

PART FOUR

If thou openest not the gate to let me enter,
I will break the door, I will wrench the lock,
I will smash the door-posts, I will force the doors.
I will bring up the dead to eat the living.
And the dead will outnumber the living.

Ishtar approaches the gates of the Underworld

26

The ancient gates of the city of Aleppo opened at dawn, and we joined the throng of labourers going to the fields and of merchants and tradesmen setting off to work. We were glad to leave, for the second Prince of the Hittites, Viceroy of the City, had accommodated us with ill will. There was no brotherly love between him and Zannanza, for whom he displayed only a sneering condescension. Here also we had reached the border of Hittite-dominated territory. The Hittite guard, which had accompanied us from Hattusa, across the arid plains to the north, down through the poor villages and border towns, over the curling tracks of the cold mountain passes, dense with dark pines, and then across the plains towards Aleppo itself, would now turn back. They followed us a little way out of the city, suddenly stopped, stood to attention, offered a modest salute, and then simply rode away, as if relieved of a worrisome, distasteful responsibility. During the whole journey they had not exchanged one word, or one sign of friendliness with us.

Finally we were on our own. What lay ahead of us were unknown, uncertain wastelands, which for the last thirty years had been fought over, and for much longer had been extremely perilous to all travellers. Nakht had decided to take the trade road to Hamah, about five days to the south of Aleppo, and from there turn west, to rejoin the Way of the Sea at Byblos. The Hittite Crown Prince had arranged for us to be accommodated in fort-towns along the way, and given us documents to that effect.

It was a beautiful day. We set off into the unknown, our guards jogging before and behind. The road was lined with meadows, the dew was still heavy upon the fields, and birds sang in the branches of the trees and swooped along the trickling water courses. For the first time in many days, despite the perils that lay ahead, we all felt a weight lift from us. Even Prince Zannanza seemed to be touched by the beauty and the freshness of the early morning. Nakht said something politely to him, and he nodded, and almost smiled. For the whole journey up to this point he had been sunk in a profound, speechless depression; he had barely eaten, he had drunk little, and lack of sleep circled his elegant eyes with dark rings.

We rode together, Prince Zannanza in the middle, Nakht and I on either side, Simut and his guards before and behind. Nakht tried once again to engage the Prince in conversation.

'Queen Ankhesenamun's beauty is remarkable. Isn't that so? Rahotep, I was just failing to find the words to describe her grace and her intelligence. She is quick-witted, and delightful in conversation.'

'So why has she had to beg for a husband from her greatest enemy?' Prince Zannanza asked quietly, in perfect – if accented – Egyptian.

Nakht began to answer him, but the Prince interrupted.

'I am not a fool. I know what families will do for power and glory. My father has sold me; I am merely a commodity, bartered

220

for political gain. And when I am no longer useful, I know I will be disposed of without a second thought.'

'That is not so, Your Majesty. As long as I live I will serve you, and protect your life with my own,' replied Nakht earnestly.

Prince Zannanza gazed at him.

'And how long can I hope to survive in your Egyptian royal court, which is so notoriously full of assassins and betrayers?' he replied. 'And who are you?' he said, turning to me unexpectedly.

'Life, prosperity, health, Your Majesty. I am Rahotep.'

'Tell me about yourself,' commanded the Prince.

I could hear Simut coughing with amusement behind me.

'What would Your Majesty care to know?'

'You are not a noble, yet you are not a guard. Why are you here?'

I glanced at Nakht, who was following the unexpected progress of this conversation carefully.

'The Queen of Egypt commanded my presence,' I said. 'I am a Seeker of Mysteries and worked for the Thebes Medjay.'

'She must value your loyalty highly,' he replied.

I could think of nothing to say to that. He gazed at me.

'I see something else in your eyes. You carry a dark anger in your heart, don't you, Rahotep, Seeker of Mysteries?'

I was taken aback.

'I recognize the signs all too well. I, too, was not made for the darkness of men's cruelty. But the Gods make fools of us all,' he continued. And then he spurred his horse, and cantered forward a little, to return to his solitude.

Simut winked, and clapped me on the shoulder, whispering into my ear: 'I think the Prince has taken a liking to you. "The Gods make fools of us all . . ."'

'You're just jealous,' I replied.

We both laughed. Nakht was not amused.

The sun rose quickly as we travelled onwards, and soon the

land began to simmer with heat. Later, up ahead, in the dazzle and shimmer of the afternoon, one of the reconnaissance guards suddenly stopped and whistled a warning. Simut and I cantered up to join him on a slight rise in the terrain. He gestured for silence, and pointed from his eyes to a square mud-brick building in the distance. It was hard to make it out in the glare of the light.

'It's an outpost. That's a water cistern in the middle,' he said.

'So where is everyone?' I asked.

There seemed to be no watchmen, nor any soldiers moving about on duty. In fact, the place was eerily silent, as if it had been abandoned. Wiping the sweat from our brows, we scanned the parched, empty terrain.

Simut and I dismounted and, taking two of his guards with us, made our way slowly and quietly towards the fort. There was nowhere for us to hide if we came under attack. The guards held their bows at the ready. The desert land was utterly silent all around us, and we made no sound either. I examined the dusty ground, step by step; it was heavily marked with the prints of horses' hooves, and sandals, and bare feet, running crazily in all directions. As we came closer to the fort itself, spots, arcs and trails of dried black blood decorated the dirt. It was the diagram of a battle. But where were the dead?

Simut scanned the place, then motioned the two guards to cover us, their bows aimed at the walls; then, swift and silent as shadows, Simut and I ran across the dangerous open ground until we had our backs against the wall of the gatehouse. I wiped away the sweat dripping from my forehead; we listened for any sound within the fort. Still there was nothing. All I could hear was the buzzing of flies. Simut instructed the guards to position themselves directly before the gateway, and then, with a nod, he and I burst through into the inner court, our weapons raised.

Instantly we were overcome by an appalling stench, and we pulled our linens to our noses. We were confronted by the scene

of a massacre: a platoon of Egyptian soldiers had been slaughtered, their limbs, hands and feet indiscriminately severed with
crude blows from their torsos. The bodies had begun to putrefy in
the intense heat. This was a recent event. And then it struck me.

'There are no heads,' I whispered to Simut.

'So where are they?' he answered.

We searched the fort. Everything was destroyed: the crude
wooden benches were smashed, the storage jars and bowls were
shattered, and the straw sleeping pallets were slashed open. There
were smears and pools of blood on the floor and across the walls.

I held up my hand for silence. Something was bothering me;
a remote buzzing sound. I approached the small circular water
cistern. With the tip of my dagger I lifted the lid. Instantly, a black
cloud of flies swarmed out. I stepped back quickly, waving them
away. When they had settled again, with my linens wound around
my face and head, I pushed open the cistern lid and glanced
inside. Crammed into the dark, dank well of the water hole was a
platoon's-worth of severed heads, staring sightlessly up at me, still
dripping with blood, poisoning the once-fresh water below.

27

Simut sent out his men to reconnoitre the land around the fort. They found nothing in the immediate vicinity, having followed the horse tracks for some distance, heading away to the west. So he posted the lookout guards, and they crouched down in whatever shade they could find and gazed intently at the shimmering land. We needed to rest in these hours, before we began the next day's journey in the dark. But we were all wide awake, listening for any sound that might betray the return of the attackers. Nakht organized a couch for Prince Zannanza, and tried to improvise an awning for him. He explained why the tents could not be erected, but the Prince just waved him away disconsolately, and turned his back on everything.

The heat of the afternoon was unbearable. Nakht, Simut and I sat together, batting the incessant flies away, and whispering so that he could not overhear us.

'This barbarity is familiar,' I said. 'It fits with what Paser told us about the Army of Chaos.'

'I agree. So how can we best defend ourselves against the possibility of another attack?' asked Nakht.

'I'll send scouts ahead to reconnoitre the land around us as we proceed. We have twenty men; they're far better trained and far more deadly than any horde of undisciplined mercenaries,' Simut replied.

'This wasn't a random attack. Whoever they are, they know we're coming,' I said. 'And I don't want to say this, but there were more than twenty soldiers in the garrison here, and look what happened to them.'

We sat in silence contemplating our predicament.

'There's no water here. The horses are thirsty. We have no choice, we need to press ahead. Better to travel by night. The bow guard must be fully armed at all times. We will put cloths around the horses' hooves, and no one will speak. We will travel in silence. Our ultimate duty is to protect the Prince, and that means both of you must guard him at all times,' Nakht decided.

And so, as soon as the sun set, we rose, prepared ourselves, ate a little bread, and set forth into the cooling desert darkness. The stars were shining brilliantly in the sky, but the moon was new, just a sliver of white, giving us little light to travel by – and fortunately little light to be seen by. The horses' hooves were muffled, and in the strange silence we listened intently for anything that might alert us to the presence of enemies on horseback in the shadows. Our nerves were wound tight; I blinked and rubbed my eyes as I stared into the darkness. Slowly, we covered the distances; the stars turned in their spheres, and then, after hours of tension, the darkness of night began to change. The rim of the world took on a blue tint, which gradually spread, until the horizon brightened, and light began to reoccupy the world. Ra, the Sun, was reborn into a new day. But what it revealed, up ahead of us, in the blinding white and gold of sunrise, was the image of our nightmare; in the distance, a dark line of shadowy figures on horseback were waiting for us.

Simut raised his hand, and the caravan instantly halted. Prince Zannanza, who had been nodding with sleep, stirred.

'Why have we stopped?'

Then he blinked, and saw the dark figures.

'No, no, no . . .' he whispered.

'Shut up,' I snapped, without thinking of protocol. Simut gave a signal, and his bow guards dropped into formation in front, and raised their bows. Their arrows pointed into the sky, their tips glinting with the new light. Others stood behind them, their long spears poised. And then we heard coming from all around us a barbaric noise like I have never heard before, a drumming of weapons on shields, and a chanting and shouting. We turned in our saddles; in the distance, and from all around us, horsemen appeared up out of the shimmering desert dawn, surrounding us in every direction.

Simut gave a swift order, and the bowmen trained their arrows on the shadowy figures; but we were vastly outnumbered. There must have been more than a hundred of them. Four of our men moved to protect Prince Zannanza and Nakht, their leather shields raised, their swords ready to defend them both to the death. I caught a glimpse of Nakht's face, his arm protective and reassuring around the Prince's shoulders.

The shadowy horsemen continued to make their hideous war music as they slowly tightened the circle that surrounded us; they were still too far away for us to see their faces clearly. But then a commanding figure on horseback cantered forward into the open desert within the circle. I shaded my eyes; I could make out long hair, and flowing robes. This figure made its horse dance before us on its hind legs, while waving a long curved sword threateningly in the air, and shouting, calling out incomprehensible threats and ululating wildly. The huge circle of men responded with jubilation, rattling their weapons against their shields, and screaming with rage and fury.

Simut waited, intently focused for the first sign of movement. His men were poised, disciplined, their weapons ready. And suddenly it came – the leader screamed a ferocious howl of delight, and then they were charging at us from every direction. Simut bellowed orders, and arrows sprayed up into the blue sky, glittered at the peak of their arcs, and then showered down accurately into the charging horde. A number of the horsemen were hit, and fell sideways off their galloping horses, to be trampled under the hooves of the others. At Simut's command another round of arrows was fired, not this time into the air, but directly at the attackers; and many hit their targets, bringing down men and horses in a mortal tangle. But still they came forward, and now I could just make out their wild beards and hair, their screaming mouths, and their faces crazed with the ecstasy of battle.

My heart was pounding. Nakht appeared beside me suddenly, and shouted: 'What should we do?'

'Where is the Prince?' I shouted back.

'He's with the guards!'

'That's where you should be!'

'We need every man to fight,' he replied, his eyes shining.

'Hold up your sword. Stay behind me, stay close!'

Nakht drew out his sword. I suddenly remembered that in the past he'd flinched from the use of the knife and abhorred violence of any kind, but he must have taken training since, for he held his blade now with a new confidence. The bow archers fired more arrows into the approaching attackers, and more of the barbarians fell; but suddenly spears and axes were hurtling through the air, embedding themselves with grim thuds and cracks into the heads and chests of some of our own guards in the outer protective circle, who fell with grunts or in silence. In a moment, the assailants would be upon us.

I glanced up and saw one of the horsemen, his arm pulled right back, cast his spear with all his might – it came quivering through the air right on target for Nakht. He had not seen it. Just in time I threw up my shield, and it hit directly with an enormous thud that reverberated up my arm, throwing me backwards on to the ground, and winding me. I grabbed Nakht and pulled him down, protecting him with my body, as the storm of horsemen broke through the ring of bow archers, hacking wildly, gleefully, at them, separating arms and heads from torsos. Blood gushed and arced richly red into the fresh morning air. I glimpsed Simut attacking back, encouraging his men to do the same; they were superb marksmen and soldiers, and their weapons sliced and sang accurately through air and flesh and bone; and more of the horde fell dead from their horses. But we were impossibly outnumbered. Nakht was struggling underneath me.

'Let me fight!' he shouted.

'Stay still,' I said. For a moment, our eyes met, and it seemed to me he almost smiled.

'Death holds no fear for me,' he said. 'Not if we die together.'

The savage and relentless noise of the battle suddenly seemed very far away, the barbarity of the attackers, as they slashed and hacked their way through us, seemed to slow down. I thought of the pity of life, and of my children, and my wife. In my mind I began to say goodbye to them.

But then, even as a feeling of terrible waste flowed through me, a shadow fell across my body. I looked up, dazzled by the rising sun that framed the dark figure on a magnificent stallion, gazing down at me. From the horse's bridle hung several battered heads of dead men, the flesh torn away, the eyes missing from the sockets, the jaws hanging broken, loose. Chains of human hands had been fastened in a collar around the stallion's neck, the yellowed, gnarled fingers imploring for help, too late. The rider's scimitar was raised, glinting in the sun, ready to strike me dead.

But instead the figure laughed, and moved out of the sun. I looked into the face of the enemy, and I saw that it was not a man at all; but a woman, laughing with delight at the bloodshed and the victory. Her hair was black and thick, braided and tangled wildly around her head; her eyes were a compelling, shocking blue; and the mad fury of her expression was contradicted by the magnificence of her face. Then she looked at me directly, curiously; and a moment later, to my bewilderment, she smiled. And then everything went dark.

28

I tried to stir, but pain danced through my body. My hands and feet were bound, my mouth was gagged with a filthy rag, and I seemed unable to open my eyes; a raging thirst parched my throat, and the brutal sun burned my face. I tried to make sense of things: the rumble of cartwheels, the irregular sound of horses' hooves on the rough ground, and the casual banter, cheerful shouts and aggressive laughter of men all around, in a language I did not understand.

I managed to open one eye. The other was swollen shut. It throbbed uncomfortably. The first thing I made out in the squinting light was Nakht's face, very close to mine. His mouth was open, his face bruised, and his lips parched. His eyes were closed. Beyond him lay Prince Zannanza, awake and terrified, his mouth also gagged, his desperate, beautiful eyes pleading with mine. On the far side of the cart lay Simut, unconscious. Dried blood caked his face and beard, and flies feasted around a large, open gash on his head. His face was badly bruised. I saw his lips twitch against the flies. We four were all still alive. Why? And what of the guards?

The cart rattled jarringly over stones. I could make out little of the men on horseback who surrounded us – they were shadows silhouetted against the dazzle of the sun. But one of them saw I was conscious, and called out. The cart suddenly halted. He leaned down, unknotted the gag, and threw it aside. I gasped in the hot, dry desert air. I tried to speak. 'Water . . .' My voice was cracked and broken. One of them said something to the others, which made them laugh. Then several stood up in their stirrups, pulled aside their robes, and began to piss on me. I closed my eyes and mouth against the hot, revolting spatter, but they only laughed harder as I tried to squirm away. Then they pissed on Nakht and Prince Zannanza, too. This woke Nakht from his torpor; he coughed and cried out in revulsion. I was suddenly possessed by the strength of outrage, and, despite my hands being bound behind my back, I yanked myself to my feet, off the cart, and ran at the men, screaming with rage, trying to butt them with my head; but my legs gave way, and I fell to the ground, humiliated. This only delighted them more, and they roared with laughter. Several got down from their horses, I supposed to beat me up. I picked myself up to run at them again. But then a woman's voice, commanding and deep, berated the men, and they stepped back, obedient as a pack of snarling dogs.

She stood gazing at me, her hands on her hips, and her wild hair like a glorious mane about her face, smeared with dust and blood. She dashed water from her leather water-skin over my face, then gripped my head between her fingers and turned it this way and that, as if valuing a horse. She raised her sword, drew the point of the blade under each eye, down my nose, and across my lips, like a crude version of the Opening of the Mouth ceremony, as if she were a high priest, and I the corpse waiting to be resurrected in the Otherworld: 'You are young again, you live again, you are young again, you live again, forever.' I jerked my head back, out of her grip. She smacked me hard, but then, as if pleased about something, she shouted, in a voice that could have knocked down a stone temple, something that sounded like 'Inanna!' – and her wild Army of Chaos screamed in respect.

She gripped my face again, prised my teeth apart, held the leather water-skin from her belt to my mouth, and poured a stream of clear, cool, blissful water for me to drink. Then she nodded to one of her men, who gave Nakht and Prince Zannanza brief draughts of water from his water-skin, too. Simut was still unconscious. The man splashed the water over his face, but it made no difference. I was afraid he might be dead. But the man cuffed Simut about the face, pulled him into a sitting position, and forced water down his throat. Suddenly Simut coughed and retched. He was alive.

The others were ordered to get out of the cart, and we were made to stand in a line. Now I could see more clearly the motley militia under Inanna's command. They wore black, together with exotic assemblies of gold collars, bangles and jewels. Their hair and beards were worn braided or plaited in wild, different styles. They were extensively armed, and must have collected their weapons from a wide range of victims, for some of them I recognized as Egyptian, some as Hittite, and others were unfamiliar to me. But to the last man, they looked like brutal criminals.

Inanna walked up and down imperiously, assessing us in turn. She gazed at Prince Zannanza, marvelling and whistling at his perfect white teeth, his smooth face, and his delicate hands whose unblemished skin showed a lifetime of luxurious leisure. She called out ribald comments, and her men guffawed, and slapped each other's hands. Some approached the Prince aggressively, brandishing their weapons and mocking him. Inanna seemed curious about Nakht, too.

'What is your name, Egyptian?' She spoke in broken, strangely accented Egyptian.

'I am Userhat,' he lied.

'What are you?' she demanded.

'I am a merchant.'

'What do you trade? This delicate beauty next to you?' she said.

'He is a young scholar of the Hittite court, and we are accompanying him to Ugarit,' he said.

She laughed out loud. 'How beautiful are the young scholars of the Hittites! He must be very valuable.' Nakht said nothing. She cuffed him hard across the face. 'You lie,' she said, simply. 'I know who you are.'

But Nakht's spirit seemed to revive within him, and he stared her down.

'Egyptian armed forces will be looking for us, even now,' he said. 'The Hittite army will vow revenge against any harm that comes to this man, or us. You have committed a foolish crime against the empires of Egypt and Hatti, and it will be best for you if you supply us with horses and water, and release us now.'

During this, Inanna began cleaning her long nails with the tip of a dagger, shaking her head with amusement. But suddenly she pushed the point of the blade right against Nakht's lips.

'Open your mouth, Egyptian liar,' she hissed. He complied, and she slowly pushed the blade deep into his mouth. He gagged, desperate not to have it cut his lips or his face open. His eyes blazed with the dishonour of it. She forced him down on his knees.

'For lying to Inanna, I should slice off your tongue and your lips and make you swallow them. Your lies would not be so elegant, then.'

The moments passed in agony. Nakht tried to return her gaze, and waited for his fate.

'You understand me now,' she said. 'It is I who speak the truth.

You are all my slaves. Do not think of attempting to escape. Egypt is far away. You will not see your land again. Here lives death. She is standing before you now.'

And she withdrew the dagger and raised her fist, commanding a jubilant roar from her men.

Our path veered south, away from the westerly direction where the Way of Horus, and our chosen route to safety and home, lay. We were entering unknown territory. The chances of our being rescued or found were extremely slight. For who would venture into these wastelands, and even if they did, how could they locate us? Far in the distance rose a line of mountains, pale misty shapes like sleeping monsters in the afternoon heat. We continued through the barren wastes all day, and the sun was descending when we reached the grey and silver foothills that ran along the eastern slopes of the mountains. We slowly climbed up and up, until eventually we reached a cool, high, rocky pass which gave way to a spectacular vision: an amazing hidden valley falling away below us on the far side, its wide floor and lower slopes to the south packed full of intensely green fields, spreading as far as the eye could see to a far mountain peak, topped with snow, which shone with the light of the setting sun in the furthest distance. Everything was illuminated by the long, incongruously golden light of the early evening; after so long in the dry lands, it felt as if we had arrived in the Field of Reeds as depicted in our Books of the Dead. It looked like the promised bounty of the Otherworld.

Inanna raised her sword, rose up on her stirrups, and cried out her name down into the valley, where it echoed briefly. Her men yelled and whooped all around us, relishing the echoes that came back to them; and then we began the descent, following an established route down the rocky slopes, and around the scattered boulders. Soon we were riding down through densely cultivated fields. It was warmer on the valley floor. Poor, aggressive-looking farmers prostrated themselves in fear and awe, but turned their faces away from the sight of us, making the sign of the evil eye. Children ran alongside, until Inanna's men chased them away, and they raced, shouting, into the fields to hide. Peasants were labouring everywhere. Countless white, red and pink flowers rose from the richly green plants. And then I was suddenly struck by a revelation: these flowers were poppies. They were growing opium. *Fields of opium as far as the eye could see.* I knew now where we were: in the lost valley from which Paser had warned me no one ever returned.

Near sunset, we stopped at a spring, to refresh the horses. Our hands were unbound and we were allowed to drink, too. The cold water tasted of rocks and herbs; I thought it was the finest drink of my life. I raised Simut's head to help him drink. He looked feverish. I washed his head wound and his face, carefully. The air was fresh and scented. The evening shadows lay long across the valley floor. Inanna shouted an order, and a farmer and his wife, bowing low, hurriedly brought a straw basket full of glorious black grapes, just cut from a vine that grew in front of their hut. She threw a bunch to us, and we shared the luscious fruits hungrily. I suddenly felt a surge of gratitude and hope; we were not yet dead. I might see my family again.

'Where are we?' whispered Prince Zannanza.

'We've been taken to these people's heartland,' said Nakht, quietly. 'Somehow they know who we are. They must know we're more valuable alive than dead. I imagine they intend to ransom us – for gold, no doubt.'

'But who will buy us?' he asked.

Nakht pretended he did not know; but I did. Aziru must have commissioned our kidnapping. I took Nakht aside.

'Have you noticed the crop being grown here?' I said.

He looked at me as if he did not understand the question.

'I see flowers, that is all . . .'

235

'It's all opium!' I said.

He gazed around him. 'But this much opium would be worth more than all the gold in Nubia!' he said, amazed.

But then a command was called; the guards retied our hands and threw us back into the cart. We travelled on into the darkness, through the endless shadowy poppy fields, now silvered in the moonlight and alive with activity. Hundreds of farmers, young men and boys in simple, rough woollen robes, working backwards, moved down the rows of plants, among the millions of seed-heads, slitting them open to release white opium sap. They shouted and called to each other from field to field, farm to farm, and from one side of the valley to the other in the dark.

The moon was high in the starry night sky, and we were shivering in our light robes when we finally arrived at our destination, a fortified stronghold of low, flat-roofed mud-brick buildings gathered together within a large walled compound. The place was a mixture of opulent booty and filthy chaos. Several old decapitated heads, disfigured from the hungry attentions of birds, were stuck on poles on either side of the entrance gate. Crudely butchered goats and ducks were roasting over open fires, attended by hunched women, their faces hidden inside their headscarves. Dark figures moved malevolently around the campfires, gnawing on the bones of roasted animals, drinking deeply from wine vessels, and laughing at dirty jokes or picking fights with each other. Captured men, women and children served them, and were kicked, beaten and abused for their pains. Animals and naked infants wandered freely about the compound, chewing on discarded bones or howling hopelessly. Cats and dogs stole whatever they could find. There was also an intense, bitter stink in the air, which came from a pair of mangy, apathetic desert lions captured in a cage.

Inanna strode ahead, and everyone bowed to her. We were pushed and kicked behind her, stumbling in the dark. Inside, smoky bowls of oil gave off a poor light. Richly inlaid furniture and statues, lapis lazuli and turquoise amulets and jewellery were heaped up casually, as if their variety, huge value and rarity were meaningless. In the side rooms, I saw men and girls lying on couches, obviously in opium trances. The place was dismal, and the air itself seemed corrupted.

We were dragged into a large interior courtyard lit by torches. The ropes binding our wrists were kept tied. We were forced down on to our knees, amid much shouting from Inanna's men, who crowded around, cursing and spitting on us. Now that the attention of our kidnappers was elsewhere, I began to try to loosen the inept knots that bound my hands.

Inanna shouted, and her men were silenced. I wondered how she could exercise such unquestioned authority over these men. They cringed under her command. Without her, I had no doubt they would have torn us to pieces. I worked one finger gradually inside the knot of the binding.

Inanna had Prince Zannanza brought forward. She gripped his head, turning it from side to side, and watching how the fear played across his features.

'What will she do to him?' whispered Nakht.

'She won't harm him, he's the prize,' I replied.

'Are you afraid of a woman, pretty boy?' Inanna asked the Prince. He didn't know whether to nod or disagree. But when she produced a small knife with three blades – exactly like those I had seen the opium farmers using as they cut the seed-heads of the poppy plants – he began to howl, a high-pitched cry of pure fear that provoked delight in her men, who laughed, pointing and yelling obscenities. Inanna held the blade right next to Zannanza's face, and encouraged her men to start to chant. He was terrified. Her face was lit red and gold by the flickering light of the fires. Suddenly she brought the blade quickly upwards, expertly slashing the Prince across his perfect cheek. The men roared. Three lines of bright red instantly appeared, and blood began to drip down his chin, and on to the ground. He wailed in distress. Inanna leaned forward and licked the blood off the Prince's jaw. He recoiled in disgust, and spat in her face. She stared at him, her eyes as cold as a snake's, wiped the spittle from her cheek, and then punched him hard in the face. He collapsed to the floor, and several of the men began kicking him as he coiled into himself.

Finally, the knot binding my hands loosened. I worked my wrists against each other, enough to open up a length of rope. I ran forward, tearing it off. Prince Zannanza's attackers weren't expecting me. I grabbed the sword of one of them, kicked the others away, and found myself standing over the beaten body of the Prince, screaming at them like a Theban street fighter. The courtyard was silenced. Several of Inanna's men surrounded me, drawing out their swords, moving around me, closing in, ready to go for the kill. It was better to attack than defend. I clashed swords with the two in front, while trying to defend my back from the others. Prince Zannanza cowered next to me, trying to keep clear of the slicing blades. I managed to score a cut on the arm of one of the attackers, and with a renewed roar of rage he went for me, while the others backed off to watch and enjoy the spectacle. We fought across the courtyard, and the crowd made way for us. Out of the corner of my eye, I saw Prince Zannanza being bound and tied again. I was for a moment off-guard; my opponent's sword suddenly sliced towards me sideways. I jumped back, and then, as his sword carried on through its arc, I saw my chance and plunged mine into his undefended chest. The roar of the crowd faded. The man retched up blood. My sword came reluctantly out of his chest. The man still was not dead. He stared up at me with contempt, choking and muttering, struggling to breathe.

Inanna was suddenly standing beside me.

'You must finish what you began,' she said.

I had no choice. I raised my sword once more, and thrust it

down into the man's chest again. He scrabbled on the ground, muttering, as if trying to claw back the last moments of his life, until finally he let go, and died.

Inanna appraised me with new interest. Several of her men ran forward to apprehend me, but she shook her head. I thought I saw a touch of amusement in her wild eyes. She raised her three-bladed knife and held it close to my face, as if daring me to attack her. Her expression was enigmatic. The men started to chant again. But suddenly she began to dance and chant, whirling in circles, clapping her hands, and crying out, invoking a Goddess or a spirit of darkness. The men shouted encouragement. And then just as suddenly she stopped, right in front of me, and shouted something in a language I could not understand. And then she kissed me full on the lips.

29

Sunlight broke in splinters through the slats of the battered wooden door. We slept or dozed on piles of filthy straw, and were thrown only gnawed bones and dirty cooking pots from which to eat the burned scraps; there was a jar of stale water in the corner, and a cracked chamber-pot. We had not washed for several days now, and already the chamber-pot in the corner was overflowing.

Nevertheless, my stomach rumbled incongruously. Hunger is no respecter of disaster. Prince Zannanza still lay turned to the wall, hiding his disfigured face. The ruin of his beauty seemed to cause him more distress than the fear of losing his own life. Nakht had been unable to console him. Simut stirred, and groaned quietly, and raised himself slowly to sit next to me. I passed him a dish of the stale water and he drank slowly.

'We're in trouble,' he said, quietly, wiping his mouth.

I nodded in agreement.

'No one knows where we are,' I replied.

'Even if they did, what could they do?' he said. 'We could be held here for months, and meanwhile, Ay must be dead by now, Horemheb will march on Thebes, take power from the Queen, and there's not a thing we can do about it . . . We've failed.'

We were interrupted by voices outside the door. The door slammed open, and a couple of Inanna's henchmen entered the cell. Prince Zannanza huddled deeper into his corner. They made some extravagant joke about the stink. They were munching on legs of roasted meat, luxuriating in the good food and our hunger. We watched them with hatred. When they'd chewed off as much as they wanted, they threw us the bones – as if we were dogs. Prince Zannanza grabbed one quickly, and began gnawing the tiny scraps that remained. I picked up another bone, and threw it back with all my strength in their faces.

'Bring us food fit for human beings,' I shouted. They just laughed. So I grabbed one of the discarded cooking pots they'd thrown into the cell, and advanced on them, whirling it around my head. They retreated, laughing, and slammed the door shut. I threw the pot, but it just clattered uselessly against the door.

'Why has that murdering bitch taken a shine to you?' asked Simut, darkly.

'It's not my idea of a good time,' I muttered. 'Next time they come back, we could attack them together, make a break for it, steal four good horses from under their noses, and be out through that gateway in a moment.'

'And then come back with an Egyptian division and raze this place to the ground, and her in it . . .' added Simut, for good measure.

'We're locked in a cell, we have no weapons, we have no knowledge of this valley, and even if we did escape, we would be hunted down very quickly,' said Nakht.

'So what do *you* suggest?' asked Simut angrily.

Nakht stared at him.

'I suggest you remember who you're talking to,' he said. 'I am still in command of this mission.'

Simut said nothing.

'They're going to kill us all,' said Prince Zannanza, quietly, from his corner. Simut rolled his eyes, but Nakht, once more the diplomat, turned to console the Prince.

'You are far too important for that. You will be ransomed, I assure you. The Queen of Egypt will soon know we are missing. I was to have sent fast messengers at every stage of our journey, to keep her informed of our progress. She will interpret our silence, and she will have some knowledge of where we disappeared.'

Simut and I exchanged a brief look. There was absolutely nothing Ankhesenamun could do to save us. Our mission was secret. She had no troops to send out to rescue us. Only Horemheb had his divisions in the north. And help from him would spell death. We were on our own.

'Your father will also know we are missing,' continued Nakht to the Prince. 'He will have had spies prepared along our route, to watch your progress. He will be very angry. He will come to rescue you.'

Zannanza stared at Nakht disconsolately.

'My father despises me. I appal my brothers. None of them will rescue me. They will simply cultivate the advantage of my death for their own ends. The Crown Prince was always opposed to this alliance. Now he will be able to claim my father was wrong to trust Egypt. The King will be shamed before his people, and he will easily be goaded into adopting my brother's plan to renew Hittite attacks upon Egypt. But what does that matter to me? For I will soon be dead.'

And he turned again to face the wall. He was right. If any harm came to the Prince, then the Hittite kingdom would make good on its threat and take revenge against Egypt. The war of the last thirty years would seem like the prelude to a far greater calamity. Egypt would be held responsible. We would all be held responsible.

'We are still alive for a reason,' I said.

'And what is that?' asked Simut.

'There are two possibilities. There are two men who would wish to destabilize the prospect of peaceful relations between the two empires by means of the Prince's death. One is Horemheb himself . . .'

'Horemheb would never commission the Army of Chaos to undertake such an act of kidnapping and assassination. If he had knowledge of our mission, and our return route, he would simply do it himself,' said Nakht.

'I agree. So that leaves Aziru,' I said. 'Aziru hates Egypt because his father was executed by Akhenaten. Aziru is the King of Amurru. Aziru has changed allegiance from Egypt to the Hittites. Aziru has almost certainly maintained secret contacts with the Army of Chaos. He wants us.'

'Aziru will be dead by now. My request to the Hittites was absolutely clear,' said Nakht.

'But how can you be sure the Hittites have done what they said they would do? What if they have not assassinated Aziru? The Crown Prince proved himself a strong ally of his, and the Crown Prince now has the upper hand with his father,' I said. 'Aziru is probably still alive. And if he is . . .' I left the thought unspoken.

Nakht's face was dark. He was thinking.

'It seems to me we have one chance left to save ourselves,' he said eventually.

'And what's that?' asked Simut.

'Inanna's interest in Rahotep. She likes you. So we must consider how to play the throw of the dice to our best advantage, for it may make the difference between success and failure. Between life and death.'

'You're asking me to *seduce* her?' I said, astonished.

'Not asking. *Ordering.*'

Simut guffawed with amazement at the idea. But Nakht was staring at me seriously, coldly.

'You know my wife. You know my family. You cannot ask me to do such a thing . . . It would be a betrayal of all I hold dear,' I stammered.

'I am not ordering you to sleep with her. But her attraction to you is a prime vulnerability. We must exploit it. You must find out anything you can about her plans for us. Above all, it would give you a chance to persuade her of the advantage of doing a deal with Egypt for our safe return. She is avaricious. She wants only the best return for her possessions. She might be persuaded to take a better deal than Aziru – if he is alive – could offer. But be quick. Whether Aziru or Horemheb, or some other, as yet unknown person, is behind our kidnapping, they will soon be arriving to claim the prize,' he said. 'And either way, at that point I believe we will be killed.'

30

I called out Inanna's name all afternoon, and I was taken to her for the first time that night. Soon after dark, her henchmen came, kicked Simut and Nakht aside, and dragged me to my feet. I was stripped, doused with water, washed by two women, and thrown a tunic to wear. My hands were tied behind my back, and I was led to a place in the centre of a chamber, and left to wait.

Oil lamps had been lit, creating a low light that was almost romantic. Incense burned somewhere in the shadows. A strange assembly of divine statues from different lands had been arranged around the walls. And then the woman who killed men, rode a stallion, cut faces with knives, and licked blood, entered, wearing a fine red linen tunic. Down her back fell an ornate cloak of feathers, like the wings of a strange bird. The tunic dipped at the front: her breasts were naked. Her wild curly hair had been braided and coiled with gold thread into a kind of crown. Gold bangles glistened on her wrists and ankles. She walked around me, assessing me, smiling almost coyly. I felt like a slave for sale.

She cut the ropes that bound my hands, and motioned for me to sit on a stool. Then she sat down on a golden throne and set her feet upon two carved, beautifully inlaid, wooden lions. To either side of her were two large statues of birds with round faces, alert eyes, and sharp beaks – much like our human-headed bird, our *ba* spirit. I sat before her like a worshipper. A servant wafted an ostrich-feather fan over her.

The trays before us were piled high with roasted meats, vegetables, bunches of superb grapes and pomegranates. She cut a leg from a roasted bird and offered it to me on the end of her knife. I was ravenous, and although I was disgusted to be eating with her, I had to do it. Time was running out. I accepted the meat, and tried to eat slowly.

'They say I was born with a knife between my teeth. I made my first kill when I was ten years old,' she said quietly.

'And what did you kill?' I asked, assuming she meant animals on a hunt.

'Sometimes travellers and merchants risked the paths into our valley. So I waited, and soon enough, along came a caravan. They thought I was just a child. They were stupid. They didn't take me seriously. I took a merchant hostage, with my blade to his throat, and I made the others give me gold and a horse in exchange for their master's life.'

'And then?'

'And then I slit his throat,' she said calmly, and took another careful bite of her meat.

I said nothing. I wanted her to talk.

'Men always assumed they could beat me, and abuse me. And when I was too young to know how to take revenge, they did. Often. But as soon as I learned to defend myself, I began to kill them with my knife. And from then they learned to take me seriously.'

She let that hang in the air.

'Revenge is important,' I said.

Her eyes scrutinized mine. I made myself hold her gaze for as long as possible.

'Why do you say that?' she asked.

'Because a great friend of mine was murdered. I live with the hunger for revenge every day of my life.'

'You might yet have the opportunity to satisfy your hunger,' she said mysteriously.

'I desire that greatly,' I replied.

'Then you must please me greatly,' she said.

I tried to return her look. I knew I must try to do as Nakht had commanded me.

'How many men have you killed?' I asked.

'Why? Are you impressed by blood?'

'I am impressed by you,' I replied. And it was almost true. For all her barbarity, there was something compelling about her. She pretended to be defiantly scornful of my praise, but I saw I had touched on something. And then I realized: *she was lonely*.

'Men love fear,' she said. 'It makes them feel alive. But you are different. Perhaps you have passed beyond fear because of the power of your desire for revenge.'

The light from the oil wicks quivered. The walls of the room wavered with shifting shadows.

'The Hittite Prince in your cell is an extremely valuable prize. His father would pay handsomely for his return.'

She didn't reply, but merely poured new wine from an especially finely wrought jug. I tried again.

'Egypt has all the gold in the world. Negotiate with Thebes for his release. You will be handsomely rewarded.'

She passed one of the goblets to me.

'If Egypt and Hatti both value that pretty boy so much, perhaps I should have him write two letters, and then cut off his hands, and send them one each, holding his plea, as proof he is alive and in my possession.'

I noticed how she tested the bouquet of the wine, and drank thoughtfully.

'I do not care to know why the son of the Hittite King is travelling by such a route, in such secrecy, to the Egyptian court. Nor do I care why high-ranking Egyptian officials accompany him. Nor why the man who commissioned your kidnapping wants you all dead by his own hand. It is of no consequence to me.'

'It is of consequence to me,' I replied.

Our shadows wavered against the walls. She clasped her ringed fingers together and regarded me carefully. Her beauty sometimes shimmered to the surface, and sometimes vanished into a cold mask of anger.

'There is nothing you can do to save your friends or this Hittite Prince. They are already dead. But you can make another choice for yourself.'

'I would never choose my own survival at the price of my friends' death,' I replied.

'Of course you could. I might offer you a new life. If you joined me here, you would enjoy the best fruits of this world, and the next. By my side.'

What could I say?

'I am honoured by your offer . . .' I said. 'Give me time to consider it . . .'

'You will not refuse me,' she said quietly. 'You must choose. Death, or life.'

Our eyes held each other's gaze again, and this time I did not look away.

She clapped her hands, and a servant hurried in, carrying a beautifully inlaid wooden box, a silver dish on long, elegant legs, and a candle. She opened the lid, and took out a small piece of something dark brown, and sticky. She placed it in the dish, and let it heat and melt over the candle flame. Then, as it began to fume, she earnestly chanted a short prayer.

'To which God are you praying?' I said.

'To no god! To my Goddess. The Queen of the Underworld. To Ishtar.'

'She is unknown to me,' I said, recalling how the Babylonian Queen in Hatti had identified the symbol of the black star.

'She is the Goddess of Love and War. She has wings of many colours. Her feet are the talons of an eagle. She stands on the back of two lions. In her hands she holds the rod and ring of justice. She is all-powerful.'

Then she offered me her bejewelled hand.

'Come,' she said simply. 'It is time to meet her. It is time to dream.'

31

The time contained in a drop of water is infinite. As I stared at it, gathering itself into itself in its own time, I knew a thousand years was held in the swelling beauty of the water drop. A golden tranquillity flowed through me, and it was the warmth and light of Ra himself. My hands and feet were heavy with calm, and very far away. I could, if I desired, raise my right hand and gather the stars like jewels from the sky, or carefully pick the moon from the vast dark and hold it in my palm, delicate as a moth. The walls of the chamber swam like clear water. The flames of the lamps moved freely, like fish, through the passing of time, through the insubstantial reigns of gods and kings. That which was near was also far away. Everything was illuminated with beauty and a calm glory. I was dreaming, but more awake than I had ever felt in my life, which all now seemed a dream; the pains and fears of the past diminished to tiny figures on reed boats set to sail on the sunlit ocean of the Otherworld. I was part of the endless

sparkling glory of its waters. I moved forward, sweeping the
lights with my hands, holding the glitter up to my face, going
deeper and deeper into the endless delight of the light . . .

Very slowly I rose up from the depths of the dream. I felt I had
been with the Gods. But I felt inexplicably saddened to awake to
the world, to the chamber, to the couch. Inanna was beside me,
still lost in her own dream. Her lips were slightly parted, and her
eyes flickered under her eyelids. We were both naked. Her skin
was warm and soft against mine. Sudden fear gripped my heart in
its fist. I moved quickly away from her and stood in the dark, the
chamber spinning around me. What had happened? What had I
done? I struggled to remember the events of the night. I recalled
the invitation to partake of the drug; then wanting to vomit; but
next being overcome by a slow, golden sensation of tranquillity and
bliss. And then I remembered Inanna chanting to her Goddess, and
stripping naked before me – and I had been dazzled.

My mouth was dry. Panic danced through my body. I tried to
breathe slowly, but Inanna stirred, and rolled over, stretching like
a cat. And she saw me, and smiled, and reached for me. *And then
I knew exactly what I had done.*

Before she could see the look on my face, I bent to the wash-
bowl, and cupped water in my shaking hands, and splashed the
water on my face. I had to bring myself back. I had experienced a
kind of bliss, but now all I felt was torment. I had to get away from
her. I moved silently to the doors, but when I opened them, two
guards stood facing me, and waved me back into the chamber.
Inanna beckoned to me.

We rode out together on a pair of magnificent horses into the
fresh morning. Her henchmen watched me antagonistically, and
then turned their backs, muttering quietly to each other, as if they
knew something I didn't.

The sun blazed in the clear sky, adding a fine warmth to the cool, clear air. From time to time, Inanna glanced at me; we had been intimate, and yet now we were as distant as strangers. I felt like a stranger to myself; the world of my real life seemed far away. My friends were prisoners of this woman, and here I was, riding out with her as if I were her lover. The golden bliss of the drug still lingered inside me, but I felt as if I were trapped in a nightmare of betrayal from which I could not wake.

We rode along a busy way, passing between the fields that climbed the slopes of the wide valley. Above us, the grey and silver mountains glinted in the powerful morning light. The sloping opium fields were busy, full of men and teenage boys, their heads shrouded in cloths to protect them from the sun, working backwards through the crops, scraping the night's sticky harvest from the seed-heads into containers hanging from their necks, while younger children were set to weeding among the plants. Some workers were seeding newly ploughed fields. In others, the poppy plants bore new white flowers.

'Each crop comes to fruit in four moons. The Goddess rewards us,' Inanna said proudly.

She showed me a seed-head ready for scoring; it was dark green, and the crown, which had held the petals, was standing straight out. She produced the three-bladed knife with which she had cut Zannanza, and deftly pulled it upwards across the skin of the seed-head. It made only the shallowest of incisions, but instantly white tears of pungent sap appeared.

'The tears of joy,' she said.

'You need many hundreds of labourers to harvest the crop . . .'

'Everyone here belongs to me. This is my kingdom.'

'And they have no idea that each of them is harvesting something that could earn them fortunes beyond their dreams, in the cities of Egypt, and no doubt elsewhere?' I said.

She turned to me.

'And what would they do with such knowledge, or with such fortunes? I give them all they need, all they desire.'

'Surely some of your men know the value of the opium?' I suggested.

'They get their share. And besides, they would not dare to confront me,' she replied.

'Why not?'

'Because I would kill them,' she said, and spurred her horse forward.

We rode on until we reached a small collection of simple shacks surrounding an open area, and a mud-brick storehouse. Farmers had come to exchange their harvest of opium sap for food and grain, some lengths of cloth, and primitive tools. Poppy seeds were raked out in large areas in the sun to dry. Big cauldrons were boiling over open fires. Inside these, I saw to my astonishment, the opium sap was being cooked. I watched as a cauldron was skimmed of leaves and debris, and then the liquid strained through a cloth. What emerged was a steaming brown broth, which was heated again, until it thickened into a dark-brown paste that was shaped into bricks. She offered me one to hold; I turned it over in my hands, fascinated. It was sticky, but dry and relatively light – and above all, far more easily transportable than its liquid form, which required heavy clay jars.

We went into the storehouse. Shelf upon shelf held hundreds of blocks of the brown resin. At last I knew how the Theban gang had been able to supply such quantities of opium, and transport it across such distances.

'You are amazed!' she cried, delighted by the look on my face, and slipped her arm through mine.

'You are as rich as a goddess,' I said.

She nodded happily.

'Where do you sell it?' I said, nodding at the stacked shelves.

'Why do you ask so many questions?' she said. 'Why do you need to know such things?'

I had to be careful. If all of this were to save us, I had to remember Nakht's command. I knew I must take my chance, so I kissed her, and held her in my arms. She gazed at me warily, and finally allowed a wide smile to appear on her face. Her blue eyes shone. I kissed her again. Who was this traitor, who was doing these things? What was this feeling inside him? How could it be pleasure?

She led me out of the building, running with excitement. We cantered quickly away, and then followed a path, bordered with fruit trees and wild flowers, higher and higher, until we turned, and looked down at the valley, illuminated in the midday sun.

And then she pulled a jug of wine from her saddle and, arching her head back so that the red wine flowed expertly from jug to mouth, drank deeply. She wiped her lips, and passed it to me.

We sat on the grass in the sun, and looked down at the great valley of her extraordinary domain. Lying back, the echo of the opium's golden bliss still alive in my veins, I confess I suddenly felt a terrible temptation to let the weight of my old life fall away, as if into the earth and stones beneath me; all I would need to do would be to allow this strange, golden light in my body to enter my soul.

Suddenly Inanna was astride me, her magnificent hair glowing around her shadowed face as she gazed down. I reached up and held her breasts, then ran my hands down her body. She leaned down to kiss me lightly, her hair brushing my face.

'What do you see?' she asked.

'I see you,' I replied.

'You please me,' she said. And then she laughed, an open, honest laugh of delight. She offered me her hand. I took it, and we rose to our feet. But then she stopped me, and gazed intently into my eyes.

'But I do not yet trust you. The shadows of the past are still alive in you. I see it. But they will fade, as shadows do. You are here, now. You have awoken to a new world and a new life. You cannot go back.'

I assumed I would be returned to the cell, and to my friends. As we cantered into the stronghold, Inanna leapt from her horse, and shouted orders to her men. I jumped down from my own horse, but even as my feet touched the ground, I was surrounded, and my hands bound with cord. I was pushed into a different cell, and left there for the rest of the day. I shouted out to Nakht and Simut as loudly as I could, but received no reply. I sat with my head in my hands, in remorse at what I had done. The golden bliss had gone, and instead I felt gripped by a terrible new darkness. My body was wretched with tension. I paced the cell, trapped, desperate to be freed, kicking at the walls, trying to think what I could do to save us all, before it was too late.

As the evening light began to fade, the guards came for me; I was bathed once more by the women. The fresh water brought me to my senses. When the women's backs were turned to me, I grabbed my tunic and slipped away. I ran silently into the passageway, and then across the open ground of the forecourt. I made it most of the way to the cells before the men noticed me. They gave chase, and before I could get to my friends I was tackled to the ground, bound at the feet and wrists, and carried back towards Inanna's chamber.

Inanna was waiting for me. She seemed unconcerned by my attempt to defy her. She simply melted more opium over the oil lamp, and offered it to me. I refused, but I confess this time my blood cried out for it. Inanna summoned her guards, and they held me down. As soon as the golden calm, the slow bliss, the annihilation of all pain and anger hit me, I felt myself falling with a horrifying gratitude and relief into its beautiful embrace.

32

As we lay together once more, beside the lit lamp, a memory flashed through my mind of men and women, dazed with dreams, lying together in dark shadows. And then suddenly a woman's face, sorrowful, rose in my mind's eye, looking at me sadly. It was my wife, Tanefert. A door back to my old life opened briefly, and the pain of what I had done, as I recognized it in her eyes, touched me. But then the golden bliss persuaded me away into its glorious light, I felt my bones soften, my skin become light, and long waves of pleasure began to pass through me.

Much later, I awoke in the dark. The oil lamp had gone out. Suddenly I was certain someone else was in the room. I heard a sound, like a small laugh. I listened to the silence, my nerves straining. The darkness seemed alive, shifting with presences. I sat up.

'Who's there?' I whispered.

Again the strange little sound – laughter, or perhaps something moving in the dark like a tiny animal. My skin prickled. I stared into the blackness, seeing brief stars of light, and passing patterns of colour; and then I made out a small, dark shape standing at the edge of the couch. I stared harder. A little face suddenly swam out of the shadows: my son. Amenmose. He looked at me, and I was so happy to see him; but he was not smiling.

'When can we go fishing, Father?' he whispered.

I heard the words, but his mouth didn't move at all. He began to cry, and as he did so, his face crumbled and began to dissolve before my eyes. Fear like freezing water poured down my body. I leapt up to catch him, but he was gone, vanished; and in the darkness I suddenly discovered something else waiting at my feet. It was heavy. I lifted it up. Khety's dead head was in my hands. His eyes were shut, but his mouth was wide open, a sticky brick of opium wedged in it, and he was screaming with rage –

Inanna had her arms around me. I was shaking and shouting, my breath jagged, panic trapped like a wild animal in my chest. My legs moved madly, as if spiders were running all over them. I pushed her off, and ran across the room, desperate to escape; I threw the doors open, and ran down a passageway, hitting walls, feeling nothing, until suddenly I found myself in the compound yard. I looked up. The moon was high in the sky. Her bony white light illuminated the figures passed out on the ground; but these began to rise up before me, muttering, their hands reaching out to catch me. I ran towards the compound gates, but suddenly Inanna was standing there before me. I stopped. She came towards me, but I panicked again; then someone gripped me from behind, and dragged me to the ground. I heard myself screaming from far away, and I heard laughter and curses. And then I was trussed like a captured animal by my wrists and ankles, and carried back inside, back into Inanna's chamber. She made me lie down beside her, and she soothed me. I knew what I needed to restore me to peace: a new draught of golden liquid. She prepared it for me, and like a baby I took it; and I once more let go of the world, and entered the golden light. And somewhere deep inside me, I knew I was now truly lost.

33

'He is here,' Inanna said, shaking me awake.

She was already dressed, and the sun was high in the sky. I struggled to come to my senses; every morning when I awoke now, the walls wavered, and the floor rose and fell with each breath. Inanna looked apprehensive. She led me quickly to a smaller chamber, away from her own.

'Whatever happens, promise me: do not show yourself. Stay hidden here until I return for you. If he finds you . . .'

For once she looked strangely vulnerable. She kissed me, and vanished from the chamber. Outside, I could hear the shouts of men, the clattering of horses' hooves, and laughter. I lay back on the couch, and closed my eyes to stop myself feeling sick. But my legs itched with anxiety. I could not keep still. Then, in the blank space in my head, Khety's face appeared to me again. We were in the dark alleyway in Thebes; he was staring at me, with a look of terrible disappointment. I sat up, feeling a sharp stab of guilt. There was something I had to do.

I rose, and dressed myself, and carefully made my way along the passageway that led to the compound yard. The buildings were empty. The women and children had vanished. When I looked into the yard I saw Inanna and all her henchmen gathered together. Three men were lined up, on their knees, bound like captives, their heads hanging down. *Simut, Nakht and Zannanza.* How many days had passed since I last saw them?

Inanna was conferring with a man. He had red hair. I recognized his face at once: I had seen him in the great shadowy hall of the Hittites. Now he was here. Aziru. He turned to examine his prizes, one by one. His face was animated by an intense anger that seemed to burn through him. He nodded at the scar deforming Zannanza's beautiful cheek.

'Greetings, pretty Prince. Your brother, the Crown Prince, sends his greetings,' he said sarcastically.

'My brother?' stammered Zannanza, confused.

'Of course. He and I are close associates. Do you not know the depth of his contempt for you?' said Aziru, enjoying the cruel import of his words.

'My brother – *betrayed me*?' said the Prince, slowly.

'Well, yes. He has sentenced you to death, for fraternizing with the enemy. I am here to execute his command. And I must say, it will be a curious pleasure.'

He ran the point of his sword slowly down the Prince's cheek, and across the wounds made by Inanna's knife. The Prince flinched.

'I see my friend has already had some pleasure with you. I'm sure that's the first time you have given pleasure to any woman.'

'You disgust me,' said the Prince.

'The feeling is mutual,' replied Aziru. And then he turned to Simut, and placing his boot on my friend's head, ground his face painfully into the dirt, in the traditional gesture of kings to their defeated enemies.

'And this is the big man, the man of honour, the Commander of the Palace Guard.' He pressed his foot down harder on Simut's head.

'Not so big now . . .' he said, his face twisting.

Simut was silent. Then Aziru turned to Nakht.

'And here at last is the Royal Envoy himself. The great and noble Nakht. We meet again,' he said. 'Although in such altered and, for you, unexpected circumstances.'

And then, without warning, he kicked Nakht with all his might in the stomach. Nakht doubled over and collapsed on the ground, gasping for breath. Aziru stood over him.

'You thought you could manipulate me. But I am Aziru, King of Amurru. And I want revenge for my father, and for my-self.'

And then he kicked Nakht hard in the face. The royal envoy went flying back, his head twisted to one side.

'You thought you could use me. You thought I would do the bidding of Egypt. How foolish you were. How easily I convinced you. And then, when all was lost, you thought you could trap me, and have me killed. You thought you could negotiate my assassination with the Hittites. But you underestimated me. It is you who is caught. Now it is you who will die.'

With every sentence he administered another vicious kick to Nakht's body. Then he stepped back to admire his captives again.

'Is this not a pitiful sight? The effeminate little Hittite Prince, runt of the litter, bartered to the lonely soon-to-be widowed-Queen of Egypt. Imagine the dynasty of such a creature! A dynasty of females and eunuchs . . .' He kicked Zannanza hard in the groin, and the Prince gasped and gagged with the pain.

'All in all, it was a very witty move on the part of your brother, I must say, to persuade your father to send so useless a specimen in answer to his enemy's prayers.'

Then Aziru turned to Inanna, as if he had just thought of something.

'Four men were taken, and you have only offered me three,' he said.

'One died from his wounds,' she replied, quickly.

They stared at each other.

'I paid for four men, alive.'

'My men were over-zealous. Pay me for two men, then. I will give you the third for free!' said Inanna, lightly.

'Show me the bones of the missing man.'

'We left him in the desert,' replied Inanna.

There was a moment of tense silence; then Aziru said clearly: 'You are lying.'

'I am not,' she replied. And then, to my astonishment, she kissed him passionately, like a lover. Aziru responded, embracing her possessively, but then winding her wild hair in his fists, and dragging her head back, painfully. Her men bristled.

'The truth has never passed your foul lips,' he said, a nasty grin on his face.

Inanna shook herself free. He nodded to his men, who dragged Nakht apart from the other two men. Simut attempted to defend him, but he was kicked and punched to the ground. Then they dragged Nakht away by the feet, his head bouncing against the hard ground, until they disappeared into the main building of the compound.

'Keep them here in the sun, and give them no food or water. I will deal with them later,' ordered Aziru, nodding at Simut and Prince Zannanza. He disappeared into the building, his arm possessively around Inanna.

I ran around to the back of the compound buildings. Women and children were cowering there, terrified; they huddled away from me. I found a doorway and slipped into the rear of the building. A golden statue stared at me, its yellow eyes unblinking, accusatory.

I could hear distant voices. I slipped along the shadows of the passageway, away from the unreal light of the day. The voices were closer now.

'You are a traitor.'

'You trained me well. You thought you could send me back to the Hittites, as your trusty spy. And I made you believe I was loyal. All those reports I sent to you? *I made them up*. They were all lies.'

'I always knew your reports were lies. Do you think you were the only contact I maintained in Hattusa? Did you think I was ever fool enough to trust you?' It was Nakht's voice.

Then I heard the sound of a deep punch, and a sudden series of gasps. I glanced around the corner and saw Aziru squatting down over Nakht while Inanna watched. He grabbed him by the hair, yanking his face towards him.

'You offered me my freedom in exchange for betraying my own people. My father died at the hands of Akhenaten, and yet still you believed I could be controlled by Egypt. But I am my father's son. Amurru will be great again. Chaos will rule. Know this: all your plans have come to nothing. Egypt and the Hittites will always be at war until the stones of Egypt's temples are fallen. I will take pleasure in cutting off the pretty head of the Hittite Prince and sending it in a box, with my compliments, to your hopeless Queen, so that she will know her last chance has gone. She carries the future of Egypt in her empty womb; and that future is a desert.'

Nakht looked at him.

'You fool,' he said, with a new, dark contempt in his voice. He sounded unlike himself. 'You have understood nothing. You will never know the truth.'

'Oh noble Nakht, orator and master, your skills are of no use to you now. Words will not save you. I am going to make you confess all your secrets, so-called envoy of the royal court, spider at the heart of the web of secrets. And you will tell me them all, as I cut off your fingers, and then your hands, one by one.'

But Nakht's response to this was simply to close his eyes. Aziru was incensed.

'Don't you *dare* close your eyes,' he screamed, brandishing his polished scimitar. 'I am Aziru. I am a King! Look upon me. And know this: there is a force of darkness awake in this world. There is a great man whose shadow will fall upon this world, and none shall escape his vengeance.'

Aziru's face bore the mad grin of an enchanted fanatic, as he raised the blade high into the air, and held it there, the more to torture Nakht with fear and anticipation; but Nakht's eyes still remained closed. From where did my old friend find such strength to face his own death? He looked like a man at prayer, invoking from deep within himself the support of his God. Suddenly I felt anger rising up inside me like a storm. Aziru, too, was now beside himself, shouting: 'He will destroy all that has been. He will bring his darkness to the world. Do you know his name? You, envoy, keeper of the secrets, Scribe of all Truths? You do not know his name. Names are powers, and I invoke his name . . .'

Neither he nor Inanna saw me as I ran at him, tackling him from behind, and throwing him to the ground. His scimitar clattered away across the floor. I gripped his head in my hands and beat it with all my strength against the floor. He struggled like a demon, but rage gave me strength, and, though he turned to face me, I held his writhing body down like a snake's. My knees on his arms, I smashed his skull against the ground, over and over; his expression went from astonishment to rage, and as the back of his skull cracked open and caved in, to agony, and finally emptiness.

'You can stop now. He is dead,' said Nakht quietly.

Blood spread silently all around Aziru's shattered skull. I looked up. Inanna had disappeared. Nakht was standing very still, with Aziru's scimitar in his hand, a strange look on his face.

'Your loyalty is commendable,' he said.

'Come, let us find Prince Zannanza and Simut,' I said. 'Now is our chance to escape.'

But then, out of the blue, the remarkable, long, splendid note of a single Egyptian war trumpet reverberated through the air; and in the silence that followed, the sound of a thousand furious, hissing serpents rising up from the valley floor; and then we heard cries and shouts of confusion from inside the compound walls.

I ran to the entrance in time to see a second glittering volley of arrows rain down into the compound, thudding into the bodies of more of Inanna's men who fell like slain animals. The attackers had set fire to the compound gates.

'Who is it?' I shouted.

'*Horemheb*,' replied Nakht. There was a new light shining in his eyes.

If that was true, then everything was lost.

Without warning, units of Egyptian archers armed with magnificent bows and elite soldiers with shields, spears and curved swords leapt through the flames that had already consumed the wooden gates; the archers quickly and accurately picked off Inanna's men as they scrambled in wild confusion towards the compound buildings. More units of soldiers followed, fanning out with perfect discipline, killing everything that moved with merciless, scrupulous precision.

'Give me the scimitar!' I shouted. 'I'll hold them off for as long as I can.'

Nakht hesitated.

'I can't let you do that,' he said.

'You have to. Get back to Thebes. Warn the Queen. Look after my family. Tell them I love them.'

We stared eye to eye. For a strange moment I felt I was looking at the face of a complete stranger; something in his expression and in the poise of his body had changed, and I did not know him. He glanced along the blade of the scimitar, admiring it in the light, and fleetingly I imagined he might even strike me dead. Smoke was everywhere, and behind Nakht, along the corridor, I could see the red glow of fire. Suddenly he smiled.

'It is only by dying that we find everlasting life,' he said, mysteriously.

'This is no time for philosophy. Go now!' I shouted.

He grinned, and then, brandishing the weapon, he turned and ran into the billowing smoke.

Suddenly the chamber was full of Egyptian soldiers. They surrounded me, their swords at my throat; but I shouted: 'I am Egyptian! My name is Rahotep. This is the body of Aziru of Amurru. I killed him!'

'Don't move!' shouted one of them. 'Face down on the ground. Now!'

I complied. Then, from a side chamber, I heard Inanna shouting, as the soldiers dragged her out by her feet. She stared wildly at me and Aziru's corpse.

Another trumpet blast sounded the call of victory from inside the compound. I heard the clatter of more soldiers running in, hurriedly assuming a formal position; and then, when all was absolutely silent, someone entered the chamber.

'You have deprived us of the pleasure of capturing and interrogating this great enemy of Egypt,' said Horemheb, General of the Armies of the Two Lands. I was about to reply, but he pressed his foot down on my face. 'Be silent. Say not a word. I know exactly who you are, Rahotep. Your own interrogation will come soon enough.'

And then he turned to Inanna.

'Bring this revolting creature outside,' he said. 'And put that man in chains.'

34

My hands and feet were bound like a captive of war, and I was dragged out into the courtyard, and thrown down next to Prince Zannanza and Simut, who were both bound and gagged. Simut stared at me in amazement and something like contempt, and then turned his face away.

The compound buildings were on fire. Gusts of bitter smoke drifted into my eyes. Beyond the walls, in the great opium fields, fires raged hugely, turning the great sky dark red and black. The sun was a pale disc, trapped among the thick, billowing clouds of smoke. Everywhere, I heard screams and cries. I knew then that Nakht could not have escaped alive.

The Egyptian troops moved confidently and swiftly around the destroyed ground of the compound. I watched them pick up crying children, and the women who held them close, and hurl them by the arms or legs into the burning pyres, where they fell screaming amid little explosions of bright sparks, and rushes of crackling flame. It seemed to me the God Seth had truly returned to the world, destroying everything in his rage.

Horemheb strode among the horror, issuing orders, and calmly assessing the progress of the massacre. He turned to a line of Inanna's men, and one by one smote each of them like a king, caving in the backs of their skulls. Their bodies were cast on to the pyres as well. Inanna watched the execution of her army and the destruction of her kingdom with her head held high. On her face I saw a noble melancholy that touched me. And when it was all done, Horemheb ordered his men to hold her up by the hair. Her face was lit by the light of the fires. She looked around her world, knowing this was the end of her life. Finally, her gaze rested on me, and she gave me a look I will never forget, of pity and of loss. And then Horemheb slashed his sword across her throat; blood flowed down her bare breasts, and slowly she slumped forward. Then, in a final act of remorseless triumph, before she was dead, an officer hacked her head from her neck, impaled it on a pole, and stuck the pole in the ground. The soldiers cheered obediently.

And then Horemheb turned his attention to us. His blue-black hair was combed precisely from his imperious forehead. He wore a cuirass made of many overlapping black leather scales that imitated the feathered wings of a falcon. His shield, slung over his shoulder, was covered in cheetah skin, gilded along the edges, and with a gold plate in the centre bearing his name and office. These were the self-conscious trappings of a King; and he looked utterly self-possessed and confident wearing them.

His eyes were stony with contempt as he glanced at the three of us. He nodded to one of his men, who quickly removed the gags from Simut and Prince Zannanza. They coughed and spluttered, gasping at the smoky air.

'The Prince Zannanza, pointless son of our great enemies, the Hittites. The Commander of the Palace Guard, Simut. And

Rahotep, Seeker of Mysteries,' he said. 'I remember you well. You are a loyal servant of the Queen. And that of course is why you are here.'

'I am here by her command,' I said. 'Life, prosperity, health to her. I am truly her loyal servant.'

'Much good it will do you now. For with those futile words you have condemned yourself. And speaking of loyal servants, where is the Royal Envoy Nakht?' he said.

None of us replied.

'I know he was here with you. He cannot have escaped. My soldiers have conquered this valley and encircled this miserable hovel; they have orders to bring him to me alive. He will then be interrogated and executed. Stand up, Prince Zannanza, son of the Hittites.'

Zannanza did so, mustering all his courage to confront the general.

'So this is the weak boy they thought to marry to the Queen of Egypt,' he said. 'They thought with this trivial juvenile they could prevent my great victory.'

He paused and glanced at his men. They laughed subserviently, coldly. But Horemheb did not laugh.

'What should I do with you?' he said, his face now very close to Prince Zannanza's.

'Let me go home,' whispered the Prince. 'Let me go home . . .'

Horemheb cupped his ear, as if he had not heard properly.

'Speak up! Don't whisper like a girl.'

'Let me go home!' cried Zannanza.

'The Hittite prince wishes to go home!'

Horemheb's men sniggered. Horemheb made an exaggerated gesture to the Prince.

'Go, then. Please, sire. You are free! Do you know which way is home? I suppose it is a long way, so you had better start now.'

Prince Zannanza's face took on a new depth of despair.

'Go!' yelled Horemheb, whacking him hard on the back of the head. The Prince shuffled forward, his ankles and wrists still bound, taking tiny, terrified steps. Horemheb's men, in silence, opened up a path for him to pass through, towards the gates. Once he fell, but was hoisted to his feet, and pushed on. Finally he lost all strength, and sank slowly to his knees in despair. Horemheb came to stand before him.

'Are you still here, Prince?' he said mockingly.

The Prince raised his face. Horemheb slowly produced his sword. It was long and sharp.

'What are we going to do with you?' he said, as if to a truculent child.

'He is innocent. Do not kill him. Release him to his people!' I shouted.

Horemheb turned to me.

'None of you will be released. You are all traitors.'

And then he turned back to the Prince.

'Your time has come. Pray to your Gods now.'

Prince Zannanza uttered a few words of a prayer in his own language, and then the sword sang through the air, separating his head from his body, with a gust of blood, which spattered across the ground and raised a grim, mirthless cheer from the assembled soldiers.

Horemheb picked up Zannanza's head by the hair.

'Send this to his father, Suppiluliuma of the Hittites. And tell him there will be no marriage between Egypt and Hatti. Tell him there will never be peace. Tell him I, Horemheb, hold the royal crook and flail of the Two Lands, and Egypt has no need of his weak son!'

The officer bowed briefly, ran to a horse, and swiftly galloped out of the compound, Zannanza's once-beautiful head dangling from his fist and staring back sightlessly, as if he wanted to tell me something. The hairs on my neck bristled; I suddenly remembered Khety's screaming head in my opium dream; and an idea came to me.

Horemheb turned to Simut and me. The opium was betraying me again. I felt an intense frustration in my skin. I was crawling with something – it felt like spiders, or ants. I desperately needed to scratch myself, but my hands were bound.

'And here we have the leftovers. Kill them, and then burn everything. Leave nothing but ash,' said the general, and turned away. His men approached us, calmly unsheathing their swords for yet more bloodshed.

'If you kill us, you will never hear what I know,' I shouted to his back.

Horemheb turned back to me.

'What has happened to you, Rahotep? You are an opium addict – look at you, shaking like a lunatic. You are a disgrace to Egypt,' he said.

He turned away again.

'A platoon of the Egyptian army is smuggling opium into Thebes,' I said.

An expression of authentic surprise slipped unguarded across his haughty face.

'What did you say?'

'The General of the Armies of the Two Lands would wish to know if one of his own platoons had betrayed him,' I said.

'You are lying to save your skin,' he sneered. 'Besides, I have heard this story before. It was not true then and it is not now.'

'I am not lying. It is a platoon within the Seth division,' I said.

'You dare to accuse the Seth division of such corruption?' he drawled.

'Release me, and I will tell you why,' I said.

He hit me across the face.

'Do not bargain with me.'

I was beginning to feel awake again. My mind was clearing.

'The opium is not transported as a liquid, in jars. They have found a way to distil it into bricks, which are transported to the southern end of the valley, where they are collected, and paid for. These opium bricks are then smuggled all the way to Thebes, where a new gang has taken over the whole business from the old gangs.'

'How do you know this?' he demanded.

'It started with an apparently simple murder, in Thebes. Just another execution of five street kids, who were working for the cartels. They had been decapitated, as usual. But I saw it had been done expertly. Then a close colleague, a friend, was also assassinated, by the same gang. By the same killer. And everywhere they left their sign. I have it on a papyrus in my robe. Release me, and I will show you.'

He gazed at me for a long moment. Then he cut the ropes round my hands and I produced the papyrus of the black star, now tattered.

'This is the sign of the Army of Chaos. But the cartel in Thebes operates with similar ruthless efficiency and skill. They also leave this sign on the bodies of their victims,' I said.

Horemheb stared at me.

'Then the Army of Chaos has a foothold in Thebes, which is impossible.'

'Impossible. But there is another explanation . . .'

'Continue,' he said.

'Until recently, only relatively small, unreliable quantities of opium could be smuggled across the desert, or by river; just the usual petty black-market operation. But suddenly all that's changed,' I said.

'If you have a point, make it now,' he interrupted, glancing up at the sun, as if he had somewhere else he needed to be.

'A rogue platoon within the Seth division is smuggling the

opium. They buy it from here. They transport it themselves down to Egypt. They also control the Thebes operation.'

For a long moment he said nothing.

'Kill him,' he ordered, and began to walk away again.

'They are smuggling the opium inside the corpses of dead offi-cers, killed in the wars, and then repatriated for burial . . .' I shouted.

Horemheb stopped in his tracks. My life was in the balance. He could laugh, and then slice my head from my neck in the next moment. But he did not.

'What evidence do you have for such a grotesque, insane accusation?' he said.

'I am sure of what I say,' I offered. 'Evidence could be found. I know where to find it.'

'Where?' he demanded.

'In Bubastis. In Memphis. And in Thebes,' I replied.

'All you have is a series of assumptions and suspicions.'

'I have information. I make interpretations. It is what I do. I am a Seeker of Mysteries. And I know I am right,' I replied.

Horemheb considered me carefully.

'I despise the corruption of opium,' he said. 'It causes weakness and it undermines order. If there is any sign of this corruption within my army, it must be annihilated. I will see to it.'

Suddenly I felt my position slipping.

'There is no point destroying the supply chain! You have to attack the heart of the problem. You have to identify the culprits. There is a man, in Thebes. He is the overseer of all of this. They call him "Obsidian". Let me go, and I will bring you proof. And then you can annihilate the entire cartel. If I fail, kill me,' I said.

He turned his cold grey eyes on me.

'You have ten days. If you bring me this evidence, then I will act, and your life will be saved. If you do not, then I will arrest your family, and you will never see them again in this life, for they will be sent to Nubia, to labour in the gold mines for the short time left to them before the heat and the disease kill them.'

He approached closer.

'There is much at stake in these last days of the Queen Ankhesenamun's corrupt and dying dynasty, and my triumph will not be denied,' he said.

'I need the help of my colleague, Simut,' I said quickly.

'He is a prisoner of war, and he will be returned to Thebes for trial as a traitor of the new order,' he responded brusquely.

'He is essential to my investigation. He carries royal authority. Without him, it will be impossible for me to examine the army ships, to infiltrate the warehouses, to question witnesses . . .'

'I will give you that authority,' he said.

'I must not be identified with you in any way during the course of this investigation. It would reveal too much, if I were caught. This has to be clandestine. I must remain invisible, and all connections between us must remain secret,' I said, trying not to plead.

'Do not try my patience. I will not release him. He will still stand trial. He is a traitor. As are you.'

'If I succeed, grant me his life,' I said.

'There is a new order coming to Egypt, and I will not be persuaded by arguments of care. There will be no forgiveness. There will only be retribution. Starting with those who undertook this treasonable mission to marry the Queen to a Hittite and bring him to the throne of Egypt.'

And then he was gone.

PART FIVE

My mouth is given to me that I may speak with it in the presence of the Great God, the Lord of the Underworld.

The Book of the Dead
Spell 22

35

It was early evening. The oppressive heat of the day refused to lift from the port town of Avaris, just inside Egypt's border.

I had tracked the military convoy on foot along the last part of the Way of Horus as they transported another consignment of the dead. But I was in trouble: Nakht's death haunted and obsessed me. I had been sent on the mission to protect him, but I had failed him, as I had failed Khety. Now both my dear friends were dead. If Nakht had survived, he could have supported the Queen in her fight against Horemheb's occupation. But now she would be alone. I kept remembering the strange look on Nakht's face as he brandished the sword, and then ran into the smoke and flames. I could not stay still; I toyed with my dagger, over and over. My body shivered continually; an uncontrollable shaking tormented my legs; and the skin on my arms and legs was bleeding from the endless scratching. I had been unable to sleep or find any rest for days. I knew what was wrong with me. I craved the golden bliss of the opium dream. I had become the addict I once condemned.

I expected the cargo of coffins to be loaded directly on to a military ship bound for Bubastis; but instead they set off towards the military camp, accompanied by soldiers who peremptorily cleared their way through the crowds. They continued past a long row of warehouses, then turned a corner as if making for the huge tent city of the military camp; this occupied every free space between the port warehouses and grain silos, the massive new barracks under construction, and the ruins of the old citadel which lay behind. Despite the heat, bonfires burned in the shimmering late light, and sweating red-faced cooks toiled at brick ovens, serving the lines of soldiers waiting for food.

But the soldiers and their carts did not enter the camp compound either; instead, they moved towards the burial grounds, and the ruined walls of the citadel ahead of them. I followed behind, keeping within the lengthening shadows. The soldiers and carts continued beyond the burial grounds, too, until they passed through the citadel's broken gateway, and the old wooden doors creaked closed behind them. Then two soldiers discreetly appeared and stood guard.

Keeping to the shadows like a jackal, I scouted further away along the walls, until I discovered another way into the citadel: a section of wall had collapsed inwards into a broken slope of crumbling stone and mud-brick. I pulled myself up the outer wall of the citadel by my fingers and toes, grasping the crevices between the stone blocks, until I just managed to reach the top. Having hauled myself over, I scrambled down the slope of collapsed blocks, and was inside.

I crouched against the wall, sweating. My guts felt twisted and knotted inside me. The interior was haunted by shadows; everywhere animals had left their scents and their dung. Birds squawked and roosted in the crevices. In the distance I made out the sound of voices calling brief commands; I crept carefully through the darkness, feeling my way over the broken ground, until, around a corner, I found myself looking into a large courtyard. The carts with the coffins stood in the middle, and along one wall empty coffins were stacked upright, as if waiting for re-use. The foot soldiers were unloading the last of the coffins from the carts into a storage magazine. When this was accomplished, they loaded the carts with the empty coffins and, with a salute, drove away, accompanied by the officers on horseback. The great doors creaked closed behind them. The two soldiers who had stood guard at the gateway remained behind. The sun had now passed below the horizon, and the last golden light of the evening occupied the arch of the sky; but it would soon be dark. The two soldiers lit an oil lamp, and found comfortable places to sit and rest, while keeping their attention turned to the gateway doors.

Keeping to the shadows, I slipped silently along the wall of the magazine behind them, and entered. The interior stretched back into darkness. It was cool, but the stink of putrefying meat was overwhelming. The coffins – twenty of them – were stacked inside. Each one had the same hieroglyph drawn on it – Seth, God of chaos, storms, darkness and the desert, with his curved snout, forked tail and body of a dog. In the underworld of the abandoned citadel, before the marked coffins of the dead, I shivered; I could almost feel the dark presence of the God at my back, and his stinking breath on my neck.

The last of the evening light was fading fast; I prised off the crude wooden lid of one of the coffins. The almost-sweet stench of death instantly invaded my hair and skin. I forced myself to look inside: the body was wrapped in a thin layer of white linen bandages, stained and mottled yellow. Turning the body on its side, I slipped my dagger blade between the layers and as quietly as possible cut through the bandages. I carefully lifted them away, but the dead man's skin peeled from the body, too, where it had become stuck to the linens. The officer's side had been sliced open from his armpit down to his hip, and then crudely stitched together

279

again. The wound was yellow and blue. I quickly cut through the stitching, and the body cavity opened up. Some crude work had been done to preserve the body for its journey: all the viscera had been removed; the flesh had turned grey and green under the desiccation of the natron salts; and the corpse had been drained of its blood. Willing myself not to gag, I reached inside; to my profound relief, my fingers quickly discovered several wrapped packets. I withdrew one and, with the blade of my dagger, opened the packaging. And there it was, at last: a brick of sticky, brown opium. Evidence; proof of my contention, and the key to everything that lay ahead. I felt stupid tears of relief filling my eyes. With this, I could return to Horemheb, and save myself and my family.

But even with the relief of the discovery, something else possessed me: an overwhelming need to return to the golden bliss of the opium. My hands holding the brick were shaking. Hurriedly, I reached inside and took out three more packets. If each body held four packages, then this consignment of coffins alone would yield eighty packages of opium; a quantity of vast value on the streets of Thebes. How clever they had been to think of this grotesque method of transportation! Once the body cavity was emptied, I could see how the soldier's spine, ribs and thorax created an efficient storage area. The muscles of the abdomen looked like old leather.

And then it occurred to me to wonder how this officer had died. There seemed to be no bloodstains on the linens around the body. I unwound the bandages from his head. At the back they were hard and cracked with a mass of dried blood, and it was difficult to peel them away without also pulling off hair and skin. The man's dead face was dark blue and black, like a massive bruise. The muscles of his lips had shrunk and peeled back, revealing his poor teeth. His eyes were no longer white, but faded black orbs in the sockets, seeing nothing. Despite this, I could still tell he was young, perhaps eighteen years old – and definitely not an officer of any kind. This was a conscripted foot soldier, and there would be no reason to return his body to Egypt for an expensive burial. Usually he would have been buried where he fell. The platoon were not only smuggling opium; they were also using the bodies of low-level soldiers as the container. I looked at the ruin of his face, and tried to imagine him alive: a kid without prospects, who would have chosen soldiering, despite its reputation for misery and hopelessness, as the best, perhaps the only, way forward in his life. I managed to lift his head enough to peer at the skull at the back. I could see at once it had been smashed in with a single blow. This was not a battle wound, but a summary execution. And now I knew the secret within the secret. The platoon were murdering their own, to provide transportation for the opium.

Suddenly the stench of death, and my terrible desire for the opium, were too much to endure. I buckled over, gagging, trying to hold my bowels together, desperate to make no noise. But the guards must have heard something. They appeared together at the entrance, holding up their lamp, listening intently.

'You're imagining things,' I heard one of them whisper.

'No. I heard something,' said the other.

'Maybe they're not all dead. Maybe they're coming back to life . . .'

He made a noise like a spirit and suddenly gripped his friend around the neck. His companion laughed, shook him off, and stepped further inside the darkness.

'We'd better take a look.'

'Not a chance! This place scares the life out of me. There's nothing going on here. Come away . . .' said the other.

The suspicious one, holding the lamp, peered one last time into the dark, then shook his head, muttering: 'The sooner we get this consignment back to Memphis, the happier I'll be. I've had enough. I want out. I want to go home.'

'Once you've joined up, the only way out is in a coffin, isn't that what they say?' his friend replied.

'Obsidian has us all in his grasp,' said the one holding the lamp. 'Whoever he is . . .'

'They say he's not a man at all, but Seth returned to the world. They say he kills all who oppose or disobey him by cutting them to pieces while they are still alive. He has a blade, a black scimitar, which is so fine, so sharp, that it can slice open the air itself. They say it can even cut through time, and that is how he enters our world again, wherever and whenever he wills . . . He hears everything, he knows your thoughts, and he could even be here, now, right behind us . . .'

'Stop it! All I know is this: he demands loyalty, and those who fail him disappear, never to be heard of again,' said the other.

The men were briefly silent.

'Come. We're scaring ourselves. Let's do our job, and we'll have nothing to worry about,' said the suspicious one.

I froze in the shadows, hearing the name of Obsidian again, as if he had been conjured right before me. I knew he was not a god returned to this world. He was a man, and the murderer of Khety, and I would return to Thebes and destroy him, if it cost me my life.

I replaced three of the bricks and rewrapped the corpse, then slipped out of the magazine, made my way back along the dark passages of the citadel and, with the mad energy in my legs, clambered up the broken stones of the wall. An almost full moon had risen; the night was full of stars, and from my vantage point I could see across the dark burial ground to the camp bonfires and torches beyond, and further away in the distance the dark shapes of ships moored at the harbour, awaiting their secret cargoes. In my shaking hands I held one precious brick of opium. I knew I could never complete my mission if I tried to survive without it. I told myself I had no choice.

36

The following morning, the soldiers returned to the citadel, loaded up the coffins on the train of carts, and accompanied them back to a military vessel newly docked in the harbour. I watched as they carried each coffin up the gangplank and inside, with a performance of military honours. No port or military overseer examined the coffins or questioned the officers. I knew their destination: *Memphis*. I had to arrive first.

I took a space on the first passenger ship I could find; it was already crowded with traders, merchants and their goods, and as soon as I stepped aboard, and the Official of the River had checked our authorizations, we set off into the Great River, the big sail over our head, among its taut web of ropes, gathering the afternoon breeze into itself, and carrying us south, against the strong current.

As I sat listening to my fellow passengers on the deck, all were alive with rumour and speculation: Ay was dead, Ankhesenamun was isolated and hopeless, the End of Days was nigh, said some;

others, that Ay was still alive. No one spoke Horemheb's name aloud, although he was surely on everyone's minds.

I found a space apart; I wanted to be alone, to think, and to take more of the opium without being seen. I constantly felt the small bundle inside my bag to make sure it was still there. But an elderly pot-bellied merchant, whose business was in the trade of wood for shipbuilding, spotted me, introduced himself, and immediately started talking.

'The latest reports from Thebes are bad, very bad,' he said, with the strange pleasure men take in the discussion of impending disaster.

I said all I had heard was rumour. I had been away from the Two Lands for several months.

'Well, you might have done better to stay away. They say King Ay has died, but the palace is not revealing the truth for fear of what the uncertainty of the succession may provoke in the people. But in my opinion, by not saying *anything* they surely provoke even *greater* uncertainty!'

'But whether or not that is true, Queen Ankhesenamun still holds power,' I offered.

'How can she hold power, man? She's just a girl! I mean, yes – I wish it could be so, for her sake. And it's unfortunate the dynasty has come to a sad ending. It began with the great glory of Amenhotep the Magnificent – who I recall vividly, for I was a boy when he ruled – and all the great monuments of his reign. The processional colonnade, the great pylon at Karnak, and of course the royal palace of Malkata, which they say is a great miracle of a place, all were his works. But since then? We've had the disastrous days of his son, whose name I shall never be persuaded to utter, with all that nonsense about a new religion, and the madness of the priests turned out of their temples. Everything was thrown up in the air, and nothing came down right.'

He leaned closer towards me, his index finger raised like a teacher.

'And then it got even worse with his son – Tutankhamun. You can't tell me that wasn't a sign from the Gods. I mean, I'm sorry he died young, and the tragedy was very great, of course; but I don't think he'd ever have made a strong king. He was weak as water. Can you imagine him smiting the enemy? Destroying them in battle? Having the guts to execute the opposition?'

'Perhaps it's time we had a king who didn't do that. Perhaps it's time we had a king who had other values on his mind,' I said, playing nervously with my dagger to calm the growing anxiety inside me.

'Like what?'

'Reform of corruption. Civil order to prevent the abuses of power. Justice.'

The old man waved his hands dismissively in the air.

'What world are you living in? This is *Egypt*. Justice is for children. At the end of the day, gold talks,' he said, rubbing his fingers together. 'We need a strong king now, not a pretty girl. Don't get me wrong, I pity the Queen, I do – imagine sharing a throne and a couch with Ay, who's even older than I am! That can't have been a pleasure, can it? Although I do know women respect a powerful older man . . .'

And he prodded the grumpy woman sitting next to him, who pitched in: 'Do they? Well, I'm this one's wife, and I can tell you it's no pleasure sharing a throne and a couch with *him*,' she said. 'When he's not talking, he's snoring and keeping me wide awake. That's the long and the short of *his* powers.'

The old man shook his head.

'Well, mark my words. We're going to have to celebrate the festival of a new king very soon. The general's a man of the world. He knows one end of a sword from the other. He's fought wars. He's beaten the enemy. He'll bring back order,' he said.

'I pity the Queen,' said the wife, sadly. 'She's only a young woman alone in a world of bad men. I hate to think what they'll do to her now. I wouldn't be her for all the gold in Nubia.'

Once I had taken more of the opium and its golden bliss had calmed me, I sat looking out at the passing fields, where it seemed the terrible history of kings and generals never mattered, for the crops were ever the same, and the men and women toiling there unchanging in their endless labours. As I listened, the children along the water's edge seemed to be calling into the golden dusk of a different world. I glanced back up the river, looking north. At this moment only fishing boats and a few cargo ships occupied its shining, languid waters. But in the next few days, Horemheb's ships, loaded with thousands of soldiers in their divisions, would be sailing into Memphis, in preparation for the taking of Thebes. I thought of Ankhesenamun alone in her palace, and I wondered what I, an opium addict, and a disgraced man, could do to save her from the general's revenge.

37

Hundreds of ships were crowded along the wharves of the great harbour of Memphis; regiments of soldiers marched down the gangplanks of transport boats and gathered in long lines on the quays awaiting their next orders. Horses and chariots were driven from their stalls, and the rich booty from the wars was unloaded by dockers and then swiftly transported away to the army depots by stevedores. Vast cargoes of grain were being measured by the weighers and their overseers, while scribes noted the trans-actions.

I went to the northernmost point of the docks, and settled down to wait, with a fresh roll to eat and a jug of beer. The jitters in my legs, and the crawling of invisible spiders through my hair and across my skin had faded as more opium calmed me. Around mid-afternoon, I spotted the military ship carrying the coffins among the busy river traffic. She negotiated a space on an outlying wharf, and docked. I watched as the gangplanks were lowered and a small military escort swiftly drew up with carts.

Once more, there was a performance of military honours. The Official of the Dock and his scribe merely bowed their heads, and signed a papyrus of authorization; then the coffins were unloaded and driven away on the carts.

As they passed swiftly through the dock gates I saw one of the officers dismissing the port guards, who bowed and let them pass without checking their authorizations, and they set off along the paved stone ways of the city. I hailed a passing cart, loaded with vegetables, and bribed the driver, a surprised young lad, to follow them.

'Where to, master?' he asked enthusiastically.

'No questions. Just follow those carts,' I said.

He grinned. 'Yes, boss!'

We followed them into the centre of Memphis, towards the district of the Temple of Ptah, whose pylons, enclosure walls and huge statues towered above the rooftops of the city's buildings. But they did not pass across the open, western forecourt, choosing instead a series of side streets containing small businesses, and leading away from the city centre. They continued onwards until, just beyond the edge of the great city, they finally paused outside a well-kept workshop behind high enclosure walls; the gates were swiftly opened, and they disappeared inside.

'Go on, tell me what this is all about,' said the boy.

'Sorry. I can't,' I said. 'But know this; you've served the empire well today.'

His face lit up. I paid him off, and he drove away. The area I found myself in was inconspicuously ordinary; other workshops were scattered around, dirt tracks led in different directions, the shadows were occupied by sleeping dogs and unemployed men, and the dusty, derelict grounds between the buildings shimmered with heat.

I walked up to the entrance of the embalmers' establishment, and saw the hieroglyph of Anubis, the Jackal, the One in the

Place of Embalming, carved over the lintel. From inside I heard the sound of women weeping. I could smell death over the high wall. I knocked on the door.

Groups of mourners were gathered in the long, low public room. Some were waiting for the delivery of their relatives, ready for burial after the long rituals of mummification, while others, newly bereaved, keening and weeping, had come to negotiate with the embalmer. Two young men, neatly dressed, moved among them, taking orders, noting details, discussing the choice of coffins, and applying their consolations and commiserations with practised finesse. One nodded respectfully to me, indicating he would attend me as soon as possible.

Along one wall were displayed various coffins with different prices: cheap, simple boxes of roughly cut timber painted over with white plaster; and more costly ones in the form of a person, thinly gilded all over, with bands of painted inscriptions, and the wings of the Goddess Nut spread protectively over the lid. And then there were offerings of other necessary paraphernalia: canopic jars and chests of various qualities; gold-leaf eyes and tongues; gold finger-caps; masks; much funeral jewellery; heart scarabs and necklaces of scarabs; protective *wedjat* eyes; amulets of Isis suckling the baby Horus, of Anubis, the Jackal, and of Bes, the little ugly spirit who scares away demons; and tiny glazed hands, legs, feet, and hearts.

The two men – who looked like brothers – were preoccupied with their customers, and when both were turned away, I slipped through the doorway at the back. In contrast to the neat order of the public room, here everything was a mess of planks of wood and piles of supplies and materials. Ahead stretched a shadowy passage; I made my way carefully past a small, empty office where papyrus scrolls were scattered in great disorder. Next came the carpenters' workshop; the sweet scent of wood shavings briefly masked the stench of dead bodies. I saw coffins in different stages

289

of completion. An old man was focused upon his work, hammering and carving.

I continued down the passage, until it opened out into an open yard. On the far side, two bandagers were chatting casually as they quickly bound the feet of a desiccated corpse that had come to the end of the embalming process. Other withered, blackened bodies were waiting for their attention, stacked together on a cart. One worker sneezed, taking no care to protect the corpse, and the other laughed, and I took the chance to move past them, beyond more storage buildings, and peer into another courtyard. Here the stench intensified, for this was where the embalmers' first work was undertaken. Perhaps ten corpses lay in the shade, on sloping slabs, their sides slit open, their internal organs not yet removed. Others, already eviscerated, were hidden under mounds of natron salt. And several new arrivals simply lay, undignified, naked and dead, in the open air, awaiting attention. There was a large guard dog chained in the corner, his head on his paws, watching and waiting.

I could smell resin being warmed; and then a man appeared, carrying a wide pot of resin with a brush in it, along with a flint knife and a sharp, pointed instrument. The guard dog immediately sat up. Seemingly oblivious to the appalling stink, the man set the pot down, laid the knife alongside the naked corpse of a fat, middle-aged man, and then, as if this were the most normal thing in the world, he inserted the point of the tool up the man's nose and jabbed hard. I heard the sound of bone cracking. Whistling, he took out the tool, inserted a long, thin spoon, and began to scoop out brain matter, scraping around carelessly inside the dead man's skull; and this he flung casually at the attentive dog, who eagerly gobbled up the offering. This work completed, he sliced along the side of the corpse, and the yellow fatty flesh opened up quickly. He rummaged around inside the body with his knife, tugging and cutting and drawing out organs, which he threw equally casually into a pot at the foot of the table. Then he set about painting the face of the man with the warm resin.

While the guard dog was preoccupied with his snack of brains, I quickly moved across the courtyard towards another opening on the far side. I hurried down the darkness of a passage, but quickly backed into a doorway, for just ahead of me, soldiers were unloading the coffins from a backyard area into a storage room. I listened to their feet coming and going, and their grunts as they worked, carrying and setting down the heavy burdens. And I heard two men's voices, speaking in a low tone to each other. I couldn't make out what they were saying. There was clearly a problem. And then their voices faded as they walked back into the yard. I inched my way along the wall, and peered into the storage room; inside, the coffins marked with the sign of Seth were laid out on the ground, with their lids removed. The twenty dead soldiers gazed up sightlessly at the ceiling. And along one wall, as I knew, seventy-nine packages of opium were stacked. One was missing, because it was in my satchel. No doubt they had now discovered that.

I made my way back as quickly as I could; but the guard dog spotted me and barked furiously. The embalmer looked up. I offered a confident greeting, and continued back towards the shop. Suddenly, footsteps hurried towards me, and the two brothers appeared, alarmed. The embalmer approached, too, knife in hand. I raised my hands.

'I was looking for somewhere to piss. I got lost. If you're free, can we discuss arrangements for my brother now?'

Attended by the man with the knife, the brothers surrounded me, questioning me loudly. I continued to protest my innocence, and to talk about my dead brother. Then a large man appeared, quickly coming up the passageway; obviously the father of the brothers. He had a face made for dealing with the dead – cold, pious and hard.

'What's going on?' His was the voice of one of the two men in the backyard.

'He says he's here for his brother's body,' said one brother.

'He says he needed a piss,' said the other.

'This is a private area. Why didn't you ask, like any other customer?' asked the father.

'These gentlemen were busy with other customers – I see how very busy you are – by the Gods, death has much to answer for in these days, doesn't it?'

They stared at me. I allowed my shivering to turn into a fit of grief. 'I'm sorry. The truth is – I don't know what happened – I was suddenly overcome, and I didn't want to show my grief in public. I am sure you understand. We were notified my dear brother had been killed in honourable battle, and his coffin would be returned here. I have come to reclaim his body.'

I stared at the ground, shaking my head sorrowfully, and drying my eyes. The father considered me.

'My condolences. Your brother gave his life for the greater good of Egypt. Now, if you will just return to the front office with my sons, they will take down your details, and we will gladly assist with the necessary arrangements.'

38

I stood before Horemheb, in his office within the Memphis military compound. At first his handsome, cold face betrayed nothing as he stared out of the window. 'These men will be arrested immediately! I will interrogate them myself, and then they will be executed. They have disgraced the army and the Two Lands of Egypt.'

But this would not serve my purpose.

'Consider again, lord. Only two people know about this: you and I. These men have no idea we know about their activities. But they are not the important ones. They are the workers, not the head. We must track the shipment of opium to Thebes, to see where it goes – to see who receives it. To see who is behind the operation that is selling the opium on the streets. Those are the key men. The killers.'

He stared suspiciously at me. I had to persuade him.

'There is still more to this. There is a commander who runs it all. He has a code-name. *Obsidian.* I believe he's one of *your* men. He is extremely dangerous. He created and instigated everything, inside the Egyptian army itself, inside the Seth division, for his own profit. Such a man is extremely dangerous to you. Imagine how much power he commands. Imagine the disastrous effect of his work. Imagine what could happen if he has power in Thebes, *especially at this highly sensitive moment for the Two Lands . . .*' I said.

I let the implications of that do their own work; for if Obsidian were not caught, Horemheb's ability to command the city would be severely compromised. Worse still, if the corruption came to light, his claim to the royal succession would be profoundly damaged, no matter how many divisions he ordered to take over Thebes, no matter how brutally efficient the martial law he might impose. Horemheb's face was taut with suppressed rage at this unexpected flaw in his grand plan.

'*Find this Obsidian.* But I want him alive. Keep me informed at all times, and when the moment comes, I will personally command the troops that attack these traitors, and I will destroy them and their filthy trade. All corruption will be wiped out in the new Egypt; none will be tolerated. And I will personally silence this Obsidian. Be sure you deliver him to me. You know the price of failure,' he said quietly.

I nodded and turned away. He had given me what I wanted: permission to track down Obsidian. But he was *my* prize, and I would never give up the satisfaction of my revenge for Khety's death, not to Horemheb or anyone else.

As I passed through the doorway, he called out: 'And remember this, Rahotep. I don't trust you. I won't hesitate to destroy you if you put one foot out of place. You have three days to accomplish everything. Ay is dead. A storm is coming to Egypt now, a storm that will cleanse and purify the corruption and the chaos into which we have descended as a result of the selfish decadence of the so-called royal family and those fat, self-satisfied priests. Their time is over. My time is now.'

39

When the pylons and great walls of the temples of Thebes finally appeared before me, rising above the river waters and the surrounding cultivation, after so long away my heart brimmed over with the emotion of homecoming. Ra shone brightly upon the city that held my wife and my family.

But I confess, too, that the beautiful light seemed a cruel illusion. Little did the citizens of this great city know of the dark storm that would soon change everything: Horemheb and his divisions were on their way, to occupy the streets, palaces and offices of the city, and bring the arrests, executions and wholesale destruction that would surely follow, as he grasped power, took the Crowns, destroyed the carved names and faces of the statues of the old dynasty, and asserted his new dynasty. But more than even that, I was the only one of the original party to return alive: Nakht had died at Inanna's compound; Simut was in chains, condemned; Zannanza had been brutally assassinated. And now Ankhesenamun was doomed.

And as for me, I was an opium addict, and until I was no longer in the grip of such craving, I would not allow my family to know me. Still worse, how could I find the courage to tell my wife of my actions? Before I could walk through the gate and back into my home and my old life, I would somehow have to atone for the dark truth of what I had done. And so, as I set foot once more on the stones of the city of my birth, I felt I was more a shadow than a living man: a thin black silhouette, separated from my old self and my old life.

News of Horemheb's impending occupation, and of Ay's death, must already have circulated, for there was a strange, new tension in the air of the city. Many smaller ships were being loaded with trunks containing personal possessions, as the rich tried to save their families and worldly goods by shipping them out of the city and down to their country houses. Crowds of merchants clamoured to buy cargoes of grain as if they were the last ever. Fear had already begun to grip the city. We had lived like gods on borrowed time, and now that dream was over.

In the small hours, three nights earlier in Memphis, I had watched the opium packages being transported from the backyard of the embalmers' and loaded on to another, smaller commercial ship. I had watched the Official of the Dock sign the papyrus of authorization for the cargo, and give it back to a man dressed in military clothing. I had not recognized him. He and several other accomplices had then boarded the boat to accompany it to Thebes.

It had arrived at noon. I stood in the shadows and kept watch. Nothing happened until the sun set. Then, in the dark of the night, more men appeared, and carried ten wooden crates down the gangplank to a waiting cart. I followed it into the city. The moon was full, and its bone-light lit the streets. The single cart was accompanied by armed guards, running before and after in silence. They did not travel far. They turned past the Southern Temple, and then followed its eastern wall before turning into the spreading labyrinth of the eastern suburbs and their narrow side streets. I knew these streets and passageways well, for I had lived and worked there as a Medjay officer all my life. Some were thoroughfares with shops and markets, others were dedicated to different trades where the workshops opened directly on to the street; others still were low passages only wide enough for one man. So I ran through these, following the map of the place in my head, glimpsing the progress of the cart down dark alleys and side ways.

Finally, it stopped at the high wall of a merchant's warehouse. The great wooden doors were immediately opened, and it drove in. I waited, breathless, listening to the sounds of the night city, which I seemed to hear intently, in enormous detail – the barking of the dogs across the districts, the cry of night birds, and the uncanny silence of the streets. I approached warily. Nothing distinguished the house from any other, except that its walls were high, it was separate from the buildings around it, and there was only one entrance. Disappointed, I found a discreet doorway in the shadows, and settled down to wait. The cart did not reappear, but all through the night, men in groups appeared in silence, knocked quietly, and were admitted – perhaps twenty altogether. None, however, left.

As I waited in the darkness, Ankhesenamun's face began to haunt me; I remembered the warmth of her greeting, all that time ago, before we began our journey north. I remembered the fear in her eyes, and her noble call upon my loyalty to her. She was alone, in that lonely palace. Perhaps she had intelligence about Horemheb's imminent arrival in the city; perhaps she was preparing to escape. But perhaps she was trapped there, unaware. Without Nakht to support her, or Simut to protect her, maybe I was the only man in the world who could help save her from the coming storm.

So when the night sky began to turn blue, and the first workers appeared in the dark streets, coughing and hawking and spitting phlegm, and still no one had appeared from the merchant's house, I made my choice. I gambled that Obsidian would not appear in daylight. I had very little time.

40

The palace corridors were crowded with men and priests, followed by servants and assistants carrying piles of papyrus scrolls, going about their duties with an air of desperate purposefulness, as if even now meetings and high-level decisions could somehow make a difference to the coming catastrophe. Probably they were all jockeying for position, stabbing each others' backs, and working out how they could plausibly ingratiate themselves with the general, when he finally occupied the city.

I walked through the crowds without being questioned; and no one stopped me until I came to the doors to the royal apartments themselves. The guards took one look at me, and barred the way, calling to their colleagues to send more officers to arrest me for trespass. I tried to use Nakht's name, and I invoked Simut's authority, but they only glanced at me quickly, evasively. They forced me down, their knees in the small of my back, until I was pressed flat to the ground, and could not even speak.

'What is happening here?' I suddenly heard a superior, commanding voice. 'Who is this man?'

I recognized the voice. It was Khay, Chief Scribe to the palace.

The guards twisted me until my face was revealed.

'*Rahotep?* Is it possible . . . ?'

Khay was suddenly, imperiously, in command.

'This man has essential business with the Queen!' he exclaimed to the guards. He set about their heads with his staff of office.

He took me through into an antechamber of the great Audience Hall.

'We learned the news of your death. How is it you are alive, and standing here before me?'

'I have to speak to the Queen. I will speak only to the Queen.'

He considered me, and finally nodded.

'Come.'

And so I was announced and admitted into the Audience Hall, and into Ankhesenamun's presence once more. I walked towards her, between the columns, and once more past the walls inlaid with coloured tiles depicting the great victories of Egypt over her captive enemies.

The Queen was seated on her throne, upon the raised dais, wearing the Blue Crown with its worked decoration of discs, and at the front she wore the gold cobra head. She held the crook and flail, because she was now indeed ruler of Egypt. She was surrounded by her advisers and hangers-on, wearing their insignia of office, whispering confidentially to each other, or addressing her with desperate advice – all trying to save their own skins. But when she noticed me, she suddenly stood up. All stared at me, as at a spirit returned from the Otherworld. I prostrated myself.

'Life, prosperity, health.'

The words of the formula had never before had such intense meaning for me.

The Queen dismissed her advisers with a gesture of her bejewelled hand, and they backed away, bowing and muttering along the length of the columned hall. Once they had all left, and the doors were closed, we were alone.

'Stand up, Rahotep. Approach the throne.'

I did so. To my astonishment, she suddenly threw her arms around me. I carefully held the slim body of the Queen, our living God, in my arms. Rage and despair had kept me going all these days. And now her extraordinary gesture moved me so deeply, I almost cracked and wept. When she looked up, her face was wet, her eyes shining. A lock of her own black hair, which had been hidden under the crown, hung down around her ear.

'I knew you had arrived safely in Hattusa. But when no news came to me of success, or of your return, and there was only silence from the messengers, I believed the worst had come to pass . . .'

Suddenly the events of the journey ran through my head in a wild spool of impressions and emotions. Something very painful was welling up from deep inside me, and I found I could not speak. She motioned me to sit on a chair. I gripped the goblet of wine she offered me with both hands, to prevent my attack of the shakes becoming apparent.

'But you are alive, Rahotep, and you can tell me everything that has happened, and how you have been able to return, at last . . .' she continued.

I wanted to tell her about Prince Zannanza, Aziru and Nakht, but first I said urgently: 'I have come to warn you. Horemheb is massing his forces. He will soon march into Thebes . . .'

'I know,' she replied. 'I have known for some time. His deputies are loyal to him. The divisions will support him.'

'So you must prepare . . . There is still time . . . Or else you must take refuge. Or sail out of Egypt, find a secret place . . .'

She raised her hand to silence me.

'No, Rahotep. You have seen how things are. My allies are in disarray. My palace guard has lost its finest, now that Simut cannot command it. All is lost. But I am still Queen of Egypt. I will not run and hide,' she said proudly. 'I will face my destiny with dignity.'

'And Ay?' I asked.

'Ay died soon after your departure. We kept it a secret for as long as we could. His tomb was finished long ago, and his body is now being prepared for eternity. And Horemheb will soon be here. I know he will not let me live.'

I saw fear suddenly slip across her face, even though she was trying to look strong and composed.

'I can tell you, of all people, the truth, Rahotep. I am afraid. But at least I have seen you once more . . .' she said.

Foolish tears startled my eyes. I felt the uncontrollable shaking threaten to possess me again.

'All is not lost. I will command your guard. We will fight. You must speak to the people: there are still many in the city who will oppose the general . . .' I said.

She gripped my hand hard.

'You are a loyal man, Rahotep. But listen to me now. I have no troops. I have no forces with which to contend against the general. I have learned enough to know that when power starts to slip away, it is very soon gone. Those who have been so faithful, so loyal, must now choose – not for my sake, but to save their families, for survival. You have done me great service, and I wish I could repay you better. But you, too, must go to your family and be with them. They need you now,' she said.

'I will not abandon you!' I said.

'I command you to. You must go!' she said firmly. 'If you do not, I will call the guards.'

'*I will not go.* There is one last chance. Listen!' I shouted. I suddenly realized I was gripping the Queen by the shoulders, and almost shaking her.

'Horemheb released me for a reason. There is a platoon within the army that is corrupt. They have been smuggling opium into Egypt, under everyone's noses. Horemheb, the famous general, had no idea! But I know where they are based, and how they operate. I know where they store the opium, and no doubt the gold they earn from the trade. You can use this information against him. His claim to power will be fatally undermined . . .' I said.

She stared sadly at me as if I were mad.

'But, Rahotep, this is an old story, and, besides, it isn't true.'

'It is. The platoon is here, in Thebes. It has a leader, his code-name is Obsidian, he is at the heart of the mystery . . .' I said.

'What has happened to you, Rahotep? You have changed. I hardly recognize the man I knew.'

She was crying silently now. I could not bear it.

'I will not give up! I will prove this, and then we will confront Horemheb. It is what Nakht would have done,' I shouted.

'Nakht?' she said.

'He died for you. He was killed by Horemheb's men. And I will not let his death be in vain.'

She looked at me strangely.

'But it was Nakht who told me of your death, and those of Simut and Zannanza,' she said carefully. 'He told me you died saving his life. It is he who has advised me there is no hope.'

At these words, something dark clicked into place deep inside me, and the blackness in my heart was complete.

41

I stood, a shadow in the shadows, and watched Nakht's mansion. The golden strength of the opium coursed through my veins. With shaking hands, I had taken the last of it. Now everything was vivid and pin-sharp once again, my mind lucid and my heart clear. I welcomed the perfect God of Revenge as he took possession of me. The time had come.

The guards were on duty at the gateway. The street was thronged with the usual traffic of carts and chariots, and the crowds of mid-afternoon. I was waiting to see my children. Soon I saw them walking towards the house, accompanied by armed guards. They held hands, but they weren't smiling; their faces were heavy, and they didn't speak. All their usual vivacity had vanished. Then Tanefert suddenly appeared at the great door to the house, waiting to greet them. She was wearing a robe in the pale-blue of mourning. She held herself tightly, as if something was broken, and she was holding the parts together. She looked thin and exhausted. As the girls arrived, she enfolded them into her embrace, kissed their heads, and then, as if the noise and life of the world was too much to bear, hurried them inside. I desperately wanted to call out to them all, to reveal myself, to run across the street and sweep them into my arms. But suddenly Nakht himself appeared in the doorway; his smooth face, his perfect robes, his hawk eyes, gave nothing away. He glanced up and down the street, and then disappeared inside.

I settled down to wait. Darkness would reveal the truth. I had not slept for several nights now, but the opium gave me a new intensity of wakefulness and animal power. My long vigil was eventually rewarded. In the late hours of the night, the great door opened briefly and a dark figure, his head covered, slipped out and moved swiftly along the empty street, accompanied by two guards. They were well-armed; but now so was I, with weapons borrowed from the palace armoury. The figures crossed into the shadows of a side passage and disappeared. My hunting instinct was alive in me now, and I already guessed where they were going; I followed, tracking their progress through the dark labyrinth of the city. I arrived at the merchant's house in time to see the figures slip through the big wooden doors.

I stood in the shadows, listening intently for any sound from the house. I watched the full moon as she moved slowly across the dark ocean of the night, and the great stars wheeled around her. Eventually, in the darkest hour of the night, when she was about to sink below the horizon, the doors opened once more, and the cloaked figure slipped out, accompanied by his two guards. I ran silent as the moon through the dark ways of the city, found the place I had decided upon in my head, where several lanes merged into a small open space, and waited. I was ready.

As the group of figures appeared, I sent an axe hurtling through the shadows with all my strength; it thudded exactly into the centre of the first guard's forehead with a crack, and he slumped to the ground. The cloaked figures of Nakht and the other guard stopped in their tracks, trying to identify their attacker; the second guard moved quickly on his feet, fully-concentrated, coming towards me, his curved blade slicing at the shadows before him. I tormented him with a scatter of small stones cast against the wall beside him. He turned, and I plunged my scimitar deep into his belly, jerking the curved blade sideways until his guts spilled out, warm and slippery, into his clutching hands. His face tipped up to the stars; it was Nakht's manservant, Minmose. Perhaps he recognized me, for he muttered something; but the blood in his mouth choked him, and he died. I lowered his body to the ground.

The hooded figure had already disappeared silently into the narrow streets. But he didn't know his assailant was me; nor did he know I knew exactly where he was going. And above all, I knew how to get there faster. I ran like a jackal, with the supreme power of the opium surging through me; and I was waiting for him in the shadows opposite the door of his mansion when he arrived, breathless and silent. The moment had come. Just as he reached his door, and safety, I stepped into the street and revealed myself. He stared at me.

'Show yourself,' I said.

'Why?' he replied. 'Do you not know who I am?'

'I want to look upon the face of Obsidian.'

'Obsidian has no face,' he replied.

'We have that in common, then. I, too, am a shadow returned from the Otherworld to feed upon revenge. So show yourself. Or is the great Obsidian afraid?'

He slowly slipped off the hood. In the moonlight, the face was familiar, and yet now it seemed possessed by a stranger. I knew him and I did not know him. His eyes were black stones.

'Names are powers. You should use them carefully, with respect,' he replied. 'They bring the forces of eternity to life in this world.'

'You lied to me. You left me to die.'

Obsidian's face betrayed no emotion.

'Have you not discovered there is so much more to yourself than you ever believed? And is it not so much darker than you could ever have imagined?' he said.

I took another step closer to him. I could see a faint sweat on his skin. His right hand held on to a hidden weapon. He stood poised, like a different man entirely.

'I have lost my family,' I said.

'All earthly things end. But the way forward calls you now to something far greater . . .'

'Don't talk that rubbish to me. I know you too well,' I said.

'You do not know me at all.'

'*I want my life back*,' I hissed.

Obsidian almost smiled.

'Your old life is gone. It's finished. But there is a place for you, in the future of a new world, without dynasties – if you join me now.'

I tightened my grip on my scimitar.

'What future? Ankhesenamun cannot prevail now. Horemheb will occupy Thebes. Nothing you have done will prevent that calamity. You have simply made it possible,' I said.

'The royal dynasty is finished. General Horemheb is a soldier without imagination. He believes he will bring "order" to the land. It is a shallow ambition. He would stifle the priesthood, and impose his own dynasty. Egypt is the greatest of all empires. But it has for too long been ruled by kings and dynasties, beset by vanity and jealousy. That shall be no more. There will be no more kings. And that is not all. There will be no more worship of the Gods, for they too have failed. Only Osiris, Lord of the Dead, eternally incorruptible, will rise again at the midpoint of the night, reborn in me. When Ra ascends tomorrow, time itself will begin again, a new age and a new world,' said Obsidian. 'It is I who will prevail.'

Somewhere in the distance a dog howled, and another answered. It would soon be dawn.

I took another step forward. With the next I would be close enough to slay him. But he was prepared, too. He watched me carefully. The city was silent all around us. I looked up at the eternal ocean of the night, glittering with stars. A harrowing sorrow entered my heart.

'I have one last question,' I said.

'Of course you do,' he said.

'Why did Obsidian kill Khety?'

'You already know the answer to your own question,' he said, simply. 'Because *you* told me about him. Your own words condemned him. And now here we are.'

He might as well have cut my heart out with his knife. I had told Nakht about Khety for the first time on the boat, on our way to the palace. I had trusted him.

He took one more step towards me.

'You have looked into the dark mirror of the truth, so you now understand.'

He touched his heart. And when he smiled, I attacked.

Our swords sliced through the moonlight. His was made of obsidian; a long, black, deadly, shiny blade, honed to the finest edge. This was what had cut off the head of my friend. This was the blade that had sliced him apart, while he was still alive.

We fought intently, closely, our faces almost intimate, our breaths close in the cold air, our swords desperate to find each other's hearts.

The obsidian blade whispered through the silence and I twisted out of its dark path, parrying each brilliant thrust and slice with my own curved blade, battling to maintain momentum. Suddenly his sword sliced into the muscle of my right forearm. My blade clattered across the stones, and blood slipped from the perfect cut.

He leapt back, light as a cat on his feet, and disappeared around a dark corner of the street. I tore a piece out of my robe to bind the wound, and stood still, listening to the silence. Then I picked up my sword in my left hand and moved slowly around the corner. The shadowy doorways seemed empty. Up ahead was a derelict space between two buildings, where a large house was being reconstructed. I knew he must be in there. I knew he was leading me away from his mansion.

As I entered the darkness, sand and grit crunched lightly under my sandals. I peered into the gloom. Here and there slants of moonlight entered through the timbers of the roof. I inched forward, my sword ready, trying to see into the gloom. And then I heard something, the faintest whisper – the obsidian blade slicing through the air. Just in time, I threw myself down, and as it flashed over me, catching the moonlight, I twisted around on the ground, drew my old dagger from its place across my chest, and threw it, left-handed, with all my strength. There was a moment of silence; and then Obsidian's face loomed out of the shadows. The dagger was planted in his chest. He looked curiously at the bloom of black blood that stained his linen robe, made luminous by the moonlight. And then, to my astonishment, he offered me the obsidian blade.

'Take it. Kill me. For Khety. For the dead boys. Taste your revenge. *Do it now* . . .' he said quietly, with a strange remorse.

I hesitated. Was he now himself again? But then the wrong smile crept over Obsidian's face. He began to draw the dagger out of his chest. Blood followed. He hissed in some kind of dark rapture. Then he pointed the dripping blade at me.

'I knew it . . . you are too weak even to take the revenge you have sought for so long,' he said. 'But I am perfect.'

And in the moment it took him to smile, I grasped the obsidian knife with both hands, and with one absolutely silent motion, the blade cut through the dark air, and through his flesh and bones as if they were insubstantial as a spirit's. His torso remained standing, his arms moving as if in apology or confusion; his blood pulsed out of his neck in gushes that quickly lost their strength, until his body slipped over and fell to the ground. It jerked a few last times, and then lay still.

His head had rolled away; I scrambled to find it, then ran into the street with it still warm, still full of secrets, in my hands. I held it up, dripping, by the hair, in the last of the moonlight. His eyes were open wide, staring, as if he had seen something that truly surprised him.

'*What do you see now? Do you see the truth and the light? Or just the darkness?*' I cried.

But his features were changing again. Slowly, and in death, I could once more recognize not Obsidian, but Nakht, the man I had called friend nearly all my life.

I walked to the Great River. The vast waters were black under the late-night sky. I sat down, and studied the head: this simple skull, with its once-mutable, lively face, had contained secrets, and languages and ideas, and the knowledge of the stars and the Gods; it contained brilliance and mercilessness, crimes and cruelties, and somewhere, somehow, even love. But those things were all gone now. With the last of my strength, I threw the head as far out as I could. It landed with a faint splash, and vanished.

I stayed there watching the great mysteries of the perpetual waters running by me in the last of the darkness of the night. I was shivering uncontrollably again. The opium sang in my blood, demanding to be satiated. But I would never take it again. I had to face myself before I could return home. I felt unclean. So I stood in the Great River, and began to pour its waters over myself, over and over, scrubbing at the agony in my flesh, and heard myself begin to scream.

42

Horemheb's divisions occupied the city the following day. Before dawn his ships sailed into the harbour in silence. As Ra rose upon a new day, his regiments moved through the silent streets quietly and efficiently. There was no resistance. There was no disorder. Shops remained closed, and people stayed at home, afraid, waiting to see what would happen, hoping the storm would break and pass into a new peace. The Medjay submitted obediently. My old foe Nebamun remained at the head of the force, and was ready and waiting for the general himself, offering his congratulations. Horemheb's officers marched into the bureaucracies and the temples, and new men, who swore their loyalty to the army, were given positions of authority. Those who were associated with the old regime were marched out, under arrest, in daylight, to await their trials in the jails of the city. But no one disappeared in the dark of night. There was no violence. There were no summary executions. Elite men hid in their mansions, and waited to see what would happen. Horemheb's reign began, as he had said it would, with the restoration of order. And the next day the shops opened, and people returned to work.

I visited the general, and gave him the location of the merchant's warehouse. That night, after the fall of the new curfew, he commanded his most elite squad. They took their positions along every street and every alleyway in the moonlight, armed with axes, staves, swords or spears. Up on the rooftops, archers waited, poised and silent. But instead of breaking down the great wooden doors with a battering ram, Horemheb commanded the archers to fire arrows dowsed in flaming bitumen into the compound of the warehouse. These hissed up into the night sky, brief shooting stars, and arced down into the unseen interior. After a moment, there were shouts from within as fires sparked; then another round of arrows shot up into the sky, and down into the warehouse. As the fires took hold, smoke began to rise up, and a glow could be seen inside the building; the shouts of men trying to rally their forces came clear over the high walls. A third shower of arrows lit up the sky, and now fierce red flames took possession of the warehouse, shooting up above the walls.

Horemheb nodded, and his foot soldiers gathered before the doors. A figure suddenly appeared at the top of the high wall, his tunic and hair on fire, dancing in agony, and dropped to the ground; instantly the back of his skull was dashed by Horemheb's men. There were more shouts within, and then the great wooden doors began to open; thick smoke billowed out, and a gust of heat and flame, and men, blinded and staggering, many on fire, ran screaming towards Horemheb's men, and were swiftly dispatched with blows to the skull. Quickly there was a long line of dead bodies laid out neatly in the street, and the fire burned on, lighting up the night sky; but Horemheb had imposed a curfew, and no one dared to come out to see what was happening.

By dawn, the fire had gutted the warehouse, and burned itself out. Horemheb strode among the ruins, and I followed him, taking in the carnage and chaos around me. Many more bodies, burned into twisted, inhuman shapes, lay scattered about. We looked at the ashy remains of cages and cells, where kidnap victims must have been held; we found the storage rooms where the opium would have been kept; and finally we stood in the treasury, where the vast golden profits of Nakht's opium trade, tarnished by the heat of the fire, spilled across the floor. There was enough gold there to buy a new army. Horemheb kicked at it, contemptuously.

'And they thought they could destroy me with this?'

I said nothing.

'Where is "Obsidian"?' he asked, suddenly, turning on me. 'I have a feeling he is not here, and that you know where he is. Do not lie to me.'

'He is dead. I killed him.'

Horemheb's sword blade was suddenly sharp and cold against my throat.

'I gave very clear orders he was to be taken,' he said.

'He killed my closest friend. He betrayed me. He left me for dead. And he had my family, living in his house,' I said. 'He was my prize, and he was about to kill me. I don't regret what I did.'

'Who was he? Name him . . .' he insisted.

For some reason, perhaps the last traces of loyalty to the memory of a former friend, I hesitated for a moment. But I wanted the world to know the truth.

'His real name was Nakht.'

Horemheb laughed briefly, like a jackal, at the cruel irony.

'How perfect. The Queen's royal envoy turns out to be the spider at the heart of the dark web of secrets. I suppose he would have exposed and disgraced me, and then proposed himself as leader, as the restorer of order after the time of chaos.'

'He wanted to start a new age. Without kings, without Gods . . . the errors of the past all purged away. He thought he could make the world perfect in his own image. He thought he was incorruptible. But he wasn't. He discovered he liked killing...'

We stood in silence for a moment. 'All his secrets died with him. No one else knows the truth about Obsidian, and the opium-smuggling within the Seth division,' I said.

'Except you,' he replied.

'Yes.'

I supposed he would now have me arrested, and sent bound like a captive to his darkest prison, never to return. But instead he reached into a leather purse, and produced a fine gold ring.

'Here. Recompense,' he said.

I held it in my palm. 'I don't want it,' I replied, and flicked it carelessly into the great mound of gold before us.

Horemheb looked genuinely surprised.

'Then what do you want?'

'I want you to release Simut. I want you to allow the Queen to live out her life in privacy. And then I want to go home.'

For a moment, he considered.

'Even now, when you should be grasping your rewards, you remain loyal to that disastrous dynasty...'

'I am loyal to *her*.'

He stared at me.

'Your loyalty is commendable. But I'm afraid you must mourn her. She is dead. She died by her own hand. Poison. Supplied, I am reliably informed, by your old friend Nakht.'

I turned away.

'This was the inevitable ending. Let us not be sentimental. All this was business. And now it will finally be possible to rebuild Egypt. I will, of course, destroy the names of her dynasty, and I will usurp their monuments. The stones of their temples will be demolished to build new temples, in my name, and in the name of my dynasty. I am King now, but I was born an ordinary man. I remember that. I will proclaim a new edict of excellent measures.

I will appoint new judges, new officials and new regional tribunes to oversee the improvement of the laws. Wrongdoing will not be tolerated. Theft will be severely punished. Corruption within the instruments of justice will be severely punished. Crimes against justice will be severely punished.'

'And what of those who oppose you?' I said. 'What of men like Simut, good men, honourable men? Will you torture and execute them? Will those of the old order disappear in the night, into dark prisons, never to be seen again? Will you target and assassinate your enemies?'

'There will be public trials, and those who opposed me will answer for their wrongdoing before a judge, if necessary with their lives. Those who repent could be freed, on condition of absolute loyalty,' he said.

He came closer.

'I have had many years to think what to do with my kingship. I have no interest in personal acquisition. Gold has never delighted me. I am only interested in Egypt. There is much to do. I have need of reliable men. Men who are not in love with gold. Your allegiance to the Queen has impressed me. I know very well that the Thebes Medjay has been governed poorly. This city needs a new hand to restore faith in the laws, and security on the streets.'

'Nebamun has welcomed you with open arms,' I said.

'Nebamun is no fool. He is an old hand, and he knows his time is over. He will accept a decent settlement of the gold he has always coveted, and the status he has always aspired to. He will retire to his country villa, and drink himself stupid,' he said. 'So there will be a vacancy. I would need someone reliable to appoint to his office . . .'

He was offering me the great prize. I stared at the piles of gold at my feet. So much had been lost for the sake of its terrible glory.

'I am not reliable,' I replied.

'And perhaps that is why I respect you. These are the days of reckoning, Rahotep. It is time to make choices, and swift changes. Think about it carefully,' he said.

I stood before the great wooden door of Nakht's mansion, and hesitated. And then I knocked three times. I heard footsteps. The door slowly opened. Tanefert stared at me. I could not speak. Slowly, she raised her hand, and carefully touched my cheek, not yet daring to believe I was alive. Then she beat her fists against me, in fury and grief; but, suddenly, she crumpled. I caught her in my arms, just in time.

43

We crossed the Great River in sunlight for Khety's funeral rites; Khety's wife, Kiya, and her daughter, and his younger brother Intef, and my own family. We were all dressed in white linens. Kiya's belly was swollen now; the baby was growing. The girls sat together, Khety's daughter folded into the generous company of my girls, her face alert to the strange seriousness of the ritual. Tanefert tried to comfort Kiya; but to her the river traffic all around us was simply unreal.

I found myself gazing into the dazzle of the light on the waters, mesmerized and apart. Since my return home, and from the dead, three weeks ago, I had kept myself apart. The grim agony of separating myself from the addiction was finally over; but I felt empty and detached. The darkness was still inside me. I had told Tanefert everything on my first night home. And her silence had taken possession of the house as surely as Horemheb's soldiers had taken possession of the city. We slept like strangers, and her eyes avoided me during the day. As I sat on the boat,

317

my son insisted on sitting with me, his hand in mine, as if he were afraid he would lose me again. He gazed up at my face, perhaps searching for the father he remembered and could no longer recognize.

At the embalmer's shop on the west bank, we met Khety's coffin, and the cortège of priests and mourners who would accompany it. The coffin was placed on its covered bier, decorated with bouquets, and pulled by the embalmer's men to the cemetery. I insisted on joining them in their labour. I wanted to feel the true burden of Khety's death as I dragged my friend's coffin to his tomb. The professional mourners went ahead of us in their blue robes, tearing their hair and beating their breasts. I hated their high wails and cries, so rehearsed and inauthentic. The chest containing the canopic jars was dragged on a bier by more of the embalmer's men. The priest, wearing a panther skin thrown over his shoulder, went before the coffin, sprinkling milk on the ground, and wafting incense in the bright air of the morning. Behind came the funeral servants, carrying the trays, foods and flowers, jars of wine and jugs of beer, and the other necessities of the funeral feast. And behind that, others carried the few objects from Khety's life that would be left in the tomb with him.

We came to the cemetery, and the tomb. The lector priest was waiting for us, chanting prayers and spells from the papyrus roll he held out before him. Khety's mummy was propped upright, and the priest set about preparing the instruments he would need for the Opening of the Mouth ceremony. The lector priest began to recite the Instructions, and the priest approached the tomb statue of Khety. I tried and failed to find his face in the generalized features the embalmers had given him. He was one with the innumerable dead, now. Following the prescribed gestures, the spells and libations, the priest took his instruments from their alabaster tablet, one by one, and touched the face of the statue with the forked *pesesh* knife, the chisel, the adze and the rod ending in the snake's head – restoring the senses to the dead man so that he might live again in the Otherworld, and eat, and speak his name. He made offerings of incense and natron, of food and wine, and the traditional cuts of meat – the foreleg and the heart. All this was intended to reunite the parts of the body and the spirit; and I could only hope the magic would work powerfully, restoring the butchered parts of Khety's body to his new, whole self, in the beautiful light of the Otherworld.

It was hot. The children, who had been awed and fascinated, began to look around, slightly confused and bored. Tanefert gave them each a drink of water. Intef looked dazed. Kiya stared straight ahead, holding her daughter's hand. The child must have been puzzled by the elaborate rituals, and by the disappearance of her father into this anonymous wooden shape.

Finally, the rites were concluded; Khety's coffin was carried down the small steps into the tomb chamber. The canopic chest was settled in its niche. I descended into the small space of the tomb; there, around the mummy, I placed his *senet* game board, over which we had spent many hours of play, and his staff of office, and his knife, which, according to ritual, I broke so that it could not be used against him in the afterlife. And then I laid in front of Khety the papyrus scroll of the Book of the Dead which I had commissioned especially for him, with his name written throughout, and whispered my earnest prayer for his afterlife, that he should pass the trials of death, and arrive at the Field of Reeds, and that it should bring him all the pleasures and the peace he dreamed of, but never quite achieved in this life; and that, if he could, he might one day forgive me my failure of friendship.

Kiya and Intef kissed his headrest, and then passed it to me to place gently beside the coffin. But when her daughter gave me his favourite old sandals, Kiya suddenly began to weep in terrible and uncontrollable jolts. Her daughter embraced her, and Tanefert went to her support. Then all the girls began to cry together.

Quickly, the funeral feast was prepared; back up the stairs, in the light of day, they stood at the chapel door together, eating and weeping, weeping and eating. I could do neither.

The priests and embalmers whispered their condolences and excuses, and made their way back to the river, with all the tools and paraphernalia of the rites. The professional mourners had already gone to another engagement, another burial. Death was everywhere, of course.

There was nothing more to do. There was nothing else to be achieved. Tanefert came to my side. We didn't speak. Very carefully I took her hand in mine, and this time she allowed me to do so. We remained like that for a few, vital moments. Then, with a brief squeeze, she withdrew hers, gathered the children together, and led them away.

Kiya remained behind, unwilling to leave. We stood together in the heat. She looked at me.

'I loved him,' I said.

She nodded.

'He knew that.'

She touched her belly. Her words, and the sorrow on her face, and the sadness of the unborn child inside her who would never know its father, suddenly passed into me, into my dead, black heart. And then bitter tears poured out of me, despite myself; my cries of grief were wordless and helpless as a child. I wept for what I had risked, and what I had lost, and for who I had become. She held me, as I buckled, as best she could.

As we walked back to the Great River, arm in arm, we were silent. But just before we came to the boat, she turned to me.

'When the child is born, if it's a boy, I will name him after his father.'

'It is a fine name to carry through life,' I said.

'He will live for his father. He will be a good man, too. You will take care of him. You will stand in for his father,' she said simply.

Epilogue

Year 1 of the Reign of King Horemheb, Horus is in Jubilation
Thebes, Egypt

Our skiff lolled on the edges of the Great River, among the reed beds, a little way south of the city, in the dappled shade. It was a quiet afternoon. Amenmose and I lay back with our fishing rods in our hands. Thoth crouched in the prow, gazing suspiciously down his long nose at us, and glancing swiftly aside at the sudden ripples made by the fish as they snapped at insects. He hated the open water. Ducks argued and birds sang invisibly within the dense stands of papyrus; across the water we could hear the calls of other fishermen, and further off the farmers and their children at work in the fields. I offered my son some bread, which he took and chewed thoughtfully.

'Father?' he said, in the way he usually commenced a long enquiry into philosophical matters.

'Son . . .'

'What happens when we die?'

'Well, it's a long story. First our hearts must be judged in the presence of Osiris himself, and the forty-two judges.'

'Why?'

'To see whether we have lived a good life,' I answered.

'And how can they tell?'

He squinted up at me in the strong sunlight.

'Your heart is weighed in the scales, against the feather of the truth, which belongs to the Goddess Maat, and you have to make a denial of wrongdoing,' I said.

'And then what?' he insisted.

'If your heart is heavy with evil or wrongdoing, then it will tip the scales against the feather, and it will be gobbled up by Ammut, who stands waiting by the scales; she's a monster with the head of a crocodile and the hind legs of a hippopotamus. But, if you're clever and quick, before she gets it, you can also ask for forgiveness,' I said.

'How?' he asked, curious.

'You have to make an offering to Osiris, because he is God of Truth. You have to say: "Oh lords of justice, put away the evil harm that is in me. Be gracious to me and remove all anger which is in your heart against me."'

'So next time you're angry with me, or with any of us, we can say that?'

'You can try . . .' I said, smiling.

He was silent for a long moment.

'So what's it like in the Otherworld?' he asked.

I looked around, at the wide sky and the shining waters, and the city in the distance, with its temple pylons, and its stone palaces and poor districts. I looked to the east, and the mystery of Ra's rebirth, and to the west, the great desert, where Ra set each night in the place of the dead. I looked up at the dark, perfect shape of a falcon silently sweeping across the face of the sun. I thought about the future in which my son would live his life, under a new King, and a new dynasty. I looked down into the green waters of the Great River, ever flowing, and remembered my dead. I remembered my father, and the dead Nubian boys, and Khety, and Ankhesenamun. But their faces didn't haunt me now. I could look them in the eye. I thought about Horemheb's offer. Perhaps, after all, I could make a difference to the world my children would grow up in.

I looked at my young son, staring at me, waiting for a good answer.

'It's like this,' I replied. 'It's like this moment.'

Suddenly he called out in excitement. A fish was pulling on his line. And then, to my surprise and his delight, he reeled it in with a skill he must have learned from his grandfather, on those long fishing days without me. And he stood – holding up the silver fish, as it danced and struggled on the line – laughing and grinning proudly.

AUTHOR'S NOTE

The King's Wife to Suppiluliuma of the Hittites –
'He who is my husband is dead! I have no son! I do not
want to take one of my subjects and make him my husband.
I did not write to any other land, I wrote to you! They say
sons are plentiful for you. Give me one of your sons. He will
be my husband, and he will be King in Egypt!'

From the Seventh Tablet, The Deeds of Suppiluliuma
As Told By His Son Mursilis II

This letter (actually a clay tablet in Akkadian, the lingua franca of international diplomacy at the time) from an Egyptian queen to Suppiluliuma I, the King of the Hittites, was discovered in the Hittite archives, and is a tantalizing clue to one of the most mysterious and compelling unsolved mysteries of the Ancient World.

It is in every way an extraordinary, audacious communication – not least because the Egyptians and the Hittites had been at war for decades, battling for control of the Syrian territories and kingdoms between the borders of their empires, and so such a letter could have been seen as treacherous. But even more significantly, no Egyptian royal had ever made such a request to a foreigner, let alone an enemy; the trade in international royal brides was strictly a one-way affair. And yet here is an Egyptian queen asking her enemy for one of his sons to join her on the throne. It is an extraordinary mystery to rival that of the death of Tutankhamun.

In the letter, the queen is called 'Dahamunzu', which may be a translation of the Egyptian title *Tahemetnesu* (the King's Wife). For complex reasons of Egyptian chronology and the uncertainty surrounding the translation of the Hittite rendering of Egyptian names, the attribution cannot be certain; some scholars propose a chronology according to which the King's Wife might have been Nefertiti. But the letter is thought by others to have been sent by Ankhesenamun, widow of Tutankhamun, and daughter of Akhenaten and Nefertiti. The latter attribution forms the historical basis of this novel.

Ankhesenamun became the last surviving member of her dynasty, the eighteenth, when her husband Tutankhamun died aged around nineteen. She was probably only twenty-one years old herself at that moment; and she had no heirs. It is thought she was then married to Ay, the powerful courtier who had been closely involved with the royal family since the Amarna period – indeed he might even have been her own great-uncle. Already an old man by the time of the marriage, Ay ruled for only four or five years. His death must have presented Ankhesenamun, at this point perhaps twenty-five or twenty-six years old, with a grave set of dilemmas. How could she rule alone? How could she continue her line? How could she ensure the stability of her own position, and that of Egypt, domestically and internationally? Who could she trust? The elite men of the nobility and the priesthood might well have seemed more like a threat to a young and relatively inexperienced queen, than a source of support. Above all, how could she defend herself against the ambitious challenge for the crown by Horemheb, the general of the Egyptian army? No wonder she wrote in one of the Hittite letters, 'I am afraid!'

In the eighteenth dynasty other royal women had achieved great power, including Queen Hatshepsut (1473–1458 BC), who had enjoyed the full support of the Amun priesthood in crowning herself; Queen Tiy, consort of Egypt's own Sun King, Amenhotep III; and, most famously, Nefertiti (c.1380–1340 BC), principal wife of Akhenaten, whose story is told in *Nefertiti: The Book of the Dead*. But perhaps, due to her youth, relative inexperience of power, and lack of a stable royal marriage and heirs, Ankhesenamun's position at this moment was much more vulnerable.

Egypt in the eighteenth dynasty was the greatest power of the Ancient Near East, and the Hittites were their most confrontational enemy. But after the later collapse of their empire, the Hittites disappeared from history, and not until the late twentieth century did they become the focus of archaeological and historical research. Kingship was hereditary, and the king, addressed as 'My Sun', acted as high priest for the kingdom. Among his responsibilities were the supervision of annual festivals and the maintenance of the sanctuaries and temples.

Hattusa, the fortified capital of the Hittite homeland, was in central Anatolia (modern Turkey); through the might of their armies (a mixture of professionals, men answering the call of feudal obligation, and mercenary troops), and their control of vassal states and territories, they conquered northern Syria and extended their empire so that it stretched from the Aegean coast of Anatolia as far as Babylon. By the time of the setting of this novel, they had established themselves as one of the key players on the international stage. King Suppiluliuma I (c.1380–c.1346 BC) was one of the great warrior kings, who corresponded on equal terms with the other kings of the Ancient Near East. But the astonishing success of the Hittite expansion brought them into direct conflict with Egypt.

At the time this novel takes place, the Egyptians and the Hittites had been at war for years. At stake was control of Syria, the crossroads for all the commerce of the Ancient Near East. From the great port of Ugarit, goods from all over the eastern Mediterranean – cedar, grain, gold, silver, lapis lazuli, tin, horses, etc. – would arrive to be sold and distributed via a network of trade routes that stretched south to Egypt, east to Babylon and north-east to Mittani. So Syria was vital for commerce, but it was also strategically indispensable, and the great empires warred and negotiated with each other for influence and dominance over it.

Egypt had long controlled southern and central Syrian territories, which were a source of great profit and political prestige. But Suppiluliuma, in a series of what must have been daring military campaigns, quickly took control of the northern kingdoms and cities of the region from the empire of Mittani. The status quo was threatened, and the region became politically volatile. (It is not hard to recognize the parallels with today's Middle East.) Characters such as Aziru of Amurru, as historically attested, grasped the opportunity to forge alliances that suited their ambitions, and to extend their own territories.

So Ankhesenamun's letter to Suppiluliuma requesting him to send her a son to marry was unprecedented, and came at a time of escalating conflict between the two superpowers. Suppiluliuma was, understandably, very suspicious of her request. According to the annals, he sent a high official to Egypt to investigate. And the following spring, the high official (the Ambassador Hattusa in this novel) returned with a representative of the Egyptian court (Nakht, in the novel) with a further letter:

Why did you say 'they deceive me' in that way? Had I a son,
would I have written about my own and my country's shame

to a foreign land? You did not believe me and have said as much to me. He who was my husband has died. A son I have not. Never shall I take a servant of mine and make him my husband. I have written to no other country, only to you have I written. They say your sons are many: so give me one son of yours. To me he will be husband, but in Egypt he will be King.

According to the annals, Suppiluliuma remained suspicious:

You keep asking me for a son of mine as if it were my duty. He will in some way become a hostage, but King you will not make him.

But we know that, after further negotiations, a deal was agreed, and his son Zannanza was sent back to Egypt. But then, disaster struck, for Zannanza was murdered on the journey. The Hittites blamed the Egyptians, of course:

When Suppiluliuma heard of the slaying of Zannanza, he began to lament for Zannanza, and to the Gods he spoke thus: 'Oh Gods! I did no evil, yet the people of Egypt did this to me, and they also attacked the frontier of my country.'

And in the end, what Ankhesenamun might have intended as a radical solution to the problem of her succession, and an attempt to forge a peace treaty through marriage between the two empires, actually raised the stakes of the conflict, and would eventually lead to one of the most famous confrontations of the Ancient World, the Battle of Qadesh, in 1274 BC.

The dramatic geopolitics of the region – and the sophisticated diplomatic methods of the time – make up the historical panorama of this novel; and I hope the resonances for our modern world, with today's great powers vying for influence for commercial and political reasons in the Middle East, are part of the pleasure of the story. I've drawn on the best available historical and archaeological evidence to reconstruct both the daily world and the drama of high politics in Egypt, Syria and Hatti; and through the eyes and mind of Rahotep, Seeker of Mysteries, I have imagined my way into the events as they might have been experienced by the key players. Above all, I have attempted to tell the story behind Ankhesenamun's mysterious letters, and to solve the twin mysteries of what might have compelled her to resort to such desperate measures, and of who killed Zannanza, and how, and why.

There is no evidence, other than the Hittite annals, for what happened on that return journey to Egypt. However, the Apiru (or Habiru in some translations) are well-attested in Egyptian, Hittite and Mittanian sources. Inanna (known in Akkadian as Ishtar) was the Sumerian goddess of love, fertility and war. She is stunningly depicted in the British Museum's Queen of the Night relief (also known as the Burney Relief), winged, with taloned feet and a headdress of horns topped by a disc, her hands raised to the viewer. (You can see the life, head and heart lines on her palms.) She is holding rod-and-ring symbols. (These appear frequently; what they symbolize is uncertain, but they were only ever held by gods.) She is also attended by lions and owls, standing upon a range of stylized mountains. Her symbol was an eight-pointed star, which in the novel becomes the sign of the Army of Chaos. 'She stirs confusion and chaos against those who are disobedient to her, speeding carnage and inciting the devastating flood, clothed in terrifying radiance,' according to the 'Hymn to Inanna'.

My character has borrowed the name and the powers of her goddess. For her, opium is both a commodity and something sacred. Of course psychotropic drugs, especially hallucinogens, have been used for religious and shamanic purposes from prehistoric times. 'Soma' was a ritual drink of great importance among the early Indo-Iranians, for whom it had the status of a god. There is wide evidence for the cultivation and ritual use of opium throughout the Ancient World – in Neolithic settlements in western Europe, and then in Mesopotamia where the Sumerians called it the 'joy plant'. The Assyrians and Babylonians also collected 'poppy juice'. The Ancient Egyptians used mandrake (a fruit) and the lotus (blue water lily) for medicinal narcotic purposes, although it must be said that any exact identification of opium within the herbals and medical papyri is problematic. One likely reference appears in the Ebers Papyrus as a 'remedy for driving out much crying [in children]'. Base ring juglets, which were shaped to resemble an inverted poppy seed-pod, were probably used to import opium juice from Cyprus. It has also been proposed that opium and lotus flowers were mixed with wine for recreational as well as religious use, because the effective alkaloids were soluble in alcohol. In the novel, the 'lost valley' of the Army of Chaos is based on the Beqaa valley, where the production of wine and opium, and the rule of tribal militias, remain as active today as they were in the Late Bronze Age.

Alas, there is no other evidence at the time of writing to suggest what might have happened to Ankhesenamun after the murder of Zannanza. Horemheb (1323–1295 BC) succeeded Ay on the throne of Egypt, and she disappears completely from the historical record. And with her vanishing the great eighteenth dynasty of Akhenaten and Nefertiti, of Tutankhamun and Ankhesenamun, also came to an end; Horemheb, in the iconoclastic custom of new kings, dismantled their temples and usurped their monuments. And then he adopted as his heir a military officer from the delta (Horemheb's own home), who would found a new dynasty: the Ramesside, which would comprise eleven rulers in the nineteenth and twentieth dynasties.

Ankhesenamun's tomb and mummy have never been found. She was neither named nor depicted in Tutankhamun's tomb, and despite the custom of burying personal items belonging to the Great Royal Wife in the tomb, nothing of hers was found there. The very absence of such things is significant. Similarly, as Ay's Great Royal Wife, she should have been depicted in Ay's tomb; but its walls are decorated with images of another wife, Tiy. KV63 (i.e. the sixty-third tomb to be discovered in the Valley of the Kings) lies near Tutankhamun's, and some fragments of pottery suggest a possible connection to Ankhesenamun. Another recent nearby excavation has also been identified as a possible tomb: in February 2010, DNA tests encouraged speculation that one of two late eighteenth-dynasty female mummies from the Valley of the Kings might be Ankhesenamun. But as of the time of writing she remains missing. All we have are fragments of evidence, some glorious images of her such as that on Tutankhamun's golden throne, and the great mystery of the Hittite letters. 'I am afraid,' she wrote; and she had good reason to be.

BIBLIOGRAPHY

Andrews, Carol, *Egyptian Mummies*, British Museum Press, 1998

Bryce, Trevor, *Hittite Warrior*, Osprey Publishing, 2007

——, *The Kingdom of the Hittites*, Oxford University Press, 2005

——, *Life and Society in the Hittite World*, Oxford University Press, 2002

Cohen, Raymond and Westbrook, Raymond (editors) *Amarna Diplomacy*, The John Hopkins University Press, 2000

Collins, Paul, *From Egypt to Babylon*, British Museum Press, 2008

David, Rosalie, *Religion and Magic in Ancient Egypt*, Penguin, 2002

Faulkner, R. O. (edited by Carol Andrews), *The Ancient Egyptian Book of the Dead*, The British Museum Press, 1985

Jones, Dilwyn, *Boats*, British Museum Press, 1995

Kemp, Barry J., *100 Hieroglyphs*, Granta, 2005

——, *Ancient Egypt, Anatomy of a Civilization*, Routledge, 2006

Manley, Bill, *The Penguin Historical Atlas of Ancient Egypt*, Penguin, 1996

Meskell, Lynn, *Private Life in Ancient Egypt*, Princeton University Trust, 2002

Nossov, Konstantin, *Hittite Fortifications*, Osprey Publishing, 2008

Nunn, John F., *Ancient Egyptian Medicine*, British Museum Press, 1997

Pinch, Geraldine, *Egyptian Myth, A Very Short Introduction*, Oxford University Press, 2004

——, *Magic in Ancient Egypt*, British Museum Press, 1994

Redford, Donald B., *Egypt, Canaan, and Israel in Ancient Times*, Princeton University Press, 1992

Reeves, Nick, *The Complete Tutankhamun*, Thames and Hudson, 1990

Shaw, Ian, and Nicholson, Paul, *The British Museum Dictionary of Ancient Egypt*, British Museum Press, 1995

Vernus, Pascal (translated by David Lorton), *Affairs and Scandals in Ancient Egypt*, Cornell University Press, 2003

Wilson, Penelope, *Hieroglyphs, A Very Short Introduction*, Oxford University Press, 2003

ACKNOWLEDGEMENTS

Howard Belgard inspired the writing of this story in many ways, and guided me through to the end with patience and generosity. I can't thank him enough.

Carol Andrews, BA, PADipEG, once again scrutinized the drafts, meticulously correcting the factual errors of my ways, and constructively disputing some of my ideas and decisions. Any liberties taken with the known facts are my responsibility.

My thanks to Bill Scott-Kerr, and to Sarah Adams – my wise, patient and encouraging editor; and to Alison Barrow, Vivien Garrett, Lucy Pinney, Ben Willis (tour manager supremo), Matt Johnson and Neil Gower at Transworld.

Thank you, too, to my agent Peter Straus, and Jenny Hewson; also to Laurence Laluyaux and Stephen Edwards at Rogers, Coleridge and White; and to Julia Kreitman at The Agency.

Walter Donohue and Iain Cox read drafts of the novel, and their responses helped me to find my way.

And thanks to Cara, Grainne and Siofra, the glorious girls, to Dominic Dromgoole and Sasha Hails, to Broo Doherty, Paul Sussman, and Jackie Kay.

Thank you from my innermost heart to my partner Edward Gonzalez Gomez.